The Sacrifice of Constellatia

Book 1 of The Constellatia Saga

Bianca K. Gray

CONTENTS

To those looking for freedom
And to my wonderful street team

CHAPTER ONE

Emira never thought she, of all people, would end up being a murderer. She was raised by Priestesses of the Night, a little orphan girl left outside of the Temple of Aeluris. Always was covered, head to toe, in a gown made of the night sky. There was no one more loyal, more dedicated, to Constellatia than she. She was supposed to become a priestess herself, one day.

And yet, here she was. Running for her life with an ornate, golden dagger dripping with blood in her hand.

She couldn't help but think that this wouldn't have happened if it were not for that day at the parade. If it were not for that boy who tried desperately to save her.

"EMIRA, PLEASE," PRIESTESS IRENE BEGGED EXASPERATEDLY. SHE threw open the curtains, letting the harsh rays of sunlight shine through and fill the darkness of the teenager's room. Emira groaned, covering her face with her bony hands. The sunlight managed to get through them anyway.

"I can't have you running late, not today," Priestess Irene said, throwing back the covers, revealing Emira's fetal-like position. "You need to get up, my sunshine." Priestess Irene had always called her this, ever since she was a young girl. Emira figured it was probably because of her hair color, and not really for her winning personality. Though she prided herself on being an excellent listener, a true rule follower, she always tended to push the boundaries when it came to Priestess Irene.

"Incanvantus is supposed to be a fun day. A day where we can sleep in," Emira moaned. Irene physically had to get her to sit up as she flopped backwards, dramatically.

"Not for us priestesses," Irene grunted as she pushed Emira into a sitting position. Emira immediately turned over and tried to grab the covers like they were shields from the threat of day.

"Emira!" Irene scolded.

"I'm not even a priestess yet," Emira complained, letting the soft blanket go. With it went her hope for the dreamworld to take her once more. Irene gave her an exhausted look, a look Emira was, unfortunately, very familiar with.

"You will be soon," she said. "Now, please." Her chestnut brown eyes were wide with desperation and sunk in from exhaustion, or from the years of life slowly killing her. She gestured to what Emira was doing, and Emira sighed, loudly.

"Okay, I'm up," she begrudgingly said. There was always a limit with Priestess Irene, and Emira never wanted to reach that limit.

"Good," Irene said, smoothing out her gown. She readjusted the veil on her head, which glittered like a star-filled night and nearly completely covered her hair, besides a few brown-gray strands near her hairline.

"Please get dressed and come out and help," Irene said before leaving the room. Emira forced a smile on her face, though it probably was more of a grimace, and then promptly flopped back down on her bed once Irene closed the door shut.

It was Incanvantus today. That meant Emira would be joining the Priestesses of the Night in three days. Three days and she would be dedicating her life to Ophelia, the Idol of Night and Magic.

A feeling of finality knotted in the pit of her stomach. It didn't matter if it was what Emira wanted or not. She used to have dreams of becoming a warrior, of being magical and having ichor in her blood. But, she woke up to reality quite quickly. Emira didn't really have a choice. No one had much choice in Constellatia. She was going to become a priestess because she was raised in a temple, and that was that.

After a few moments with her eyes squeezed shut, she finally got up and started to get dressed. Priestess Irene was right. There was much to do on the Idol of Night's holiday. She grabbed her gown made of dark velvet that also shimmered like the night sky. The sleeves covered up to the palm of her hands, and the skirt went down to her ankles. The neckline was high, covering her long neck. She gathered her unruly, blonde curls into the veil, some curls daring to peek through. Emira was sure High Priestess Ethel would comment on them. She always did. Emira blew upwards and made the stray curls dance across her forehead.

She stared at herself in the cloudy mirror. Her bright, violet eyes stuck out on her face. They glittered, like polished amethyst. Sometimes, Emira liked to think it was the most attractive feature of hers. They were beautiful. But, it didn't help that her eyes were like goldfish eyes, bulging out for everyone to see. And they were the first thing that anyone saw on her. And once people looked into her eyes, they immediately looked away. Not out of fear, but out of deep respect. Well, maybe a little bit of fear. Who would want to look straight into the eyes of an Idol?

See, Emira was the spitting image of Mali, the Idol of Luck and Agriculture. At least, that's what everyone had told her. She never met the Idol, herself. But, few ever did.

She had seen paintings of the Idol though. And, to her dismay, she did agree with those who would murmur the comment behind her back or who would say it to her as a compliment. Besides Emira's thick blonde curls, pale complexion, and golden freckles that dotted her face and body, she did look eerily similar to the Elephant Idol. Down to the jewel-like eyes.

Emira tore herself away from the mirror and rushed down the stone steps. The temple was abuzz with activity. A black cat cuddled against her legs, and she stooped down to pet the purring beast. Cats were always around the temple as the priestesses weren't allowed to shoo them away. In the province of Aeluris, cats were considered holy. Any one of them could be the Idol of Night and Magic herself.

"Emira, could you go check on the entrance? People have been camped out for ages, and we need to make sure the entrance is going to be fixed on time," High Priestess Ethel said. Emira bowed her head in response, not wanting her wrath to be directed towards herself, but before she could rush towards the entrance of the temple, Ethel had something else to say.

"And Emira?" Emira turned around, questioningly, though she knew what the high priestess was going to comment on. Ethel motioned towards her own head and gave a slight scowl. "Adjust your veil."

Emira nodded her head, once, and ran towards the entrance

of the temple, her hands desperately pushing back the stubborn curls. The black cat with blue eyes followed her, tail up high.

"Aren't you a nosy thing?" she muttered towards the cat. She dodged all the other priestesses who were carrying decorations as deftly as a pro Volani player—not that she ever watched the winged violent game—as she made her way towards the entrance.

The temple was the busiest place in all of Aeluris during Incanvantus. It was because people from all over Constellatia would come to this temple in order to possibly meet the three Sybils and ask a question about their future. It was the only time of year where the Sybils would be able to have a vision, as the herbs they ate took a huge toll on their bodies. Only the Idol of Night was able to access the future at all times—as well as, of course, her sacrifice.

Emira wondered if she'd have time to ask a question this year.

When she finally made it to the entrance, there was a boy, who couldn't be older than her, standing at the bottom of a ladder. She looked up to see another man at the top of the ladder carving out the face of a giant black cat. Last month, one of the two giant black cat statues on either side of the entrance had broken. She guessed these two were the ones who were tasked in fixing it.

"The high priestess would like to know when this will be finished?" Emira said, her voice lilting into a question. The boy holding the ladder turned towards her. A black eye patch covered one eye, and Emira vaguely wondered what happened to it, but that wasn't what bothered her about the boy. What bothered her was the fact that he was staring directly into her own eyes. The only people who would look into her eyes were the priestesses she grew up with. Not a stranger. Never a stranger.

He brushed his brown hair from his one brown eye before looking up at the other man.

"Nicky!" he called up. "When do you think this will be finished?"

"It'll be finished when I say it's finished, Solus," grunted the man from high above. Emira winced at hearing the last name. Solus. It was her own last name. The name they gave to orphans. A stamp of eternal embarrassment. She never understood why society needed to know she didn't have a home to go to just by saying her full name.

The boy shrugged. "Nicky doesn't know."

"Well, can you tell Nicky that the high priestess is the one asking and that we need it to be finished soon so we can start with the Incanvantus celebrations?" Emira asked. She gestured to the long line of people, which wrapped around the streets, who were waiting outside the entrance of the temple. The boy marginally looked at them, his disinterest and indifference obvious, and then looked back at her. It was still unnerving how comfortable he was looking into her eyes.

"Nicky!" he shouted, still staring at her.

"What?"

"The high priestess wants you to be finished soon!" he said, finally looking away. His gaze was unnerving, to the point where when he looked away, Emira realized she was holding her breath. When was the last time she held uninterrupted eye contact with someone who wasn't from the temple?

"What is this world coming to, Mateo?" Nicky lamented as he chipped away at the stone. "Rushing art? Do you want me to rush *art*?" The boy, Mateo, once again shrugged.

"Nicky is really passionate about his art," he said. Emira did her best not to show the irritation threatening to surface. She was a priestess in training. She had to control her emotions. But, anger was always a tricky one for her. It bubbled incessantly underneath her skin, like an itch that refused to go away.

"That's nice," she said, through gritted teeth. She stared up at Mateo, directly staring into his one eye, hoping to unnerve him as much as he did her. "If you could just convey the urgency to the artist, that would be great. I'll go talk to the high priestess."

"Sounds good," Mateo said, turning back towards the ladder, not fazed by her own gaze in the slightest. Emira bit the inside of her cheek as she pivoted sharply on her foot. The black cat decided to stay outside with Mateo and the annoying artist.

Before she could step back inside the temple, the boy called out, "Priestess, could you get this cat away from me?" She paused. Her eyes lingered on the black cat before dragging her gaze up to him. *He wants a holy animal to be taken away?* She had never heard of anyone asking for a holy animal to be removed from one's presence.

"I'm sorry?"

"Are you not a priestess? You're dressed like one," he said, his one brown eye looking her up and down. Her eyes narrowed.

"No, I'm not a priestess, *yet*, but that's not…" Emira gathered her thoughts. "You want the cat to go away?" Mateo glanced down at the cat whose ice blue eyes were staring up at him, large and almost pleading. She wondered if the boy had snacks hidden in his pockets.

"Yeah," he said, looking back up at her. "I'm allergic. And to be honest, I'm not that fond of cats." He said that last bit, seemingly, to the cat. The cat gave a small meow.

"Are you not from here?" Emira asked, dipping her voice low. She didn't want anyone in the line hearing their conversation.

"Is that okay?" he responded.

"No, yeah. That's fine," she said, standing up straight. "I've just never... I've never met anyone not from Aeluris. What province are you from?"

He shrugged. "I'm from around." Whatever that meant.

"Well, for the record, in Aeluris, people *love* cats," Emira said. "Any one of them could be the Idol of Night and Magic, so you should be careful which cats you talk to."

"I don't really care if any of them end up being Ophelia," he muttered. Emira swallowed the gasp that almost escaped her mouth. No one called the Idol of Night Ophelia unless they knew her, like High Priestess Ethel. Not in a familiar tone like that. And those who knew her, personally, all called her Mouse.

"Well," she said, grabbing the cat from Mateo's feet, "I'll just take her then."

"Thanks," he said, directing his attention to something Nicky was saying from above.

Emira's eyebrows knitted together as she walked back into the temple, absentmindedly petting the cat in her arms. She had never met someone who had a clear distaste for the Idols before. She didn't know there *was* anyone who didn't care about them. Everyone respected and worshipped the Idols of Constellatia, at least, that was what she had always thought.

The cat jumped from her arms as High Priestess Ethel came towards her. Her veil was slightly out of place, which was abnormal for the high priestess, and bags clung to her eyes. To put it lightly, High Priestess Ethel looked stressed. And when she was in that mood, Emira knew not to mess with her.

"The entrance?" Ethel asked, her voice as sharp as ever.

"The *artist*," Emira put a sarcastic tone on the word, "says he can't be rushed."

"Nonsense," Ethel said, her ebony eyes flashing as she walked past Emira. Emira heard some shouting, perhaps some choice words that a high priestess should never say, and in a matter of minutes, Ethel walked back and clapped her hands.

"The doors to the temple will be opened momentarily," the high priestess said. "Could someone grab Sybil Mirabel, Sybil Selena, and Sybil Yuka please?"

"I'll get them," Emira volunteered, as it was clear the high priestess was passive aggressively ordering her to do it since everyone else was busy. Plus, she wanted to see the Sybils. Ethel let out a breath of relief.

"Thank you, Emira," she said, like Emira was doing her a huge favor.

Emira had only spoken to the Sybils a few times in her life. They weren't much older than her, but they lived in the palace of the Idol of Night, in the center of Aeluris. They didn't hang out at the temple all that much, opting to stay indoors with their beloved Idol. But, what excited Emira more than anything, was that they had graduated from the Leliara School. Only those who had ichor in their blood went there. And the Sybils had the ichor of Ophelia in them, which was even more appealing for Emira. The Sybils would be the closest she had ever been to an Idol.

She found them in the gardens that connected the Palace of Night with the temple. They were wearing dresses made of starlight and glittering veils which covered their faces along with their hair.

"Is everything ready?" Sybil Mirabel asked. Her voice was faraway, indicating she had already eaten the herbs they were supposed to take.

"Yes," Emira said, bowing slightly. "Right this way." The three Sybils followed her back into the temple. She stood, as they passed by, with her head bowed to show respect. The last of them, Sybil Yuka, stared at Emira, her eyes disturbingly blank. She could feel Sybil Yuka's eyes on her, and she shifted uncomfortably from foot to foot. It was risky, as Emira didn't want to be impolite, but she dared a look into the Sybil's face.

"Gold. Freedom," Sybil Yuka said, once their eyes met. The veil covered her face, but Emira could still see her glazed over brown eyes.

"What?" she asked. But Sybil Yuka couldn't clarify, or wouldn't, and continued to walk past her. The three of them sat down in their respective seats behind another white veil that separated them from the people asking their questions.

Emira was frozen to the spot on the ground. She wanted to go up to the three of them and ask what Sybil Yuka meant. The desire was so present, that she felt herself take a small step. But, she stopped herself. The first of the people were already asking their questions. And they had been waiting for days, if not weeks, outside of the temple to ask them.

But, what did Sybil Yuka mean?

It was well known the Sybils only spoke in words, words that didn't necessarily make sense or go together. Words that any skeptic could say were merely random. However, the high priestess was the one who translated for them, was able to make sense of their words.

Perhaps, Emira would ask High Priestess Ethel what the words meant. It seemed important to her future, since she never asked Sybil Yuka a question.

"You don't have to wait here," Priestess Irene said, from next to her. Emira, like the other priestesses, were standing against the walls, watching the people come in and ask their questions. The brown-gray strands sticking out of Priestess Irene's veil were gone. She half-wondered if High Priestess Ethel got to her, too.

"I always wait here with you all," Emira pointed out.

"I know," Irene shrugged. "But, you should enjoy Incanvantus. Like you did when you were a kid. Just one last time." Irene pushed her towards the door. Emira's eyes darted around the room to watch out for the tall and commanding high priestess.

"But, what would High Priestess Ethel—"

"I already cleared it with her. You're free to go," she said, a warm smile twinkling in her eyes. *Freedom. Gold.* Was this the freedom Sybil Yuka was talking about? Didn't seem too important. And Emira didn't see any gold.

"Thanks, Priestess Irene," she said, enveloping the old lady into a hug. Irene hugged her back and smiled.

"Go and have fun," Irene said, waving her away. Emira rushed out of the temple, the line to get in still as long as ever, and walked down the festive streets of Aeluris, not knowing this was the beginning of the end for Emira.

CHAPTER TWO

The people of Aeluris always left a wide berth for the Priestesses of Night, and Emira was no exception. Sometimes, she wished she had something other than her priestess gown to wear as she looked down at the gown which shouted at everyone in Aeluris that she belonged to the Idol of Night, but she didn't possess any other clothing. She never had worn civilian clothes before.

When Emira was only a baby, she was left outside of the temple. The priestesses took her in, and Emira, while thankful, had never known what a normal life was like. She never had friends and had never been to a proper school before.

"The Priestess with Idol eyes, how are you?" a shopkeeper asked as Emira walked by. It was what a lot of people called her, as they didn't know her name. The shopkeeper kept his eyes low, not meeting hers, as he gestured towards his wares. Because it was Incanvantus, he was selling outside—for the tourists—little black and white statuettes of cats. They all had ice blue eyes.

Emira picked up a black one with eyes like ice crystals and

turned it over in her hand. It reminded her of the cat she met earlier in the day, the one the boy couldn't stand to have in his presence, and she handed it to the shopkeeper.

"I'd like this one," she said.

"That'll be 10 stellae," the shopkeeper replied. Emira raised an eyebrow at the price. The shopkeeper gave a half-hearted shrug. "Prices surge when it's Incanvantus."

"Of course," she said, handing over a gold coin with a 10 stamped in the middle of the intricate star. Though, her irritation once more bubbled underneath her skin. The price was a rip off, and the shopkeeper knew it. But, her expression remained the epitome of cordial.

"Pleasure doing business with you, Priestess," the shopkeeper said, taking the coin and handing her the cat statuette. She put it in her dress pocket and continued down the street.

The streets of Aeluris were decorated with tons of streamers that sparkled more than diamonds in sunlight and images of cats and the moon. People were crowding the streets, waiting for the Incanvantus parade to go by.

Emira remembered when she was a young girl and Priestess Irene would take her to see the Incanvantus parade. Unlike most Idols, the Idol of Night was one who liked interacting with the people of her province. And she would sit on a float at the end of the parade, waving to her citizens.

Everyone waited for that moment, to see the Idol, to get the chance to look into the Idol's ice crystal eyes that were said to be truly jewel-like. Emira had never been close enough to see the Idol up close, not close enough to make out the features in the Idol's face, and could never put a cat statuette onto the Idol's float.

Perhaps, this year would be different. It *was* her last Incanvantus she would be able to attend. And she hadn't been able to go to one in years.

She stood at the edge of the street, having pushed by people in order to get to the coveted spot. The parade had already begun, and the floats were going down one by one. Each float was different and portrayed different kinds of magic. Some had a bunch of plants on them, to represent the Idol of Night's ichor in turning plants into something else or using plants. Some had cauldrons with potions brewing to represent potion-making. Emira's favorite float had magicians leveraging their Idol of Night ichor, which gifted some the ability to transform regular items.

It started to go by, and Emira watched in fascination as the magicians turned a chair into a suit of armor. She clapped along with the rest of the crowd as a cup of red wine turned into a standing firework. And she watched in awe as the colorful fire rained down into little sparks onto the float. It was magical. That was the only way she had ever been able to describe Incanvantus.

"I didn't know they let you guys out during Incanvantus," a voice said from beside her. It nearly startled the life out of her as she whipped around. It was the boy from earlier. Her eyes lingered on his eye patch before scowling up at him. He was, unfortunately, much taller than her.

"I'm surprised you want to watch the parade, since you don't care for the Idols," she said. She whispered the last part, not wanting anyone to overhear. *Could you imagine?* She thought. If someone did hear them? A future priestess talking to someone who didn't care about the Idols?

"You shouldn't worship them either," Mateo muttered back. She gave him an incredulous stare.

"They saved our world from being overrun by *belluas*," Emira hissed. "I think it's safe to say that we should continue to… at least respect them."

"I respect that they're warriors," he said. He gave her a cold glance. "But there's nothing more to them, besides that."

"T-They also have immense power," Emira sputtered. "Their ichor, that they so graciously gave to us humans, is… is…"

"What? Magical?"

"It *is* magical," she insisted. "The only ones who don't think so are probably the ones who have ichor, since they're so used to it. Where were you raised? Inficium?"

"Inficium's a great place," Mateo said, quirking an eyebrow. "They don't have blind worship like Aeluris does." Emira swallowed. He must have been well traveled if he wasn't from Inficium. And part of her envied him, as she wished she had the ability to see the rest of Constellatia, too. She narrowed her eyes.

"They don't respect their priestesses, you mean," she retorted. "And how could you say they don't have blind worship? Their province holiday is the Idol of Wisdom's birthday. That's plenty worship to me."

Mateo chuckled, the sound surprising Emira. She was starting to wonder if he was able to feel joy. "I guess that's true. But, the people of Inficium aren't as fascinated with the ichor as other provinces."

"The Idols' ichor is what helps protect the walls of Constellatia, currently. If we didn't have enough humans with their ichor, we wouldn't be able to protect Constellatia from the *belluas*," Emira said, her chin held high. He clenched his jaw and looked away from her, like she was an annoying fly buzzing around his head.

"You don't understand," he said, clearly irritated. Emira opened her mouth to argue against his point when people started to shout. Her head whipped around as she looked over and saw the sapphire float coming down the street. Anything she wanted to say to the boy evaporated as she looked upon the Idol of Night.

The float moved slowly, slowly enough for people to place their cat statuettes onto the shelves of the float. Emira reached into her pocket and grabbed the cat statuette she had bought earlier.

"You're going to place that onto her float?" Mateo asked.

"It's an offering," she said.

"An offering to… Ophelia?" he asked, his voice revealing his shock. She looked over at him, biting back the urge to say, *"Obviously."*

"Yes, of course," she said, instead, ever the perfect priestess. "She's my patron Idol."

"Your eyes are violet," he pointed out. Emira tried not to roll her eyes.

"That has nothing to do with her being my patron Idol," she said. "I am a Priestess of Night."

"You said you weren't yet."

"Well, I'm not going to travel all the way to Sapiem and become a priestess for the Elephant Idol just because my eyes are purple."

"But you'll dedicate your life to the Cat Idol just because you were raised here?" Emira bit her tongue.

"Do you have a purpose being here or are you just trying to annoy me?" she asked, sharply turning towards him. He smirked.

"You're gonna miss your chance," was all he said. She turned back around, black cat statuette in hand, and moved through the crowd that was starting to form around the float. She made eye contact with the Idol of Night, the Idol's ice blue eyes even more glacial than Emira could've ever imagined. Those eyes were like crystals, jewel-like, like her own. The Idol of Night's ebony eyebrows knitted together as Emira and her stared at each other. Guards, no doubt from Pyrinia due to their large stature, flanked both sides of the float and started to push through the crowd to keep it moving.

A person bumping into Emira shook her out of her trance. The Idol of Night continued to look at her, as if she were studying her, as Emira desperately tried to put the cat onto the float. It was going by, and the people around her weren't moving. It was her last chance. The last chance to show the Idol of Night her allegiance and worship. She will never be allowed to see this parade once she became a Priestess of Night, as they were supposed to help with the Sybils.

Invisible hands seemed to start pushing people out of Emira's way, as if her desperate thought was forcing them out of her path. People shouted while she walked through them and placed her black cat onto the float. Relief flooded Emira's body, the tension running away, as she stared at the black cat's crystal eyes. But, eventually, she felt eyes on her.

She looked over and saw the guards staring. Emira felt the burning of the Idol of Night's eyes. And the people around her looked upon her with mouths agape and furrowed eyebrows. Her own eyebrows started to knit together from confusion. Why was everyone staring at her?

"We need to go," Mateo's now familiar voice said from beside her. He grabbed her wrist and pulled. From that, the moment of silence was broken. The guards were shouting. The Idol of Night stood up on her float and started saying something Emira couldn't hear. Her heart was pounding wildly in her ears, and Mateo just kept repeating that she needed to follow him. One guard grabbed him, but he slipped out of his grip, his eye patch falling off.

Some sort of feeling like dread started to settle into the pit of her stomach at seeing him without an eye patch. Mateo didn't cover that eye because something horrendous had happened to it, like Emira had assumed. He covered it because it was gold. The color of pure gold.

"Mateo... You're..." she stammered. The grip on her wrist tightened.

"Priestess, we need to get out of here. *Now.*" Emira wasn't sure what was going on, or what the danger was. But she trusted the fear etched into Mateo's face. Whatever was going on frightened him to his core.

"I know where to go," she said to him as they ran through the streets, guards chasing and shouting at them.

"Lead the way, Priestess," he said, pulling her to be in front of him. She ran with Mateo at her heels towards an alleyway. She pulled on the black sewer cap and gestured towards him.

He looked at her with disgust. "You want to walk through the sewers."

Emira rolled her eyes. What was this guy? Rich or something? Born with a golden spoon that matched his one eye? He wants options on escaping? What kind of an orphan was he? Like a good priestess, she didn't dare voice any of these thoughts out loud.

"It's not actually a sewer. It's a secret passageway to the temple," she said instead, her voice flat. Mateo raised his eyebrow and gestured for her to enter first. Sighing, she got in and held out a hand to him.

"C'mon," she said. They could hear the guards getting closer. Hesitantly, he put his hand into hers, and she dragged him into the sewer. He fell onto the floor with a thud as she covered the opening with the sewer cap once more.

"You could've let me go down that ladder," he muttered, pointing to what she was getting down on.

"You didn't want to go first and I had to put the cap back on," she pointed out. Plus, it did fill her with a little bit of joy inside that he fell on his butt.

The lights in the fake sewer flickered on from the sconces on the stone walls due to the movement. They walked down the passageway towards the temple in silence.

Emira glanced over at Mateo. She couldn't stop staring at his one golden eye. No wonder why he hid it. If she could get away with hiding her eyes, she would. But, it would be weird to wear two eye patches. Also, inconvenient.

"Could you stop staring?" he asked, without looking at her. Heat rushed to her cheeks as she looked ahead.

"Sorry," she said. "I've never met someone who is…"

"Like you?" he finished her sentence.

"So, you're related to—"

"Balan, yeah," he said, his tone cold. Balan, the Idol of Law and Fate, though his ichor had nothing to do with law and fate —the titles for the Idols never did have anything to do with them personally. Though, Balan was the scariest Idol that ever lived. His mere presence probably created laws of the universe.

"I guess you don't have ichor either," Emira said.

"Either?" Mateo's face was the personification of confusion. She didn't understand why he was looking at her like that. If he had ichor, he would be at Leliara. An idiot would know that.

"Yeah," she said. "I was tested as a child for the Idol of Luck's ichor, but I didn't have it. Were you also embarrassed? For people to recognize that you're related to an Idol but not have a lick of their power?" His eyes squinted as his mouth opened.

"Do you not know why we were running away from those guards?" he asked.

"No," Emira said. "But, whatever it was, I could see it frightened you so."

"Frightened me?" Mateo asked, incredulously. "No, I was more than frightened. I was petrified." She resisted the urge to roll her eyes.

"That's why I followed you," she said wanting to add *"duh"* to it, but refrained. "Here's the temple." She started up the ladder to open the sewer cap that was in the Temple of Night.

"Priestess—"

"My name's Emira," she said as she pushed the sewer cap open.

"Emira," his voice was soft, "I was petrified for *you*." This comment gave her pause. Before she could process what he meant, Priestess Irene's face looked down into the sewer cap.

"Emira!" she exclaimed. She grabbed Emira's arms and pulled her out of the sewer. Mateo climbed out after her.

"I was worried sick about you! There was all this commotion in the street. And someone was saying that the guards are looking for a person with…" Priestess Irene's words came to a stop as she stared at Mateo. Her eyes quickly looked away from his, down towards the ground.

"I apologize for staring," she said, her voice trembling with reverence.

"I don't really care if you do," Mateo responded, irritation lacing his words.

"Where's Emira?" High Priestess Ethel's faraway voice could be heard throughout the temple. Irene's eyes seemed to glaze over with realization.

"The person they're looking for… with the Idol of Luck's ichor…" she muttered as she looked up at Emira. Tears started to prick at the corners of her crow-footed eyes. That frightened Emira, Priestess Irene crying, because she had never once seen the woman cry. Not even when her own mother died.

"Yeah, they're looking for her," Mateo said. "Do you want to help save her? Or are you going to let them take her away?" Priestess Irene wrung her hands as she took a step back.

"I can't betray the Idols again," she whispered. She fluttered her hands over Emira, as if she wanted to hug or touch her shoulders, but then pulled away. "I can't do it again."

"What can't you do again?" Emira asked. "What are you talking about?"

"Oh for Idols' sake," Mateo whispered under his breath. "The temple isn't safe for you either. I thought the women who raised you might want to protect you, but I guessed wrong."

"What is going on?" Emira asked, planting her feet where they were. Mateo pulled at her. She could feel he was stronger than her, much more, but he didn't pull hard. More like it was a suggestion, a suggestion she wasn't going to go along with. He looked down at her with a permanent scowl on his face.

"We need to go before the guards get us."

"And *why* do we need to go? Why are you scared for me?"

"I'm not just scared for you now. I'm also scared for myself at this point," he grunted, gesturing towards his gold eye. "If they see me..."

"Someone needs to explain to me what's going on, right now," Emira nearly ordered. Tears were running down Irene's face, and Emira couldn't understand it. She had never seen Priestess Irene full out cry, and it was wreaking more stress on her mind than listening to the high priestess scold her.

Irene took Emira's hands into her own as she heard commotion coming from deeper inside the temple.

"Emira, when they came long ago, I switched your blood for

another orphan's," Irene said. "I didn't want them to take you. You were so young, and the Tenth Year was so close. I didn't want you to…" The Tenth Year. It was when twelve people with the Idols' ichor were sacrificed to their respective Idol. It happened every ten years, and the next one was happening soon.

"Wait, you think that I… You think that *I* have…" Emira could barely process what was happening.

"I worried, based on how closely related you must be to the Idol of Luck, that you might be the one with all of her ichor. I didn't want you to be sacrificed so soon, you would've only been eight years old, but now… Well, you're nearly a woman now, my sunshine," Irene said. Her grip tightened. "It's a good fate to be sacrificed to the Idol of Luck."

"A good fate? Are you out of your mind? You want her to… You know what? Screw it. I'm leaving," Mateo said. Before he could, the guards turned the corner with High Priestess Ethel behind them.

Mateo quickly moved the sewer cap and started to jump in, but a guard who was definitely from Pyrinia, as all people from that province were nearly giants and this guard was no exception, grabbed him by the shirt.

"Where do you think you're going?" the guard asked.

"Well, I thought I was going to leave, but I guess I thought wrong," Mateo said, still being lifted by his shirt. The guard put him down and stood at attention as the high priestess got closer.

"Emira, what is going on here?" High Priestess Ethel said. That was what Emira also wanted to know. She wondered if this was all a joke. Some kind of cruel joke before her life was locked in on being a priestess and never leaving this temple until the day she died.

Behind her, a small woman moved to the side. Her ebony

black hair was piled on top of her head in an updo that Emira only saw in the movies, and her ice crystal eyes sent daggers into her soul. Even up close, she was impossibly beautiful, and her features were otherworldly. It was right, what they said about her. An Idol with the looks of an alien. She moved with the gracefulness of a cat, towards the two of them.

"Emira, is it?" she asked. She looked over at Mateo, her eyes roaming over him, but focusing on his one gold eye.

"Mateo, we meet again," she said. He only let out a grunt. Emira turned towards him and gave him a questioning glance, that probably looked more like betrayal, before directing her gaze towards the floor.

"Your holiness," she said, bowing low to the ground.

"Mouse, it can't be her, I swear to you. Emira doesn't have any ichor. We tested her when it was her time," Ethel explained.

"Ethel, my good friend, I believe that *you* believe that," she said. Her crystal eyes darted over towards Irene who was still sniffling. "We'll get to the bottom of it, eventually. For now, I know what I saw with my own two eyes."

"And that is?" Mateo drawled. The Cat Idol ignored him.

"Emira, it looks like we missed you when you were a child. Unfortunately, you'll be behind everyone else at Leliara but it's a good school to go to. And it will teach you how to handle the ichor flowing within you," the Idol of Night said. Emira still didn't look at the Idol directly in her eyes, but butterflies appeared in her stomach. Leliara? *She* was going to Leliara?

"Am I really being accepted into Leliara?" Emira dared to ask. Were her childhood dreams honestly coming true?

"Of course. You have the ichor of Mali within you, child."

CHAPTER THREE

Saying goodbye to Priestess Irene was probably the hardest thing Emira ever had to do. She was the only mother figure Emira had ever known.

Irene helped her pack up her things as Emira's hands shook, which wasn't much as priestesses weren't allowed to have worldly objects. The only thing she had was her silver necklace of a crescent moon, which she fingered as it hung around her neck.

When Irene started to pack up Emira's priestess gowns, the Idol of Night or, "Call me Ophelia or Mouse. Not this holiness nonsense," as she had told Emira, unpacked some of them and said, "She won't need these in Leliara. We'll get her some new clothes on the way."

Emira tried to prolong the packing, asking Irene about different memories in her childhood, but it went by too quickly. And soon, she was saying goodbye to everyone she had ever known, to the only home she'd ever known.

"I'll miss you more than you know," she said as she hugged

Irene tightly. She could tell Irene was trying to hold back tears that flowed so freely earlier.

"I'll miss you. And please know, I have always loved you as if you were my own," Irene whispered, hugging her back. Her words nestled their way into Emira's soul.

"Take care of yourself," Emira said, trying to keep her own tears from escaping. Once she pulled away, she grabbed her little suitcase and headed towards Mateo, sadness and excitement intermingling within her. He was flanked by two guards and his expression was twisted, sour. *He really doesn't want to go back, huh?*

"Don't worry, we'll take good care of Priestess Irene," High Priestess Ethel called out. There was a flicker of worry that passed over Irene's face, but Emira didn't think much of it. She waved to the other priestesses as they shouted out their goodbyes and was led to a black carriage with intricate designs of cats chasing one another on the side door.

The Idol of Night, or Ophelia (Emira wasn't comfortable calling an *Idol* by her nickname), was the last to enter the carriage. She took her time in saying goodbye to her priestesses and had a hushed conversation with the high priestess in the corner. It had looked serious, as Ethel's eyes were never that wide. Then, she entered the ornate carriage and sank into the blue velvet seats as the horseless carriage started to move, guards sitting in the front and back.

"Mateo, Mateo," Ophelia tsked. "Did you really think we wouldn't find you?" He was looking out the window, the side with his gold eye facing Emira. She really had to stop staring at it. She imagined how she would feel if someone kept looking at her just because of how unusual her eyes were. But, it truly looked like melted gold, it was mesmerizing. It must've been what others felt when looking into her own.

"I had hoped," he muttered, not looking at her. "Considering it seemed like you didn't know it was me this morning."

"Oh, I knew it was you. I was simply curious what you would end up doing," Ophelia said.

"And if I had escaped? I've heard the wrath of Balan is a sight to see," Mateo said, his voice falsely upbeat. He had finally looked over at the Idol, his expression colder than ever. Ophelia scoffed, but it looked much like how a cat would cough a little due to some hair in their throat.

"Ah, I knew you wouldn't be able to resist another one like you. Especially after Cassandra," Ophelia said, absentmindedly. Though she had a cavalier attitude about this Cassandra, Mateo had a visceral reaction. His body tightened and his fingers curled into a fist.

"Don't mention her name," he warned. And something in his voice made Emira want to shrink and disappear from the conversation entirely. Like if she listened for any longer, she was going to be sick.

"It's been nearly ten years, Mateo," Ophelia sighed, not moved in the slightest from his tone. "You must get over it. She did her duty, like you will do yours." *Duty?* Emira wondered what it was that Mateo was expected to do.

"A duty that shouldn't be expected of any of us ever," he spat. Ophelia shrugged, staring at her pointed nails. Something was emanating out of him. Something that was making Emira's stomach churn. She cleared her throat. She needed to change the subject.

"I'm sorry to interrupt this..." Emira tried to think of the word, "...somewhat happy reunion? But, what exactly is going on? How do you know I have the ichor of the Idol of Luck within me?" Ophelia looked shocked.

"Well, for one, she's been watching you for a while," Mateo said, jabbing a thumb in the Idol's direction.

"She has?" She wouldn't admit it to Mateo, of all people, but it warmed her heart to hear that an Idol had taken an interest in *her*.

"When I heard about a child with an Idol's eyes, I had to see for myself. When it was said you didn't have any ichor, well, that fascinated me even more," Ophelia admitted.

"But, I've never seen you before," Emira said, her eyes wide.

"You *have* seen her," Mateo said, his expression in a permanent scowl. "Just, not her human form."

"Yes, you saw me as a cat. All the time," Ophelia said. "Including this morning."

"And the ichor?"

"To be honest, you never showed any signs," she said, her hand on her chin. "It is quite interesting to think about, I'm sure Mali would be more insightful about this, but I've never seen you have a lick of ichor until today." Emira wracked her brain on what she could've done earlier that showed her ichor, but came up with nothing.

"Today?"

"Do you not remember what happened?" Mateo asked, incredulous.

"I just remember everyone staring at me after I put my offering onto the float," she confessed. "And then you grabbed me and we started running."

"Yes, because I was—"

"*So* shocked," Ophelia said, finishing his sentence. "So shocked that you had ichor and weren't ever found out until this moment. And we're so glad we found you!" Mateo looked like he wanted to say something more, his mismatched eyes pleading something, but he didn't say another word. Instead, after staring desperately at Emira, he turned his head and continued to look out the window. It felt like he was trying to convey some kind of message to her. What it was, Emira had no idea. She tore her gaze away from him.

"I've always wanted to go to Leliara," she said, turning towards Ophelia. Ophelia looked pleased at this, which made Emira's goody-two-shoes heart soar.

"Of course you have," she said. "It's a great school and a *great* occupation once you reach graduation."

"Great occupation? We have to fight *belluas*," Mateo retorted, before quietly adding, "If we live long enough." Emira refrained from rolling her eyes. She didn't want to be impolite in front of an Idol.

"It's a noble job," she argued, keeping her voice even. "Like how a priestess is noble, but more so because the warriors are protecting Constellatia."

"Yes," Ophelia said, leaning back in her velvet seat. "This girl knows her stuff. You should strive to be more like her, Mateo." Emira tried to hide her smile while Mateo made a face that read that he couldn't believe what they were talking about before listlessly staring out the window once more.

But his next words made the whole carriage quiet, "Was any of it noble when it happened to Leliara?" Ophelia looked like she had been sliced into pieces.

Everyone knew the myth about Leliara. The daughter of two Idols, Balan and Ophelia, she had immense power due to her ichor. She had all the powers of Balan and the power of transfiguration from Ophelia. Leliara fought the *belluas* that surrounded Constellatia, and she was nearly an Idol in her own right. She was a hero.

And when the Tenth Year came around, and the only person who had all of Balan's ichor and power was her, she was the one who was nobly sacrificed. In order for the Idols to persist and to continue to protect the world, those who had their ichor must sacrifice themselves so that the rest of the world could continue to be protected and so that humans could still have the ichor of the Idols, which Constellatia needed more than anything as protection against the *belluas* was paramount.

Emira remembered the painting she had seen titled "Leliara's Noble Sacrifice." Light covered her dark hair as her hands were placed into Balan's. It was a beautiful painting and a beautiful moment. It defined how the sacrificial ritual was perceived. Even the school was named after her. So, she didn't understand the icy tension that stretched between Mateo and Ophelia after he mentioned her.

"It *was* noble," Emira finally spoke. Mateo didn't even look at her, not that she wanted him to. "She sacrificed herself so that Constellatia could survive and continue to be protected."

"Did she?" he asked, staring still at Ophelia. Ophelia looked outside the window herself now, her expression like a stone statue's. "*Did* she sacrifice herself? Is that how it happened? Tell us how it went down, Ophelia. Tell us about how your daughter *willingly* sacrificed herself to her father."

But, Ophelia didn't say a word. Emira could feel the immense sadness that emanated from the Idol. Something started to twist inside of her. She smacked Mateo's knee lightly.

"Stop it," she hissed. "Can't you see you're hurting her?" Mateo gave Emira a weird look.

"*I'm* hurting her? What do you think *she's* about to do?" he asked. She didn't understand his question, and she didn't want to. Slumping against the blue velvet seat, she realized she was tired. Too tired for this boy's antics. Incanvantus didn't go exactly how she planned, and she wasn't going to get to go to the magician show at the end of the night. He didn't have a monopoly on disappointment. There was no need to make everyone else miserable.

As she thought this, the carriage was nearing the walls of Aeluris. Excited, she leaned forward to look out the window. Emira had never left Aeluris before. She had heard about the underground train to different provinces, but she had never once been on one.

"We're here, your holiness," a guard said from outside the carriage.

"This is as far as I'll go with you," Ophelia said, her voice cold. "The guards will make sure you get to Leliara." Emira couldn't help but think about what Ophelia had said before, about taking her shopping. The glare she directed towards Mateo was almost natural at this point.

"Guards?" Mateo scoffed.

"Guards with ichor, Mateo," Ophelia said, a forced smile on her face. "Drink this." She handed him a glass that seemingly appeared out of nowhere.

"I'm not drinking it."

"If you don't drink it, I'll kill you," Ophelia said, smiling big enough to show her elongated canines. Mateo stared off into the distance for a while, but then downed the liquid.

"Let me see your mouth," she said, leaning towards him. He scowled, swallowed the liquid, and then opened his mouth wide.

"There, happy?"

"Extremely," Ophelia said, but without emotion.

Emira guessed that the drink was a potion which paused one's ichor for a while. She glanced over at Mateo and couldn't help but wonder why he hadn't used his ichor up to this point. Was it because it was an Idol? He didn't think he'd be able to fight one? Emira's thoughts got interrupted once the Idol of

Night turned her attention onto Emira, and with that uninterrupted, intense attention, she could feel all the hairs on her body stand up, as if a predator was hunting her. Something about the Idol felt dangerous.

"I should be able to trust you not to use your ichor on this train, correct?" she asked.

"Of course, your holiness," Emira said, obedient.

"Kiss ass," Mateo muttered under his breath only loud enough for Emira to hear. She cut a glare towards him.

"Good. I'll see you two soon, I'm sure," Ophelia said as she stepped out of the carriage, to let the two teens out. Emira and Mateo followed after her. She nodded once at the two of them before re-entering the carriage, and the two of them followed the guards into the underground train station.

"What was that about?" Emira muttered, bumping into him. His eye twitched as he looked down at her.

"That? That was just good old fashioned emotional revenge," he responded, walking ahead of her. Emira rolled her eyes and scoffed before catching up to him.

The underground train station was exactly what she had read about. It was beautiful, the ceiling and walls made of red brick and adorned with silver decor. The trains were sleekly black and they were bigger than Emira had imagined. There were so many people from all different provinces rushing about.

"Let's go," a guard grunted, pushing Emira forward. Mateo didn't seem impressed by the sight.

"How many times have you been on the underground train?" she asked him, in a hushed whisper.

"Oh, now we're friends?" he asked, his mismatched eyes glittering. Emira looked away from him, her lips twisted.

"It's just a question. Let's not get ahead of ourselves," she muttered.

"The underground train? A lot," he responded, uninterested. People who walked by glanced quickly at the two of them, curious about the guards, but when they caught their eyes, they immediately looked back down at the ground. Emira wondered if Leliara would finally be the place where people would be comfortable enough to actually look her in the eye. She thought about asking Mateo, but when she saw his expression, she thought better of it.

The guards led them to a train which had black fox statues on the sides of it, showing that they were going to the province of Astutera, the Fox Idol's residence. After pressing the paw of the fox reaching out, the fox statue turned inwards, revealing the inside of the train.

"Get in," the guard said.

"Milo, let's talk about this," Mateo finally said, turning around.

"There's nothing to talk about."

"If you let me go, I'll get you whatever you want. You want the newest sword in Pyrinia? I'm your guy," he said. "You know I know a lot of different people. I could get it to you for a good price."

Milo grunted.

"Okay, I'll get it for you for free. You don't gotta twist my arm or anything," he said, raising his hands.

"Get on the train, Mateo," the guard called Milo ordered.

"C'mon," Emira said, pulling on his shirt. He sighed, loudly, as he was forced onto the train. She and Mateo found their seats, and the guards sat very close by. The inside was beautiful with orange leather covering the seats.

"I've read that there's a cart that comes by that sells pastries from Krachelle!" Emira exclaimed happily. She couldn't contain her excitement. She had always wanted to try the pastries from Krachelle, as everyone has said they taste otherworldly.

"I can't believe you stayed in hiding all these years," Mateo muttered.

"Sorry?"

"Never mind," he said. "I hope you know the pastries aren't that good."

"You just don't like anything nice, do you?" she muttered back. Mateo mimicked what she said in an overly high voice, and she retaliated by sticking her tongue at him.

No matter what this guy's problem was, Emira would be dead before she'd let him ruin her excitement.

CHAPTER FOUR

Emira forced herself to eat the whole pastry she bought from the cart that had come by. She didn't want to admit to Mateo that he was right and that the pastries weren't good at all. In fact, they were incredibly dry. But, she would rather have her body be buried outside of the wall after death than to admit he was right.

Unfortunately, however, he was watching her as she swallowed and forced a smile onto her face, and his expression was amused.

"You hated it," he pointed out.

"I actually really loved it," Emira lied. "It was delicious. The most delicious pastry I had ever eaten."

"Oh really?" Mateo's eyes twinkled. "I should get you another one. My treat."

"Sure," she said, dread filling her stomach as she called his bluff. "Go ahead."

"Hey Milo," he called over his shoulder at one of the guards, calling her own bluff.

"Mateo," the guard said without looking up from his book.

"Could you go get another one of those pastries? Get the one with the cream in it, would you?" he said. He dug around his pocket for some stellae and then put the coins into Milo's outstretched hand. Milo, without another word, went looking for the pastry cart.

"The one with the cream is even better," he winked. Emira smiled, though she felt like it was more of a grimace.

"Perfect," she responded. The two of them silently stared each other down, as if they were about to duel, as they waited for Milo to come back with the pastry. When he did, he handed it to Mateo who immediately gave it to Emira.

The pastry looked innocent enough. But, after the last one, she wasn't itching to eat it right away.

"Go on," Mateo said. "Eat it, since you love it so much." She swallowed her hesitation and then took a giant bite out of it. The cream was nearly enough to make her gag. The texture of it was already something that made her stomach turn, but the lack of flavor also made her feel like she was eating goop mixed with some sand.

You can't throw it up in front of him, she thought with conviction. *Imagine his smug face. Do you want to see that smug face burned into your memory for all of time?*

She forced herself to swallow it with minimal chewing required.

"Did you like it?"

"Yeah, *loved* it. But, I'm getting kind of full so I think I'll save this for another time," she easily lied, putting the pastry back in its wrapper before putting it off to the side. The corners of Mateo's lips twitched upwards, but not into an actual smile. Because Idols forbid he actually smiled at her.

"It's not from Krachelle," he said.

"It's not?" she asked, hopeful. She had always heard good

things about Krachelle's tea and pastries. The fact that these pastries weren't as good as she had heard made her heart fall.

"Yeah, it's made on the train. They follow the recipe, but I think the ingredients aren't good quality. Or, as my friend Atlas would say, they just give the wrong recipe so it can't be recreated outside of Krachelle," Mateo said. "I was telling the truth when I said the pastries aren't all that good."

Emira made a face at him and then turned away. They sat across from each other in silence as the darkness whooshed by them. She found herself sneaking glances at him as he stared out into the darkness, silently. He looked almost regal, in a messy-on-purpose kind of way, not so much like an orphan. And she had never spent this much time with someone her age. She couldn't really say she enjoyed it.

As their destination got closer and closer, Emira felt herself getting restless. She tapped her foot, rocked back and forth, and couldn't seem to get comfortable in her seat. Time was moving more slowly than a sloth trying to get to its destination. Mateo's eyes darted over to her, looked her up and down. His permanent scowl melted some.

"Are you terrified now about where we're going?" he asked, his expression surprisingly genuine.

"No," she was confused as to why he would think that. "No, I'm excited."

"Oh," he rolled his eyes, leaning back into his seat.

"What is Leliara like?"

"Prison."

"No, seriously," Emira pleaded. "Is it everything they say it is?" Mateo made an expression of disbelief before thinking about how to phrase what he wanted to say. She sat with bated breath as she gave him the space to think.

"I know how they market it. Leliara is the school for those

who are special enough to have ichor in their blood, either from being directly related to the Idols or from being one of the families that was granted ichor during the Dark Ages. And sure, yeah. We might be different from others. We might have ichor in our blood. And maybe they teach us how to control that ichor, that power. But, what is it all for? Just for us all to die someday. Either by an Idol or by a *bellua*," Mateo said.

Emira stared at him for a long while. *I mean, what did I expect?*

"Thanks," she managed to finally say.

"You're welcome," he responded. She decided she wasn't going to ask him anymore questions about the school since he apparently hated the whole thing and, apparently, all of Constellatia. Well, maybe she was being too dramatic to say he hated Constellatia, since he never said anything of the sort, but he might as well have said it.

They sat in silence until they reached their destination. She couldn't help but notice that Mateo had a pained expression on his face when the train stopped. *He really hates this place, huh?* Part of her couldn't help but wonder why.

A kind voice over the speaker said, "We have reached Astutera. Please make sure you gather your belongings before exiting." Astutera. The Fox Idol's province. Emira grabbed her small suitcase from the compartment above them and hurriedly exited the train, a guard in front of her and a guard behind Mateo.

"Milo, last chance," he said, turning towards the guard. "The sword offer still stands."

"Get off the train," Milo responded. Mateo sighed, dramatically. The underground train station in Astutera was exactly the same as the one in Aeluris. Emira didn't know what she expected, really. But, it was a slight disappointment.

The guards led them to another carriage, but this one was bright orange, with carvings of foxes playing with one another. The velvet seats inside were white, and Emira found herself subconsciously petting them. They were the softest seats she had ever sat on. The guards sat in front of the carriage, and once everyone was settled, it started to move.

Mateo looked out the window before quickly turning towards Emira. She jolted backwards at his sudden movement.

"Okay, you cause a distraction. Say that you're hurt or something and you need to go to the hospital. That will be my chance to slip away," he said, gripping the edges of the carriage door. She looked him up and down.

"I'm not going to do that," Emira said.

"Why not?" he asked, pinching the bridge of his nose.

"Because I don't want to get in trouble on my first day," she argued.

"Look, this is a win-win scenario. You want to go to Leliara. I don't. If you want to die, that's your prerogative. I would rather not die. I feel like I'm allowed to make that choice for myself. So, since I'm making my own choice and you're making your own choice, could you *please* help me escape?"

Emira thought about it, her eyebrows knitted together. She pursed her lips into a line. On one hand, it didn't matter to her if Mateo came with her to Leliara or not. She would be incredibly glad to get rid of him. On the other hand, she *really* didn't want to get in trouble. Emira hardly ever got in trouble. The only thing she did back at the temple that would be considered bad would be sleeping in. She always slept in. Well, and also having her hair out of her veil, but that happened to everyone. High Priestess Ethel was just a stickler for order.

But, she doubted she'd get in trouble if Mateo got away. The guards would. However, then thinking about that, she felt bad for the guards.

"So what's it going to be?" Mateo asked as the carriage was illuminated by the setting sun. She looked out of the window at Astutera, a province she had never been to. It was breathtakingly colorful. Aeluris was mostly dark buildings with some blue decor. But, Astutera had orange and red buildings. And the buildings looked regal, not like they were haphazardly put together. Emira looked back at the pleading Mateo. For some reason, even though she desperately wanted to, she couldn't say no to him.

"Okay," she said, betrayed by her own mind. "I'll try."

"Excellent," Mateo's lips spread into a big smile. He was sort of handsome, in a devilish way, when he smiled like that. Okay, he was lot handsome. Probably the most beautiful man she'd ever laid eyes on, not that she'd seen a lot of men in her life. He pounded on the wall behind him. The carriage stopped.

"I think something's wrong with the Priestess!" he called out. He motioned for her to hold her stomach. Emira immediately did as the carriage doors opened.

"What seems to be the problem?" the other guard asked. Mateo looked meaningfully at her. She blinked and then held her stomach tighter.

She groaned. Mateo motioned with his hand to turn it up a notch. Emira groaned louder as she leaned over.

"Oh, my stomach," she said, unconvincingly. The guard raised an eyebrow.

"I think she needs to go to the hospital. Her stomach seems to hurt real bad," Mateo said. Milo pushed the other guard out of the way and stuck his head in there. It felt like he was staring into her soul.

After a while, he said, "She's fine," and slammed the carriage door shut. A moment later, the carriage started to move once more while the two teens were still staring at the door, shocked.

"You're a *terrible* actress," Mateo muttered, after shaking his head.

"I'm *sorry*," Emira said back, with the same kind of attitude that he had given her.

"My death is on your hands," he said, pointing at her. She made a face at him and then scooted to the other side of the carriage to look out of the other window. *What an obnoxious boy,* she couldn't help but think. At least she *tried* to help him. He *could* thank her. It wasn't necessarily her fault she didn't know how to be an actress. She wasn't from Fonsia, where all the entertainers were from.

They sat in silence as she watched Astutera go by. Astutera was known for their teachers. Knowledge was everything to them, and they liked to know everything, too. The best and biggest libraries were here, and Emira half-wondered if she'd be able to explore the city some time.

The carriage halted to a stop, and she looked out of the window at the golden gates. "Leliara" was written on the gates in a fancy script. For a moment, they sat in front of them, and then they magically opened, and the carriage continued up the hill. Incanvantus marked the end of the month of Ophia, and so the trees lining the cobblestone road were adorned with red and orange leaves that were starting to fall to the ground.

In the distance, Emira could see the school of Leliara. It was made of dark stone with gothic architectural design that didn't really match the rest of Astutera. It was far removed from the city and the grounds were gated with guards flanking all sides.

But Emira's heart nearly burst. She was born an orphan, without parents. She was raised in a temple and was told that, even though her eyes were special, the rest of her wasn't. She had dreams of being able to fight *belluas* outside of the wall. She had wished she had powers of her own, that ichor flowed through her blood. And to find out all her dreams were coming true, that she was going to attend the school of Leliara, it was enough for Emira to nearly pass out from excitement.

"Come on out," Milo said as he opened the doors. "We're here." Emira stepped out of the carriage as Milo had to drag Mateo out. The doors to Leliara opened, and the headmistress stood in the doorway. Emira, of course, knew who the headmistress was.

In her prime, Headmistress Alessia was the strongest warrior there was. She was born in Pyrinia, making her taller and stronger than the average woman. And she had Nyro's, the Idol of Power and War, ichor running in her blood. She had the ability of controlling earth and could move rocks, plants, and anything else that had to do with the ground. Alessia had fought hundreds, if not thousands, of *belluas* and lived. Stories had been written about her quests. And someday, when she dies, she would live on with other legendary warriors in the form of myths.

Now, in her older age, Headmistress Alessia was in charge of the Leliara School and the education of future warriors. And as she stepped towards Emira, Emira couldn't help the awestruck look on her face as she stared up at the magnificent woman. Her gray hair was tied into a tight bun on the top of her head, and she wore a black dress that was similar to the priestess gown Emira had on. She seemed to appraise Emira, her expression stoic.

"Ophelia didn't take you shopping? She usually loves to do that," Headmistress Alessia said. *Does everyone at Leliara just call Idols by their first name?*

"I think Mateo might've chased her away," Emira said. Headmistress Alessia made a sympathetic expression.

"Mateo has that effect on people," she said. "Come this way. I'm sure your roommates might have something you could wear." Emira followed Headmistress Alessia through the doors of Leliara. The indoors looked a lot like how Aeluris buildings looked. Dark with arched windows. A crystal chandelier hung from the tall ceilings. And the high ceiling was painted with images from the Idols' adventures from many millennia ago.

Three boys sitting on one of the staircases near the entrance stood up once Mateo walked in.

"You were gone for a month," the one with piercing blue eyes said.

"That's a record," the one with the shaved head said.

"Yeah, but they still caught me in the end," Mateo muttered as they all did some kind of complicated handshake with one another.

"It's okay," the one who was incredibly tall and had black eyes said. "We'll figure out a different plan." The one with black eyes perked up as a girl with curly, black hair walked by him.

"Hey Darling," he said.

"Get a life, Kanoa," she responded cheerily, as she walked up to where Emira and the headmistress were.

"I swear, we're going to get married someday," the boy who Emira now knew was named Kanoa said.

"Darlene isn't going to be the one to tame you," the boy with the shaved head responded. Emira was concentrating more on Mateo's friend group than the headmistress, who was explaining the history and rules of Leliara. As if she didn't already know it, had it memorized since she was a child. Hoping and praying she'd be able to someday come here.

"Ah, here's one of your roommates now. Darlene Polaris, this is your new roommate, Emira Solus," the headmistress said. Emira tried not to cringe at hearing her surname that showed she was an orphan. Darlene smiled elegantly at Emira. She was small and slight, like how one would think a ballerina would look like. Darlene held out an umber brown hand to her.

"Everyone is talking about the girl who got accepted in their last year," she said. "It's such an honor to have you as a room-mate." Emira shook Darlene's hand and smiled back at her, though it was unnerving to know everyone was talking about her already.

"Where's Shiloh?" Headmistress Alessia asked.

"She's studying for the history test, Headmistress. She said she couldn't be bothered," Darlene said.

"Well, good thing it's a holiday today or I would punish her accordingly," Headmistress Alessia responded, her expression annoyed. She turned her attention back onto Emira. "Shiloh Astoria is your other roommate. I hope you all become good friends and that you'll enjoy your time here, at Leliara." *Astoria?* Emira's other roommate was a descendant of one of the human families first given ichor. Her roommate was a legacy.

"C'mon," Darlene said, linking her arm with Emira's. "I'll introduce you to Shiloh. She's a mess, but she's a lovable one."

CHAPTER FIVE

arlene led Emira up the staircase and down multiple long hallways which seemed like they would stretch out forever, like if someone didn't know where they were going, they could easily get lost. The hallways were decorated with all different styles of paintings which depicted past adventures some of the former famous students had been on.

"So, how did you and Mateo end up meeting?" Darlene asked. Emira looked over at her. The way she said it made Emira's interest pique.

"He was working at the temple I was raised in, and then something happened during the Incanvantus parade—"

"Oh, I've always wanted to go to the Incanvantus parade in Aeluris! I hear it's *such* a magical experience," Darlene gushed.

"It is! But, yeah, something happened and he grabbed me and we started running. And then we were caught and we were sent here." Emira could feel Darlene's interest waning. "So, Mateo has always gone here?"

"Yeah," Darlene said, brightening up at the mention of him.

"He and his three knuckleheads he calls friends have been here since they were tested." Everyone in Constellatia had their blood tested at five years old in order to determine whether they had ichor or not. And if they did, they were sent to the Leliara School in order to be trained to be the next generation of warriors.

Darlene looked Emira up and down. "I don't think we've ever had a student that came in at your age. Everyone arrives at testing age." Emira's lips twisted in response. *Great.*

"Does he escape often?" she asked.

"Ever since Cassandra, yeah," Darlene answered. Her voice was normally upbeat, cheery, but it slightly faltered when she mentioned Cassandra.

"Who's Cassandra?" Emira asked.

"You don't remember the sacrifices from the last Tenth Year?" Darlene answered with another question. She had the vague feeling of being judged as Darlene's expression turned stoic.

Emira was eight the last time the Tenth Year was conducted. And the sacrifices were always celebrated in the week leading up to it. But their names... No one really ever remembered their names. Granted, they were documented in history, and they were always considered noble and holy, but unless it was a famous, legendary warrior who was sacrificed—which happened some years—no one really remembered them.

"I don't," Emira admitted. Darlene seemed to stiffen at those words.

"Well, Cassandra was Balan's sacrifice," she said. "She was related to Mateo. Gold eyes and everything." Now that Darlene described her, she roughly remembered a sacrifice with pure gold eyes that were so bright against her tan face.

"Oh, I think I know who you're talking about," Emira said, her voice small. She remembered watching the broadcast of the sacrifices and how she stared at the girl with gold eyes, thinking about how she had different eyes like her. And she watched as a light encased the girl and she was gone, absorbed by the Idol of Law and Fate, Balan.

"Since then, it's been known that Mateo would be the next sacrifice," Darlene said, nonchalantly. "And he doesn't want to fulfill his duty." *So that's why he keeps escaping,* Emira thought. *He would be the type of person to try and skirt his duties.*

Emira tried to swallow the envy that twisted in her abdomen. He was a sacrifice, the highest of honors. She'd do anything to be one, herself.

"But why? It's such an honor to be a sacrifice," she said, aloud. Darlene smiled at her and patted her arm.

"It is," she responded. "But, sometimes, your instincts kind of kick in. I think that's what's happened with Mateo." The will to survive. Every human had it.

She stopped in front of a room with three symbols on the door. A pegasus, a kraken, and an elephant. They represented what ichor flowed through their blood. Darlene opened the door to reveal a room in utter chaos.

Everything was broken apart, but not like something had crashed into everything. More like the pieces that went together were pulled apart. The bed pieces were in a pile on the ground, the desk, the bookshelf. And standing in the middle of it was a girl with brown hair that reached her shoulders and square glasses covering brown eyes. Her head was in her hands.

"Shi…" Darlene said, utterly disappointed. Shiloh's head popped up, a look of helplessness on it.

"I'm so sorry, Darlene. I'll go find Edgar and see if he can—"

"I thought you had this under control already. You know we

graduate this year, right? Shouldn't you know how to control… this?" Darlene asked, gesturing to the state of the room. It was jarring to hear her upset, as her voice was still so melodic.

"You have the Idol of Mystery and Death's ichor," Emira breathed. She had never met anyone with the Idol of Death's ichor flowing through them, let alone a descendant of one of the first families. And if the kraken on the door represented Shiloh, then the pegasus must've represented Darlene. Emira looked over at Darlene and wondered what power she got from the Idol of Music, Poetry, and Light.

"After a couple of weeks, you won't be saying *that* with as much awe as you are right now," Darlene sighed. "She only has the deconstruction part, not reconstruction, as most of Lysto's disciples."

"Edgar can reconstruct. I can ask him to fix everything," Shiloh said, nearly pleading.

"Edgar is twelve. I doubt he is able to control anything at this point, especially while going through puberty," Darlene muttered. She took a hair ribbon from one of the broken desks and tied her tight curls into a ponytail at the top of her head.

"I'll fix it," Shiloh said, dejected. "I'll put everything back together." Darlene smiled a little.

"No worries. I have someone in mind to help us."

IT WASN'T LONG UNTIL MATEO AND THE THREE BOYS FROM earlier were standing in their doorway, Kanoa leading the charge.

"Thanks, Kanoa," Darlene said as he entered the room.

"It's no problem, Darling," he said, pushing his sleeves up to his elbows. "We can put everything back together in no time."

"Are we really doing this again?" the boy with piercing blue eyes said. His black hair lightly fell into them. "Didn't we help Darlene last week with this?"

"And you guys did such a wonderful job. I just thought you wanted to help… But, if you don't… it's fine…" Darlene said, dramatically. Kanoa held up his hands.

"No, no," he said. "We would love to help, wouldn't we, Silas?"

"The things I do for friendship," the boy with blue eyes who was called Silas said. Silas was a scrawny thing, compared to Kanoa who was built like a brick wall.

"Are you from Pyrinia?" Emira couldn't help but ask. Kanoa looked at her and shrugged.

"I was born there," he answered.

"This is the girl," Mateo said, gesturing towards her as the other three sat down on the floor, trying to find the screws to piece the furniture back together. "The girl who got me caught." Emira frowned at his words and threw him another glare. A smirk simply played on his lips, like he enjoyed irritating her.

"Ah, the priestess," the one with a shaved head said. His features were sharp, like a lion's. But he had the kindest brown eyes, and his skin color was beautiful, a rich sepia brown.

"Oh, where are our manners?" Darlene exclaimed, clapping her hands. She gestured towards Emira. "This is Emira."

She then gestured towards the boys. "You've met Mateo." As if on cue, he rolled his eyes, leaning against the door frame instead of helping the others find the many different screws that were needed.

"And these are his equally stupid friends, Silas, Kanoa, and Atlas." Atlas was the name of the boy with the shaved head.

"We're not stupid, first of all," Silas said, rolling his own eyes at Darlene.

"Well, you guys are a little bit not right in the head," Shiloh piped up. The three of them looked at her.

"Why do you say that?" Atlas' voice was quiet and reserved, much like Shiloh's.

"Because your leader would be able to do this in five seconds," Darlene said for Shiloh, whose ears had turned bright red from all the attention being placed on her.

"Oh, right," Silas muttered, dropping the screws he had in his hands. "It's been so long since we've seen you, man. I totally forgot."

"It's fine," Mateo said, his expression amused. He took both his hands and raised them. As he did, the pieces on the ground raised, too. He brought his hands together, and the pieces magically found their way back to one another. The nails and screws were put back into place, and in a matter of seconds, the furniture in the room were all restored once more.

"I thought you had the Idol of Law and Fate's ichor," Emira said, awestruck. He cringed at her expression.

"Please don't look at me like that," he said.

"Like what?"

"Like I performed some kind of miracle," he said. "And don't call Balan the Idol of Law and Fate," he mocked her voice as he said the last words, "Just call him Balan." Idols, she wanted to throttle him.

"Well, I have never seen anyone use ichor like that before. I've only ever seen magicians," she argued. Magicians were what people called those who had Ophelia's ichor running through them. The rest were usually called disciples or warriors.

"He does have Balan's ichor," Darlene said, interrupting. "He just has all of it." All of it? *That makes sense*, Emira thought. Of course he had all of Balan's ichor. He was the future sacrifice. That meant he had the power of imitation. But not just imitation, he could retain it. Any power he saw, he would have forever. Balan wasn't considered the King of all the Idols for nothing. It was because he had nearly every power in his back pocket.

If someone had Balan's ichor, but wasn't the sacrifice, it was like they didn't have a power at all. The only way they could use theirs is if they see someone else use a power. And then they were able to copy it, but only for a few minutes to a few hours. After that, the power was lost to them forever. Mateo, being the future sacrifice, had the ability to keep every power he'd ever saw in his lifetime. She twisted her lips as she regarded the brunette. His mismatched eyes met hers, a twinkle in his eyes.

She wondered how dangerous this boy could be.

"Good thing Edgar came in or Mateo wouldn't have that trick," Silas said, wiping his hands against one another.

"Are we done now?" Mateo asked, rolling his head towards Darlene. She shrugged.

"If you want to be," she said, her eyes twinkling.

"Let's go. We only have eight months to go before I'm dead," he ordered.

"We'll figure out another way," Silas said, throwing his arm over Mateo's shoulders as they walked out. "Atlas will think of something."

"I don't think I want to be involved this time," Atlas responded as he followed his friends out the door. "I nearly got expelled the last time."

"But you're the smartest of us," Emira heard Silas' pleading from the hallway.

"Hey, so, if you want, you and I can hang out a little longer,"

Kanoa said, leaning against the door frame. Darlene scoffed and pushed him through.

"In your dreams, Kanoa," she said. He held his heart as he walked backwards while Darlene slammed the door.

"Boys," she said, rolling her eyes.

CHAPTER SIX

"So-o-o, that's her," Silas said as the four of them walked back to their dorm room. Mateo shrugged his arm off of his shoulders.

"Yeah, that's her," he said, sticking his head out from around the corner. Boys weren't allowed on the girl's side of the dorm rooms. There was a magical barrier, but Kanoa was able to disable it. For someone who wasn't Avish's sacrifice, Kanoa definitely had the brains. The only thing he really used it for, though, was for girls.

"She's pretty," Silas murmured.

"Pretty? Did you see her eyes? Those orbs are mesmerizing," Kanoa piped up from behind Mateo.

"Who calls eyes 'orbs?'" Atlas said.

"Eyes *are* orbs, aren't they?" Kanoa retorted, uncertain.

"They are, but no one calls them that," Atlas said.

"I can see why you came out of hiding for her," Silas teased, poking Mateo's arm. He seemed to be fishing for something.

"I didn't come out of hiding *for* her," Mateo corrected. "I was trying to help her."

"What exactly happened out there?" Silas asked, becoming more subdued. Silas knew Mateo better than anyone. They had been best friends since the moment the two of them were born, as their moms were good friends. So, Mateo could feel that he knew it was something deeper than just the fact that Emira was pretty. And she *was* pretty. Mateo wasn't going to deny that. He had eyes.

He didn't answer until they were out of the girl's side of the dorm rooms. Then they were able to walk leisurely. Atlas and Kanoa were still arguing about the word "orbs" behind Silas and Mateo.

"Eyes are round, like orbs are, so I called them orbs," Kanoa said.

"Yes, I agree. They are orb-like. But I'm only saying that if you went up to a girl and said 'hey girl, I like your orbs' I don't think it would work very well," Atlas responded.

"You think I can't pick up a girl by calling her eyes orbs?" Kanoa said.

"No, I don't."

"I'll prove you wrong, Hawke," Kanoa responded, calling Atlas by his last name and pointing at his eyes and then at Atlas' with two fingers. "I'll prove you wrong." Mateo ignored the two of them.

"She used her ichor," he finally answered Silas. "That's what happened. During the parade, where everyone could see her."

"How did she not know before?" Silas asked. "That can't have been the first time she used it."

"I don't know," Mateo murmured. "But, she didn't know she was using it. Like it flowed out of her without her permission. I don't know if she was even feeling anything, emotionally. Her face didn't change."

"Her face looks like it'd be hard to read," Silas said, stroking an imaginary beard.

"With those jewel eyes and ichor, I had to help her. She might've been... I mean, she might still be..." Mateo couldn't finish his sentence.

"A sacrifice," Kanoa said, interjecting. He and Atlas seemed to have finished their argument as they all entered their dorm room. Their door had the images of a fox for Silas, a snake for Mateo, a hydra for Kanoa, and a phoenix for Atlas.

"For all we know, she could be one," Atlas responded as the door shut behind him.

"Does it matter to her, though? She was going to be a priestess," Kanoa pointed out, flopping onto his bed. "Aren't they devoted to the Idols or whatever?"

"Well, devoted to *their* Idol, the one they worship," Atlas corrected.

"Yeah, whatever," Kanoa said. "But, like, she believes in them."

"Well, to be honest, we're the only ones who don't believe in them," Silas pointed out.

"We're not the only ones," Mateo said. "If a warrior is chosen, they don't go quietly. And even they don't know the truth. Not like how we do." They all stayed silent.

"So, what are we going to do? If she is a sacrifice, are we going to help her escape, too?" Kanoa asked. "Because, that seems like a lot... to me."

"Yeah, me too. Because of you three, and because of Mateo's... situation, I've gotten detention *so* many times, my mother has written to me—"

"How *is* your gorgeous specimen of a mother, Atlas?" Kanoa interrupted. Atlas winded up his arm and stopped it before hitting Kanoa's bicep.

"Stop mentioning my mother, Kanoa, or I swear to Lystos you'll be buried outside of the wall," Atlas said. Kanoa feigned a look of sadness.

"Oh *no!*" he said with fake distress. "Not outside of the wall!"

"You still want your body to be burned with the 'healing hand' of fire on a boat in the waters of Krachelle, Atlas?" Mateo asked. "After everything we've found out?"

"The afterlife still could be real," Atlas said, grabbing his history textbook from his desk. "And I want the opportunity to get there. If I'm buried in the ground, my essence will never reach the sky."

"You can't be serious right now," Silas said.

"Deadly," Atlas responded, before opening up his textbook.

"So, are we?" Kanoa asked.

"Are we what?" Mateo responded.

"Going to help her? The priestess."

"I mean, we should wait until we know for sure, right?" Silas asked, looking towards Mateo. Mateo laid down on the bed in the room he so desperately simultaneously wanted to leave and wanted to live in for the rest of his life. After thirteen years, this room was like home, but it was also his prison. Emira's violet eyes flickered in his mind.

"No," he said, finally. "No, we're not going to help her."

CHAPTER SEVEN

"I've only seen Pyrinian guards before. Not just a casual Pyrinian teenager," Emira said after she unpacked her suitcase. "Seeing him is like seeing a giant." The three of them were still talking about the boys. Mostly because Darlene kept talking about them.

"Kanoa *is* pretty tall," Darlene mused. "But, everyone's tall to me."

"And don't fall for his height," Shiloh said to Emira, opening back up her history textbook. "All the girls fall for his height."

"*And* that charming smile of his," Darlene sighed.

"But he breaks hearts quicker than Orion built the walls," Shiloh said. Orion was a legendary warrior who was granted the ichor of Phaethon, the Idol of Fortune. He had super speed and super strength, and built the walls around the provinces in a few days. At least, that's what the myths say.

"What about Mateo?" Emira asked, trying to keep her voice light.

"What *about* Mateo?" Darlene said, her dark eyes twinkling.

"Does he… get around?" Emira asked.

"Did he hit on you?" Darlene responded, her eyes narrowing.

"Sorry," Shiloh said, turning halfway around in her seat. "Darlene is obsessed with Mateo. Has been since, well, since this year."

"Oh," Emira said. "I didn't mean... I don't *like* him, if that's what you thought. I was just... It seems like..." She took a deep breath. "I just think he thinks pretty highly of himself, that's all." Shiloh snorted.

"He does," she said.

"Mateo isn't like that, not deep down," Darlene said, laying back down on her bed. "But, he does get around." Emira wasn't surprised.

"Between the three of them, they probably slept with most of our year," Shiloh mused.

"Three of them?" Emira asked. *Aren't there four?*

"We don't know about Atlas, actually," Darlene said, turning onto her side. "If he does sleep with girls, he doesn't talk about it. And the girls keep it to themselves, too." Shiloh's face turned a deep red before she turned back around again.

"Can we stop talking about the hellions?" Shiloh asked. "I'm trying to study."

"Sorry, Shi," Darlene said but rolled her eyes at Emira. "C'mon, let's go to the bathroom. We have to get that veil off of your head and do something fun with your hair before dinner!" She grabbed Emira's wrist and then dragged her out of the room.

When they got to the communal bathroom, it wasn't long before Darlene tore Emira's priestess veil off and took a good look at her hair. Emira's long, thick, curls came flowing out like a lion's mane.

"Oh the Idol of Life herself," Darlene said, holding her hand to her chest as she looked at Emira in the mirror. "You have such beautiful hair." She looked at herself in the mirror, her hair a wild bird's nest. *This was beautiful to her?*

"It's a mess," Emira said, lightly touching her hair as she looked at herself. "I never know what to do with it."

"Well, you probably grew up with people who didn't have hair like yours," Darlene said as she grabbed a caddy from one of the lockers. She took out some hair products and a wide-tooth comb and started going at it. She also detangled the curls with her own fingers.

"What was it like? Growing up in a temple," Darlene asked as she worked with Emira's hair.

"Oh, it was normal to me. Priestess Irene raised me like I was her daughter. She's the only mother I've ever known, really. I was left outside of the temple when I was a baby and I grew up following their teachings. They were Priestesses of Night, so there was a lot of ritual stuff regarding the moon and every-thing," she explained, fingering her crescent moon necklace. "I've actually never hung out with people my age before."

"That explains your awkwardness," Darlene said. "But, that's okay. You'll get acclimated." Emira tried to contain her expres-sion from revealing how insecure Darlene's sudden blunt honesty made her.

"What about you? How was your upbringing?"

"Weird question, but I was raised here," Darlene said. "I mean, we all were on some level. Although, during the Winter Solstice we have vacation and go home to see our families. I'm from Fonsia, actually."

"Oh, and your ichor—"

"Yup. Raila's ichor. Pretty weird coincidence. I think Silas is the same. He has Hemlock's ichor but was also born here, in Astutera," Darlene said. "He's a legacy though." Legacy was short for being a descendant of one of the first families.

"He is?" Emira couldn't hide her shock.

"Yup, he's a Silver," she said. A Silver? They weren't just one of the first families. They were also pretty prominent politicians. *Remind me not to get on his bad side*, she thought to herself.

"Oh," was all Emira could muster.

"That's why he and Mateo are such good friends," she said. "Them legacies stick together."

"What do you mean? Mateo is an orphan," Emira pointed out. Granted, *possibly* a rich orphan, but an orphan all the same. Darlene's eyebrows knitted together. Her long, delicate fingers worked through her hair.

"He's not an orphan. He's a Cordero." A Cordero. Another legacy. Emira melted in her seat from embarrassment. He's a legacy, not an orphan. He wasn't a wealthy orphan or an orphan who had a lot of misplaced pride in themselves, he was a Cordero. *No wonder why he thinks so highly of himself*, she thought. He was probably richer than most in Constellatia, as all the twelve families were. He must've been calling himself a Solus when he was in hiding.

"Oh, I guess that was his disguise," she muttered to herself. Darlene smiled big as she finished with Emira's hair.

"Tada!" she said. "And *that's* how you do hair." Emira's unruly curls were pulled back into a singular intricate braid. She looked at herself for a while. It was going to be the first time in a long time that people were going to see her hair. She didn't know how she felt about it.

"And with those eyes," Darlene said, "Emira, you're going to be a killer."

"A killer?" she asked.

"Them boys are going to drop dead, I'll tell ya," she laughed. Emira wondered if her thoughts would eventually revolve around boys after being in this place for a while. She never really spent long periods of time with boys before.

When the two of them went to dinner, it wasn't what Emira expected. Back at the temple, the priestesses would wait until everyone got there before eating. And the high priestess would always say a long, sprawling prayer to the Idol of Night before they were able to dig in. Here, at Leliara, it wasn't like that.

Emira sat down at a dark, wooden circular table, much like the ones back at the temple. But, what was different was the food magically appeared on the table as Darlene and her sat down. And the food hall wasn't filled to the brim with students or faculty members. There were some here and there, but not everyone was eating all at once. And there wasn't a long prayer that made the food go cold.

Emira almost didn't know what to do with herself as she waited for someone to speak. Darlene started eating, glancing over at her.

"Are you all right?" she asked, warily.

"Sorry, is there not going to be a group prayer?" Emira asked. Even as she asked, she felt like it was a stupid question. Darlene raised an eyebrow.

"A prayer? To the Idols?" she asked.

"Yes," Emira answered, sheepishly. "Back at the temple, we always had a prayer to the Idol of Night. I thought... I mean, this being Leliara and everything... I figured there would be *some* kind of prayer..."

"What? To all twelve Idols?" Darlene said, almost in disbelief. "That would take forever. And you know they would all want a separate prayer, not for just one of them." What she said made sense. Emira guessed people who weren't a part of the temples didn't pray before eating.

She gingerly ate a bite. It felt like a crime, to eat without prayer. But, some part of her enjoyed it. Reveled in the rebellion of it all.

"Priestess, Darlene." Emira heard Mateo's voice before seeing him. She looked up to him staring down at her, his mismatched eyes widened at seeing her and then they seemed to glitter. She was very aware that his gaze was on her hair, and she refrained from touching it.

"I don't get a cute nickname?" Darlene asked, leaning forward on her elbows, her head in her hands.

"Kanoa gives you a pretty cute nickname," Silas said, from behind Mateo. Mateo didn't seem to be paying any attention. He pointed at what Emira was eating.

"I didn't see you pray beforehand. Don't priestesses pray before eating?" he asked. She tried very hard not to roll her eyes.

"Darling is not a cute nickname," she heard Darlene say to Silas who had walked around the table to be closer to her.

"How isn't it cute?" Silas asked.

"It's what everyone calls their significant other," Darlene huffed.

"So?" Mateo said, bringing Emira's attention back to him. "Why didn't you pray?"

"Who would I pray to?" she answered, honestly. She repeated what Darlene had said, "Do I pray to all twelve of them?" His eyebrows jumped, but a smile played on his lips.

"I thought you were dedicated to Ophelia?"

"I am," she said without thinking. Then she pulled back, "I mean, I was. I'm not a priestess anymore. Or rather, I never was one." Her heart fell at those words. She had lived her whole life thinking she'd become a part of the priesthood. Now, the trajectory of her whole life had changed.

"That's too bad," Mateo almost whispered. "You would've made a great priestess." And with that, he went over to Silas and nearly dragged him away to where Kanoa and Atlas were waiting at another table.

"Ugh," Darlene groaned, taking another bite. She chewed it as she glared from under her eyebrows at Silas. She swallowed before turning back to Emira. "That boy is always getting in the way."

"Who?"

"Silas, obviously," she said, sighing. "He's always trying to get in between any conversation I have with Mateo." Emira glanced over at Mateo, who was seemingly joking around with the other three.

"What is it about Mateo that you like so much?" *He's obnoxious,* Emira almost said. Darlene shrugged, her dark brown eyes glistened with some kind of sadness.

"I don't know. I feel like it'd be easy," she said, quietly. She glanced over at Emira and seemingly dusted off any sadness that lingered on her body. "I don't do deep feelings, and the boy's attractive." Frowning, Emira glanced over at Kanoa, but she didn't say anything.

Darlene grabbed some food from the table and put it in a glass jar that she had brought with her. When Emira gave her a sidelong glance, Darlene said, "It's for Shiloh. That girl doesn't eat enough." After they both left the food hall, Darlene turned towards Emira and handed her the glass jar filled with food after making eye contact with someone.

"Make sure Shi eats this," Darlene said. "You know your way back now, right?" Emira nodded, as she tried to mentally remember the maze of hallways they went through to get to their dorm room. Darlene waved goodbye and darted down the hallway, off to meet someone.

The moon was rising in the sky, and she stared at it through the window. At the end of Incanvantus, she and Priestess Irene would go outside, just the two of them, and leave an offering to the moon, the symbol of night. It was what a lot of families back in Aeluris did.

A pang appeared in Emira's chest as she saw the half moon illuminating the sky. She missed Priestess Irene. She missed all the cats around the temple. She even missed High Priestess Ethel, even though she did terrify her a lot growing up. Emira wished she had something to offer the moon. The only thing she had was the silver necklace around her neck of the crescent moon. The only worldly item she owned from the temple.

She fingered the pendant on the necklace for a minute. But eventually, Emira slowly unclasped it from around her neck and left it at the window sill.

Priestesshood was her old life. And she was walking into her next one.

CHAPTER EIGHT

"Emira Solus?" the teacher said at the front of the classroom. Emira partially raised her hand. How she wished they wouldn't announce her last name to everyone. The teacher, Mrs. Hawthorne, looked at her through her small, rounded glasses.

"I'll have you do the history test with the rest of the class, to see where you stand in your education," Mrs. Hawthorne said, adding quietly, "Though, I doubt you were highly educated at a temple." Emira felt her whole face heat up at those words, and with everyone staring at her, the embarrassment rose.

It didn't help that she seemed to be the only one in her year with an elephant symbol on her uniform. Everyone wore a uniform at Leliara. The skirts were knee length long, a dark brown, which added another form of embarrassment that she didn't foresee—the idea of her calves being shown off to every-one. And on their white blouses, there was a patch sewn on the pocket representing what ichor one had. Most people in her year seemed to have griffins on their uniforms.

"Phaethon has such a giant umbrella when it comes to his

ichor. Physical powers? That's nearly everyone," Darlene had explained as she, Emira, and Shiloh walked down the hallways to their first class. Phaethon was the Idol of Fortune. "And it doesn't help that he's a man whore."

"*Darlene!*" Shiloh had chastised.

Darlene stood up straighter before biting back, "What? You know it's true. That man has more children and grandchildren than all the other Idols combined."

"What Darlene is *trying* to say," Shiloh said, glaring at her friend before turning her attention to Emira, "is that a lot of people who have ichor tend to have Phaethon's. That's why the two of us get along so well. We're both the only ones in our year to have Raila's and Lystos' ichor."

"Plus, the *others*," Darlene said with distaste, "tend to stick with those who have the same Idol in their blood."

"I'm sure if there was another one in our year with Raila's ichor, you'd be hanging out with them rather than me," Shiloh muttered.

"Shi-Shi!" Darlene had exclaimed, hugging her from the side. "I would never!" Shiloh clawed at Darlene's death grip before escaping.

"Although," Darlene had said, looking up at the ceiling, "I already hang out with people other than you." Shiloh didn't respond.

Emira glanced down at her patch as the history test was passed out. An elephant's head stared back at her. Loneliness didn't begin to explain what she was starting to feel at Leliara. Even though she didn't know anyone her own age back at the temple, at least she was never alone.

The history test wasn't as difficult as Emira thought it would be. The questions were all about the Idols and how they helped create Constellatia. How the Idols were first animals as they were lowered to the ground from the heavens, and when their feet touched our world, they turned into the human-like creatures the people of Constellatia knew today. They gave twelve families their ichor to help them defeat the *bellua*, and those twelve families protected Constellatia while the Idols rebuilt the nation to its former glory.

I guess being raised in a temple makes me highly educated, actually, she thought, bitterly, as she handed in her test to the teacher. *At least when it comes to the history of the Idols.*

After the history test, Emira had a survival class with the rest of her year, but it was about creating bombs. She didn't understand what bombs had to do with being a warrior and fighting *bellua*, but that's what Mr. Summers had instructed.

Mr. Summers, another legacy, in a matter of minutes demonstrated to Emira how to create a bomb out of things she would find in the forest. But, she was pretty sure he was using his own ichor to do so.

"It's important for a future warrior to know this," he told her. Emira didn't respond, just watched with a confused mind. The others, in her class, were working on their own bombs made from various items.

"And with this," he produced a black powder from his lab coat, "it will complete it." He poured a little bit over his makeshift forest bomb, and it started to glow a little. *Ah, so that's why it could be used on belluas*, Emira thought.

"Never go anywhere without some of Nyro's dust," Mr. Summers said. "It turns anything into a bomb." Emira put some of the dust in between her fingers, phoenix ash definitely present in it. She wasn't sure why it was called Nyro's dust when this was clearly created and used by magicians. Though, she wasn't going to bring it up to the teacher.

By the time lunch came around, her head was pounding.

Violence wasn't something she was raised with, so using a bomb... She had never imagined using one in her wildest dreams. Adjusting to this school was going to be a lot harder than she had previously thought.

Food appeared on the table once Emira sat down. She held her head as she stared at the soup magically sitting in front of her. Rain pelted down on the arched windows surrounding the food hall.

"That history test was so hard," Darlene moaned as she sat down at the table with Emira. "How am I supposed to know how many *bellua* Phaethon killed in the Battle of Solstice?"

"It was two thousand and fifty three," Emira answered. Darlene looked over at her, her doe eyes appraising her.

"Okay," she said. "Ms. Smarty Pants."

"I think I aced that test," Shiloh said, sitting down with them. She pushed her glasses back up her nose. "I think I got everything right."

"I hope you did, after all that studying," Darlene pointed out.

"So, survival class..." Emira changed the subject. "Do you all usually create weapons in that class?"

"Just bombs," Darlene said, shrugging. "Although, if you don't like weapons, you'll absolutely hate sword-fighting class."

"There's a sword-fighting class?"

"We're training to be warriors, Emira, not priestesses," Darlene responded, popping a fried potato into her mouth.

"Right, of course." Shiloh put a comforting hand on Emira's shoulder.

"It's hard to get used to the idea of killing *bellua*. We forget that we were raised since the age of five to understand that we will be taking lives someday. You weren't raised that way," she said. "But, you'll get used to it. Besides, the *bellua* are disgusting creatures." The idea of killing any living creature made Emira's stomach churn, demon-like or otherwise. As she felt the bile rise up in her throat, she closed her eyes and tried not to gag.

"I think I'm going to take a walk," she responded, standing up from the table. Darlene shrugged and started to excitedly tell Shiloh the gossip she had heard.

Emira walked through the mostly empty halls, as everyone was eating lunch. She walked out into the courtyard that was in the center of the school. Standing outside, underneath the porch that led into the courtyard, she watched as the rain poured down.

Of course, she knew warriors took lives, at least, demon lives. She had seen paintings of the *bellua*, their shadowy figures and their glowing white eyes. They didn't look living or dead, simply a creature in between. It shouldn't be hard for her to take a *bellua's* life. But, it was like the reality of what a warrior had to do was starting to sink in. And she wasn't sure if she was strong enough to do it.

Out of the corner of her eye, she saw someone wearing a hooded cloak place a circular object behind one of the plants. As they looked up, piercing blue eyes stared stricken at her.

"Silas?" she asked. He put a finger to his lips before bounding over towards her. He shook the rain off of his cloak, letting droplets fall onto her. She wiped them off of her skin, annoyed.

"What are you doing?"

"I was never here," he said to her, winking.

"O-kay-y," she said, dragging out the word. He leaned towards her, his impish smile spreading across his lips.

"Although, you should probably get out of here," he said, looking back at where he placed the circular object. "It's about to get dicey." He flashed her a final smile before lowering his hood and entering the school. Emira stared at the circular object for a moment more, and then decided to follow Silas' advice and go back inside.

As she did, the circular object opened, much like how an egg would hatch, and what crawled out was a giant black snake. She stared up at it, frozen with fear.

What the twelfth circle of hell is that?

The snake's golden eyes seemed to look right at her, and then it started forward, fangs first. Letting out a bloodcurdling scream, Emira ran inside and shut the door. But the snake went through it, like it was cardboard, and she ran for her life.

Screams around her were heard everywhere and suddenly, someone grabbed her arm and pulled her into a classroom. He shut the door as the snake went by.

"Silas, that was some great work, I have to tell you," Mateo said, after he let go of Emira's upper arm. She rubbed where he was holding as Mateo and Silas high-fived each other.

"Are you two *insane?*" Emira hissed. "Why in the name of the Idol of Life would you let a giant *snake* go through Leliara?"

Silas had a blank stare. "Because it's funny."

"And it's the first day of Balia," Mateo pointed out. The month of Balia was named after Balan, the Idol of Law and Fate —who was also known as the Snake Idol.

"I tried to talk them out of it, but..." Atlas shrugged his shoulders. Kanoa was nowhere to be seen.

"I could have *died,*" Emira pointed out.

"No one is going to die," Mateo argued, rolling his eyes.

"Besides you, in eight months," Silas joked.

"Ha, ha. You're hilarious," he said before getting Silas into a headlock. Emira looked through the little window on the door of the classroom. She didn't see the giant black snake anywhere, but her heart was still pounding from seeing the sinister-looking beast.

"Shouldn't you guys be doing something about this snake in the hallways?" she asked, her voice starting to go shrill. She could still hear it running into the walls around the school.

"Eh, not yet," Silas said.

"We're testing something out," Mateo muttered.

"What? Another escape? You got here yesterday," Emira pointed out.

"And I didn't want to be here yesterday," he argued. "*You* brought me here."

"I don't think it's fair to blame *me* for *you* getting caught." Mateo's eyes narrowed.

"You don't think it's fair?"

"No."

"I saved you from a very terrible fate—"

"And what fate would that be? Coming to Leliara? Getting to be a warrior?"

"If you even live that long," he muttered.

"You didn't *save* me. You were trying to get me to run away with you," Emira pointed out. Mateo narrowed his mismatched eyes once more.

"How many times do I need to tell you that I was terrified for you?" he said in a low voice. She didn't know when they started standing so close to one another. She could see the gold flecks floating in his one brown eye and took a step back.

"You don't need to be scared for me," she muttered.

"Yeah? What if you're a sacrifice?" he asked. His eyes seemed to be studying her as he waited for an answer. Something twisted in her abdomen, poisonous and angry. She glared at him. *He* was a sacrifice, he had the highest honor of all of Constellatia. And he was *worried* she might be one?

But, the idea of not existing, a small part of her felt cold at the thought.

"It would be an honor," she bit, glowering up at him. His eyes roved over her.

"Would it be?" his voice was barely above a whisper.

"If you two lovebirds would stop arguing—" Silas interrupted.

"We are not lovebirds," the two of them said at the same time.

Silas cleared his throat before continuing, "I think the snake would be an *excellent* distraction for your escape."

"Silas Silver," the headmistress' voice echoed throughout the school. "Please come see me in my office."

"I think it's too flashy," Atlas said, looking up from his book. Silas hung his head, sighing deeply at being caught. As he left the classroom, the snake was behind him, racing towards him. But with a flick of his hand, the snake disappeared into thin air. Emira watched with her jaw hanging open.

She had to admit that it was pretty cool what Silas could do.

"Silas, you better not say I was involved in this because if I get another letter from my mother, I will be hanged and slaughtered in minutes," Atlas called after him. Silas simply waved his words away. Atlas slumped against the door frame, his head against it.

"Are you okay?" Emira asked.

"I will never be," he answered, still facing the door frame. "My fate was solidified once I met these two."

"It'll… It'll be okay," she said, patting his back as she walked by. She had to stifle a laugh, but she looked over at Mateo who was still in the classroom and his expression subdued her. He stared at her, one brown eye and one golden. Both looked haunted.

She tried to shake his gaze off of her as she went to the next class. But the look he had given her, stayed. She believed him when he said he was terrified for her, a stranger no less. But she couldn't figure out why.

Though, that image stayed with her, Mateo standing in the darkness of the classroom, looking like he had aged ten years. Haunted. That was the only word Emira could think of when she remembered his expression. Mateo looked haunted. But by what, she wasn't sure.

CHAPTER NINE

Mateo watched as Emira hit the wooden dummy with a wooden sword while he took a break near the water fountain. Silas, next to him, downed three cups of water and poured the fourth over his head.

"She's not very good," he murmured.

"She'll die in an instant," Mateo concurred.

"When's the next outing?" Silas asked, looking up at the ceiling. "Is it next month we're supposed to go outside of the walls with the other warriors?"

"I don't think I would be allowed to go," Mateo said, finally tearing his gaze away from Emira. Sacrifices very rarely were allowed to go on dangerous trips, considering they needed to stay alive until it was time for them to be sacrificed.

He watched as the wooden sword slipped out of her hands and landed on her foot. She stifled a yelp and jumped around for a little before getting down and grabbing the sword once more.

"Yeah, she's going to die," Silas confirmed. Mateo put a hand to his forehead and rubbed his temples. He wasn't sure what it was about this girl, but she did everything in her power to worry him.

Kanoa bounded up, covered in sweat, as he threw his sword into the "Return" pile. He also downed some water before he started talking and threw a thumb over his shoulder.

"Silas, do you think your cousin would go out with me?" Kanoa asked. The three of them watched as Silas' cousin, Celeste Silver, cleanly sliced off the magical *bellua* dummy's head. Her light blue eyes, the same that Silas had, looked murderous.

"I mean, if you want to, be my guest," Silas shrugged. Kanoa pointed at Atlas who was still finishing up his assignment. Atlas just gave Kanoa an exasperated look before dodging his dummy's blow, not knowing what they were talking about.

"Celeste!" Kanoa called. Celeste's blue eyes glared at him as she returned her sword.

"Kanoa," she said. She looked over at Mateo and Silas, but didn't say a word.

"I think you have the most beautiful orbs," Kanoa said. Celeste's hard gaze faltered.

"You do?" she asked.

"Yeah and you know, I have to say, you're the most beautiful in your year," he continued. Celeste was in the year below them. Her pale skin had a slight pink tinge to it upon hearing his words. Mateo made eye contact with Silas. He was convinced Kanoa could charm a *bellua* if he tried to.

"What about Isla?" Celeste asked in a small voice. She looked over her shoulder at the girl with red hair glaring over at them. Silas mouthed "Isla?" to Mateo. Mateo shrugged. He didn't remember Kanoa ever talking about or to an Isla.

"Isla and I are over," Kanoa said. "We've been over for a

while. But, would *you* like to sit together for dinner tonight? It would be nice to have a pretty girl's company." Celeste tucked a dark lock behind her ear. It was weird seeing the future warrior Celeste acting like a girl in front of them.

"I mean, sure," she said.

"Celeste, are you insane?" Silas said, interrupting.

"What?" she asked, her glare exacting from her cousin interrupting. Silas put his arm around his cousin's shoulder as he nearly glowered at Kanoa.

"Stay away from my cousin, Kwan," Silas said, calling him by his last name before dragging his cousin away.

"You said it was all right!" Kanoa called after him.

"I didn't think she'd cave to your showman-like advances," he said. To his cousin, he muttered, "I thought you were better than this."

"I'm sorry that your friend is really attractive," she mumbled. Silas' jaw dropped. He turned back towards Kanoa.

"Stay away," he warned. The two of them watched as Silas was clearly arguing with his cousin as they walked out of the auditorium. Atlas, finally finishing his assignment, walked over to them.

"What did I miss?" he asked, looking over his shoulder at Silas and Celeste leaving.

"What you missed is that I successfully pulled a girl by complimenting her orbs," Kanoa said, proudly.

"What? With Celeste?" Atlas asked, rubbing water onto the back of his neck. Kanoa nodded his head. Atlas looked over at Mateo for confirmation with those quiet eyes of his.

"He did lead with that, yeah," Mateo said.

"Weird," Atlas mused. "So, you're attracted to Silas."

"Yes—What?" Kanoa said.

"You're attracted to Silas," Atlas repeated.

"I'm not… I'm not attracted to Silas," Kanoa said, confused.

"Celeste and Silas look the same."

"No, they don't," Kanoa laughed. But his laugh slowly disappeared as he continued to think.

"Atlas is right. They look pretty similar," Mateo said, cocking his head as he looked at the back of his friend and Celeste, standing in the far end of the auditorium, in the doorway. Still, very clearly arguing. He glanced over at Emira who was still trying to finish her own assignment by hitting the wooden, non-moving dummy a certain amount of times in certain spots.

"They… They don't look similar," Kanoa said, unconvincingly.

"Same black hair, same blue eyes. They even have the same nose," Atlas said. Kanoa's expression was frozen.

"So, you're attracted to Silas," Atlas confirmed. Kanoa looked out into space.

"*Am* I?" he whispered to himself. Mateo shook his head, looking back at Emira. Mr. Killian was instructing her, but the former warrior looked frustrated and Emira looked lost.

"Are you coming with, Mateo?" Atlas asked. The two of them were about to leave.

He looked at her once more before responding, "Yeah, I'm coming."

MATEO PUT THE BOOK ON THE SHELF WHERE IT WAS SUPPOSED TO go. He sighed as he looked back at the cart filled with books. His punishment for escaping was having to help out the school librarian, Mrs. Foxweather. He put another book on the shelf.

He hated doing mundane work like this. Not when he should be trying to figure out his next escape.

He heard a book thud to the ground and a small yelp of pain from a few rows away. Mateo looked over at the grand clock at the front of the library. It was too late for anyone to still be studying there. He quietly walked over to where the sound came from.

Peeking his head around the corner, he watched as Emira grabbed the book and put it back in its place. She rubbed her foot, the same foot she dropped her wooden sword on earlier. Mateo massaged his temples before revealing himself to her.

"Priestess," he said as a greeting. She looked over at him, her violet eyes prominent on her pale face. Golden freckles scattered across her cheeks and nose. She pushed her curls out of her face, glaring up at him. He hadn't seen her curls at their full glory, as she always had them pulled back into a singular braid. He breathed in sharply upon seeing her.

"Mateo," she said, rather coldly.

"What are you looking for?" he asked. He was amused by her tone. Most people liked Mateo, when he wasn't causing trouble. Though he wasn't sure if people liked him because he was a Cordero, the grandson of Balan, or because of who he really was. It was nice to be under someone's skin for once.

"None of your business," she said, holding her nose up high. He shrugged and pointed over to the row he was at.

"If you need help, I'm over there," he said.

"I won't need your help, but thank you," she retorted. Mateo went back to his cart of books and watched as she pivoted on her foot and walked to another row. She had her head sideways, reading the spines of the books. Her long curls hung down like a curtain of sunlight.

He moved his cart to be in her row and when she gave him a death stare, he shrugged and pointed to the books.

"I have to put them away," he said. She rolled her violet eyes and continued to look sideways at the books in the row. He watched her as he put away the other books. He couldn't help but watch her, like she was some strange, mythical creature. After a few minutes of this, she started to reach up towards the top shelf. Her fingers barely grazed the book she was trying to grab. He watched her struggle for a little before walking over and grabbing it, letting it drop onto her head.

"Ow!" she said, rubbing her head as she picked the book up from the ground. She threw him a glare. Mateo smirked.

"*The Twelve Steps to Sword Fighting*," he said, reading the title of the book she picked up. "If you think that'll help you get better, it won't."

"What would you know?" she muttered, opening the book up. She started to thumb through it.

"Yeah, what would I know," he said, returning to his cart of books. "It's not like I'm the top swordsman at Leliara or anything." He glanced over at her for a reaction. She stopped turning the pages of the book, her amethyst eyes curious.

"You're good at this?" she asked, holding the book up a little.

"Yeah," he said. He walked over and grabbed it from her. "And I didn't use a lousy book to do it." Her eyebrows knitted together and she snatched the book back.

"Whatever," she muttered.

"I could help you," he said the words before he even thought about it. *Help her? Why would I help her?*

"I don't need your help," she said. Mateo rolled his eyes, and she had the audacity to look offended by it.

"Listen, if you want to fail at being a warrior, that's up to you," he said, raising his hands. "I don't care if you're a part of the Idols' army or not." She bit her lip and glanced over at him before shaking her head.

"If I need your help, I'll ask," she said, holding the sword fighting book close to her chest. She pivoted away and went to check the book out. Mateo half hoped she wouldn't take him up on his offer. He had this sinking feeling that if she did, he wouldn't be able to leave this place.

CHAPTER TEN

Emira pored over *The Twelve Steps to Sword Fighting* while she half-heartedly ate a biscuit. She had been reading it every day, to the point where she was sure her eyes were swollen from all the straining she was doing. Mateo's words had been ringing in her ears the whole time. *"Listen, if you want to fail at being a warrior, that's up to you."* It was her worst nightmare.

"You've been reading that all week," Darlene said, half awake. She rubbed the sleep from her eyes.

"Is it informative?" Shiloh asked, only opting to eat a biscuit with grape jelly smeared over it. Darlene was right, she ate like a bird. A book about the myths of Constellatia was open to the left of her brunette friend, her eyes gently roving over the words every so often while she ate. Emira looked down at her own book that she had open. *Am I turning into Shiloh?*

"I don't know," Emira responded, closing the book. "I need to advance faster. How am I supposed to graduate with everyone and be a warrior if I can't use a sword?" Darlene and

Shiloh exchanged a glance. Whatever they knew, they weren't saying anything to Emira about it. Her heart sank. They probably thought she wasn't going to succeed as a warrior as well. *"If you want to fail at being a warrior, that's up to you."* Damn that Mateo.

"Well, you aren't going to learn by reading a book," Shiloh said, gesturing to it, her own book still open. Emira squinted her eyes at her comment. She always learned things from books, but Emira didn't want to be the person to point that out.

"Why can't I?" she asked, putting her head into her hands. Darlene pulled Emira's hands off of her face, a cautious, yet pitying, smile on her lips.

"You learn sword fighting by doing, not by reading," she said, tapping Emira's book with her fingernail. "When you get your physical strength up, it'll be easier."

"Says the one who fully plans on not using a sword once she's a warrior," Shiloh said. Darlene shrugged, grabbing a biscuit from the table.

"Why use a sword when I have this?" Light illuminated from the tops of Darlene's fingertips. Phoenix ash and intense light were the only things that could penetrate a *bellua*, at least, that's what Emira had read.

Seeing Darlene easily manifest her power, Emira thought about her own ichor. So far, she hadn't been able to replicate whatever she did that got the attention of Ophelia. She wasn't sure if she even truly *had* ichor at this point, Mali's or otherwise. Something twisted in Emira's chest as Darlene's light faded. Something sharp and torturous, like envy.

Kanoa grabbed the biscuit out of Darlene's hand before she could take a bite out of it. She looked up at him as he took a big bite and then handed it back to her. The three of them looked at him with disbelief creased into their expressions. He didn't seem to notice it.

"Hey Darling," he said after he swallowed. She dropped the biscuit in disgust.

"Are you for real, Kanoa?" she said, getting up from the table. She turned towards Emira and Shiloh. "I'll catch up with you guys later." Kanoa watched as she stalked away. Emira was surprised her little steps didn't leave burn marks into the marble floor.

"Do you think taking a bite out of it was too far?" Kanoa asked, his charm disappearing. Shiloh shrugged.

"Maybe don't get in between a girl and her food in the future," she said, softly. "What is with you, anyways? You usually know exactly what to say to a girl."

"I don't know," he muttered, watching Darlene leave the food hall. "Something she does to me, I guess." Shiloh widened her eyes at Emira, who shrugged in response.

"You'll talk me up to her, won't you Shi?" Kanoa asked, patting Shiloh's shoulder. She winced at his heavy hand. "She keeps avoiding me, ever since last year." *Last year?* Emira's curiosity was piqued, but she didn't want to ask him about it. She hardly knew them enough to ask something as personal as that.

"Yeah, Kanoa. I will," Shiloh said, dismissive. He winked at her, back to his usual confident self, before walking away.

"I have to go," Emira said, grabbing her book as she finished eating her biscuit. She quickly drank a glass of orange juice. "I have to meet with the headmistress." Shiloh winced once more.

"Good luck," she said.

Emira pressed her lips into a line. "Thanks."

They both knew what the headmistress wanted to meet

Emira about, considering all the meetings she had with her prior. Emira's ichor hadn't shown up at all. Most people's ichor manifested around eight, or nine, or—at the latest—ten. Some were lucky to have it manifest earlier than that. But, Emira's hadn't at the age of seventeen, at least, not purposefully. And she could feel that everyone seemed nervous and tense about it.

As she was leaving the food hall, Mateo was walking in. Emira ducked her head, hoping he wouldn't see her, but he grabbed her arm and gently turned her around.

"You hiding from me?" She wanted to rip his smirk off of his face. Instead, she stood up straighter and cleared her throat, her chin raised minutely.

"I don't know what you mean," she said. "Why would I be hiding from *you*?" She tried to put the book behind her back. His quick eyes clocked it, and he grabbed it, pulling it out from hiding.

"Looks like you were," he said, gesturing to her book. "You still trying to teach yourself how to fight by reading?"

"You can learn a lot from reading," she retorted.

"I don't doubt that," he said, crossing his arms as he leaned against the wall. *Does he ever stand upright?* "How is it working out for you?"

"I feel like you know the answer to that," she said with a grimace. She didn't like admitting it to him, but he could clearly see her struggle in Mr. Killian's sword-fighting class. She sometimes would see him looking at her, like he was amused at how terrible she continued to be. He tapped a knuckle on the cover of the book.

"If you need help, you know you could just ask," he said, softly. She bit the inside of her cheek. She really, *really* didn't want to be in close quarters with this guy. Ever. And yet, she kept finding herself in the position of being around him. And, if she admitted it to herself, she *did* need him.

"Let's say I did need your help," Emira said, her voice barely above a whisper. He raised his eyebrows. "Where would we meet?"

"If I were to help you," he said, slowly, going along with the hypothetical, "we'd have to meet outside after curfew."

"Right," she said. Emira hated breaking the rules. It was basically ingrained in her at this point in her life. But, she desperately needed a win. Some kind of win.

"What time?" she asked. Mateo blinked, his mismatched eyes softening. Part of her felt proud for thwarting his expectations.

"Eleven," he said.

"Fine," Emira said back. "I'll be there." She pressed the book into Mateo's chest. "You better not be all talk." He smiled, lopsidedly, as he took the book from her.

"I've never been just talk, Priestess," he whispered. Emira shivered as she walked away from him, towards the headmistress' office. She could feel his eyes on her as she continued down the hallway.

EMIRA SAT STILL AS THE SYRINGE PUNCTURED HER SKIN, THE small pinch not warranting her flinching like a maniac, though a deep part of her wanted to. She was terrified of needles. Dark crimson blood filled the syringe, and she watched with fascination. Blood was something Emira hadn't seen much of, as she didn't go with the other priestesses to the hospitals in Aeluris because she was "too young." The liquid was interesting to her.

The crimson fluid was what held her power, was what was keeping her and all other humans alive.

"This is the fifth test we've done, Felix," Headmistress Alessia said, interrupting Emira's thoughts.

Felix Sharpe was not only a legacy, but was a fearsome warrior. As far as Emira knew, he was still fighting *bellua* outside of the walls. She wasn't exactly sure why he kept coming to Leliara to take her blood.

"Every test we've done has said she has ichor," Felix said. "I'm not certain why it's not manifesting itself."

"Do you think it matters?" Headmistress Alessia asked, her voice low.

"I'm not sure," he said. "We've never had a case like this, plus we don't know about the powers she possesses yet." They exchanged silent looks with one another.

"Will I be able to be a warrior if my ichor never manifests?" Emira asked, breaking the silence. Felix glanced over at her, the sharpness in his eyes diminishing.

"Of course," he said, a kind smile appearing. "We need all kinds of people in the ranks." Which meant he didn't think she'd be able to fight *bellua* with everyone else. Emira tried not to sink into her seat. The two of them exchanged another unreadable look with one another before the headmistress got up from her desk and grabbed a cup. Emira already knew what was about to happen, and the greasy feeling of dread settled into her chest.

"Let's move on to some tests," Headmistress Alessia said, gesturing towards another seat. Felix wiped down the area where he took blood to get rid of any residue and pressed down with a soft gauze as Emira moved from one chair to another.

"Try to move this cup from one end of the desk to the other," the headmistress ordered. This was the fifth time this week she had Emira do this.

Emira stared hard at the cup and tried to will it to the other side. *Please, please, please,* she thought. It didn't move an inch. A feather would've done more damage to it than her mind. After a grueling few minutes of this, the headmistress removed the cup.

"Okay," she said, obviously disappointed. "Try to read my mind." She stared into Headmistress Alessia's green eyes. She strained her eyes to try to see beyond her face and into her head, but she heard nothing.

"Do you hear anything?" Headmistress Alessia asked. Emira shook her head. Heat flushed her cheeks. She was an embarrassment. Not only to herself, but to Ophelia, the Idol of Night, who was sure she had Mali's ichor within her. Who was so sure, she had brought Emira to the school of Leliara. Headmistress Alessia only sighed in response, deeply.

For the last test, the headmistress brought Emira to her giant fish tank she kept in her office. Emira could see her watery reflection in the glass of the tank. Her violet eyes stuck out, like always, but there was a dullness to them. Her lips were curled downwards, and even to herself, she looked like the picture of defeat and failure.

"Control one of the fishes to jump out," the headmistress ordered. A blue fish with a beautiful flowing tail caught Emira's attention.

Jump out, she ordered in her mind. The fish stared at her with its one eye as it swam along the length of the tank.

Jump, she thought. The fish continued on its way.

Please, just jump, she thought, desperate. But, there was nothing. Emira didn't feel magical in the slightest. She glanced over at the headmistress, whose disappointment was palpable.

Emira did her best not to hang her head. She hated disappointing people. Especially those in charge.

"Let's stop for today," Headmistress Alessia ordered. Emira straightened and stepped away from the fish tank. Felix scribbled some stuff in his notebook. *Probably about how the Idol of Night made a huge mistake and that the girl with Idol's eyes is just that, a girl with weird, abnormal features,* she thought.

"You're free to go," the headmistress said. Emira left, but before she could close the door all the way, she heard Felix and the headmistress talking.

"It might be that she's repressed it all these years," she heard Felix say.

"If that's the case, how are we supposed to find out if..." and the headmistress' voice morphed into hushed whispers. Emira quietly shut the door and headed back to her dorm room. There weren't any classes today, thank Kali, the Idol of Life. All she heard lately was how she wasn't good enough, and she'd rather not hear it from her teachers as well today.

"How did it go?" Shiloh asked once Emira came in and shut the door. Emira shrugged. *It was a disaster,* she could say. *Turns out, I'm probably a normal human who doesn't belong here in the slightest.* She could feel the fiery tears start to burn the back of her eyes. How dare she think she was remotely special, like Darlene and Shiloh. How dare a priestess-to-be, an orphan, ever believe herself to be more than just that. The headmistress' disappointed pursed lips flashed through her mind.

"Still hasn't manifested itself," she answered, instead of revealing her own vicious thoughts. Shiloh twisted her lips in thought.

"Maybe it's because you haven't used it much. You don't know what it feels like," Shiloh mused. Easy for her to say. She was a legacy. Her ichor probably manifested before the age of eight.

Emira tried not to sound bitter. "What does it feel like?"

"Well, every power feels different to each person. Though, it is hard to explain. When you're a kid, it's easier for the power to flow out," Shiloh said, using her hands to demonstrate the flow. "And if you use it enough, your power grows. Although, I still don't have a handle on mine yet. For me, big emotions cause it to just flow right out. Maybe that's the same for you, too."

"Maybe," Emira said, flopping down onto her bed. She stared up at the sage green ceiling, deciding to reveal her insecurities. "Or maybe I don't have any power."

"You wouldn't be here if you didn't," Shiloh said, crossing her arms on the back of her desk chair as she rested her head on them.

"Maybe the test is wrong. Maybe it's possible to have ichor but not have any power that comes with it," Emira wondered.

"You had to have shown your power for Ophelia to bring you here," Shiloh pointed out. Emira thought about the day of the parade. She didn't do anything, really. She was frustrated about putting the statuette on the float and then, suddenly, the people parted ways and she was able to do so. There was nothing that she could feel come out of her. Maybe it was fluke. Or maybe…

"Maybe they got the wrong person," she said, her voice a whisper of a sound.

"No, don't say that. They didn't get the wrong person," Shiloh responded, getting up from her chair and sitting down on Emira's bed. She stared at her for a moment, her brown eyes searching, before saying, "C'mon, let me show you something."

Emira groaned a little. "Leave me here to wither and die." Shiloh laughed as she pulled on her arm.

"C'mon, you're starting to sound like Darlene," she said.

Emira reluctantly followed Shiloh out of the dorm room, pulling on her shoes as she did.

"Where are we going?" she asked. Shiloh looked at her, her normally even bay brown eyes glittering.

"A place where you can let your ichor flow," she answered. Emira followed her out of the girls' side of the dorm rooms and down the swirling steps that led towards the back of the school.

They walked in silence as Emira studied her newfound friend. Shiloh didn't talk to many people. She had only seen her speaking mostly to Darlene and sometimes to Atlas.

"Did you ever have trouble? Adjusting here?" Emira asked as they walked out the back door. The sweet smell of the ground after rain filled her nose. It was nearly always raining during the month of Balia. She wondered, albeit selfishly, if they had that in common. Hardly anyone spoke to Emira at school. She had heard whispers of people talking about the fact that she was raised in a temple, and a gaggle of laughter following it. An uneducated orphan with no family to support her. It was why she spent so much time in the library after hours, reading everything she could get her hands on.

Emira didn't want to admit she was having trouble to anyone. That moving from everyone she'd ever known, and suddenly becoming someone different than she thought she was, was making her head spin. But, she wanted to know if it was normal to feel that way. If everyone did, at some point. Or if she really was simply different from the rest. And even though Shiloh wouldn't be able to relate entirely to Emira, she just needed to know she wasn't alone.

"I did," Shiloh responded, to Emira's relief. "When we first got here, it was hard for me. I was only five years old, and I was ripped away from everyone I grew up with and loved. And I was never someone who fit in, really." The wet leaves underneath their shoes squished in the silence.

"Darlene is actually who made me feel better about being here. She came up to me one day, talking about my shoes of all things, and we've been best friends ever since," Shiloh continued, a small smile spreading across her face from remembering the moment.

"Darlene seems really friendly," Emira said. Shiloh looked over at her.

"She is," she confirmed. "She wants to be friends with everyone and be liked by everyone. And it's hard not to, when she tries." The image of Darlene flashed through Emira's mind. She really was like what they used to say about fairies. Darlene was all light and love, flitting around from person to person. But, like fairies, Emira was sure that if anyone crossed Darlene, she wouldn't let it go.

"This is it," Shiloh said. Emira looked at where they were. It was the lake that was in the wooded area of the school grounds, and near it was a giant willow tree. Its leaves were scattered on the ground below it, with some still hanging on for dear life.

"You come here to practice using your power?" Emira asked, looking around. For some reason, it felt almost creepy to be there during a cloudy, fall day.

"Yes," she answered. She picked up a stone near the lake's edge. "This lake has a lot of useless stuff like this to practice on." And then, without another word, she concentrated on the stone in her hand. And a few seconds later, the stone had broken into pieces.

"Do you want to try?" Shiloh reached down and grabbed another stone from the water, holding it up to Emira.

"I don't think it would do anything," Emira mumbled. Shiloh furrowed her eyebrows.

"It's a tangible feeling," she said. "It's not just a thought. It comes from within." She put the stone on the ground a little ways away and then stood next to Emira.

"Go ahead and try to move it. And focus on the feeling as you do it," Shiloh instructed. Emira's face scrunched up. She didn't know if she should trust Shiloh's words. And she didn't particularly feel like embarrassing herself further.

"It's okay if you don't move it," Shiloh reassured. "But, there should be a certain feeling you get somewhere within your body when you try. Focus on that feeling and hold onto it."

"What if I don't feel anything? What if there's something wrong with me?" Emira asked, quietly. Shiloh smiled, the light coming through the gray clouds reflecting off of her glasses.

"If you feel nothing, there's nothing wrong with you," she comforted. "It just means that your ichor is different from mine." Emira stood there for a little longer, her eyes on the stone. She held her arm, something she did when she was feeling insecure. *Everyone's ichor is different,* Emira thought to herself. Shiloh wasn't there to judge her, she reassured herself, she was there to help. And Emira desperately needed help.

"You can do it," Shiloh said softly. "It's just us two here." Emira swallowed her fears down to the pit of her stomach and focused her attention on the smooth stone. She focused so hard she thought her head was going to explode.

Focus on that feeling, Emira thought to herself. She held onto the feeling of her head splitting open, her eyes straining as white filled her peripheral vision. The feeling changed to a lightheaded feeling, like her head was floating above her somehow. Emira rocked forward, but the stone didn't move an inch.

Did she...? Relief washed over her as she stared at the stone. She was feeling something, something that she could hold onto. Maybe she wasn't a hopeless case after all.

"Okay, let's stop," Shiloh said, concern lacing her words. She picked up the stone and closed her fingers around it, breaking Emira's concentration. Emira immediately sat down in the wet grass, not worrying about her skirt getting wet in the process. She held her head, but looked up at Shiloh, beaming ear to ear.

"I think I felt it," she whispered. Shiloh smiled back at her.

CHAPTER ELEVEN

A knock came at their door. Darlene opened it to a tall girl with long, straight black hair which was pulled back into a tight ponytail. Her blue-gray eyes stood out on her pale face, causing her features to look even more sharp than they already did. Like cold marble, or white porcelain, she looked like she was made of stone.

"Celeste, what are you doing here?" Darlene asked. Celeste held up a white piece of paper, folded in half, nudged between her pointer and middle fingers.

"This is for someone named Emira," Celeste said. *For me?*

"Ooo, who from?" Darlene asked, taking the note. Emira wracked her brain trying to figure out who would be sending her a note at this hour. The only person she could think of was Mateo. He said to meet him at eleven, she just didn't know where. She stood up from her desk chair, having finished her assignment for the evening. Darlene handed the note to Emira who immediately opened it.

> *Meet me by the back door.*
> *The spell will be broken around 10:50 pm.*
> *It'll only last for five minutes, so don't be late.*

Emira looked at the spiky scrawl briefly and then folded the note back up and put it in her back pocket. He didn't sign it, which for some reason bothered her. It showed how arrogant he was. A true aristocrat. She refrained from rolling her eyes.

"I don't know. Kanoa told me to deliver it," Celeste said, bored. Darlene's obsidian eyes cut over towards her.

"Kanoa?" she asked, her voice uncharacteristically sharp. Celeste, who looked like she could already be a warrior, looked taken aback by Darlene's change of tone.

"Yeah?"

"Are you sleeping with him?"

"Hopefully."

"Do you not realize he's your cousin's best friend?"

"Technically Mateo is Silas' best friend," Celeste responded. Her stormy eyes narrowed. "Are you into Kanoa or something?"

"I'm not," Darlene scoffed. She looked Celeste up and down. "Are you done here?"

"I... I guess so," Celeste muttered. Darlene promptly let the door close, hard. She stared at it, seconds ticking by, before she took a deep breath, fluffed her hair up, and turned around. Shiloh and Emira exchanged glances with one another. *That was... weirdly aggressive for Darlene.*

"What does Kanoa want with you?" Darlene asked. Her voice still had some bitterness attached to it.

"It's not from Kanoa," Emira said.

"Oh." She looked a little lost. "Who's it from?" She looked like she was calming down a bit.

"Oh, uh, it's from Atlas," Emira lied. "He's helping me with sword fighting."

"Atlas?" Darlene said. Her eyes lit up. "Maybe he likes you! He's not even that good at sword fighting. I mean, he's all right. But, he's no Mateo."

"Maybe," Emira said, glancing over at Shiloh. But Shiloh had turned around, her ears redder than a chili pepper. It was okay if she let Darlene think Atlas was into her, right?

Emira glanced over at the clock on the wall. Thirty minutes before she had to leave the dorm room.

"Good luck sneaking out," Darlene smiled, laying down on her bed. She picked up her book that she was reading before Celeste had knocked on the door. Emira smiled back, but it didn't reach her eyes.

She didn't know why she lied to Darlene and Shiloh about who the note was from. For some reason, Emira didn't want them to know she was meeting Mateo. Maybe because she thought Darlene would get the wrong idea. At least, that's what Emira told herself.

MATEO WAS WAITING RIGHT BY THE BACK DOOR, LEANING AGAINST the brick wall next to it. Emira nearly had a heart attack, seeing him there. He always seemed to sneak up on her.

"Don't do that!" she exclaimed. He stood up straight.

"Do what? Stand here?"

"Yes," Emira said, clutching her chest. She looked at his smug, arrogant face and rolled her eyes. She knew she was going to severely regret this. "Idol of Life, let's just get this over with."

"Don't need to invoke Kali," Mateo said, a shit-eating grin on his face. He grabbed the two wooden swords that were resting on the wall next to him and started to lead the way.

"So, how long do you think this lesson of yours will be?" Emira asked from behind him. He was wearing a navy blue sweatshirt, and she found herself realizing that she never noticed how broad his shoulders really were. He was a lean guy, lithe. But, also, built like a strong warrior. She blinked away the thought as she rubbed her arms. Her long-sleeved shirt was probably a little too thin for the autumn night.

"It'll only be for an hour," Mateo said, looking up at the moon. Emira unconsciously went to hold the crescent moon necklace charm that had been around her neck for as long as she could remember, forgetting she had left it on a windowsill. She saw Mateo glanced over at her, noticing her hands reaching up and touching nothing. Blood rushed to her cheeks, and she hoped he would think it was because of the chill air.

"It's this way," he said, not mentioning it, gesturing towards the wooded area.

"Do we have to?" Emira asked, meeting his eyes.

"What? Are you scared?" he teased.

"I'm not scared of anything," she lied.

"Yeah," Mateo said. "I can see that. Considering you walked straight into your death."

"I don't know why you keep saying that," she mumbled, grabbing a branch as they walked into the woods. She pulled it off the tree and used it to move any other low hanging branches out of her way.

"You could be Mali's sacrifice," Mateo pointed out. Emira opened her mouth to respond, but he held up a hand. "Please don't say it'll be an honor to be her sacrifice." She closed her mouth.

Emira studied him for a moment and could see the angry, bitter boy that still lived within his body that was becoming a man. She couldn't help but wonder what it was that made him this way. It made her uncomfortable, how comfortable his presence was becoming. How she wondered about his childhood. Knitting her eyebrows together, she looked down at her feet as she walked.

"I don't think that I am," she said, trying to hide her disappointment. "If that's what you've been worried about." He was quiet, and there was a tightening around his face that appeared whenever the topic of the Idols came up, she noticed.

"They haven't found the one with all of her ichor yet and then you come along, with her eyes and everything. You're clearly related to her," he said. *Trust me*, she wanted to say, *I wish I was the sacrifice, even if it is your greatest fear. You truly don't know how lucky you are.*

But, she didn't say that. She couldn't.

"Yeah," she said, scratching the back of her head. "But, there's no way to see if I have all of her ichor from blood tests. And I'm not able to do anything that falls within her powers." *And we don't know how closely related I really am to her*, she wanted to say. The Idol of Luck could be her great, great, great grandmother, and she simply had the genes for her eyes... and her entire face.

"What do you mean?" Mateo asked, his mismatched eyes searching hers.

"I mean, Headmistress Alessia and Felix keep testing me to use my ichor, and I haven't been able to yet." He furrowed his thick eyebrows, looking away from her, at the mention of Felix. She didn't know why the name bothered him, but she decided not to press about it.

"You might've repressed it too much," he muttered.

"Well, if I've repressed it too much, then I don't think it'll come out by the time the Tenth Year arrives," Emira said. At her words, he looked relieved, like a weight was lifted off of his shoulders. His lips curled into a smile, but it didn't reach his eyes.

"I hope that's the case," he said softly. And as he said this, Emira was filled by some kind of sadness even though she smiled back at him. His eyes, his eyes looked so empty. *Did they always look that empty?* And something hit Emira like an underground train.

Mateo was a sacrifice. He was going to die.

She swallowed the pang deep into the recesses of her body. She had gotten too used to him, too comfortable in his irritating presence. He wasn't going to die, and part of her chastised herself for immediately thinking it.

It was an honor that he was a sacrifice. He was going to be absorbed by Balan in order for Balan to continue to protect and guard Constellatia, in order for his life to be prolonged. And so were the other sacrifices. They all had an important job to do. Mateo wasn't going to die. He'll live on in Balan. He'll live for an eternity. It was what she was taught. It was also what she told herself whenever she looked at him a little too long.

He's arrogant, probably had everything handed to him on a silver platter, and he hates the Idols and everything good about Constellatia, she reminded herself. But, even to her, the words were starting to fall flat. Idol of Fate, she knew she shouldn't have spent time with him.

"Here's a good spot," Mateo said, gesturing to an empty field in the woods and interrupting her spiraling thoughts.

"Why the woods?" Emira asked, looking around at the shadows in between the trees.

"Because the guards don't patrol around here," he said.

"Shouldn't that clue you into thinking it *might* be dangerous?"

"Dangerous? Priestess, there aren't any *bellua* here," he scoffed. "Although, the creatures that Mrs. Halloway teaches about are kept here."

"Aren't the creatures she teaches us about dangerous?"

He shrugged. "They're not too difficult to handle if you know what you're doing."

"I don't know what I'm doing. She's barely taught me about the creatures outside of the walls," Emira said, hands on her hips. And Priestess Irene didn't teach her about them either, not realizing she'd need the knowledge someday. He handed her one of the wooden swords and put his down by the base of a tree.

"You're not going to fight me?" she asked. He raised an eyebrow.

"I need to see if you can even handle it first," he said. Emira held her chin up.

"I can handle it," she said. "You're not *that* good. And in class, you're fighting a fake, dummy *bellua*. It's not the same as a real life person." Mateo couldn't help the laugh that escaped his lips. She glowered at him.

"What?" she asked. His one gold eye glittered in the dark.

"You think you can beat me?" he nearly whispered. He was closer than she wanted him to be.

"I think I can," she replied, holding her chin high as she held his gaze. The corners of his lips twitched.

"You? Who let a sword fall and hit your foot the other day." Emira could feel heat burn her cheeks.

"You saw that?" she said, almost under her breath. A smirk played on his lips. He turned around, creating distance between them, grabbed the wooden sword, and lowered himself, bouncing from leg to leg.

"Let's do it, then," he said, his eyes turning cold. It was as if his whole face changed, from his boyish charm to a full blown warrior ready for battle. Emira held her sword with two hands, cursing herself for saying anything. She couldn't sword fight to save her life, and she knew it. And she knew Mateo knew it. She was simply bluffing, like she always seemed to do in front of him. And he was the number one swordsman in all of Leliara.

"Great," she said, with gritted teeth. *Why do I keep doing this to myself?* She groaned within. *Just remember what the book said, dodge and slash,* she thought.

But, what the book said did nothing to help her. Mateo came rushing towards her like she herself was a *bellua*. She clumsily tried to dodge his attack but his wooden sword hit her, and she started to fall forward. She dropped her sword and braced herself. With one arm, he grabbed her and pulled her towards him.

"Guess you couldn't handle it," he smirked down at her. His chest was somehow simultaneously hard and soft. And warm. Very warm. Looking up at him, she never noticed how sharp his jaw was, or how the knot of his throat jutted out. He was handsome, devilishly so. It was a fact that she could no longer deny.

Emira was aware how hard her heart was beating, and afraid that he could hear it, too, she immediately pushed off of him.

"I guess the book didn't really help," she muttered, brushing the wrinkles off of her clothes. She avoided looking at him, her heart pounding all over. She had never been that close to a boy before, and she didn't know how to comprehend how it made her feel.

It's not because it was Mateo, it was because it was a boy, she told herself. *You'd feel that way with any boy.*

"Let's just start with dodging and slashing," he said, putting his wooden sword back at the base of a tree. His previously smug smile was gone, and he looked a little rattled himself.

"So the book was right," Emira said. "Dodging and slashing."

"You gotta practice it, not read about it," Mateo said, in his know-it-all tone. She rolled her eyes. She leaned down and grabbed her wooden sword, determined to put the thought of Mateo holding her against his chest out of her mind.

"Let's practice then," she said.

Mateo made her practice slashing forward and then dodging his outstretched arm. But he moved in slow motion, not like how he did earlier. Emira did this for an hour, and by the end, she felt like her arms were going to fall off. But, the thought of her against him refused to leave her mind.

"Good work," he said, grabbing the other wooden sword. "In a few months, I'm sure you'll be able to fight one of the sixth years."

"In a few months?" Emira panted. "What do you mean? I don't have that kind of time."

"You can't rush a skill," he shrugged. He started to walk out of the clearing, towards the school.

"Wait," she said, grabbing his arm. He looked down at her hands, and she immediately released him. She held her own arm instead. "Are you saying we're doing this again?"

"Do you want to be better?" he asked. His mismatched eyes burned holes into her.

"I don't know if I can keep sneaking out like this," Emira said, rubbing her arms. The workout made her body heat up, but now that she had stopped moving, the sweat on her skin made it feel like ice was clinging to her.

"Well, if you want to get better, we need to meet every night," he said. He glanced down at her rubbing her arms and then started to take off his sweatshirt.

"What are you doing?" she asked, her eyes wide.

"What does it look like I'm doing?" he said, his words laced with annoyance. He finished taking off his sweatshirt and handed it to Emira. She held it an arm's length away from her, like it was a dead animal.

"You don't need to look so disgusted," Mateo sighed. "It's so you don't catch a cold."

"I don't need this." She shook her head and handed it back to him. She didn't want this, she didn't want to have her nose filled with his scent. He flashed her a smile.

"If you can keep up, I'll take it," he said, and then he started running through the woods.

"Mateo!" Emira whisper-yelled into the darkness. "Mateo! This isn't funny!" All she heard in response was his laughter. She started forward, as she put on his sweatshirt. Despite not wanting it, she was, admittedly, very cold. And his sweatshirt *was* very warm.

They both ran through the woods, catching glimpses of each other as they did between the gaps of the trees. Emira hated every minute of it, and Mateo seemed to know it, a gleeful smile on his face every time he turned around.

By the time she reached the back door of Leliara, she was covered in sweat. She definitely didn't need his sweatshirt at this point. She tried to take it off, but Mateo shook his head.

"You keep it," he said, a smirk playing on his lips. "I don't want it anymore."

"Why not?" she asked, anticipating his answer.

"Because it's covered in your sweat stench." Emira purposely bumped into him as she opened the door.

"Tell me how I knew you were going to say that," she said, over her shoulder. "You're predictable, Cordero."

"Ah, don't say that," he said, clutching his chest. "You're gonna hurt my feelings. I strive to be unpredictable."

"Keep striving," Emira responded, letting the door close behind her.

CHAPTER TWELVE

"*H*elp me!" Cassandra's voice was haunted, tortured. "*Mateo, help me!*"

Mateo sat up in a cold sweat. He wiped his forehead as he got out of bed. Silas, Atlas, and Kanoa were still sleeping.

He rubbed his temples as he got up. The nightmares were getting worse and more frequent. He didn't know how to make them stop. Carefully, he got dressed and walked towards the door. The floorboards squeaked underneath his foot, and Kanoa sat up straight. Ice cold fear filled Mateo's veins.

"It's okay, Kanoa," he whispered, holding up his hands. "It's me, Mateo. Just had a nightmare."

"Maateeoo," Kanoa moaned slowly before laying back down. Mateo breathed a sigh of relief.

Kanoa was always too light of a sleeper due to his upbringing in Pyrinia. Mateo wasn't exactly sure how Kanoa was brought up, but from what he had said about it, it seemed tough.

Pyrinia was known for being fighters. And if someone was

"

born in that province, the one ruled by the Dragon Idol Nyro, they were trained from the moment they could walk on how to be, not just a fighter, but the strongest one someone could be. Their methods were considered... strict, at best. Considering Kanoa had knocked Mateo out while still half asleep a few years ago, his upbringing had to be pretty bad.

Mateo left his dorm room and walked out of the boys' dormitory and down the spiral steps. Going out the back door, he leaned against the brick wall and pulled a cigarette out from his pocket, a habit he picked up at the age of thirteen. He lit it with his finger, one of the many powers he had the pleasure of being able to mimic. And he breathed in deep while Cassandra's voice echoed in his head.

"You'll help me, won't you?" he remembered Cassandra had said when it was announced she was the sacrifice for Balan. *"You wouldn't let me die, right?"*

He blew out slowly, waiting for the cigarette to relax his body. Emira's violet eyes flickered in his mind, mixing with Cassandra's gold ones. *Shit.*

He closed his eyes and tried to get Cassandra's voice out of his head. Maybe he couldn't save Cassandra, but Emira had nothing to do with it. She said it herself, she wasn't a sacrifice. And even if she was, she would have ten years before the next ritual.

Mateo took another drag from his cigarette. If Emira had powers, it wouldn't come out until after this Tenth Year ritual. He would be long gone by that point. At least, he hoped that would be the case.

The back door opened, and he flinched. Darlene walked out in her pajamas. Baby dust pink, predictable for her. She looked startled to see Mateo standing there beside her.

"What are you doing here?" she asked, accusing. He quirked an eyebrow.

"I could ask you the same thing," Mateo pointed out. She sighed, deeply.

"I can't sleep," Darlene muttered.

"Is it Kanoa?" He saw the way she looked at him. The way she had looked at him since last year. And now, with Celeste in the picture, she didn't look at Kanoa as much anymore. Darlene glanced at him and sighed again. She held out her hand and gestured impatiently. Mateo hesitantly gave her a cigarette, and she put it in between her teeth. He didn't know she smoked.

"A lighter, please?" she ordered. Mateo, instead, turned his finger into flames and lit her cigarette. She took a long drag.

"I hate him," she finally said. "I want nothing to do with him. And yet, here I am. Unable to sleep because of the hellion." She glanced over at Mateo.

"What are *you* doing out here?"

"Same thing," he answered. She raised an eyebrow.

"You also can't sleep because of Kanoa?"

"No," Mateo let out a laugh. "No. Nightmares."

"Oh, Cassandra again?" Darlene asked. It was well known that after Cassandra's death, Mateo would wake up screaming in the middle of the night. Everyone in his year knew about it. It was hard to hide something like that.

Mateo took another drag from his cigarette, hoping the effects would kick in faster. Cassandra's voice started to enter his mind again.

"Mateo, help me!" He winced.

"Yeah," was all he said. Darlene took a good look at him and nodded her head.

"Because of Emira," she said, definitively. That was Darlene's charm. In front of everyone, she was the happy-go-lucky, boy crazy, almost ditzy kind of girl. But, she was observant. Nothing escaped her gaze. And not many people knew that about her.

"I couldn't save Cassandra," Mateo whispered. "I *could* save her." For some reason, he didn't want to say her name. As if not saying it would protect her from whatever darkness took Cassandra.

"Emira isn't even a sacrifice," Darlene pointed out. "There's no need to save her. And with Cassandra... there was nothing you could've done."

A flash of Cassandra struggling against a guard and Balan's eyes keeping him in place went through his mind.

And then blood, so much blood.

Mateo's breath started to quicken, and Darlene looked over at him, concern marring her brow.

"Mateo? Are you all right?" she asked. Her voice sounded faraway. He nodded his head, but he couldn't answer.

"Help me, Mateo!" Cassandra had screamed. *"Mateo! You promised! You promised me!"*

"I'm sorry, I just..." he stammered out. There was a ringing in his head. He looked up at Darlene but her face flickered between Cassandra and Emira. Her brow wrinkled together as Mateo felt himself sinking to the cold, hard ground. It felt like his head was being pulled apart.

Darlene got down on her knees so she was eye level with him. She held his face and stared into his eyes.

"Hold your breath," she said.

"I—"

"Hold your breath, Mateo," she ordered. Mateo held his breath, the little that he had. She held her breath with him and they stared at each other in the silence. Then she breathed out, and he breathed out, too. And his heart slowed down. But the voices...

Darlene gave him a long look and then removed her hands from his face. "You hear voices, don't you?"

Mateo stared at his hands that were still trembling a little. He didn't meet her gaze. "How do you know that?"

"My mom heard voices," she said, her voice hard. "She was a warrior."

"Oh," he said, softly.

"Mom said the best way to get rid of the voices was to do something that took your mind off of them. Easiest way was making love," Darlene said. She was silent for a moment. "Maybe we can help each other."

"Help each other?" he asked.

"I want revenge on Kanoa. You want the voices to stop," she said, simply.

"You'll help me, won't you?" Cassandra had said to him, holding his face in between her hands. *"You'll help your favorite cousin, won't you, Mateo?"*

"Does that offer still stand now?" he asked, his voice breathless. Darlene's eyes widened but then she nodded.

"I'll help make the voices go away."

CHAPTER THIRTEEN

Emira rubbed her head while she stood outside as Mrs. Halloway lectured about the creature she had in front of them. Mrs. Halloway was short and stout, and Emira was surprised to see how short Mrs. Halloway really was when she first met the Creatures teacher. Considering Mrs. Halloway was known for her ability to talk to animals and for being extremely determined to kill *bellua*, Emira imagined her to be taller.

"Now, baby griffins are not as deadly as an adult one," Mrs. Halloway continued her lecture. The baby griffin beside her looked around the field, its bird eyes curious. It was almost as tall as Mrs. Halloway was.

"When you see griffins outside of the walls, they are not domesticated. Those griffins will kill you, especially if they see you as a threat. And they see most warriors as threats," Mrs. Halloway said. "The way to get around a griffin, or to keep a griffin from killing you without killing them, is to give them something valuable. Always keep at least one valuable thing with you whilst in the field. It could save your life." A boy named Ezra Wilson raised his hand.

"Yes, Mr. Wilson?" Mrs. Halloway said.

"Couldn't we just kill the griffin if it's going to attack us?" Ezra asked. Mrs. Halloway's hazel eyes hardened.

"You could," she said. "And gathering the feathers and claws from your kill would make you a very rich man indeed. However, griffins don't forget. And every time you're out in the field after that, you will be hunted down by the family of the griffin you murdered in cold blood." It looked like the blood drained from Ezra's face.

Mrs. Halloway's expression melted into child-like joy once again. She clapped her hands together.

"Who wants to go first to offer this griffin a valuable object?" she asked.

"We don't have any valuable objects," Janice Clifton, another student, said.

"Oh, no matter," Mrs. Halloway said, pulling a box out of her bag. She opened it to reveal gold nuggets. The baby griffin's eyes widened at the sight.

"You can give him these," she said. "Now, come, come. Grab one and line up!"

Emira rubbed her head once more as she grabbed a golden nugget and stood in line. Darlene stood behind her.

"Hey Darling, do you think you could grab me a nugget?" Kanoa said from behind Darlene. She turned sharply and glared into his face. Emira wondered why Darlene always had her anger so present in her expression, why every feeling was written plainly on her face. It was something Emira so carefully practiced, to hide what she was feeling.

"Emotion is a human flaw, my sunshine," Priestess Irene had

told her. *"Priestesses have to master it, in order to truly be molded for the Idols to use, to trust."*

"What do I look like? Your lackey? Get yourself a nugget," she spat, bringing Emira back to the present. "And don't call me Darling." His dark eyes widened and he looked over her head to exchange looks with Emira. Emira merely shrugged her shoulders in response. She rubbed her head once more, the dull pain refusing to go away. Darlene grabbed Emira's hand and looked at her head.

"You have a nasty bruise there, creeping out of your hairline," she said, almost accusatory. Emira felt herself blush. Embarrassment and anger, two emotions that were hard for her to master. And her body always betrayed her, her face flushing easily.

"Uh, it's from those sword fighting lessons," she muttered. She didn't want to go into detail on how she got it because it was the most embarrassing thing that had ever happened to her.

She had raised her wooden sword over her head to try a new over-the-head slashing motion that Mateo had shown her. And instead of going down, the sword slipped out of her sweaty hands and landed hard on her head. Mateo had melted into a fit of laughter when that happened.

"From sword fighting?" Darlene asked, aghast. She looked over her shoulder at Kanoa. "You need to tell Atlas to be more careful with her."

Confusion filled his face. "Atlas?" Emira laughed nervously as she tried to think of some way to change the subject. She didn't know if Kanoa knew Mateo was the one teaching her or not. And she couldn't let Darlene find out about it.

"Ahaha," Emira laughed, feeling beads of sweat appear around her hairline. She wiped them away. "It's fine. I'll tell

Atlas myself." Kanoa narrowed his eyes and looked up at the sky, thinking.

"Anyways," she changed the subject so that Kanoa would stop thinking about Atlas supposedly teaching her, "How are you and Celeste?" Darlene threw her a glare riddled with betrayal.

"It's good," he said, the previous comment already gone from his mind. "She's nice to me." That comment seemed to be directed towards Darlene. Darlene's mouth dropped at that and she pivoted to angrily point her finger in Kanoa's face.

"I *am* nice to you, Kanoa. The difference between Celeste and I is that you want to kiss her until her lips fall off and I'm just not that type of girl," she said. "There isn't any kind of emotional connection between the two of you, so if you think I feel some type of way about it, you're sorely mistaken." Kanoa smirked and leaned down so that his face was inches away from Darlene's.

"Darling, you *are* that kind of girl," he said, flashing her a smile. "Everyone says so." She scoffed and turned around once more.

"I swear to Lystos, Emira, I will kill him," she muttered.

"And, for the record, I *do* have an emotional connection with Celeste," he added. He couldn't see her face, but Emira could. And her expression... It looked like he had run over a beloved pet. Her face flickered, crestfallen, before hardening, and she didn't say another word.

Kanoa went to poke her in the cheek from behind, and Emira shook her head as a warning. He did it anyway. Darlene turned around and glowered at him. Light started to emanate out of her. Emira shaded her eyes as she got brighter and brighter, like a little ball of sunshine fury to light up the dreary fall month of Balia.

"Get your own damn nugget and stay out of my sight, Kwan," she hissed. And she turned back around, shaking her head as the light slowly dimmed. Kanoa stood there for a moment, confusion etching his brow. And then he clenched his jaw and walked out of the line.

"Are you okay?" Emira asked, softly.

"I'm fine," Darlene snapped. "Don't I look fine?" Emira chose not to answer. It was better to not get in between Kanoa and Darlene. She didn't understand their dynamic anyway.

"Again," Mateo ordered. Emira sighed deeply as she did the lunging slash again with her wooden sword. Then, she let it hang at her side, wiping the sweat from her eyes.

"Can we take a break?" she whined.

"Do you want to be a great warrior and serve Constellatia?" he asked.

"You don't even believe in the safety and protection of Constellatia," she pointed out. He shrugged.

"I don't believe that the safety and protection should be done by the Idols, no," he said. "But I do think the citizens of Constellatia should be protected from *bellua*, of course."

"The Idols are the only beings that can keep the *bellua* away," Emira said. He raised an eyebrow.

"When have any of the Idols gone into the field and killed *bellua* in the last century?" he asked. She scrunched up her nose. Well, he did have a point. But, Emira wasn't one to back down from an argument.

"Well, the warriors are outside of the walls fighting the *bellua*, but if there was ever a creature that the warriors couldn't fight, the Idols would do it. Plus, we wouldn't have ichor if it weren't for the Idols," she said. Mateo rolled his eyes. He gestured towards her arm that held the wooden sword.

"Just practice," he said, leaning against a tree. "There's really no point in arguing with you."

She rolled her own eyes and started again with her lunging. And when her lungs started to burn once more, she stopped. Darlene's vulnerable, hurt expression flickered through Emira's mind. Mateo threw up his hands.

"Now what?"

"What's going on with Darlene?" she asked. Emira could've sworn he looked like he saw a ghost.

"Darlene?"

"Yeah, what's the deal between her and Kanoa?" she asked. Mateo let out a breath.

"Oh, her and Kanoa," he muttered. Emira furrowed her eyebrows.

"Yeah, who else would I be referring to?" she asked. He shrugged as he played with his wooden sword.

"I don't really know. Kanoa has teased her from the very start, calling her Darling and everything," Mateo said. Emira waited for him to say more, but he didn't. The two of them just stared expectantly at each other.

"That's it?"

"What do you want me to say?"

"I mean, does he like her?" Emira asked.

"I don't know."

"You don't know?"

"I never asked him," Mateo said, shifting uncomfortably.

"You never asked one of your best friends if he likes the girl he calls Darling?" Emira asked.

"Why does it feel like you're accusing me of something?" he muttered, mostly to himself.

"Shouldn't you know if your best friend likes someone?" she pointed out.

"Do you know who Darlene and Shiloh like?" he asked.

"Well, I haven't known them very long but I definitely know who Darlene *says* she likes," Emira murmured.

"Who does she like?" Mateo asked. She simply stared pointedly at him. He pointed to himself and raised his eyebrows.

"Me?" he asked, almost in horror. His mismatched eyes glazed over as he stared at the ground, like he was contemplating his own existence. "No, no, that's not true."

"Well, that's what she says," Emira mused. "But, I do suspect that she likes Kanoa."

"I agree with you," Mateo nodded his head, looking more relieved. He looked up at the almost bare treetops. "Although, now that I think about it, whenever Kanoa starts something up with someone, Darlene does, too."

"So, nothing's ever happened between the two of them?" Emira asked.

"If something has, Kanoa hasn't said anything about it," he answered. "Now, could we get back to practicing?" She held up her sword and then continued to think about Kanoa and Darlene. She wished the two of them would simply communicate with one another. She had this deep need to help the two of them, she just didn't know how. Her sword slowly lowered. Mateo let out a long sigh.

"What is it that you guys talk about if you don't ask personal questions?" Emira asked. He gave her a dry look.

"We talk about other stuff," he said, his voice bored. "Please, Priestess, can we just practice? I don't have all night."

"You say 'we' but I'm the only one having my lungs get torn

out of me," she muttered. She practiced her lunging some more as Mateo watched. She could feel his eyes on her and then he suddenly stood up and grabbed his wooden sword.

"Try this," he said. He slashed the air twice and lunged with a quickness that Emira could only dream about. Whenever he showed off his sword fighting skills, she thought he looked like a predator. Ready to tear out the throat of his next victim. And she shuddered at the thought.

Emira tried to copy his technique, but clumsily—and much, much slower than he did it. He circled her as she did, but he was careful not to touch her like the first time. He would hit the wooden sword on her hips if they weren't straight and tap it on her arms to remind her to hold it a certain way. But, he was very careful not to touch her with his hands or stand too close.

Though, she could still smell him. Like mint and cedar mixed with laundry detergent. He always stood close enough to where she could memorize his scent, whether she wanted to or not.

CHAPTER FOURTEEN

Emira groaned as she sat down at the round table for breakfast. The food immediately appeared as she did. This morning was Krachelle Toast, a delicious sweet bread with syrup and powdered sugar on top. To the side were fresh strawberries that she could put on it, if she wanted. She took a bite out of it and had to stop herself from moaning. The pastries from Krachelle were exactly how people described them tasting: godly.

"Atlas is really working you hard," Shiloh commented as she sat down next to Emira. Emira rubbed the crick out of her neck at Shiloh's mention.

"If being a warrior doesn't work out for him, he seems like he could be a coach or a sword fighting teacher," Darlene said. It had been a few weeks since Emira started her secret lessons with Mateo. Darlene and Shiloh thought that, after the first lesson, Atlas had been the one to give her the blue sweatshirt. Darlene was convinced Atlas was in love with Emira while Shiloh always got really quiet when the topic was brought up. Luckily, neither of them had brought it up to Atlas himself. And she hoped and prayed every day Kanoa didn't say anything either.

"My whole body hurts," Emira moaned, putting her head into her hands. Shiloh sympathetically patted her back.

"At least you're getting better," Darlene said. Emira's head popped up.

"Do you really think so?" she asked, hope dripping from her words. Darlene gave her a small smile and also patted Emira's back.

"You definitely are," she said, her smile making Emira think she might be exaggerating how well she'd been doing. "It'll pay off for sure. Not just your sword fighting skills, but maybe you'll get a boyfriend out of it, too." She nearly squealed. Emira's face crumpled, but she tried to smile.

"Yeah," she said. Shiloh didn't say anything. And before Darlene could mention anything else about Emira's secret sword fighting lessons, Kanoa put his hands onto Darlene's slight shoulders and leaned forward, smiling.

"What are you girls talking about?"

"Hey Kanoa," Shiloh said, glancing over at Darlene. Darlene looked like she wanted to stab someone. She turned around, shrugging Kanoa off of her shoulders.

"What's wrong, Darling?" he asked.

"Don't you have a *girlfriend* to bother?" Darlene pointedly asked. Kanoa's dark brown—almost black—eyes glittered. It was the newest rumor on the gossip train in Leliara. Kanoa Kwan, notorious lady killer, finally had settled down with one terrifying Celeste. Some of the other girls were hoping the other hellions would follow suit.

"Why? Does it bother you that I have a girlfriend?" he asked, his voice low.

"Why would it bother me?" Darlene scoffed. "If you want to

make the first official woman of yours be your friend's *cousin*, that's your business. Besides, I have someone else to scratch my back, too." Kanoa's eyes darkened for a moment before flashing a smile.

"She seems kind of bitter about it, doesn't she?" he said to Emira and Shiloh.

"Please leave me out of this," Shiloh said, taking a last bite before getting up and leaving the table. Emira pleaded with her eyes, everything in her expression reading: *Please don't leave me alone with these two.* But Shiloh shook her head.

"Have you guys dated before or something?" Emira asked, almost desperately, after failing to keep Shiloh there with her.

"*Dated?*" Darlene's voice was nearly shrill.

"*Her?*" Kanoa said at the same time. They both looked at each other and then looked away quickly. *I guess that's a no...* Emira's eyebrows curled upwards. The way the two of them acted, something must've happened at some time.

"I'm gonna... I gotta go," he said, going to Celeste who was sending swords through her eyes towards them.

"Why would you ask that?" Darlene said, sharply turning towards Emira.

"I'm sorry, should I not have asked that?" Emira asked, slowly. Darlene's jaw clenched, looking over at Kanoa once more.

"To answer your question, no, we haven't," she said. "And I would never date him. Even if he was the last fucking man alive." And with that, she got up and left the breakfast table like a hurricane, emotionally destroying everything in her path. Emira swore that Darlene was almost glowing, light emanating from every part of her body. She stared at her food. *Note taken,* she thought, *don't talk about Kanoa and Darlene in a romantic way.*

When she looked back up, she saw Darlene standing near

the entrance of the food hall, talking to Atlas. The light that was coming out of her earlier had dimmed. She looked back at Emira, and Atlas looked confused. Emira's eyes widened.

For the past few weeks, she had successfully been able to make sure Atlas and Darlene weren't within a few feet of each other. She had stuck to Darlene like glue, desperate to make sure the truth didn't come out. Anytime she saw Atlas walking in their direction, she made sure to steer Darlene and her down a different hallway, which was surprisingly easy. Darlene was able to be moved, seemingly, without knowing, if she was talking. She didn't notice anything else around her but the person she was talking to, including where she was stepping.

But now, the two of them were face to face. Emira immediately jumped out of her seat. She tried to casually walk over to them but was sure the concern was written all over her face.

"What's up?" she tried to say ever so carefully. Atlas raised his eyebrows, looking over at her. *Shit, he knows.*

"Oh, I was just telling Atlas that he should be a sword fighting teacher instead of a warrior," Darlene said.

"Oh, really?" Emira replied, her voice shaking. She glanced over at Atlas. She could feel beads of sweat start to appear near her hairline.

"Yes," Atlas said. "Apparently, I'm doing a really great job teaching you." She wanted to disappear underneath the floorboards. Darlene looked back and forth between the two of them and then pinched Emira's arm lightly.

"I'll leave you two alone," she said, winking, before walking down the hallway. Atlas turned fully towards Emira, arms crossed over his chest and eyebrows raised.

"So, funny story," Emira said, laughing awkwardly. "I kind of told Darlene and Shiloh that you've been helping me sword fight for the past couple of weeks."

"You said that *I* was?"

"Yeah, and also I said that the sweatshirt that I got on my first lesson was from you as well…"

"They think you have my sweatshirt," he said.

"Yes."

"Okay." He put a hand to his temple and rubbed it. He closed his dark eyes, lost in thought or perhaps annoyance, before opening them once more. "Mateo is teaching you, isn't he?"

"Yeah," she said, pretending that she was *really* interested in the color of her skirt.

"Why didn't you just tell them that he was teaching you?" Emira took a deep breath as she looked up at the ceiling. It was a good question. Why did she do this to herself? Why even agree to Mateo's teachings in the first place?

"See, the thing is, and I don't want to betray Darlene's trust by telling you this," Emira said, looking up at him. *Especially since I've already told Mateo, it'd be bad if everyone knew about it,* she thought. Atlas gestured for her to go on. She took another deep breath. "The thing is, Darlene likes Mateo. Or, at least, she says she does. And I didn't want to tell her that he was teaching me in the middle of the night. I mean, think about how that looks."

"How does it look?" Atlas asked. A muscle around his lip twitched, like he was amused.

"You know how it looks," she said, her voice dipping low. "I'm sneaking out of the dorms in the middle of the night to spend alone time with Mateo Cordero in the woods doing Idols know what."

"Is that what you're doing?"

"*No!* No, I'm not spending alone time with him just to spend alone time with him," Emira said. Atlas finally broke out into a grin.

"Calm down," he said. "Let's take some deep breaths."

"I'm just saying that—that's just what it could look like... to Darlene," Emira managed to get out.

"I understand," he said. "Mateo is a hot commodity around here." Emira rolled her eyes.

"Be serious," she said. "Any of the girls could do better than Mateo. I mean, you're also here." Atlas laughed.

"I'm also here?"

"Yeah, you're tall and good looking," she said, gesturing to him. Atlas laughed even harder. His dark brown eyes twinkled.

"I think Shiloh might even be into you," Emira continued. Atlas' smile faded.

"Emira, since you've confessed something to me—"

"I didn't really confess anything."

"—I should probably return the favor," his voice was quiet. He pulled Emira into the hallway as the breakfast rush started to come out. He cupped a hand around her ear and whispered into it.

"I'm gay."

Emira pulled away and looked at him.

"What do you mean?"

"I like men."

"No, I mean, I know *that* much," she stammered. "You're... How long have you known?"

"Uh, probably since I was young. Once Mateo, Silas, and Kanoa started to get interested in girls, I realized that I wasn't. I was more interested in... boys, like them."

"Like them?" Emira's voice was hushed. Atlas made a face and then laughed.

"No, no I don't like *them*. They're like my brothers. Although, they are conventionally attractive, I'll give them that, though I would never tell them. Do you know how big their heads would get?" Atlas joked. "But, uh, yeah. No one knows, for the record. Only Shiloh."

"Shiloh?"

"Yeah, she's the only person I've told." She had seen Shiloh talking to Atlas, one of the only three that she talked to regularly (Emira included), but...

"I didn't know the two of you were friends," Emira muttered.

"Yeah, we're really close," he said, to her surprise. "Since we were young. But, she can't keep a secret to save her life. So, if she looks uncomfortable when I'm brought up with the topic of girls, it's because she knows and she's doing her best to keep her mouth shut. Not because she likes me. I've had a lot of people tell me that they think she likes me, when I know it's not the case." Emira mouthed *"Oh,"* at him. That made so much more sense. Every time Darlene talked about Atlas, Shiloh consistently would get red.

"Why haven't you told your friends?" she asked, gently. He stuck his hands into his pocket as he looked around.

"I don't want them to think I'm different," he muttered. "I don't want our friendship to change."

"You think it would?" she asked. He shrugged.

"I don't know. But, I don't want to take that chance," he quietly said.

"You hardly know me. Why did you trust me with that information?" Emira asked.

"Well, like I said, you confessed something to me—"

"Again, I didn't confess anything," she insisted. Atlas gave her a long look. "I didn't."

He crossed his arms over his chest. "You like Mateo."

"I don't... I don't *like* Mateo," Emira laughed, awkwardly. "That's... That's ridiculous." *How in the world did he get that from what I said?*

The feeling of Mateo's chest against her suddenly flashed through her mind. It was a memory that lingered sometimes at night, but one that she would quickly shake away. They had been so careful not to touch one another like that again, but there were other moments, lately. The feeling of his hands on her arms, adjusting her position. His mismatched eyes so close to hers as he did. And she could sometimes feel his body warmth emanating from him, electrifying every part of her body. Then, there was the fact that sometimes she would smell mint and cedar mixed with laundry detergent, randomly throughout the day. Like his scent lingered in her memory. Emira could feel the heat rise to her cheeks.

No, no. She didn't like Mateo Cordero. She couldn't. She was devoted to Constellatia. She was devoted to the Idols. He wasn't. He was an arrogant ass who caused trouble for the sake of it. He hated the Idols for reasons she couldn't understand. He would've become a social pariah if he wasn't a sacrifice. *If he wasn't a sacrifice.* And that thought hit her harder than anything ever could.

Mateo was a sacrifice. He was a sacrifice. So no, she didn't like him. And even if she did...

"I don't like him," she said again, but still to herself the words sounded false. Atlas raised his eyebrows.

"Sounds like you might like him," he said. He put his thumb and finger close together. "Just a little bit."

"I don't," Emira said, deadpan.

"Don't worry, I'll keep your secret. I have a lot of secrets that I keep from the three of them," he said. "And I'll keep up your lie."

"I seriously don't," she stubbornly said.

"I mean about the sword fighting," Atlas clarified.

"Right," she muttered. She and Atlas stared at each other for a moment.

"Atlas!" Mateo called over his shoulder as he and the other two walked out of the food hall. His eyebrows furrowed together once he saw who Atlas was with.

"Gotta go," he said.

"I *seriously* don't, Atlas!" Emira called after him, hoping he would know what she meant. He simply smiled and waved a hand. Mateo and him started talking to each other, and Emira's heart pounded wildly in her chest. Hopefully, Atlas could keep a secret.

"Do you think you've gotten to the point where you could spar with me?" Mateo asked, leaning against his tree as Emira practiced different lunges. She looked him up and down. The moonlight made his one gold eye glow in the dark while the brown one was shrouded in shadow.

"I don't think I even want to try," she said, honestly. She grunted as she lunged forward with her wooden sword and then practiced a dodge. Her breath could be seen in the cold air. The trees in the woods had lost all their leaves, and the air had gotten colder in the past few weeks. It was nearly the month of Lystia and the end of the year. The beginning of the Tenth Year was coming soon. But, Emira didn't want to think too much about the Tenth Year. Not when... She glanced at Mateo.

Mateo laughed at her words. He straightened up and walked over to where she was practicing. He put a large hand on her arm that was outstretched and another hand on her hip. She didn't know when he stopped using his sword to direct her, but she was hyper aware of it after her conversation with Atlas. He adjusted her, and Emira prayed to the Idol of Fate that he couldn't feel her heartbeat. After a second too long, she pulled away sharply. His brow wrinkled.

"Did I hurt you?" he asked.

"Sure," Emira lied. Though it wasn't a total lie. The electricity she would feel whenever he touched her would get uncomfortable after a while. She took a good few steps away from him and tried to calm whatever it was that was stirring within her. He made a confused expression, but didn't say anything.

As she practiced, she would glance over at him. Atlas was wrong, she didn't like him. What was there to like about Mateo, personality-wise? Was he attractive? Sure, Emira could admit that. Mateo even knew that about himself. There was no point in denying a fact. And after spending weeks together, of course the proximity would make one feel certain feelings towards another. She just needed to put some space between them.

That's right, she thought. *Space.*

"So, Atlas," Mateo said, casually, after barking out orders for the past thirty minutes. Emira's heart nearly stopped.

"What about him?" she asked, in what she hoped was the most nonchalant tone in all of Constellatia.

"I saw the two of you talking this morning. I didn't know you guys knew each other like that," he said. He studied Emira's face. She let out a breath of relief.

"Oh, yeah," she said. "We're friends, I think."

"Friends?" he asked.

"Sure," she said, shrugging. Friends were people who shared secrets amongst one another, weren't they? She could say the two of them were friends. But then, why did admitting that seem to make Mateo's expression fall? "Are we done yet?"

"Just do another set of dodging and lunging," Mateo said, leaning back against a tree. He crossed his arms over his chest and seemed to glare at the cold, night air—like somehow the nonexistent wind was bothering him.

"When did you and Atlas become friends?" he suddenly asked. Emira stopped her practicing and put a hand on her hip.

"Mateo," she said.

"Yeah?"

"Can you stop asking me questions when I'm trying to concentrate?" she asked.

He raised his hands. "Sorry."

Emira finished her set, and by the end, she was bent over, panting. Her body was warm, and she knew she had ugly splotches all over her face from the exercise. She never felt self conscious about it before, but in front of Mateo, she couldn't help but think about it.

"We're done, now, right?" she asked, breathing heavily in between breaths. Mateo nodded his head.

"We should start you with real swords tomorrow," he said. Emira wiped her brow as they started walking back to the school. She glanced over at him, her gaze lingering on his sharp jaw. Atlas' teasing words echoed in her mind. She forced herself to look away.

"Yeah," she said, trying to think of the best way to phrase this. "I think, actually, maybe we should take a break on the whole sword fighting lesson thing." Mateo glanced at her for a moment.

"Why?" he asked, his gaze straight ahead.

"I feel like I know the basics now. I learn better in class, and I don't think it's necessary anymore," Emira said, quietly. She tried to figure out how he felt about it. Was he upset? Did he also like spending time with her? Did she *want* him to like spending time with her?

Mateo shrugged before flashing her an easygoing smile, "If that's what you want."

"Yeah," she said, her face falling. "Yeah, I just think it's time." No, of course Mateo didn't think anything about their time together. Space was exactly what she needed.

CHAPTER FIFTEEN

"What were you talking to the priestess about?" Mateo remembered asking Atlas earlier in the day.

"Who? Emira? Oh, just some stuff," Atlas had said after joining them that morning. Mateo had glanced back at Emira who was red-faced and clearly embarrassed.

"I didn't know you two were close," he had said.

"We're closer than you think," Atlas said with a smile as he looked over his shoulder at her. At those words, something in Mateo fell to the pit of his stomach.

Mateo thought about that conversation as Emira told him she didn't want to do the sword fighting lessons anymore. Part of Mateo wanted to convince her that they should keep going. It would be beneficial to her, sure, but the main reason, a reason that he himself wasn't even completely aware of, was that he wanted to spend more time with her.

He glanced down at Emira as they walked back to the school. Her curly, blonde hair was tied back into a singular braid, but some curls popped out, sticking up everywhere and framing her small face. And her violet eyes were even more crystalline in the moonlight.

Atlas never talked about girls. He was pretty secretive about his relations, if he had any. And if Emira was one of his secret ones… Well, Mateo wouldn't have been surprised. Atlas would be crazy not to like her.

"Hey, I hope you and Atlas stay… friends for a while," Mateo said when they reached the school's back door. She looked at him, her cheeks turning a darker shade of pink.

"He's a good guy," he added.

"Right," she said, her eyebrows knitting together. "I'll see you around, Cordero." And with that, she disappeared into the school. Mateo stayed outside, the cold air seeping into his bones. It was going to snow soon. He pulled out a cigarette and lit it with his finger.

It would be good, if Atlas and Emira were close, he tried to convince himself. He had death hanging over his shoulder, Atlas didn't. And if Emira did have all the ichor of Mali, and it appeared after this Tenth Year ritual, he trusted that Atlas would save her from the fate he couldn't save himself from. Mateo always knew he wouldn't be able to escape the Idols, no matter where he went. It didn't stop him from continuously trying, however.

He blew the smoke out slowly as Emira's face filled his mind. And the memory of her morphed into Cassandra. He winced. He needed to escape again. Sooner rather than later.

When he returned back to his dorm, the boys were still awake talking about something or other.

"Yo, Mateo," Silas said, leaning against the wall behind his bed. "We're having a debate. Who do you think would win in a fight? Avish, the Idol of Wisdom, or Alexios, the Idol of the Sea and Animals?"

"Personally, I think Alexios because he could call an army of animals to fight Avish," Kanoa said.

"Atlas thinks Avish," Silas said for him. Atlas' dark brown eyes met Mateo's. The image of him smiling warmly at Emira flashed through his mind.

"Why Avish?" he asked, plopping down on his own bed.

"Same reason as Kanoa. Avish can clone himself into an army," Atlas shrugged. "He's also extremely intelligent, so he would be able to devise a sound battle strategy."

"But, what if Alexios called a dragon? Would be game over. No need for battle strategy," Kanoa pointed out.

"I agree with Kanoa," Mateo said. He didn't actually. Mateo, as a sacrifice, had met the two Idols for the first time a few years prior. And, even though Alexios was quiet, he was brutal, that much Mateo could see in his eyes. They both were. And there wouldn't be a winner in that battle. The two would keep going until they both were dust. Atlas shook his head and chuckled.

"You two are so wrong," he said.

"Silas?" Mateo asked, raising an eyebrow. Silas held up his hands.

"I'm just the one asking the question," he said. "I have no opinions on this."

"Speaking of Idols though," Atlas said, looking over at Mateo. "Have you thought about it? You haven't planned anything in a minute." Mateo stared at Atlas for a moment. Did he want Mateo to leave? Because of Emira?

"My escape," he finally said. "I've thought of a plan."

"It *has* been a while since you've talked about it," Silas said. "I was getting worried that you'd given up."

"Given up? No way," Mateo said. "But... my plan heavily involves Pandora."

"Not Pandora," Silas groaned.

"She's crazy, bro," Kanoa said, absentmindedly as he worked on his assignments.

"She's not crazy, she's just…" Atlas couldn't find the word to describe her.

"Pandora is the only one I can ask to help me with this," Mateo said. "Silas and I have known her since she was a baby. She wouldn't say no, and she's the only one with enough ichor to do the kind of transfiguration I need her to do, which I'll then be able to mimic."

"She might not say no, but it's going to take a long time for her to come to a decision, especially if she's not offered a reward," Silas muttered.

"Plus, that little dragon of hers scares the shit out of me," Kanoa said.

"That's because you tried to hit on her a couple of years ago and her familiar, rightfully so, blew fire in your face," Atlas pointed out.

"I still don't think I deserved that," Kanoa muttered.

"You literally said 'looks like puberty finally hit ya,'" Atlas said.

"It was a true statement that I stand by," Kanoa responded. Atlas hit him in the shoulder. Kanoa looked over at him and dramatically said, "*Ow.*"

"I already know what you're going to ask," Silas said, his face wrinkling once he met Mateo's gaze once more.

"Can you, please?" Mateo pleaded.

"You need to ask her yourself," he said.

"Do you want me to die?"

Silas sighed. "You can't keep using that."

"Yeah, the last time you had Silas ask Pandora something, she was obsessed with him for a month," Kanoa said. Mateo ignored him.

"What if I come with you?" Silas looked up at the ceiling for what felt like an eternity.

"Fine," he finally said. "If you come with me tomorrow, I'll ask her."

AND THAT'S HOW THEY ENDED UP STANDING IN FRONT OF Pandora Lux on the grounds outside of Leliara during free time the next day. On her blouse was a patch of a black cat with ice blue eyes. Her hazel eyes blankly stared at the two of them. Her golden dragon familiar was curled around her shoulders, and he glared harshly as the two of them walked up.

It had been a long time since a magician had a familiar, but Pandora Lux wasn't any old person. She had the blood of Nyro running through her and Ophelia's ichor, a descendant and a legacy. She ran a hand through her stark white hair, still blankly staring at the two of them.

"Silas, Mateo," she said as a greeting. "Many moons have passed us by."

"Yeah, it's been a while," Mateo said, chuckling awkwardly. Silas widened his eyes at Mateo as if to say, *See? She's insane!* But, instead of saying anything to him, Mateo cleared his throat.

"Silas has something to ask you." Pandora's eyes lit up for a moment, the most emotion Mateo had ever seen emanate from her. Silas threw a glare in his direction.

"So, Pandora, uh, we were wondering if you could use your transfiguration in front of Mateo here," Silas said.

"Why?" she asked, the glow in her eyes fading. They were, again, blank.

"He wants to have that power."

"For what?"

"Yeah, Mateo, for what?" Silas asked, looking over at him. Mateo looked at Pandora. It wasn't a good idea to tell her the truth. She was a Lux, after all. They were always very neutral on every subject, unless bribed. And Pandora could very easily be bribed. Either with a valuable object or simply with a threat against Silas, who she'd been obsessed with since birth.

"For… Just for fun," Mateo lied. "You know me, I like having fun."

"You're slippery, Mateo. Like a water snake. And this water snake likes to get away," she said, tapping his forehead with her pointer finger. She cocked her head to the side. "Is the snake escaping?"

"No, no," he said, waving the words, and her finger, away. "Me? I would never try to escape *again*. That just seems futile at this point."

"Twenty times the snake has left," Pandora mused.

"And twenty times was enough for me," Mateo responded. Her empty hazel eyes stared at him for a time, and he shifted under her gaze. He had wondered many times if she had more than transfiguration in her wheelhouse. Perhaps, she was a future Sybil herself considering the way she seemed to see through everyone. But, then again, the whole Lux family was odd.

"If we were to transform an object, what would you want us to do?" she asked, referring to her and her dragon as "we" and "us". Mateo looked around them and then grabbed a pine cone that was nearby.

"Could you turn this invisible?" he asked. Her blank, hazel eyes stared at the pine cone.

"The water snake strikes again."

"No, I just think it's funny to turn things invisible," he shrugged.

"As long as you promise not to turn the Elephant's things invisible," Pandora said, her brow wrinkled in concern.

"Emira? I didn't know you knew her."

"I don't. But you do," she said. Mateo felt a chill run down his spine. She stared at him for a moment, like she was studying him, before revealing, "The Elephant is going to the exercise."

"What exercise? The one outside the walls?" Silas spoke up.

"The blood of the Idols hasn't shown itself yet," Pandora said, turning her blank stare towards him.

"What? Her ichor? And they're going to send her outside of the walls?" Silas asked. Pandora shrugged. Her golden dragon whispered in their soul language into her ear.

"Power comes to protect when in danger," Pandora said. Mateo's blood froze as he realized what she was implying.

"She'll die," he whispered. She shrugged again.

"Do you still want us to turn your pine cone invisible?" she asked. Mateo stared at her for a moment.

"Yes," he said. Though, his plan was turning into a different one.

CHAPTER SIXTEEN

"**W**hat exactly are we supposed to bring with us outside of the wall?" Emira asked as her roommates were packing for the exercise that was starting tomorrow morning.

"Comfortable but warm clothing," Shiloh said. "You can borrow some of my clothes."

Emira didn't have many clothes besides the uniform of Leliara and her priestess gown. Headmistress Alessia had given her some hand-me-downs, but she still didn't have much. Emira held up Mateo's sweatshirt and stared at it. The smell of mint and cedar mixed with laundry detergent was gone now, replaced with her own scent. But, she didn't have many warm clothes, it was the excuse that she told herself. *I hope Darlene doesn't say anything,* Emira thought as she packed it quickly into her small suitcase.

"And the swords will be provided to us by the warriors at Camp Elemence," Darlene said. The camps outside of the walls were all named after the twelve Idols. Darlene tried closing her suitcase that was nearly bulging with stuff.

"Do we really fight *bellua* there?" Emira asked. Fear was clawing at her chest, despite this being what she wanted. She wanted to be a warrior, to help protect Constellatia. It was what she used to dream about as a young child. She would run around with a wooden stick pretending to be a warrior while Priestess Irene pretended to be a *bellua*. If she would have been given a choice before arriving at Leliara, Emira would've chosen to be a warrior. But, not yet. She wasn't ready yet.

"Last year, we really only went out on patrols, but we weren't expected to actually fight any *bellua*, the warriors kind of demonstrated it to us. But, this year, since it's our last year, we do actually go out and fight *bellua*," Darlene said. "Don't worry, though. They don't let us be too far away from the actual warriors. And no one has died on these trips, as far as we know."

"That's good to know," Emira muttered. *As far as we know,* Darlene had said, which could only mean that it was a possibility someone had died, just not recently. She inwardly cursed herself for telling Mateo to stop having those lessons. She was nowhere near ready to fight anyone, let alone an actual *bellua*.

"Good thing Atlas taught you the basics," Darlene said, winking. "And, you'll be able to spend a lot of time with him, too, if you want." Shiloh's face turned red at the mention of him. Emira knew why now.

"Oh, does that happen a lot? People spending time with each other," she asked, not denying anything. It was better if Darlene thought she liked Atlas. Though she knew where Darlene's true affections lay, Darlene herself didn't seem aware of it. And she didn't want her newfound friend to hate her for liking the same guy she did. Not that Emira liked Mateo or anything.

"It happens way too frequently," Shiloh said, her face wrinkled in disgust.

"There aren't really any teachers and the warriors don't care what we do in our tents," Darlene said. Emira mirrored Shiloh's face.

"That's… great," she said.

"Isn't it?" Darlene said, smiling. Then her face fell. "Though, Mateo won't be there." Emira concentrated on folding her clothes and putting them away into her suitcase at the mention of Mateo.

"Why not?"

"He's a sacrifice," Shiloh explained. "They can't put him in any possible danger." Part of Emira felt relieved. She didn't need to have Darlene scrutinizing every interaction Emira had with Mateo. And she didn't want there to be a possibility of her and Mateo being alone with one another. Space was what she needed from him, and it was what she stuck with for the past few days.

Any time there was an opportunity for her to be alone with Mateo, she would make an excuse and leave. It was especially hard when Emira would go to the library after hours, because he was there, putting away books. He would look up at her, those mismatched eyes searching hers. But, it was as if he knew she didn't want to talk to him because he would look back down and continue with his assignment.

He wouldn't even say anything snarky or teasing to her as she would walk by, like she thought he would. She needed space, sure, but she wondered why he was also refusing to speak to her. What did *she* do to him?

And she worried, if they were alone, that she would ask him, breaking the supposed space that she wanted. She couldn't be curious about him. Emira needed to get Mateo out of her head.

Darlene moaned as she laid back down on her bed. "I wish he would be. The things I would do to him in a tent."

"Please, Darlene," Shiloh said, putting her hands over her

ears. "You were just crying about Kanoa the other day."

"Shh!" she said, sitting back up. Her eyes darted towards Emira. Emira looked at the two of them who were both staring at her like she had stepped into a private conversation, even though she had been there the whole time.

"You were crying over Kanoa?" she asked. She wouldn't lie, it kind of hurt that the two of them were so much closer with each other than with her. But, she did just arrive while they had over a decade of friendship. Darlene's face flushed slightly.

"He's just... He's an idiot," Darlene said, shrugging. "He's using Celeste to get under my skin and I told him that."

"He told her that at least Celeste is a human being with real emotions and he'd rather her than Darlene since Darlene is a superficial robot," Shiloh said. A pillow hit her face.

"Shi!" Darlene cried out. Shiloh adjusted her glasses.

"I guess I shouldn't have disclosed that," she muttered.

"Just hearing those words," Darlene groaned, laying back down on the bed. "I just don't ever want to see that annoying gremlin's face ever again."

"So, did they have a thing?" Emira asked Shiloh quietly. Shiloh opened her mouth but Darlene interrupted her.

"No, Emira! We never had a thing because I would never date him, *ever*," Darlene cried. Shiloh grimaced and with her gaze, Emira could tell something happened between the two of them at one point.

"Okay," she said, dropping the subject. "I get it."

"Can you believe he called *me* a superficial robot? His *girlfriend* is not human. She would eat nails for breakfast if she could!" Darlene exclaimed.

"She would definitely drink the blood of her enemies," Shiloh concurred.

"Right?!" Darlene said, gesturing towards Shiloh. "She

would. She's terrifying!"

"I don't really know much about Celeste," Emira said. Darlene crawled to the end of her bed and put her head in her hands, looking at Emira.

"Well, take it from us," Darlene said. "She will make an *excellent* warrior."

"I hope she's never in charge of me, after we all graduate," Shiloh said under her breath.

"Same," Darlene concurred.

"I guess she's not similar to Silas," Emira mused. Darlene shook her head.

"Silas is basically like Mateo, but quieter," Darlene said. "Celeste is a stone statue, like the rest of the Silvers, and Silas is a teenager, like the rest of us."

"Let's stop talking about Celeste," Shiloh said, her eyes looking around the room. "I swear she'll hear about it somehow, and I would rather not be glared at from across the food hall anymore."

"I don't care if she glares at me, Shi," Darlene said. "She can't do anything to me within these walls. But, do you think I could borrow that one top of yours? The pink one that you never wear?"

"It's yours to keep," Shiloh responded, taking the top out of her dresser and handing it to Darlene. Darlene hugged it to her chest and thanked Shiloh before trying to stuff it into her already overstuffed bag. Emira quietly put away her own items. She touched the empty spot on her neck where her necklace used to rest. Part of her wished she never left it on that windowsill. She had tried to go back for it a couple of weeks ago, but it was gone. Someone had already taken it.

Praying to the Idol of Night, Emira asked for the moon and stars to protect her during this trip. Despite knowing the warriors would make sure nothing would happen to her or her friends, she still didn't have access to her ichor. And she had a gnawing feeling at the back of her neck that something terrible was going to happen.

EMIRA HAD ONLY SEEN LONG CARRIAGES A FEW TIMES IN HER LIFE. And now, five of them were waiting outside of Leliara. It was the early hours of the morning, the sun still hadn't risen all the way. And the ebony carriages looked eerily like caskets.

"Headmistress Alessia?" Silas asked, his hand raised as students started to fill up the carriages.

"Yes, Mr. Silver?" Headmistress Alessia asked.

"I..." Silas started coughing and looking more miserable than he usually did. "I think I might be sick and would prefer to have a row to myself if that's all right with you." Her eyes narrowed.

"Yes, that will be fine," she said, moving onto the next question. Silas, behind her back, made a fist and cheered silently.

"How's Mateo?" Darlene asked, pointedly. Silas' electric blue eyes widened, his fist in mid-cheer. He straightened up and stuck his hands into his pockets.

"Mateo? What about Mateo?"

"Is he bummed?" Darlene asked. "That he's not able to come?"

"He's probably trying to escape again," Shiloh muttered from next to her. She headed into the carriage.

"Why do you care if Mateo is bummed or not?" Kanoa asked. He looked miserable and Celeste, who was standing at the entrance of Leliara, looked equally unhappy. Darlene's black eyes looked between the two of them, the corner of her lips tugging upwards a bit.

"Did you and the missus get into a fight or something?" Darlene asked, changing the subject. Kanoa rolled his eyes, but he didn't answer as he got into the carriage. Darlene moved her questioning gaze over to Atlas. Atlas nodded.

"But you didn't hear it from me," he whispered. She pretended to zip her lips together and throw away the key. But, she smiled brilliantly at Celeste before entering the carriage behind Atlas. Celeste's eyes looked even more stormy than usual, murderous intentions seeping out of them. She glowered for a moment more before pivoting on her foot and stalking back into the school.

"Is Mateo okay? *Is* he going to escape?" Emira asked, quietly, as Silas and her started to go into the carriage. She hoped he would, so she wouldn't have to deal with whatever it was that was brewing inside of her. He seemed surprised she was asking.

"Mateo's fine," he finally answered. "And he somewhat is." Her eyebrows knitted together.

"Somewhat? How do you somewhat escape?" she asked. *Idols, just escape. Just go and leave this place and never let me see you again,* she thought, bitterly. Silas shrugged, but didn't elaborate. She heard a twig snap behind her, and she looked over her shoulder but didn't see anything. *That's weird,* she thought, furrowing her eyebrows together.

Once in the casket-looking carriage, which she was sure was a bad omen, Emira took the orange velvet seat next to Shiloh. Silas took the seat in front of them, no one sitting beside him. He coughed loudly once more so everyone in the carriage knew he was sick.

"Should you even be on this trip if you're sick?" one of the boys, Oliver, said.

"Sorry, should *you* be on this trip if no one even knows you exist?" Silas responded.

"Yeah, who the fuck are you, Oliver?" Kanoa said from across the aisle from Silas.

"You just said my name," Oliver muttered.

"Turn around, Oliver. Just turn around. No one was talking to you," Silas said. Atlas had a hand to his temple and mouthed apologies to Oliver. His dark brown face seemed to darken more from embarrassment. Oliver muttered something else to himself but turned around.

Headmistress Alessia stepped onto their carriage. She called out names, and everyone raised their hands when she called theirs. At the end, she crossed her arms over her chest, her gaze exacting.

"You all better be on your best behavior. If I hear anything otherwise..." She put a finger against her neck and slashed across it. Knowing her legendary past, Emira swore she heard everyone take a small gulp.

"Emira, do you think we could switch seats?" Darlene asked once the headmistress got off of the carriage. She was sitting next to a girl with long white hair who had a golden dragon curled up asleep on the top of her head.

"Sure," Emira said, getting up and switching seats with Darlene before the horseless carriage started moving. The girl was staring at the empty seat next to Silas, her hazel eyes completely devoid of any emotion.

"Hi, I'm Emira," she introduced herself. She had to admit that she'd seen the girl around the school before and in classes. People seemed to steer clear from her, giving her a wide berth as though she were a priestess herself, though Emira didn't know why. She guessed it was her blank stare and dragon that kept people away.

"I know," the girl said, dragging her empty gaze towards her. "The Elephant." Emira blinked. Or maybe it was the way she talked that made people avoid her.

"Sure," she responded. She adjusted her cloak. "What's your name?"

"Pandora," the girl said, looking back at the empty seat next to Silas.

"You're a magician, right? The first in a couple of decades to have a familiar," Emira said, pointing at the golden dragon. The dragon opened one eye to glare at her and closed it once more. Pandora's eyes once again made contact with her. It was an eerie feeling, like she was talking to one of the Sybils after they had eaten the herbs.

"What's your power?" Emira asked, hesitantly.

"Transfiguration," Pandora answered. It wasn't what she was expecting her to say.

"Is that it?"

"Power is a tricky one, isn't it?" she responded. "There never is just one." Her head cocked to the side as she regarded Emira.

"I thought people only have one power that manifests itself unless you're one of the sacrifices," Emira said, quietly. Pandora's hazel eyes widened as she looked at Emira more closely.

"Gold, freedom," Pandora whispered to her. "The gold will give you freedom." *Gold. Freedom.* It was what Sybil Yuka had said to her. Emira stared at the white blonde.

"What does that mean?" she asked. Pandora's hazel eyes had a little life breathed into them.

"Don't you know?" she replied, her voice barely above a whisper. "The *gold* will bring you *freedom*." Emira didn't know what repeating the sentence was going to do. She squinted her eyes and shook her head.

"What gold?"

"The only gold around you." Pandora looked confused at what Emira was trying to ask her. Emira stared at her for a while, Sybil Yuka's blank brown eyes flashing through her head. Her lips whispering, barely moving, *Gold. Freedom.* But, she never told anyone at Leliara about what the Sybil had said.

"How did you know about that?" Emira whispered.

"What about?"

"About what Sybil Yuka said to me during Incanvantus." Pandora looked even more confused, and her dragon on the top of her head started to stir once more.

"I didn't know a Sybil told you that," Pandora said, looking frustrated. "It's simply written all over you." She looked Emira up and down, as if she were reading the words once again. Emira stared at Pandora in almost horror before turning away.

"She's crazy," Darlene mouthed from across the aisle. Emira shook her head. She didn't think Pandora was crazy. She thought Pandora could be a Sybil. A Sybil unlike any that Emira had ever met, considering the three Sybils were still alive and healthy. And Pandora hadn't eaten any herbs from what Emira could tell. She was simply like that. Pandora, like the Idol of Night, could access the future at all times. Yet, her power, on paper, was transfiguration. Emira dared a glance over at her.

"The water snake is invisible," Pandora said, giggling as she stared at the seat next to Silas. Emira looked over at the seat and stared hard. She didn't see a thing. Her gaze dragged up towards Silas who seemed to shift uncomfortably under both of their gazes.

"Pandora isn't crazy," she whispered to Darlene. "She's more insightful than any of us, I think."

"You've gone crazy," Darlene shook her head. Emira glanced back at the empty seat, and she could've sworn she could see an imprint, like someone was sitting on it.

CHAPTER SEVENTEEN

"There are only three rules to follow, here, at Camp Elemence," Captain Patton Emerson said. He wasn't a tall man, by Emira's standards. His blonde hair was cut short to his head, and he was so muscular Emira thought his skin would burst. Some part of her thought the captain was laughable, in build and stature. Yet, there was something in his brown eyes that terrified her. And that gaze was probably why no one ever did laugh in his presence.

"First, never leave your group," he put up a finger and continued to put up more as he told the students about the rules. "Second, don't wander out of the camp without a warrior. Third, kill at first sight."

"Kill at first sight?" Emira whispered under her breath. Shiloh gave her a look.

"It's a safety thing," she whispered to her. Emira swallowed. She couldn't access her power, and she still didn't know how to sword fight. What in the twelve circles of hell was she doing here?

While getting to Camp Elemence, Emira's anxiety was at an eleven. The long carriages went through the gate in the walls of Astutera, and the wild stretched out before them. And seeing all the empty land, holding horrors that Emira couldn't imagine, it made her heart beat erratically in her chest. Even with the protective screen made of phoenix ash that shrouded the carriages, she couldn't help the familiar fear making its home in her chest.

"Now, please put yourselves into groups of six or seven," Captain Emerson said, clapping his hands, and bringing Emira's attention back to the present.

"Us three should be in a group with you three," Darlene said to Kanoa, Silas, and Atlas who were standing nearby. She beamed at Atlas before turning her mischievous smile towards Emira.

"Sounds good to me," Silas said. Immediately after, he groaned and doubled over in pain, as if punched in the gut. Emira rushed over to him and put a hand on his back and shoulder.

"What happened? What's wrong?" she asked. He jumped back like he was electrified by her and turned away. Emira furrowed her eyebrows together, putting her hands behind her back slowly. She'd never had a reaction like that to her helping someone.

Silas started coughing. He held up a hand. "Sorry, cough attack." He glared over at the empty space beside him. Emira's eyes followed his. He glared like someone was next to him, but not a soul was. She wondered if maybe his sickness was starting to drive him crazy.

"But," he added. "Maybe we shouldn't be in a group together."

"Why?" Shiloh asked.

"That's a good question," he said. "Uhhh, because of Kanoa and Darlene."

"What about us?" Kanoa asked, crossing his arms.

"There isn't an *us*," Darlene snapped. Kanoa rolled his eyes. He turned towards Silas. "Okay, *what* about Kanoa and Darlene?"

"Are you talking about yourself in the third person now?"

"Darling, what would you have me do?" he asked, throwing his hands up. The two of them continued to squabble with one another.

"I think we should stick together as a group," Atlas said, glancing over at Emira. *Why is he looking at me?* She raised her eyebrows as a response, but Atlas didn't see. He pointedly looked at Silas. "Don't you think it would be easier to *protect each other* if we're with each other all the time?"

"Protect each other?" Shiloh repeated, her eyes darting over towards Atlas. Her brow was furrowed. Atlas closed his eyes and shook his head as if telling her, *"Don't ask."* Emira watched as Silas looked over at the space beside him once more. She narrowed her eyes at the empty space, trying to see a glimmer of something. *"The water snake is invisible,"* Pandora had said. And Emira was pretty sure the white-haired future magician was also a powerful Sybil.

No, she thought to herself, shaking her head. Mateo isn't here. He couldn't be. It was impossible. There wasn't anyone at Leliara who could turn themselves invisible, he wouldn't be able to have that power.

"Right, we're supposed to protect each other," Silas said, pointedly gesturing his head towards Emira's direction. She opened her mouth, about to ask why he was gesturing towards her but before she could, Darlene spoke.

"Ri-i-ight," Darlene said, dragging out the word. "Though, I think we all can protect ourselves, considering we're all training to become warriors. And statistically, the women survive more than the men. So, I think us 'little women' know how to protect ourselves."

"That's not what I was trying to imply," Silas muttered.

"I'm so confused right now," Emira muttered. She glanced over at the empty space next to Silas, curious once more, before dragging her gaze to Silas' piercing blue eyes, which were staring right at her. He looked like he knew what she was thinking. She shied away from his gaze.

"Honestly, that makes all of us," Kanoa said under his breath.

"If you've chosen your groups," Captain Emerson said, "Then please come and see where you're sleeping."

The six of them walked up to the warrior who was giving out the sleeping arrangements. They were assigned to the area Circle 5 and were given very strict instructions to "not have the opposite gender sleeping in the same tent."

"Luckily, there's four tents," Kanoa said, leaning an elbow against the tree trunk next to him. His leaning reminded her of someone else who was never upright. Emira stared at him and then the other two. They all were so much like Mateo. It was like they had lived with one another for so long, they eventually became one.

The tents were bright red, like the other tents at Camp Elemence, due to its association with the Idol of Fire and Healing. There was gold embroidery on the tents that depicted a phoenix, as Elemence was the Phoenix Idol.

"Do you think phoenixes still exist out here in the wild?" Darlene asked as the three of them looked at the inside of one tent. It was the size of a closet, only really big enough to fit two sleeping bags.

"Probably," Shiloh responded. "There's still reports of dragons out here."

"Phoenixes were hunted for their ashes though," Emira said, quietly. It was something she had learned at the temple. The ashes were used to dip newly made weapons into as it turned out it was one of the only ways the *bellua* could be killed.

"There were few reports before they started being hunted down," Shiloh agreed. "But, I hope they're still out there some-where. At least their species live on in captivity." Emira didn't know if that was a good thing or not. They were being raised only to be slaughtered.

"So, not to change the subject or anything," Darlene said, flipping her tight curls over her shoulder. "But, do you two care if I take the spare tent?"

"Go crazy," Shiloh muttered. Darlene blew a kiss in her direction and then left the tent to go into the other one. Once she left, Shiloh snappily put out her sleeping bag. Emira raised her eyebrows as Shiloh continued to take a pillow out of her suitcase and throw it into place.

"Do you want to talk about something?" she asked. Shiloh continued to slam things down as she placed her stuff on one side of the tent.

"What would I want to talk about?" she snapped.

"I don't know," Emira said. "It just… seems like something's on your mind." She gestured towards the things that Shiloh had noisily put into place. Shiloh sighed and pushed her glasses up her nose.

"She just always does this," she finally said, gesturing towards the entrance of the tent.

"Who? Darlene?"

"Yes," Shiloh said. "Last year, we were supposed to stay in the tent together but she took the spare one and stuck me with some random girl that didn't have a group just because she wanted to be able to sleep with Kanoa and look how that turned out!" Once she finished, Shiloh put a hand over her mouth, her eyes wide. Atlas was right. It seemed Shiloh wasn't the best at keeping secrets. Emira was glad she never told her the truth about the sword fighting lessons.

"She and Kanoa slept together?" She knew there was some kind of weird tension between the two of them. It was clear Kanoa liked Darlene, but it seemed like Darlene didn't reciprocate those feelings. At least, consciously.

"*Please* don't tell her I told you," Shiloh whispered. She ran both hands through her thin, brown hair. "I'm just frustrated that she prioritizes boys over me but... I shouldn't have told you that. No one knows about it. I don't think Kanoa has ever talked about it either."

"I don't believe that," Emira said, laughing a bit. "Kanoa strikes me as the type of person to brag about something like that."

"Well..." Shiloh looked pained but she gave up the information anyway. "Darlene came onto him because, you know, Kanoa is always calling her 'Darling' and has flirted with her for ages. And then... Well, I don't know what happened. She says they slept together, but nothing ever came from it. And things were different after that. She was... angrier with him."

"But they still seem..."

"Yeah, I don't know," Shiloh said, shrugging. "I just know that's what happened. They had some kind of long talk, too, and Darlene was crying a lot last year. And then they acted like it all never happened. Kanoa still continued to flirt with her like he didn't break her heart."

"That's... interesting," Emira said. She focused on getting herself unpacked. From all the rumors she had heard about

Kanoa, he didn't strike her as someone who would reject anyone, let alone a girl he clearly found attractive. Or maybe Darlene rejected him. *I don't do deep feelings,* she had said to Emira before.

"Well, it's shitty that Darlene ditched you again this year," she said. She smiled at Shiloh. "Hopefully, it's not too much of a disappointment that you're rooming with me." Shiloh twisted her lips and gave a meek smile, which eventually spread into a genuine one.

"Of course not," she said. "I like you, Emira. Not just because you're my roommate back at school, but because I think you're cool." Emira laughed.

"Thanks, Shiloh," she said. "I think you're cool, too." They both continued to unpack, making fun of the boys as they did—Shiloh doing excellent impressions of all four of them—before leaving the small tent together, arms linked.

"Atlas, do you know what patrol group we're in?" Shiloh asked as Atlas came out of the tent he was sharing with Kanoa. He shrugged his shoulders and looked back at the main part of the camp in the clearing in the woods.

"I'll go ask Echo," he responded. Echo was one of the warriors who was in charge of their group.

"I'll come with you," Shiloh said, unlinking her arm from Emira's. She looked over her shoulder at her. "Could you get Kanoa and Silas ready in case we're on the night patrol?"

"I really hope you're wrong about that," Atlas groaned. She smiled at him. It was one of the only times Emira had seen Shiloh look so comfortable in her skin. Only around Darlene did she look like that. She wondered, selfishly, when Shiloh would be fully herself around her.

"What? You don't want to be fighting *bellua* on no sleep?" Atlas simply groaned again at Shiloh's words. Her lips curled into a teasing smile as she bumped him lightly with her shoulder.

"Should I get Darlene ready, too?" Emira asked. Shiloh shook her head.

"Darlene is always ready," she said. Atlas started forward but then turned around to look at Emira. His eyebrows were pulled together and the muscle around his lips was tense.

"If Kanoa is asleep, which he probably is, be careful," Atlas warned. "Don't wake him up too suddenly." After that, he and Shiloh walked towards the main area, talking about something or another.

Emira stuck her head into Kanoa's tent first, and he was fast asleep. She didn't understand how he even fit into the tent, considering how tall he was. He was spread out, part of his body bent in order to fit the rest of him inside.

Don't do it suddenly, Emira thought to herself as she stared at the snoring mountain of a man. She didn't know why, but Atlas' expression made her think she should listen.

She kicked his bare foot and he moved a little. She kicked it again. His eyes lazily opened, he groaned, rolled over, and then fell back asleep. Emira sighed.

How am I supposed to wake him up? she thought. She walked into the tent, bending down so her head wouldn't hit the ceiling.

"Kanoa," she said as she shook him. That made his eyes snap open, and without warning, he grabbed her by the neck. His giant hand engulfed it and squeezed, absolute terror reflecting in his black eyes. Emira gasped for breath as she felt her airway become smaller.

"Ka...noa..." she managed to get out. Recognition flooded his expression, and he immediately let go.

"I'm so sorry, Emira," he said as she fell to the ground,

coughing. He patted her back while she tried to fill her lungs. She swallowed, her throat still feeling constricted.

"It's fine," she said, her voice hoarse. *"Don't wake him up too suddenly,"* Atlas' voice echoed in her head. Apparently, shaking him was not the way to go.

"You can't do that," he said, anger lacing his words. "You can't wake someone up like that. Not in this place." Emira rubbed her neck where his hand just was.

Well, it's not like I was expecting you to strangle me just from me waking you up, she thought bitterly.

"I'm sorry," she said, instead, her voice small.

"No," he shook his head, sighing. "No, I'm sorry. I shouldn't have had that reaction. I'm sorry."

"It's really okay," Emira said. She glanced over at him while he hung his head between his knees and took some deep breaths. A big guy like him, she wouldn't have expected him to be afraid of anything. And yet, he was terrified. *What has he seen? What has he gone through?*

"Shiloh said to get you guys ready in case we're on night patrol," Emira said, rubbing her neck. Kanoa lifted his head, his dark eyes like two black holes.

"Idols, I hope we're not," he muttered. He rubbed his face vigorously before nodding his head.

"I'll be ready," he murmured. He didn't look at her. Emira nodded and slowly backed out of his tent. She rubbed her neck again, sure that there would be bruises on it before heading towards Silas' tent. She didn't think she'd be able to feel comfortable around Kanoa once more. After what he did, some part of her was horrified by him. But, it must've been the kind of thing that happened a lot, since Atlas warned her about it.

Emira went to Silas' tent. She went to open it, but paused once she heard voices in there.

"What about Pandora?" she heard Silas' voice say.

"I swear, she sees the world differently. I'm pretty sure she saw me on the carriage," she somehow heard Mateo's voice say. *Mateo?*

"Pandora isn't a Sybil," Silas said.

"You don't know that she isn't," the person who sounded like Mateo said. Emira's eyebrows knitted together, and she opened the tent. Sitting there was Silas, and she swore she saw Mateo for a split second as Silas waved his hand.

"What are you doing here?" he asked, accusatorially. Emira stared at the spot where she thought she had seen Mateo sitting.

"Who are you talking to?" she asked, looking around his small tent for a place where someone could hide.

"Talking to? I wasn't talking to anyone," Silas said, putting his hands behind his back.

"I clearly heard you talking to someone," Emira said. She wasn't going to say Mateo because... Well, that was crazy. Mateo wasn't here and there was no plausible way he could be.

"What did you hear?" Silas asked, curious.

"I heard you talking about Pandora," Emira said as she looked underneath Silas' sleeping bag, even though it was impossible that someone would be hiding there. "And for the record, whoever you were talking to is probably right. I've met the three Sybils of Aeluris. And she looks and acts exactly like them."

"What happened to your neck?" she heard Mateo's voice say. She whipped her head to look back at Silas. He looked at her as if he were waiting for an answer.

"What?" she asked, staring at him.

"Your neck," he said, nodding his head towards her. His eyes darted towards her neck and then back up to her face. Emira shook her head. *Mateo isn't here. Stop acting crazy.* She was becoming like Darlene, letting a boy haunt her mind.

"Oh, I woke up Kanoa and he got scared," she said, absent-mindedly. Her hand rubbed the area on her neck once more.

"You're lucky he didn't pop your head off, with the strength on that guy," Silas muttered. "You shouldn't startle him when he's sleeping. He's Pyrinian."

"Yeah, I figured that out," Emira said, quietly. Though, she didn't know what being from Pyrinia had anything to do with it. "Shiloh told me to tell you to get ready in case we're on night patrol." Just as Emira said this, Shiloh popped her head into Silas' tent.

"We're on night patrol, I was right," Shiloh said. Silas groaned and laid down onto his sleeping bag. He put a pale arm over his face.

"Please tell me you're joking," he moaned.

"I wish," Shiloh shrugged. "But, since we're in a co-ed group, I figured we would be on the night shift."

"Why did I agree to being in a group with you all?" Silas muttered, seemingly to himself. "Protection? How did I get convinced by the idea that we need to protect you guys?"

"You know, we're still right here," Shiloh said. She rolled her eyes, grabbed Emira's arm, and pulled her up so that they could leave the tent. She looked over her shoulder.

"And for the record, Silas, us 'damsels-in-distress' can protect ourselves," Shiloh snapped.

"I didn't mean it like that, Shi. You don't know what I'm going through here," Silas whined. Shiloh made a face before leaving the tent. Emira followed after her.

"What happened to your neck?" Darlene asked once she saw the two of them. Emira rubbed her neck once more, Kanoa's black eyes reflecting horror flickered through her mind.

"I went to wake up Kanoa and…" Darlene's expression contorted as her dark brown eyes glared at Kanoa. He looked away, his own expression pained.

"It's fine, really," Emira said. "I shouldn't have woken up a future warrior like that. Of course he thought I was some kind of threat."

"You need to assess things before you attack," Darlene said, pointing a finger in Kanoa's face. It was funny, seeing Darlene chastise Kanoa considering she was as tiny as a fairy and he as large as a giant. He hung his head. Then he yelped and rubbed his arm. He glared at the space next to him.

"Echo is waiting for us," Atlas said, pointing a thumb over his shoulder. Emira patted Kanoa's arm as she walked by him.

"I'm okay, *really*," she whispered. It was a lie, but a lie that she knew would give the Pyrinian comfort. But her heart was hammering as if she were a rabbit in front of a lion. Kanoa gave her a hesitant warm smile. He still refused to look at her directly.

"I really am sorry, Emira," he said. She tried to return his smile and nodded. One thing she knew for sure was that she definitely was brought up differently than her newfound friends at Leliara. A childhood without any kind of significant trauma. She looked at her new friends, the sun setting in the distance.

And she felt sorry. She felt sorry that her friends had gone through unspoken horrors. That they didn't have someone like Priestess Irene to care for them day to day. That they were treated like weapons.

Because at the end of the day, they were kids. They were all just kids.

As she turned away from Kanoa, walking towards the main part of the camp, she swore she heard someone hiss, "If you touch her again, I don't care who you are, I'll disembowel you."

CHAPTER EIGHTEEN

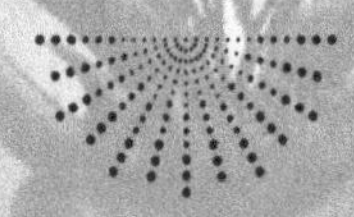

Echo was standing at the entrance of Camp Elemence. The camp was surrounded by a forcefield, made by one of the other warriors there. Her straight, black hair was pulled back into a tight ponytail and her large ice brown eyes that were slightly upturned glared over at them. She was standing there with another warrior, a man who's wavy brown hair was long enough to be pulled into a top knot on his head. The man's eyes widened as the six of them walked up to them.

"*He's* a student?" the man asked, jabbing a thumb towards Kanoa. Echo nodded her head. She put her hands on her hips and faced them.

"I'm Echo, you might remember me from last year," she nodded towards Kanoa, Silas, and Atlas. "This, here, is my partner Javier."

"Hey," Javier said, waving a hand.

"We'll show you what it's like to go on the night patrol here at Camp Elemence," Echo said, putting her hands behind her back as she stood up straight.

"And we'll keep y'all protected," Javier said, nodding. "Though, I have a feeling y'all can protect yourselves."

"Damn right," Kanoa said, fist bumping Javier.

"Okay, stop that," Echo said, slapping Javier's hand away. She put hers once more behind her back. "You can grab a sword from the weapons tent before we start."

DARLENE AND SHILOH WEIGHED DIFFERENT SWORDS IN THE TENT as Emira looked around. There were many different lengths of swords in the tent, but they all looked basically the same to her. Emira picked up one sword and the tip immediately clanged to the ground.

Why didn't I stick with those sword fighting lessons until we used actual swords? She groaned to herself. Mateo had only taught her using a wooden sword, which was nothing compared to the real thing.

Darlene pulled out a sword and handed it to Emira. It was light and a smaller sword than the one Darlene was hooking up to her waist.

"That one will be easier for you to use at your level," she said. The light, upbeat tone in her voice that was ever present was gone. Her dark brown, almost black, eyes looked icy, like Echo's. When Emira looked over at Shiloh, she had the same expression. Any personality that the two of them had were replaced by some kind of emotional armor. They were getting ready for a potential battle.

"Do you need help putting that on your waist?" Shiloh asked, pointing at Emira's sword.

"No, I'm fine," Emira said. She fumbled with it for a minute before Shiloh came over and helped her anyway.

"Sorry," she whispered. Shiloh managed to smile through her emotional armor.

"It's all right," she said. "This is your first time." Once they found their weapons, they all left the tent. Silas and Kanoa were pretending to fight one another, their swords still in their scabbards.

"Could you two stop play-fighting? Someone'll get hurt," Darlene said while walking by them. They both grumbled, and Silas hooked the sword to his waist. Kanoa simply rested his sword on his broad shoulder as he held it, and Atlas chuckled to himself at their grumblings.

The sun was long gone by the time they met up with Echo and Javier once more. They walked through the gates of the camp which was embedded in the makeshift walls around it.

"Aren't there more *bellua* at night than during the day?" Emira asked, suddenly remembering a tidbit of information that Priestess Irene had taught her long ago.

"Yup," Kanoa said, his sword resting on his shoulder.

"Great," Emira murmured, her eyes peering into the darkness before them.

"Now," Echo said, clapping her hands. "Do we need to go over the rules?"

"No," Silas said.

"I'm required to go over them anyways, so I will," Echo said as she walked ahead of them.

"Then why bother asking us?" Silas said under his breath.

"Never leave your group, *don't wander*," she pointedly said to Silas. "And kill at first sight."

"Also, keep your voice down to a whisper," Javier said, his voice low. "Some *bellua* can hear from great distances."

The eight of them walked in silence, with only the noises of the woods filling it. Emira had never been outside of the walls. She'd never seen the wilderness for what it was. The stars in the night sky were brighter than back at home. And it was peaceful. Cold, but peaceful.

Emira was staring up at the sky, her head bent backwards, craning her neck in order to have the winter night sky fill her vision. The night sky really was like the velvet priestess dress she used to don, dark velvet covering Constellatia with little white lights twinkling in the distance. She didn't realize she was slowing down compared to the others.

"Emira," she heard someone whisper. She stood upright and looked around. The others were a little ways from her, disappearing more and more with every passing second.

Somewhere, in the depths of her mind, she knew she shouldn't listen to it. But, she felt drawn, like she knew the person who was calling her name. It was resting on the tip of her tongue, who the voice belonged to. A voice that tugged in her chest.

"Emira," the whisper said from her right. She squinted into the darkness, trying to see who was there.

"Hello?" she whispered.

"Emira," the whisper said, but from her left this time. She whipped around.

"If this is you, Mateo, it isn't funny," she whispered. But there wasn't a response. She knew it wasn't him, that he wasn't there playing a prank on her. Though, she found herself wishing he was.

Having the number one swordsman at Leliara would be helpful, she thought.

"Emiraaaa," the voice whispered her name, dragging out the

last syllable. Emira slowly stepped off of the path, her hand tightly wrapped around the hilt of her sword.

"Mateo, I swear to Lystos that if you're playing some kind of prank on me..." Emira's words drifted off as she followed the voice further off of the path she and the others were on.

The dead leaves crunched underneath her boots as she walked further and further. The air seemed to get colder, and she wrapped her cloak around her body tighter. It was so crisp, the cold, that Emira wondered absentmindedly if she would get a nosebleed.

I should go back, she thought, looking over her shoulder back at the path. But the path was gone, and, looking around, she didn't know where she was. Long, spindly trees surrounded her, their shadows ominous. Swallowing the oppressive fear, she tightened the grip on her sword and continued forward.

She thought about the long carriages, how they looked like inky caskets, carrying them to their inevitable death. Perhaps it wouldn't be this trip that would take them, but it might be the next. Warriors died at an alarming rate.

Perhaps, this would be my last, Emira thought. But, she couldn't stop her legs from moving forward, towards the direction of the voice.

When her thoughts wandered, the voice would appear once more, whispering her name. And the voice got more and more familiar as she got closer.

"Priestess Irene?" Emira asked, stopping in her tracks. She waited for the voice to reappear. She knew, in the back of her mind, that it wasn't possible for Priestess Irene to be there. And yet, she couldn't explain away why the voice sounded exactly like her.

"Emira!" Priestess Irene's voice was frantic, desperate.

Tortured. Emira's eyes widened and, without a second thought, she took off running.

"Priestess Irene!" she exclaimed. Twigs scratched against her face as she ran through the brush. But, she skidded to a stop once she looked up at the creature that was before her. The face of the shadowy creature was Priestess Irene's, eyes grayed over and mouth open and elongated, unnatural.

Emira took a step back, confused about the creature's face. But, she whipped out her sword despite it. She held the blade out from her, pointed at the creature.

Slowly, Priestess Irene's face melted off of it. Underneath was a shadowy one, eyes that were pure white and looked like it was melting downwards. Two black horns sprouted from its face and it had eight shadowy legs like a spider's.

This wasn't just any kind of creature. It was a *bellua*. The magical dummy *belluas* back at Leliara didn't compare to the terror of the real thing. Her hand started to shake, causing her blade to tremble.

"A baby warrior," the *bellua* whispered, its voice morphing from Priestess Irene's to another's. "I haven't had a baby warrior in a while." Its mouth was as white as its eyes, which was also melting along the sides.

What the fuck? Emira thought. *They can talk?*

The legs stalked forward quickly, the tips piercing the cold, hard ground. Emira scurried backwards, her legs moving as fast as they could, but they weren't faster than the eight legs of the *bellua* standing tall in front of her.

"You seem more inexperienced than a baby warrior," the *bellua* mused. Both of her hands found their place on the hilt, clutching so hard her knuckles were white.

The *bellua* stood up straighter and seemed to smile widely, its completely white eyes widening.

"Are you a civilian little human?" the *bellua* whispered. "Is your blood clean?" Emira didn't respond, her legs trembling underneath her. No matter how much she strained to keep them still, they shook without permission, exposing the uncontrollable fear eating away at her. The *bellua's* voice was grating on Emira's ears, like it was clawing at her brain.

The *bellua* laughed. "It's been centuries since I've had a clean meal!"

"I have ichor, if that's what you mean," Emira managed to get out. The *bellua* somehow looked disappointed. And she was sure that it shrugged its shadowy shoulders.

"Oh well," it whispered. "A tasty snack otherwise. And I'm *starving.*" It lunged forward. Emira slashed at one of its legs, the sword only able to make contact with the shadowy creature because of the phoenix ashes it was dipped into. The *bellua* screamed.

It hit Emira with its other leg, which sent her flying. The force of it was enough for her sword to slip from her clammy hands. She was knocked into a nearby tree, the wind being ripped out of her lungs. Emira crumpled to the ground. Her sword was a few feet away from her, but her whole body felt like it was on fire.

The *bellua* took one of its many legs, lifted her up by her cloak, and pinned her high on the tree, her own body dangling, her hands clutching her collar so that it wouldn't betray her throat. The *bellua* cocked its head.

"I haven't met a warrior like you before," it whispered. It sniffed. With what nose, Emira wasn't sure. It sniffed closer, its face near hers. Up close, she could see that the whole body of the *bellua* was just air. Dark, smokey air.

"You smell like... like one of *them*," it whispered. Emira didn't know what the bellua was referring to and she didn't want to.

Instead, she closed her eyes. She needed to concentrate. She had ichor in her blood. Every test the headmistress and Felix did said so. So she had to have power.

She concentrated on the lightheaded feeling that was already present, her heart fluttering in her chest. And when her eyes opened, she didn't have a second to waste. The *bellua's* mouth was wide open, the white light facing Emira. It was like a cool calm washed over her, like she was hidden inside of her brain and the rest of her body did what it needed to.

With a flick of her wrist, the sword on the ground lifted. She could see the *bellua's* beating black heart within the swirling shadows. Emira concentrated on it, her head spinning. And with a thought, a simple thought, the sword sliced through the *bellua's* heart, without her ever touching it.

The *bellua* paused. And with its mouth still wide open, it crumpled to the ground, turning into ash. Its leg unpinned Emira, and she fell, the wind rushing past her, until she hit the ground with a thud. Adrenaline was rushing through her, but she still saw stars. She groaned, holding her arm as she tried to sit up.

She was sure it was broken. But, she was still hidden away in her brain, so much so that the pain was hardly noticeable. She recognized that it hurt, that her arm looked wrong, and she knew she should feel the pain. But, there was only a dull ache. Like her body was shielding her from it.

A twig snapped near her, and she sent the floating sword flying in that direction.

CHAPTER NINETEEN

"Mateo," a voice whispered. He cocked his head to the side. He knew better than to listen to voices when out in the wilderness. It almost always was a *bellua* trying to guide humans into a trap. But this voice was different, familiar, and it gave him pause.

Emira, he thought. He turned around, having shuffled along with the rest of them underneath his giant duvet blanket which he turned invisible from mimicking Pandora's power. When he did, he saw Emira was nowhere to be found.

I take my eyes off of her for a few minutes... he grumbled inside of his head.

"Hold up," Mateo whispered to Silas. Silas glanced over in his direction and slowed down his walking. The others didn't notice anything amiss.

"What is it?" he asked.

"Where did Emira go?" Mateo responded with a question of his own. Silas looked around before his eyes widened.

"You don't think she..." his voice trailed off.

"I don't think she knows to tune it out," Mateo said. "I'll go find her. You stay with the others."

Silas looked conflicted. "You sure you don't want me to come with?"

"Nah, I'm good," Mateo said. "I can't be seen here, and what's the point of being the best swordsman if I can't protect one girl?"

"Who says you're the best swordsman?" Silas said.

"I did. Just now," Mateo responded. He grinned, though he knew Silas couldn't see him. His best friend rolled his eyes.

"Bro, I've been letting you win all these years, I hope you know that," Silas muttered. Mateo patted his shoulder.

"Whatever gets you to sleep at night, man," he teased. "I'll see you later." Silas' smile faded as he stared in Mateo's direction. He could see the warring thoughts hidden behind his best friend's bright blue eyes.

"If you don't come back in the next hour, I'm sending a search team for you," Silas whispered. A whisper of a sigh escaped Mateo's lips.

"I'd rather be eaten by a *bellua* than killed by an Idol," he shrugged as he walked away. He paused and then whispered, "If I don't come back with Emira, let me disappear." Silas nodded once, his blue eyes somehow staring right at him.

Mateo turned around and started following the *bellua's* voice. It sounded like Emira, but without the emotion she usually put behind his name.

"I know it's not the real Emira," he said aloud as he pushed through the brush, following the voice. "You got her tone all wrong. In her voice, my name is laced and intertwined with wonderful irritation."

"Mateo," the voice said, turning his name into his favorite

sound, irritation clearly present. He cocked his head to the side as he listened to it.

"Yeah, that's a bit better," he nodded. After a few minutes, the *bellua* stopped cooing his name. His legs stopped moving as he strained to hear the voice again. But, there was nothing but the quiet sounds of the woods at night. He knew what that meant. Another human had fallen into its trap. *Emira.*

His whole head was filled with images of her, but corrupted with the vicious grips of anxiety. Her crystalline violet eyes fading, her body twisted and mangled on the ground, his worst fears coming true right before his eyes.

Mateo started running.

Running had always been second nature to Mateo, for nearly his whole life. His mother used to say that he didn't stand up and start walking, but rather took off running. Running was all he ever seemed to do.

And yet, running to Emira, knowing her fate, he never felt his heart beat that fast. He never felt the constriction of his lungs as something that was bad. He normally reveled in what his body could do.

But, his legs were burning, his breath was uneven, and it was like he had never run before. He tried not to trip over the invisible duvet that was over him. Eventually, he threw it off of him, unable to breathe.

Please, he prayed for the first time in a long time. *Let her be okay.*

He heard the voice of the *bellua,* and he stopped, his body hidden in the shadows of the woods, standing at the opening of the clearing. "You smell like... like one of *them.*" Its voice was contorted into disgust, hate. Mateo looked out into the clearing, his hand reaching for the hilt of his sword.

Emira was pinned up high against a tree, the *bellua's* head close to hers. Its melted mouth was wide open and something sheer and golden was being pulled from her. It was what all *bellua* did when they feasted on their victims. From what he learned, it was the soul of the human the *bellua* was eating, as they didn't have one for themselves.

Mateo started forward, ready to tear the *bellua* limb from limb, rip its eight legs from its body and leave it begging for death. But, as he did, something in Emira's gaze changed. He watched as the sword on the ground got lifted into the air. And with a flick of her wrist, the sword cut through the *bellua's* heart.

He watched, almost in awe, while the *bellua* crumpled to the ground, turning into black ash. He stared at it, the floating sword still resting in the air.

She did it, he thought. Her ichor manifested. And mixed with relief was a sick feeling. This is what *they* were hoping for, why Emira was sent on this trip in the first place. For Emira to get into danger and force her power to make an appearance. And here it was, making a grand entrance.

He was so lost in thought, his eyes fixed onto the ashes of the *bellua*, he didn't notice Emira falling from a great height. An audible crack filled the silence and his head whipped towards her. She was holding her arm as she stood up, and he took a step forward, something in him wanting to help her.

But as he did, a twig snapped underneath his boot. Her head whipped around, her violet eyes burning. The sword came flying towards him, and he stepped forward once more, his hands raised. If this was how he was going to die, he deserved it. One should never sneak up on a warrior, it was the unspoken rule.

Her face was always expressionless, he never could read what she was thinking. Sometimes, he could make an educated guess, but her emotions were so guarded. So kept, like a priestess's, hidden away behind a pleasant expression. It was why he liked irritating her, getting under her skin. It was the only time he could see some kind of flicker of humanity across that expression of hers.

But, here, in front of him, her face was unforgiving. Her golden freckles splattered across her cheeks and nose standing out like little flecks of sunlight. There wasn't any politeness, no pleasantness lurking behind that gaze. Just a cold, icy fury.

The tip of the sword stopped a centimeter away from his neck. He glanced over at Emira, whose eyes were like crystalline fire.

"It's me," he said, softly. "Mateo." The sword stayed there, in front of him. Her blonde, unruly curls were a mess around her head, like a lion's mane. And her skin was a stark white. But her eyes... burning crystalline amethyst. Power. Pure power. She stood there, facing him, like a golden panther.

A tug pulled within his chest. And he knew. In that moment, he knew. But, he couldn't bear to think it to himself.

"Emira," he whispered. She walked forward, power in every step. He didn't think a girl with a broken arm could bring him to his knees, and yet, here he was. Contemplating kneeling, to beg for his life.

"Emira," he whispered again.

"Mateo isn't here," she said, detached. "It's impossible."

"No, I'm here," he said. "Of course, I'm here. It's me." The tip of the sword touched his neck, pressing lightly into it. He barely flinched as it lightly broke skin.

"How?" she asked. He kept his hands raised and surprisingly, continued standing.

"You know how I can mimic powers? Technically take them once I see someone else do it? Well, I had Pandora show me how to turn something invisible. And then I snuck my way onto this trip," he explained.

"Why?" Her response was quick.

"Um," he struggled with his words. He slowly lowered his hands, before saying ever so quietly, "Because I was worried about you." Emira blinked, still standing far away from him.

"About me?"

"You aren't great at sword fighting, your ichor hadn't manifested itself yet, and Pandora said something about how danger brings power or whatever, but I was convinced you would get yourself killed," Mateo rambled. Her eyebrows knitted together. After staring at him for a bit, the sword dropped to the ground.

"The water snake is invisible," she whispered to herself. Just from how she phrased it, he knew Pandora must've said it to her.

"She calls me a water snake. Not sure why. I'm guessing Balan, since he's the Snake Idol and my grandfather, but not exactly sure where the water part comes from," he mused. Her eyes slowly were returning back to normal, her hand cradling her broken arm.

"Grandfather?" she asked, sounding more like herself. Then, she shook her head. "Never mind. Let's talk about that later." She sighed and sat down where she was. The power had stopped pouring out of her, making her seem smaller, weaker. As if the little girl that was always inside of her was coming out. Her eyes were unfocused, and Mateo vaguely wondered what it was she was thinking about. He gingerly took some steps towards her, like she was a skittish street cat, and eventually sat beside her.

"You did good," he finally said. Her eyes focused on the pile of ash that was once a mighty *bellua*.

"I almost got myself killed," she whispered, her voice faraway once more. Then, her head found its way to Mateo's shoulder, nestling itself in the crook of his neck. He stiffened, refusing to look at her, staring hard at the pile of ash in front of them. Despite the air being unbearably cold, his whole body heated up.

Emira's breathing slowed until they were heavy breaths. He couldn't move at all, in fear of waking her.

Mateo sat as still as possible, putting a hand in front of her face in case she nodded off of his shoulder. His eyes darted towards the bruises that were starting to bloom on her neck. There were some more choice words he wanted to say to Kanoa for what he did. But, those would have to wait.

His eyes found their way to her face. And he let himself look at her. He let himself have this one moment with her.

He counted her eyelashes, memorized the shape of her lips. Softly, he brushed a blonde curl off of her face. Only here, in the quiet of the woods, the moon and stars as his only witness, will he love her.

Only here. And then never again.

CHAPTER TWENTY

The crackling of a fire was what woke Emira up. She was laying on her side on the ground, something that felt like a blanket covering her. When she lifted her head and looked at her body, it was like it didn't exist. She lifted up the blanket that she felt on her, and saw her body underneath, but didn't see it when it covered her.

"You made a blanket invisible?" she asked, looking over at Mateo. He was eating something, tearing the flesh from little bones. He turned his fingertips into flames and put it into the campfire, making the fire bigger. He wiped his mouth with the back of his hand and shrugged.

"You're lucky I even found that blanket," he pointed out. "Invisible things tend to be hard to find."

"Thank you," Emira said, pulling the invisible blanket to her chin. He looked a little surprised by her genuine gratitude. She cleared her throat before adding, "It's freezing out here." Mateo gestured to himself, wearing only a long-sleeved t-shirt.

"Tell me about it," he said. He finished picking meat off of the bones and warmed his tanned hands.

"I'm sorry about…" Emira let her voice drift off. Unfortunately, she remembered everything that had happened. The bellua's wide, melted mouth, the sword piercing through its inky heart. She remembered falling to the ground, and the pain not sinking into her consciousness. The detached anger filling her limbs. And the sword pressing into Mateo's neck. She glanced over at him, looking for the spot where it broke skin.

"For almost killing me?" he asked. He leaned back against a tree. "It's all good. I've gotten used to the concept of dying."

"I didn't know if it was you or not," she said, quietly. Mateo nodded his head.

"Understandable."

"I thought you were a *bellua*," she said.

"You don't need to explain yourself," he said softly. He looked at her through his lashes. "But, just so you know, *belluas* can't shape shift."

"Good to know," she said, hugging her knees to her chest.

"And never follow a voice, even if it's someone you love," he warned. She nodded her head. It was an obvious warning, a warning she herself would've figured she'd innately follow, without any kind of direction. But, the voice… *Priestess Irene*. She wondered how a *bellua* could even know who was the closest to a human's heart. Could they read minds? Though, she remembered what Priestess Irene had taught her.

"Belluas come in all shapes and sizes, and have different abilities, like those with ichor. They came from the depths of the twelve circles of hell, and the Idols—with the help of the warriors—are chasing them back down there."

"Do you have more of whatever it is that you're eating?" Emira asked, changing the subject. She didn't want to think about the shadowy *bellua* and her brush with death. But, mostly, she didn't want to think of how it felt. The thrill of taking a life when hers was on the line. The relief of being hidden away in her brain, without emotions plaguing her. She didn't want to remember it. And, more importantly, she didn't want to talk about it.

Mateo smiled in response. She never liked it when he smiled like that.

"Oh yeah, I have more," he said. A skinned rat was pulled out of his large pants pocket. He dangled it in front of her by its tail. "Do you want some?" Emira recoiled. Her first instinct was to say no. But, she couldn't ignore the rumbling in her stomach.

"Ugh," she groaned before slowly nodding her head. "I think I have to have some." Mateo raised an eyebrow. He took his hand, turned it into flames, and then started roasting the rat while holding it.

"When did you learn to do that?" she asked. She tried to point, but then realized her right arm was bound to her body by a piece of fabric. It was like she had forgotten about the pain, boxed it up and hidden it away within her mind. Looking at it, brought it to the forefront. And she winced from it. She wanted to go back to hiding within the depths of her mind, so she didn't have to feel anything anymore.

"Fire? Oh, a lot of people at Leliara have this power. Probably acquired it the moment I enrolled," he said. "It's easy to mimic."

"When did you...?" She removed the blanket to show her arm. Mateo put the roasted rat down on a smooth rock he had been eating off of.

"While you were sleeping," he said. *Obviously*, she wanted to say but didn't. She wanted to know where he learned how to wrap up a broken arm, but thought better of asking.

"Thanks," she muttered. That was two things she was

grateful to him for, now. She watched as his long fingers picked the meat off of the bones and then handed it to her.

"Since you don't have two hands," he said when she looked at him funny.

"Thanks…" she said again, slowly, her eyes narrowed. She vaguely remembered the feather-like feeling of his finger on her forehead, pushing away her hair.

No, that was a dream, she thought to herself.

"You don't have to sound so suspicious," he mumbled. "I *can* be nice, you know."

"Can you?"

"Please," Mateo said, handing her more meat. "I'm the nicest guy around." Emira snorted.

"Maybe Atlas is, out of your group of hellions," she said. "But, definitely not you." He stiffened.

"Atlas smiles around you a lot," he said. "I think you bring him a lot of joy." She narrowed her eyes at him. Something about his tone made it seem like he was trying to say something he wasn't.

"I don't think I bring him joy," she said, laughing a bit. "But he's a good friend."

"He's a *great* friend," Mateo corrected.

"To you, I'm sure," she said, quirking an eyebrow. "How many messes has Atlas had to clean up for you?" Mateo thought about it and then laughed as he handed her some more meat. She grabbed it with her left hand and put it in her mouth. *Unseasoned roasted rat isn't too bad,* she thought, *especially when you're hungry.*

"More times than I can count," he answered. "Though, to be honest, Silas cleans up my messes more than Atlas."

"Poor Silas," Emira answered. His electric blue eyes flashed across her mind. Those eyes always looked like they knew something, and yet were devoid of any kind of emotion. Empty, like Mateo's. Almost like Pandora's.

She cleared her throat. "Do you know how to get back to the camp?" Mateo, to her dismay, shook his head.

"Nope," he said, popping the 'p'. "But, we can follow the North Star." She rolled her head towards him as a smirk played on his lips. It wasn't the best of his jokes.

"The North Star? Really?" she said in response. "Anyways, it's almost day time." Mateo nodded his head, handing her the last piece of the roasted rat.

"I know," he said, his eyes watching her as she ate the last bite. "But, at least there's less *bellua* out during the day." As the sun rose, little glowing fluff balls escaped the field they were in and started floating up to the sky. Mateo held out his hand and one of the fluff balls rested on it for a moment before continuing upwards with the rest of them.

"Sunners," he said, softly, like he didn't want to scare them. "You only see them outside of the walls."

"What are they?" Emira asked. She held out her hand to touch one of them. It tickled her palm, and she watched intensely as the sunners ended up hiding away in the branches of the trees, lighting the leafless trees up.

"Some kind of insect," Mateo said, shrugging. "They survive in any season. Even in the dead of winter."

"They're beautiful," she breathed. She watched as they stopped glowing once they were nestled into the crevices of the trees' bark.

"They're pretty cool," Mateo agreed. He stood up and brushed the dead leaves and grass off of his pants. "We should get going."

"We don't know what direction to go in," she pointed out. He nodded once, but his head was on a swivel. She saw the same kind of emotional armor wash over him that she saw happen with Darlene and Shiloh. It was different than seeing him turn from a boy into a warrior. It was more muted, less terrifying.

"There might be less *bellua* out during the day," he said, quietly. "But, there's still some. It's dangerous to stay in one spot. Let alone a dead *bellua's* nest." He gestured to the pile of ashes a little ways from them.

Emira slowly got up, wrapping the blanket around her body like a second coat. Mateo grabbed one side and started to go under the blanket, his whole body disappearing.

"What are you doing?" she asked, eyes wide, backing away from him. He popped his head out.

"I'm going under the blanket," he said.

"No, I got that," she responded. "I mean, *why* are you doing that?"

"So that I can be invisible?" he said, slowly. "You want to walk around the woods, in plain sight, with no other warriors around?"

"N-no," she stammered. "But, I didn't think that we would be sharing the invisible blanket."

"Oh, right, you're an only child," he said, continuing to go under the blanket. Emira felt his arm pressed against hers.

"I'm not an only child. I'm an—"

"I meant that you didn't grow up with other children. So, you don't know how to share," he said.

"I know how to share," Emira retorted.

"Oh? Really? Then why don't you show me by sharing the damn blanket," Mateo said, putting the blanket over both of their heads.

"I don't know where you found a giant blanket anyways," she grumbled.

"Kanoa. He needs giant blankets to cover his massive body,"

he responded. She rolled her eyes. They both started walking towards the woods, but that proved difficult when under one blanket.

"Can you stop bumping into me?" Emira snapped.

"Can you walk faster?" he retorted.

"I'm walking as fast as I can." Mateo sighed and ran a hand through his brown hair.

"Let's link arms, it'll be easier that way," he muttered.

"Link arms?" she said, recoiling away from him. "With you?"

"Why? Do you think you'll fall in love with me if you do?"

"Oh, you *wish*, Cordero," she said, grabbing his arm with her good one and linking it with hers. *Damn my anger*, she thought to herself. Now she was closer to him than she ever wanted to be.

"So, what's your plan? Just wander around until nightfall?" she asked, bitterly. Mateo put a finger to his lips and then pointed up to the sky. The blanket was invisible even whilst underneath it, so they could both see where they were going.

Emira looked up to the sky and almost gasped at what she saw. Tiny people with wings flitting from branch to branch. So fast that she almost couldn't see it.

Fairies, Mateo mouthed. Fairies. Fairies! Everyone in Constellatia were told that fairies had gone extinct. That the *bellua* had chased them all away. The little miracles that used to help humans, as well as punish them sometimes, were all gone. And yet, here they were. Right in front of Emira's eyes.

She held her breath as one of them paused in front of her. Its head was like a budding flower, and its tiny eyes were staring in her direction. It stared for a moment more, Mateo and her frozen. She wondered if it could see them through the blanket somehow, but once the thought entered her mind, it flew away with the others.

"Why did they lie?" Emira whispered, her voice barely audible. It came out of her without thinking, and the minute it did, she wanted to take it back. Part of her wondered if lightning would strike her, punish her for her words.

The high priestess used to do that to Emira, when she was younger. When she would question anything about the Idols, she was punished, severely.

"*Who do you think you are?*" High Priestess Ethel would say while a thin branch would make contact with Emira's thighs. "*What makes you think you could question the Idols?*"

Priestess Irene would always try to intervene, saying, "*She's just a child, Ethel! She's just a curious child!*"

And Emira remembered how the high priestess would look at Priestess Irene, her gaze filled with authority.

"*She's a future priestess, Irene. Curiosity will kill her.*"

Mateo and her moved quietly through the woods, trying not to disturb the little winged people, as she remembered. Her hands started to tremble, and she held onto Mateo's arm a little tighter.

"All they do is lie," he responded. She shook her head. No, no, they couldn't have. They were the Idols. God-like beings. Beings that she worshipped and had no business questioning. She shouldn't have been curious. She shouldn't have let her mind wander there.

"The Idols of Constellatia don't lie," she said. "Maybe they don't know they're here." Mateo gave her a sidelong glance.

"You just said why did they lie?"

"I was mistaken," Emira said, her voice wavering. "The Idols don't lie. I—I was mistaken. I forgot." His expression turned from vaguely annoyed to concern.

His voice dipped low. "I'm not going to hurt you." Her eyes

widened and she shook her head. The phantom feeling of blood running down her legs flickered in her memory.

"No, I know. I just—I forgot that they don't lie. They're unable to. So, they must just not know about the fairies," Emira stammered. He stared at her for a long time, his mismatched eyes searching hers, and then they hardened. His eyes squinted, and he looked away from her.

"All the warriors know they're here. So, I doubt the Idols don't know. But, fairies don't work for humans anymore, if they ever did. They hate us. And they'll attack at first sight," he answered.

"Why would they attack us?" she asked. He shrugged.

"Maybe, it has something to do with why the Idols tells everyone they're extinct." She looked away from him. The Idols wouldn't lie to the people of Constellatia. Not on purpose.

But, she dared a thought. A whisper of one. One that couldn't possibly hurt, but she winced as she did.

Would they?

"Speaking of Idols," Emira said, wanting to change the subject, once they were far enough away from the fairies. "You're the grandson of the Idol of Law and Fate?" She watched as Mateo stifled a groan. But, he couldn't hide himself rolling his eyes. He seemed grateful for the change in subject, despite acting like he didn't want to talk about it. His whole body relaxed.

"Yeah, Balan had my mom and a bunch of others throughout the years. He thought my mom would be his next sacrifice since she had the golden eyes. Luckily, she has no power whatsoever, not a lick of ichor within her, so she was saved from that fate," Mateo said. "Unfortunately, she had me and I inherited everything. So did my uncle. So did my cousin."

"Cassandra," Emira nodded her head.

"Yeah," he said, quietly.

"So, do you know him well? Balan?"

"He didn't come around for a Winter Solstice celebration when I was growing up or anything, if that's what you mean," Mateo spat. "In case you didn't realize from your own experience, the Idols abandon their kids. They only procreate to guarantee a sacrifice. You know that, right?" He talked about it a lot, being a sacrifice. But, part of her was jealous of him. Being able to sacrifice oneself to the Idols, it was an honor. Being able to live within the Idol for the rest of all time, helping them continue to persist and survive, who wouldn't be jealous of a fate like that?

"The Idol of Night and Magic doesn't," she pointed out.

"Yeah, not since Leliara. I wonder why she stopped having children after her," Mateo said, sarcasm lining his words. Emira looked at him.

"If you know something, you should just tell me," she said.

"Those beloved Idols of yours…" He stared at her, hard. But then shook his head. "Never mind."

"Tell me." Mateo looked around before letting his gaze settle onto her, again. His eyes were fixed on her, and he looked at her like he was battling within himself on whether he should speak his mind or not.

"Your power came out," he finally said, looking away.

"Yeah? So?"

"So, you don't know if that's the only power you have," he said. "And they're still looking for Mali's sacrifice. There's no one in the ranks of the warriors with all of her ichor. There isn't anyone at Leliara. The only option is that the person has been hiding all their life, or it's you." His eyes met hers. Her heart started to beat within her chest. Could she be the sacrifice?

"Okay, let's say I'm her sacrifice. So what? Why won't you tell me what you know?" Emira asked.

"It's better if you believe the lie," he muttered. "Because if you knew the truth, you wouldn't be able to escape it. It would, it would ruin your life." She furrowed her eyebrows. It was a stupid reason to not tell her. She opened her mouth to say something, to point out that he's been trying to escape *his* fate, but someone calling her name interrupted her.

"Emira!" she heard the voice say.

"Emira!" another voice called. Mateo stared hard into the distance.

"Looks like Silas sent the search party," he whispered. "For the record, I'm not here." And he pushed her out from underneath the invisible blanket.

CHAPTER TWENTY-ONE

"**O**h the twelve Idols, Emira! We thought you were *dead*!" Emira heard Darlene's voice before she saw her. She looked over her shoulder, at where she thought Mateo might still be hiding, but she didn't see anything. Just the serene view of the woods. Darlene engulfed her into a tight hug, her curls hitting against Emira's skin.

"Are you okay?" Shiloh asked, her concerned brown eyes roaming over Emira. "Gosh, Emira, your arm! At least you're not dead."

"I was lucky," Emira said, quietly. "My ichor manifested." She could hardly believe that tidbit of information herself. And Mateo's words echoed around in her brain. She could be a sacrifice. She could be the sacrifice of the Idol of Luck.

Before she met him, before she came to Leliara, she would be excited about it. High Priestess Ethel would praise her for it. And, it was the highest honor to be a sacrifice. Plus, she was jealous of Mateo, even still. But now, the reality so close, on the tip of her fingers, she didn't know how she felt.

Her friends' jaws dropped a little before smiling and hugging her once more.

"We're so glad you're okay," Shiloh whispered.

"They wouldn't let us search for you last night. Some other warriors went out looking, but they didn't turn up with anything," Darlene said. Kanoa walked up as she said this, a sword resting on his giant shoulder.

"We escaped camp anyways. We aren't afraid of a little *bellua*," he said, a goofy smile on his face.

"Speak for yourself," Silas said from behind him. "A *bellua* sees you and they run. They see me and they think 'piece of cake.'"

"We hope they run when they see Kanoa. It's why we always send him out first," Atlas said. "Glad to see you in one piece, Emira." Silas looked around her, and she raised her eyebrows at him. She gestured with her head to the space behind her, and she watched as it looked like Silas was finally able to breathe.

Atlas glanced at her bound arm. "I can heal that if you want." Emira nodded her head and watched as he bowed his head and got to work on it. She expected to feel some kind of pain, worse than the pain she was feeling now, but she didn't feel a thing as her bones fused back together. Once he was finished with her arm, he squinted his eyes at her face. He waved a hand over it.

"Scratches," he explained.

"Thank you," Emira murmured. Atlas had the ichor of Elemence, the Idol of Fire and Healing. She regarded him as he took a step back and admired his own handiwork. It fit him, healing. She was glad he didn't have the other half of Elemence's ichor. Reanimating the dead. No matter how she tried to wrap her head around that power, it still deeply disturbed her.

"What ichor manifested itself?" Darlene asked.

"Telekinesis," Emira replied.

"Oh thank the Idol of Life," Darlene said, holding her hand to her chest. "I was worried you were going to say telepathy and if that were the case, we couldn't be friends anymore."

"Your thoughts are that bad?" Emira laughed. Darlene's face remained stoic.

"The worst."

"I believe it," Shiloh said, laughing.

"C'mon," Atlas said, gesturing with his hand. "Let's get back to camp before they panic that they lost six kids." Emira followed after them, Shiloh and Darlene excited for her about her newfound power. But, she looked over her shoulder at the empty space behind them. She wondered if Mateo would take this opportunity to escape. And with that thought, part of her sank.

THE GATES TO THE CAMP WERE SLIGHTLY AJAR WHEN THEY WALKED up. The camp was busier than it was the other day, warriors running around in different directions.

"What's going on?" Emira asked when they entered the camp. It was in chaos. Warriors were barking directions at nearly every person they saw. Some of them looked like they were preparing for battle. Whatever was going on, Emira could tell the others didn't know anything about it.

"Echo!" Silas called out as the warrior ran past. "What's happening?" She turned around, running backwards.

"You kids need to get out of here," she said. "We're getting called to Ceteria."

"Ceteria?" She didn't explain further, running to the weapons tent. Silas looked at the five of them, concern weaving its way onto his face.

Ceteria was the province of Alexios, the Idol of the Sea and Animals, the Shark Idol. It was a province filled with fishing villages. Like Sapiem, it was a quiet province with hardworking people living there, feeding the rest of Constellatia. Hardly anything ever happened in Ceteria.

"What the fuck could've happened in Ceteria for *warriors* to be called there?" Darlene said, her voice low. A newspaper rolled across the ground. Atlas leaned down and grabbed it. His eyes flickered back and forth, his lips pulling into a tight line.

"There's a riot," he said, quietly. He shared glances with Silas and Kanoa.

"A riot? In Ceteria?" Darlene asked, snatching the newspaper from him, echoing Emira's own thoughts. Her eyes frantically roamed over it, widening as she read the information.

"No, he's right," she said, handing the newspaper to Shiloh. The brunette quickly skimmed the article.

"Some kid—"

"Not a kid, a baby," Darlene interrupted Shiloh.

"Right, a newborn. They think he might be the sacrifice they were looking for," Shiloh said, as she read over it. Emira's heart dropped. Something twisted in her abdomen, like a dagger coated in poison.

"A newborn?" Kanoa exclaimed.

"Mali's sacrifice?" Emira asked. Her mind was at war with itself. Part of her hoped it was true, that Mateo's fears about her being the missing sacrifice was unfounded. It was true that more than one living person could have all the ichor of any of the Idols during a generation. But another part, a very big part of her, felt greasy guilt coating over her body, mixed with the familiar ache of jealousy. She thought, especially after her ichor manifested, perhaps she was the missing sacrifice. Emira still felt she could be, or maybe, rather, she desperately wanted to be.

Shiloh nodded her head. "Yes. The baby is Mali's sacrifice."

They said it was her. They said she *was going to be the sacrifice,* Emira heard Darlene say. But, she was staring at Darlene the whole time. Her lips didn't move an inch. Emira's heart started to race.

"Sorry, what did you say?" she asked, taking a step forward. Darlene's eyebrows twitched together for a second.

"I didn't say anything..." Darlene gave her a weird look. Emira shook her head. She heard Darlene's voice, and it was as clear as if she were talking right in front of her. But, she knew Darlene didn't open her mouth, didn't voice anything.

What is going on with me?

"Oh," she replied, holding her head. "I think, I think I hit my head hard when I fell." She didn't know if Darlene believed the lie. *Am I reading her thoughts? Could it be that...*

But, Emira refused to let her thoughts get that far. Mateo's haunted, empty eyes flickered through her mind. It was his biggest fear, that thought. A fear he kept trying to unnecessarily protect her from.

"So, the baby was found in Ceteria," Silas said, grabbing the newspaper from Shiloh.

"But, ichor doesn't manifest in babies," Kanoa pointed out. "That's what they've always told us. It manifests later. Around nine or ten. It's rare if it manifests earlier than that." That familiar dagger continued to twist in Emira's stomach.

"This one came out of the womb moving things with his mind," Shiloh said. "And, he seemed to be able to control people for a second."

"Two out of three," Silas muttered.

"Power is a tricky one, isn't it?" Pandora had responded. *"There*

never is just one." The conversation with Pandora on the long carriage flashed through Emira's mind. She wondered what Pandora had meant by that. But what she said must've been the truth. *Not any one of us only have one, right?* Emira thought.

At least, she hoped. Because it looked like it was true for her. Telekinesis. Telepathy. *Two out of three.*

"No one is going to be okay with a newborn being a sacrifice," Atlas said. "It makes sense that the people of Ceteria are rioting. They have low birth rates to begin with."

"What are you lot still doing here?" Javier said, running by them. "The long carriages are here. *Go!*" Without another word, they ran towards their tents and grabbed all of their belongings before booking it to the long carriages.

Emira sat down next to Darlene, Shiloh sitting next to Silas. Pandora sat on her own, looking out the window as the carriage started to move. She vaguely wondered if Mateo would be okay out in the wild. If he truly was going to use this moment to escape, for good.

A shadowy screen, infused with phoenix ashes, covered the outside of the carriage to shroud it from *bellua* and other creatures. It also started to move so fast, the outside seemed to blur together. Everyone on the carriage was talking about the newfound sacrifice.

"It's wrong," a girl in their year said. "To kill a baby?"

"But an eighteen-year-old is fine? A five-year-old?" Kanoa piped up. She rolled her eyes.

"Mateo is a grown man. It's an honor to be a sacrifice," she said, repeating the familiar words that Emira herself had once used. *It is an honor,* Emira reminded herself. *To show devotion to your country, to the Idols who have longed protected us.* It was what she believed, to her core. And yet, why did the mention of Mateo being a sacrifice make her blood turn to ice?

"An honor? An *honor?*" Kanoa said, quickly. "Janice, you were just talking about how wrong it is to kill a baby."

"It *is* wrong," Janice said. "It's a *baby.*"

"Is the five-year-old not a baby?" Kanoa asked. She shrugged. Emira glanced over at Kanoa. Rage burned in his black eyes, as if he knew the child himself.

"It'll live on in the body of our Idols." Kanoa stared at Janice for a very long time. She shifted underneath his gaze and looked at her peers for help.

"Listen, I'm not the only one who feels this way, Kanoa. Look at the people rioting in Ceteria," she said.

"They're hypocrites," he said. "A five-year-old still has a lot of life to live."

"Which sacrifice is five years old, anyways? *I* haven't heard of them."

"Poppy," he said. "She's five, from Pyrinia, and she's the sacrifice for Elemence, the Idol of Fire and Healing. At five, Janice. Five years old. She has her whole life to live, and they decided a five-year-old should be the sacrifice for this Tenth Year. And that's somehow better than a baby?" The age of five was unusual, just like a baby not even a year old was, but it wasn't impossible. And it wasn't the same, like Kanoa believed.

"She's right, Kanoa," Emira finally chimed in. Her stomach was churning as she looked upon them. Janice relaxed, her expression pleased that someone was standing up to the giant from Pyrinia alongside her. It made the feeling in Emira's stomach even more unpleasant.

"You think it's worse that a baby is being sacrificed instead of the thousands of humans that have throughout history?" Silas asked, as Kanoa floundered, his mouth opening and closing at Emira. Betrayal flashed across his face.

"A baby doesn't understand the importance, the reason,"

Emira whispered. This was what she was taught. What she believed in.

Did she believe this?

"A five-year-old… Poppy… She understands. She understands what will happen to her in the end," Emira continued. "A baby doesn't."

"What about the sacrifices who don't believe in the Idols? They don't get a pass? The angry outrage?" Silas asked. His voice was even, the same decibel, but there was an anger simmering underneath it.

"Mateo is the only one who doesn't believe it," she said, barely even a whisper. His blue eyes twitched.

"So, it's fine. It's fine as long as they can understand what is going to become of them," Silas said, guessing at her mindset. Emira didn't say anything more. He narrowed his eyes at her.

"You really would've made a great priestess," he spat, twisting the word "priestess" into the most disgusting, vile insult and turning away from her.

No, she wasn't a great priestess. She was far from it. A great one would've been the sacrifice.

Emira licked her lips as she looked over at Darlene. Darlene shrugged, but there was something in her eyes that made her feel like she was wrong.

"It's a baby," Emira whispered.

"I know," Darlene said. "But, if it concerns you so much…" her voice tapered off. And as her lips were sealed closed, Emira still heard the words that came after.

…you should've shown you were the sacrifice.

It was a thought Emira couldn't think. A thought she wanted desperately to be true, but also wanted to be a most horrendous lie. A great priestess would be the missing sacrifice, would offer herself willingly to the Idols. And she knew. Hearing Darlene's thoughts, Emira knew. And the reality of knowing wasn't like how she thought it would be, it was like realizing the world was going to end. And then, there was Mateo…

"Do you think I'm the sacrifice?" Emira asked in a hushed whisper. A question she already knew the answer to. Darlene's ebony eyes widened. She ducked her head lower, as if the height of where her head was in regards to the seat in front of her determined whether people could hear her whisper or not.

"I thought you said you *didn't* have telepathy?" she hissed.

"I don't," Emira lied. "I just… I get the feeling." Darlene squinted her eyes at her.

"Sweetheart, I don't believe you," she said.

"If I did, I would tell you," Emira continued to lie. She couldn't let anyone find out. For some reason, a large part of her didn't want anyone to know she had two out of three of Mali's powers.

Not yet, she thought as her inner voice chastised her.

But, a baby will die in your place, her inner voice whispered. She winced.

"But, did you think I was? That… That I could be?" Emira asked, again. Darlene wrinkled her brow.

"I thought you were, when they found you," she said, quietly. "They were all talking about it. All the adults were rushing around whispering that the next sacrifice of Mali was coming to Leliara."

"That's why I was brought here," Emira said, more to herself than anything. Darlene nodded her head.

"I mean, they would've brought you to Leliara regardless, but yeah. They were convinced you were the next sacrifice," Darlene said.

Emira remembered when Mateo grabbed her. How he looked at her in the sewer, the secret entrance into the Temple of Night. How his mismatched eyes softened, his brow crinkled ever so slightly. How he whispered, *"I was petrified for you."*

She remembered that night in the woods, when they were walking to their first sword fighting lesson together. How concerned he was. *"You could be Mali's sacrifice,"* he had said to her. It was all Mateo could think about. The fear that had been plaguing him since. It's what everyone thought.

Emira swallowed. *"If it concerns you so much..."* she heard Darlene's voice echo in her head. What Emira was feeling... She knew it was the instinct that Priestess Irene had talked about when she was younger. The instinct that tormented Mateo.

"All sacrifices are human, of course. While one should be willingly sacrificed to the Idols, and while they know how much of an honor it is and how they will live on within the bodies of the Idols, humans still hold onto that instinct to survive. It's innate. And some sacrifices struggle with it for a little while," she had said.

"How do they reckon with it?" Emira had asked.

"Talking to priestesses for that particular Idol can be helpful. Prayer is helpful. And they eventually accept it," Priestess Irene had said with a smile.

A baby couldn't reckon with it, accept it. A baby didn't know what would be going on, wouldn't be willing. Plus, a riot was happening in Ceteria. The good of Constellatia was in jeopardy. Emira closed her eyes shut before looking over her shoulder at Pandora.

Pandora's hazel eyes were staring right at her, like she knew what Emira was thinking. She then turned to the side and whispered something to the space next to her. Emira looked over at the empty seat next to Pandora, and she could tell Mateo hitched a ride back.

"You shouldn't have," she whispered before turning back around. All Mateo wanted was to make sure Emira was safe, that she wasn't the next sacrifice. He thought she was in hiding all those years, and he wanted her to continue her previous life. To continue living.

All this time Emira thought she was just going to end up being a Priestess of Night, to serve Ophelia, the Idol of Night and Magic. She thought her life was going to be meaningless. But, she was important.

She could save that baby. She could save Constellatia. She could be a great priestess.

Her dream had always been to be a warrior, since she was young. To protect Constellatia with power gifted to her from the Idols. But, as she grew older, her dream changed to the reality of her circumstances. Instead, she would become a priestess, a good priestess, like Irene. But, now, she had power. And she was determined save Constellatia. Her two dreams were colliding, mixing into something she didn't ever truly want, but was the only outcome that made sense.

Two out of three. She had two out of three. And somehow, she knew Pandora would help her with the third.

CHAPTER TWENTY-TWO

"**P**andora!" Emira called. It had been a day since they arrived back at Leliara. Due to the riots and because some of the teachers were called to Ceteria to help, classes were canceled for the day.

Emira had caught Pandora staring in the middle of the hallway at a blank wall. Her golden dragon was standing up on the top of her head, staring intently at the wall as well. She glanced over at the blank wall, trying to see what it was Pandora could, but saw nothing.

"Am I interrupting something?" Emira asked. Pandora looked over at her, with those unnerving blank eyes.

"No," she said. "Just looking for something."

"I was wondering…"

"I know," Pandora said. "Two out of three. It's written all over you."

"Right," Emira whispered. She stood next to Pandora, staring at the blank wall. She wondered what it was Pandora was looking for.

"You're a Sybil, aren't you?" she asked, quietly. Pandora put a finger to her lips as her golden dragon glared intensely at Emira.

"No one ever has just one," she whispered.

"But, you have them all, don't you?" Emira asked. It was a guess, a good assumption. One that she didn't expect Pandora to admit to.

"Yes," she said. "We would be Ophelia's sacrifice, if they knew about it." She gestured to herself and her dragon. It made sense. There hadn't been a magician with a familiar in decades. She had transfiguration, the only power she flaunted in any way. But, she could also see the future. Emira was sure she was a pro at potions as well. Three out of three.

"You're the black cat," Emira said.

"And the elephant is you," Pandora said.

"You're purposefully hiding it," Emira responded. Pandora cocked her head to the side, her white hair brushing off of her shoulder.

"You can, too," she said. "Mateo messed up when he was younger. He was too excited about his power."

"He was a kid," Emira whispered. Pandora shrugged.

"Maybe," she said. "But, hiding is good for us."

"Why are you hiding? Being a sacrifice is an honor," but even to Emira, the words fell flat. Pandora blinked.

"Why are *you* hiding, little elephant?" Emira swallowed. She didn't know why she was. The only reason she could think of was because of that human instinct.

But, why was it that Mateo's mismatched eyes kept haunting her mind every time she thought about it?

"I don't want to," she whispered. "I will out myself. But, I only have…"

"Two out of three," Pandora nodded. She clapped her hands

together and turned towards Emira. She gestured for Emira to hold her hands. Emira placed them into Pandora's.

"Mind control is the third power," she said. "Try to control me."

"How?"

"The fear," Pandora said, gripping Emira's hands hard. "What if I transfigure you into something? Danger makes the power come out."

"You can do that?"

"I am the black cat," Pandora said, her hazel eyes having some life breathed into it. "I can do anything." Magic, it was a tricky power. Emira didn't even know if there were limits to Ophelia's power.

"Tap into the fear," Pandora said. "Or, I'll turn you into an elephant. I don't think I'll be able to turn you back human, though. Hadn't had many volunteers for experimentation."

"Great," Emira said. She felt the power emanating from Pandora's hands, like she was warming them up in order to turn Emira into an animal. She felt a jolt from Pandora's hands and then suddenly, her mind opened up.

She could feel Pandora's essence. And Emira somehow innately knew that she could mold this essence. Control it.

Let go of my hands, she whispered into her mind. Pandora blinked, her hazel eyes blank once more. She let go of Emira's hands, but her lips were pulled tight, like it was something she was doing against her will.

Emira rubbed her hands together and then sat with Pandora's essence. A part of her didn't want to let go, wanted to continue to mold her, to control her. A gleeful feeling in the back of her mind. And it terrified her.

Emira let go immediately.

Pandora blinked once more, and a steady smile spread across her lips. She tapped her head and nodded.

"Three out of three," she said. "A true elephant."

"I won't tell anyone about you," Emira vowed. Pandora shrugged.

"They keep trying. More power is important to the Idols," she said. "But, I don't give an inch. All we can do is transfiguration, as far as they know." She giggled and her dragon giggled with her.

"What do you mean more power is important?"

"No one has one, little elephant," Pandora purred. "It depends on more power." Emira's brow wrinkled. She wasn't sure what Pandora meant.

"Good luck," she said. "I hope you live on within Mali."

"Thank you," Emira whispered. She hugged Pandora tightly, but Pandora kept her arms down at her sides. "I appreciate everything you've done, and I'm sorry for controlling you."

Pandora didn't say anything, just poked Emira's side with her finger. Emira let her go, and she had never seen Pandora look more uncomfortable. The white blonde straightened her uniform and then, without saying another word, walked away.

Three out of three. Emira had all the ichor of Mali. She was the sacrifice. She could protect everything that Constellatia is.

And a great priestess would sacrifice themselves to the Idols. It was the pinnacle of her religion, the best way to show her loyalty.

And if she couldn't be a great warrior, she could at least be the best priestess she could be, *right?*

She started towards Headmistress Alessia's office. Headmistress Alessia was still around, too old to help with the effort in Ceteria. And her heart sank when she saw Mateo's group of hellions laughing in the main foyer. They were sitting on the steps, talking about riots, like they were glad it was happening.

"Emira, what do you think about the riots in Ceteria?" Atlas asked as she walked by, his dark brown eyes smiling at her.

"I think it's horrible," she said. Mateo rolled his eyes. He shifted a little, leaning against the step behind him, his collar revealing a silver chain hidden around his neck.

"Of course you think that way. The protection of Constellatia is the utmost priority," he mocked her. "I think it's great. Maybe the people of Constellatia are realizing how fucked up the sacrifice thing is."

"You *would* think it's great," she retorted, rolling her own eyes. "But Constellatia needs to persist. Or we'll go back to the Dark Ages."

"I'm sure the Dark Ages weren't as bad as you think they were," Mateo said. Then, his brows knitted together. The familiar creasing of worry filled his face.

"Where are you going?" he asked.

"Headmistress Alessia's," Emira responded. His mismatched eyes stared intensely at her, something like realization washing over his face. And it was like he could read every thought of hers.

No, she heard his voice say. It sounded like he was shouting it, but his mouth didn't move at all.

No, no, no. She winced from the sound. Mateo frowned, standing up from the steps. He looked over at the other three.

"I'll catch up with you in a minute," he said. "Emira?" Emira pivoted on her foot and started to walk quickly towards Headmistress Alessia's office. She heard his thoughts, and she pressed her hands against her ears. It hurt. The anguish in his thoughts, the desperation. The fear. It all hurt too much, even though she couldn't understand a word of it. His incoherent shouting in his mind was ringing around her head, and she was sure her ears were going to bleed.

"Stop," she whispered. She heard his heavy steps catching up to her.

"Emira?" he said, grabbing her elbow and turning her around. She still had her hands pressed against her ears. His mismatched eyes were wide, dilated.

"You can hear my thoughts, can't you," he whispered, like he was accusing her of something. She pulled her hands from her ears, his thoughts dimming a little.

"I can't make any sense of them," she answered, breathless.

"You have all of Mali's ichor, don't you," he didn't ask the question. It was a statement. Emira stayed quiet.

"That's why you're going to Headmistress Alessia's office," he figured out for himself. His eyes hardened. "Emira…"

"I'm the sacrifice for this Tenth Year," she said. "It's supposed to be me."

"If you're doing this because you think you can *save* Constellatia, you should know it's all a lie. Everything you know is a lie. The Idols, they—"

"Mateo, I'm doing this," she interrupted. "This is my destiny. My fate. I'm supposed to do this. And I'm okay with that." His hands raised, like he wanted to cup her face. Instead they just hovered there, his mismatched eyes melting. His thoughts were incoherent, screaming once again. She winced.

NO.

NO, NO, NO.

"Mateo, this is what I want to do," she nearly begged.

"Because you've been brainwashed," he argued. He finally did cup her face. His large hands warmed her cheeks as he forced Emira to look up at him, stare straight into his eyes.

"I can't protect you," he whispered, his voice breaking. "I won't be able to protect you."

"You shouldn't have come back," she whispered. She took a step backwards, his hands falling away from her face. "You should've stayed. Out there."

"You know I couldn't," he breathed. And she knew. She knew what he was trying to say. Even though she couldn't understand his thoughts, she could feel them. She could feel what he was feeling.

"I want to be important, Mateo," she confessed. "My whole life, I thought I was a nameless orphan. Destined to be another priestess. But, that isn't the truth. I'm someone important. I'm a part of history. I'll live on in Mali for the rest of eternity. I'll be the greatest priestess who ever lived. Who else can say that they have a fate like that?"

"A lot of fucking people, Emira," he said, taking a step closer. His face was only inches away now. "There's been thousands of sacrifices in history. And you know what history does? They forget about them. Let their names fall off the history book pages. You're not important. Let them take the baby, who the fuck cares?"

"*I* care," Emira said. "It's my duty. My destiny. I can't just hide like..." she let her words drift off. She couldn't out Pandora. It wasn't her place.

"You would've been safe as a priestess. As a true one. One without ichor," he whispered. He tucked a stray curl behind her ear.

"I wouldn't have been important."

"You would've been important to me," he whispered. And that's what it was, wasn't it? The invisible string that tied around the two of them. The string that told them they were destined for each other, in another life. But, not in this one. Never in this one.

"You're important to me," he murmured once again. He leaned in and pressed his soft lips against hers. And it was everything that she thought it would be. And she could feel his thoughts exploding. Wrapping around her, protectively. And she wanted to melt into him. To give in to the feeling. But, she couldn't. She knew she couldn't. She pulled away. And he stared at her in shock, at himself or at her action, she wasn't sure, his hands still in the air where her head once was.

"I'm sorry, Emira," he whispered. "I know… You and Atlas…"

Me and Atlas?

"Shit. *Fuck.* I'm a shitty ass friend," he muttered to himself.

"It's okay," Emira said, trying not to let his regret hurt her.

"No, I'm so sorry," he whispered, horrified. "I'm sorry. I just…"

"I'm still going to turn myself in," she whispered.

"I—" His expression was pained as he stared at her through his lashes. His one gold eye like pure melted gold. His one brown one, tortured. She touched her lips and then shook her head as she turned around. His thoughts exploded once more.

"Emira, *please*, I'm sorry," he said. She didn't turn around. "I just—I can't protect you, Emira."

She looked over her shoulder. "You don't have to. You've never had to."

And with that, she walked towards Headmistress Alessia's office. She could hear Mateo following after her. And with her mind, she reached his chaotic essence.

Stay, she forced the order into his mind. And his footsteps were no more. She swallowed, but the knot in her throat wouldn't go down. She wiped the wetness away from her face before turning the handle on the Headmistress' office.

"Emira! What a surprise," Headmistress Alessia said, taking off her glasses. But, her smile indicated that Emira's entrance wasn't quite as surprising as she thought.

"I'm Mali's sacrifice. I'm the sacrifice for the Idol of Luck and Agriculture."

CHAPTER TWENTY-THREE

ateo watched as Emira walked away from him, unable to move his feet until she was out of his sight. He struggled against the order that he heard in his mind.

Stay, her voice had said, infiltrating all parts of his brain. And he didn't have the ability to fight against it. *At least I have that mind control trick up my sleeve now*, he thought to himself, frustrated.

He wanted to kick himself for kissing her. *Why the fuck? What the fuck?* What kind of a friend was he? Atlas and Emira were... He couldn't let himself finish that thought.

Once he was able to move again, he still stood there, staring at where Emira used to be. A memory flashed through his mind.

Cassandra's hand slipped out of his tiny one. She screamed his name as they carried her away, kicking as their grandfather watched with his hardened gold eyes. His black hair was brushed away from his harsh, sharp face. She was tied down, tears streaming down her cheeks. And then, with one fell swoop...

Mateo squeezed his eyes shut. It was happening again.

Except this time… This time, he could've done something about it, could've stopped her. Instead, he fucking *kissed* her.

Why did he kiss her?

He ran his hands through his brown hair, as he paced back and forth in the hallway. He can't be in love with her, as a sacrifice, he wasn't allowed that pleasure. But, he could feel it, as his lips pressed against hers. That part of him felt like he was destined for her. In another life. In another time.

He rubbed his face. He could still feel her skin on his hands. "*Fuck*," he whispered.

"What happened?" he heard Silas' quiet voice say from behind him.

"She's the sacrifice, Silas," he said. "And she's turning herself in."

"What are we going to do about it?" Silas asked, his blue eyes wide. The memory of Emira walking away from him while he was frozen to the ground flashed through his mind. The determination in her violet eyes, the finality in her voice.

"Nothing," Mateo responded. "We're going to do nothing." Because it was what she wanted, wasn't it?

"What about you, then? You could've stayed outside of the walls. Why did you come back?" Silas asked. Mateo glanced over at him.

"Silas…"

"Don't tell me it was because of her," he whispered. "This is your *life* we're talking about."

"I'm not going to escape," Mateo muttered. "I'm done."

"Why? You saw what happened to Cassandra. You vowed that you wouldn't let it happen to you."

"There's no point," Mateo said, meeting his eyes. "There's just no point anymore. She's going to die. And I can't do anything about it." Anger boiled his blood and erupted into his chest. He clenched his hands together into fists.

"Dude, who cares? That's what she wants."

"You don't get it," Mateo said, running his hand through his hair once again. "The only reason she got it into her mind that she might be the sacrifice was because of me. I was basically shouting it at her from the moment I saw her. And if I didn't say anything, if I just kept my stupid fucking mouth shut, she wouldn't have thought that."

"She has all of Mali's ichor, I'm guessing," Silas said, his voice still. "She would've figured it out even if you didn't say anything."

"But, it would've taken her longer. Because of me... She'll..."

"You love her, don't you?" Silas said. It was as if his words sucked all the air out of the room.

"Fuck off, Silas," Mateo said, shrugging past him.

"I know you, Mateo. I know you better than I know myself," Silas said, grabbing his arm. Mateo glared at it. "And I know you're going to torture yourself. You're going to go until the end just so you can see her die in front of you before your own death."

"Let go of me," was all Mateo said.

"You're going to destroy yourself," Silas said. "All so you can be with her in her last moments." Mateo's heart was beating so hard and fast in his chest. He could hardly breathe, could hardly think.

He ripped his arm out of Silas' grip and started to walk away.

"Don't we matter enough for you to live?" Silas said, his words snaking across the hallway towards Mateo. Mateo didn't say anything else, and continued walking. All he could think about was Emira.

Silas was right, that much Mateo knew. He was going to

torture himself if he continued thinking about the would-be Priestess. He needed to get her out of his mind.

"Mateo!" Cassandra shouted. "Help me!" But, Mateo couldn't move. One look at his grandfather, and he couldn't move an inch. No word had entered his mind, like with Emira. Just pure, unadulterated fear.

It wasn't until the crimson red blood reached his shoes could he move. And he ran towards his cousin, her gold eyes dull and staring up at the sky. The other sacrifices lying next to her, in a pool of their own blood. And he cried, unable to rip himself away from his cousin. He cried until his eyes were swollen, until tears couldn't force their way out of them anymore. Cassandra's face slowly morphed into Emira's. Dull, lifeless violet eyes staring up at him.

He needed to stop thinking.

"It's my duty. My destiny," Emira's voice echoed around in his head.

"We have to find a way to save me. You'll help me, won't you?" Cassandra's voice whispered in his head from the past.

"Shut up, shut up," he whispered to himself as he continued to walk. He knew where he was going, and he didn't care if he tripped the spell for the girls' dorm room. Luckily, as he walked across it, nothing happened.

Kanoa must already be around here, Mateo vaguely thought. He continued towards the room he was most familiar with and knocked on the door.

"I want to be important, Mateo," Emira's voice whispered.

"Help me!" Cassandra's voice shouted.

Darlene opened the door. She leaned against it and smiled easily at him. Her black curls were tied up on the top of her head, some stray ones framing her heart-shaped face.

"You want to make the voices go away again?" she asked, her words soft. He didn't say a word. He gripped the back of

Darlene's head and kissed her ferociously. Washing the taste of Emira out of his mouth.

She closed the door as they continued towards her bed. And he imagined her lips were Emira's. He imagined her hands were the ones touching him.

And the voices finally shut up.

CHAPTER TWENTY-FOUR

People whispered as Emira walked by. She pressed her books closer to her chest as she walked down the hallway. The news she was Mali's sacrifice spread fast in Leliara.

"Don't mind them," Shiloh said. "They're just surprised you're the sacrifice."

"Are they?" Emira muttered. Ever since she stepped up as the sacrifice of Mali, the baby in Ceteria was announced as not being the sacrifice anymore. The riots stopped. The sanctity of Constellatia was still intact. Although, in ten years, Emira knew the child would become the next sacrifice.

"You went from not having any power to having all of Mali's," Shiloh said. "It's understandable."

"I guess," Emira said.

"Or it's because of your near death experience with a *bellua*," Shiloh mused, her eyebrows raising.

"Doesn't everyone have a near death experience with a *bellua*?"

"Sure, but yours was more recent," she shrugged. They continued to walk to their survival class with Mr. Summers. Darlene caught up to them, out of breath as she heaved.

"Where have you been?" Shiloh asked. Usually Darlene's thoughts were shouting at Emira, but lately, her thoughts were just about one thing. *Mateo, Mateo, Mateo*. And every time, it sucked the air out of Emira's lungs.

She could feel there was more behind it, behind Darlene's thoughts, but his name was the only thing that she could catch. And every time Darlene reminded her of him, she thought about the feeling of his lips on hers. The feeling of the invisible string tying them closer and closer together, suffocating her until she started to doubt the decision she made.

"Just around," Darlene said, coyly.

"You have a boy wrapped around your finger, don't you?" Shiloh said, lightly bumping Darlene's shoulder with her own.

"More like he has *me* wrapped around *his* finger," Darlene sighed, blowing a curl out of her face.

"Darlene, you could do better than that," Shiloh muttered. Darlene shrugged.

"I'm getting something out of it, too," she said. "Don't worry about me."

"Is this because of—"

"Let's just continue having a good day, Shi," Darlene said, putting an arm around Shiloh's shoulders. Darlene put an arm around Emira's shoulders, also, as they entered Mr. Summers' classroom.

Mr. Summers looked over at the three of them and gestured for them to take their seats. They all did, and Emira looked around for Mateo. Lately, she hadn't seen him and she vaguely wondered if he was avoiding her.

Perhaps it was a good thing he was. It wasn't like she wanted to see him either, see the regret that lingered in his mismatched eyes.

"Today, we're going to learn the art of making a campfire," Mr. Summers said. The class groaned, and he held up a hand. "It seems that making a campfire is helpful since some of us like to get lost." He pointedly looked at Emira, and Emira wanted to shrink in her seat as the others in her class turned around to look at her.

"We've learned this a thousand times," someone piped up.

"How many hours does it take to become an expert?" Mr. Summers asked as he paced in front of the classroom.

"10,000," they all said under their breath.

"Exactly," Mr. Summers said, snapping his fingers. "Practice makes perfect, kids." He gestured for everyone to find a partner. Shiloh and Darlene obviously paired up with one another leaving Emira with Silas.

Silas' eyes reminded her of Celeste's. Like two swords about to pierce her within a second if she wasn't careful.

"This class is a waste of time," he muttered under his breath as he put the wood pieces together.

"It's smart, this class," Emira said. "You practice survival skills until it's basically second nature. It makes sense." Silas looked up at her, the first time he made eye contact with her since they got back from Camp Elemence. He made a face and then looked away.

Emira sighed. Something was wrong, but Silas was different from others. His thoughts were so quiet, she had to really listen and dig in order to hear anything.

"If you're trying to read my thoughts, don't bother," he mumbled. Emira blinked.

"How did you know?" she asked, laughing a little, uncomfortable.

"You make a face," he said, pointing a wood piece at her. "Your nose scrunches up a little."

"Oh," she said.

"I understand why you told Headmistress Alessia," he said, after arranging the wood pieces in the right way. He started to place the dry leaves underneath the contraption he created.

"At least someone does," she said, almost under her breath.

"I understand because it's clear you're not great at lying," Silas said, glancing at her. "Besides that, no, I don't understand."

"Are you mad at me about something?" Emira asked, bluntly. His black eyebrows twitched together for a moment as he glowered at the campfire they were trying to make.

"You gave my best friend a death sentence," he said, avoiding her gaze. "Why wouldn't I be mad at you?" She resisted the urge to touch her fingers to her lips at the mention of Mateo.

"He can still escape," Emira said, quietly.

"Yeah, yeah, he could," Silas said, looking at her. His electric blue eyes were like glaciers. "He could've stayed outside of the wall. It would've been a perfect escape for him. Not being in the confines of Constellatia. And yet, he came back. I wonder why." His tongue had always felt poisonous to Emira, but today, his words were dripping in it.

"Silas, if you're trying to blame me for decisions Mateo makes, I think you're barking up the wrong tree," Emira mumbled, stuffing more dead leaves underneath the contraption. She grabbed the two stones that were given to them and started to scrape them together. Sparks flew, but they didn't ignite the leaves underneath the wood pieces.

"I do blame you," he responded, his voice low. *At least he's honest.*

"I have no control over what Mateo does in his life," Emira bit back.

"Don't you?" He narrowed his eyes. "You know he came back because of you."

"I don't know that, actually," she said, scraping the stones against one another again. "And I doubt you know that for a fact, too."

"What is it that the Idol of Law and Fate likes to talk about when one of the politicians gets married?" Silas said, almost to himself as he looked up at the ceiling. "Oh, right. There's an invisible string that pulls one to another."

Emira pressed her tongue to the roof of her mouth as she desperately tried again to ignite this damn fire. She needed to leave, to get out of there. She didn't want to hear what Silas had to say.

"There's a string pulling you and Mateo together, isn't there?" he said, quietly. Emira wanted to press her hands to her ears, as if he were shouting at her.

"Please, stop," she whispered.

"You need to talk some sense into him," Silas said, leaning towards her. His words were like the sparks that were emanating from the stone.

"What am I supposed to say to him, Silas? Mateo, I'm sorry that I outed myself as a sacrifice, but please still go and escape your duty and fate?" Emira whisper-yelled.

"You remind him of his cousin," he said. "Ever since you got here, he's been having fucking nightmares about Cassandra. It's been years since he's done that."

"Okay? That's not my fault nor my problem," Emira snapped. She tried to take a deep breath, to calm the anger simmering within. But, deep inside, something broke within her. She was hurting him. Somehow, she was hurting him.

"You need to talk to him. Tell him it's not like Cassandra. Cassandra didn't want to be sacrificed, and he couldn't..." Silas took a deep breath. "He failed in helping her. He needs to know that this is what you want."

"It *is* what I want," Emira insisted. But there was a false note in her tone, a false note she couldn't control. Silas raised an eyebrow.

"Yeah, you won't be able to convince him like that," he muttered.

"I don't know what you want from me. He's escaped twenty times. Twenty times he's been caught and brought back. And there's nothing out in the wild. Just *bellua* and danger. What am I supposed to do? Tell him that I'll escape with him outside of the walls only for us to both die there? There isn't life out there, and there isn't a life here for us either!" Emira exclaimed. She didn't know when she had started standing. But, she looked around at the classroom, everyone staring at her. Saying a silent, desperate prayer to the Idol of Night—a habit of hers that she couldn't kick—she looked up to the ceiling, and then met Silas' gaze once more.

"If you think he has a death sentence, what do you think I have?" Emira hissed before grabbing her stuff and leaving the classroom.

"Ms. Solus! Ms. Solus, you can't just leave!" Mr. Summers shouted after her. But, she kept walking forward. Her blood was boiling, and she just wanted some damn peace and quiet.

As she thought this, the group of students walking past her laughing suddenly couldn't utter another word, like her thought controlled the group of them.

She barely noticed it. She kept walking, a destination burned into her mind. She swore her steps could be heard in the depths of the twelfth circle of hell as she crossed the boys' dormitory.

The spell was turned off. She still didn't know what the spell even did since it was turned off so often.

Without so much as a knock, with her mind she unlocked the door, turned the knob, and swung the door open wide. There was a yelp, but she still walked in. In bed, next to Mateo, was a girl with red hair. Her eyes were wide as she stared at Emira standing there.

Seeing her, that poisonous dagger in Emira's abdomen twisted even deeper. It seemed its stay was permanent.

Mateo licked his lips, his eyes not leaving Emira's. "You can leave," he said to the girl lying next to him.

"Yeah, that's probably a good idea," she said, wrapping herself with his sheet and grabbing her clothes. She quickly exited his room and closed the door behind her.

"What?" he asked, once she was gone. Like it was the most casual question, like he hadn't been avoiding her for the past few days.

"*What?*" Emira exploded. "What? You sicced your guard dog on me."

"I don't have a guard dog," he said, slipping his clothes on. Emira quickly turned around, averting her eyes as he got dressed.

"Silas," she seethed.

"What about Silas?" The brushing sound of clothes was gone, and she turned around to glower at him.

"I didn't give you a death sentence, okay? I have the exact same fate as you. And for him to even think that I can... I can't do anything, right? I can't save your life. We're both going to die. We can't rewrite the stars," Emira nearly yelled. "So, why is it *my* fault that you don't want to escape one last time?"

"Priestess," Mateo said, his eyes wide from the amount of anger that was spewing out of her.

"Don't call me that," she snapped. "Besides, you know escape is futile, right?"

"What do you want me to say, exactly?"

"Say it's not my fault!"

"It's not your fault."

"Okay, that's not—" Emira took a deep breath. "*Why?*"

"Why what?" he asked.

"Why in the twelve circles of hell did you come back?" She threw up her hands. She could feel her eyes burning, and she tried to swallow the tears back down. There was another question hidden in her words, a question he probably couldn't hear since his skull was so dense.

Why did you come back and kiss me if you were going to regret it? Mateo stared at her, shell-shocked.

"I…"

"Actually, don't answer that," she said, turning around. She grabbed the door handle.

"Wait," he said, rushing to get up. He slipped in front of her, stopping her from opening the door. He still didn't have a shirt on.

She let go of the handle and took a couple of steps back, her arms wrapping around herself like she was giving herself a hug.

"I came back because… Because… I just wanted to make sure you were okay," he muttered.

"I'm fine, clearly," Emira said, gesturing to herself. "I'm alive. You didn't need to come back."

"To be honest, there isn't a life in the wild. There's nowhere to go," he said quickly, as if he were covering up something.

"So, it's not my fault," Emira said.

"No, it's not," Mateo said. He said it, but Emira knew they were both lying.

"Then, inform your guard dog," she bit. Mateo gave her that

easy smile. A smile like butter. A smile that she thought about more than she'd like to admit.

"He's not really talking to me either, right now," he confessed.

"Well, then tell him to leave me alone," she snapped. She took a step forward, looked him up and down, and said, "Move." He didn't.

"You think you're going to die," he said, quietly. His eyes were searching hers. Emira blinked.

"What?"

"You said our fates are the same. You said we're both going to die," Mateo pointed out.

"Okay, and?" she said, rubbing her arms. He took a step forward, causing her to take a step back. The thought of his lips on hers flashed through her mind.

"You've always said we live on in the Idols, that it's an honor. That's what you've always thought," he said. "But, now you're saying that we're going to die." Emira shifted, uncomfortably.

"That's what I meant," she lied.

"No, no, you *really* think you're going to die," he said. "And…" His eyes flickered from her right eye to her left. "And… you don't want to." The way he sounded, he sounded like he had just made some huge discovery.

Emira tried to push down the fear his words were making her feel. Everything she felt when she thought about the day where she would be sacrificed was starting to bubble up inside of her. Things that she was trying to bury deep within.

"It's the human instinct," she muttered. "I just need to talk to a Priestess of Luck. Please, move." He moved to the side, letting her grab the door handle.

He turned towards her and whispered, "If you're going to

stick with this, you should at least know what's going to happen."

"Whatever, Cordero," she muttered before leaving his room. She closed the door behind her and kept walking down the hallway until she was out of the boys' dormitory. And it wasn't until she crossed the threshold that was the girls' dormitory did it feel like she was able to breathe again.

CHAPTER TWENTY-FIVE

"Do you know what this is about?" Shiloh asked, holding up a note that Emira also held. They were both standing in the middle of the main foyer, staring at the giant painting of Balan ripping off the head of a *bellua*.

"No idea," Emira muttered. Darlene showed up, holding the same note, in between her index and middle fingers. The three of them held their notes up to one another.

"We all know this is from Mateo, right?" Emira asked.

"Yeah," Darlene nodded. Shiloh looked shocked.

"No, I didn't know that. I didn't recognize the handwriting at all," she said, looking at the note once again. The moonlight reflected off of the black marble floors.

"You came to a suspicious location because of a note and you didn't know who it was from?" Emira asked. Shiloh shrugged.

"My curiosity got the better of me," she said.

"Why did he want to meet us here?" Darlene asked, her whisper almost echoing around the foyer. Emira shrugged. She couldn't help but think about what he had said earlier in the day. *"If you're going to stick with this, you should at least know what's going to happen."* Especially since his note read:

> *It's time for you to know the truth.*
> *Meet me at the main foyer in front of my grandfather's*
> *stupid portrait once curfew is called.*

It annoyed Emira how he never signed his notes. And she wondered why Shiloh and Darlene were also invited if this was him trying to convince her not to sacrifice herself.

"How long is he going to make us wait?" Darlene asked, tapping her foot. Just as she did, the portrait opened up to reveal a doorway. Standing in the doorway were four cloaked figures. One of them was extremely tall.

"Why are you guys wearing cloaks?" Emira asked, cocking her head to the side. A whisper of a smile played on her lips at seeing the four boys dressed like that. Shiloh stifled a laugh.

"Just, come in," Mateo said, moving to the side. His face was shrouded in darkness, but his voice was annoyed. The smile on her face widened at his tone. Emira, Shiloh, and Darlene walked into the secret room, the sconces on the walls lighting up as they did. The portrait closed behind them.

"No, seriously, what are the cloaks for?" Shiloh asked. She did a fake gasp. "Is this a secret society?" Emira and Darlene giggled.

"This is serious business, Shi," Kanoa said.

"Oh yeah, I can see that," Shiloh said, laughing a little.

"Why did we invite all of them again?" Kanoa asked. His stare lingered on Darlene for a little too long.

"So that Emira has support," Mateo answered.

"Support for what?" Emira asked as they continued walking down the haphazardly made stone steps. The room opened up into a study of sorts, filled with dusty books. Armchairs filled the room, with little mismatched side tables next to them. It looked like a study of sorts or a small, personal library.

"For when you find out the truth," he said, pulling the hood of his cloak off of his head. Shiloh genuinely gasped when she saw the books in the room. She ran to the bookshelves, looking at the books sideways as she did.

"These are all first editions," she breathed.

"Yup," Mateo said. "This room is otherwise known as the Room of Serpentes. Also known as the room for us Corderos or anyone related to Balan."

"That's so cool!" Shiloh exclaimed. She turned towards Emira. "Do you have a secret room?"

I'm an orphan, Emira almost said. *How would I know if I have a secret room?* But, instead, she shook her head.

"No," Emira answered. "Not that I know of."

"You probably do," Mateo said, nodding his head. "Though, Mali doesn't really have an ongoing family line like Balan does."

"Or like Phaethon," Darlene muttered.

"But, the first family she gave her ichor to probably has a room like this," he mused. The family Mali gave her ichor to was the Raven family. There was a Raven at Leliara, but he was two years below them, and Emira had never spoken to him. Plus, he didn't have the ichor of Mali, his shirt donning the symbol of a dragon, Nyro's ichor.

"So, why bring us to this secret room?" Emira asked, hands on her hips.

"You said you didn't want to die, but escape is futile," he pointed out.

"You said that?" Darlene asked, looking over at her. Emira wanted to strangle his pretty throat.

Instead, she took a deep breath, her expression never

betraying her inner thoughts. Coldly, she said, "I didn't say I didn't want to die. I just said we were *going* to die."

"Right, same thing," Mateo said, waving her words away. "I have something to show you." He went behind one of the bookshelves, the shelf scraping against the stone ground as he did. And he pulled out an old, leather bound book. Shiloh gasped again.

"Shi, please," Atlas said, quietly. She smiled up at him.

"This is like a dream come true," she breathed. Mateo almost handed Emira the book but then turned and gave it to Shiloh. His lopsided, teasing smile appearing on his face as he handed Shiloh the book, his eyes still on Emira. She simply rolled her eyes in response.

"My grandfather's diary from the very beginning," he said. Shiloh gingerly held the ancient diary in her hands, her jaw wide open.

"You want... You want *me* to read it?" she asked. Emira watched Mateo's eyes dart over to her, like he was gauging her reaction. So what if he had the diary of his grandfather? What was it going to say besides probably how weird Constellatia was compared to the heavens? She kept her expression unreadable, the mark of a trained priestess. But, she dug her nails into her palms.

"I want you to read it, and then I want you to tell Emira what you find," he said. "Because, obviously, this account is a skewed one. But it's more truthful than what we learn. It actually disproves a little fact that history teaches us."

"Ah, I see," Shiloh said, carefully placing the diary on one of the side tables in the room. "You want me to dissect it. You think I can tell the difference between the truth and the lies Balan gives."

"Yes, I do," he said, honestly. "I trust you can do that more than anyone else."

"You mean, more than I could," Emira said, wrapping her arms around herself. Lately, she felt colder. Like the fact that death was close to her was making her bones freeze.

"You would believe everything Balan says in his account," Mateo pointed out. Emira shrugged. He wasn't wrong. She probably would. Because why would an Idol lie?

What makes you think you could question the Idols?" High Priestess Ethel's voice pierced through her mind. She flinched.

"So, that's why you brought us all down here?" she asked, recovering quickly from the invasion.

"Yes," he said.

"Welcome to the Order of Truth," Kanoa said, rubbing his hands together.

"That's a stupid name," Darlene muttered.

"What would you call it?"

"Welcome to the Order of Chaos," Darlene said. "Because, if you're trying to tell us the Idols lied about everything we've ever learned, well, it'll cause anarchy in Constellatia." Emira's eyebrows knitted together.

Anarchy in Constellatia would destroy it, and they would go back to the Dark Ages. It went against everything Emira believed in. The protection of Constellatia was paramount, the unwavering belief in the Idols was drilled into her from a young age. And, she was a rule follower. She wasn't an anarchist. She could never be an anarchist. Something desperate clawed up from her stomach into her throat, squeezing it.

"No, no, I don't want to be a part of this," she said, backing away. "I don't want anarchy in Constellatia."

"There won't be, because I'm sure you won't do anything once you know the truth," Mateo said. "But, you need to know it, Priestess." His mismatched eyes held her gaze. Her eyes flickered towards what he had in his hands. She didn't see it before, but a gray, blank mask was being gripped in his veiny hands. She looked back up at him, knowing her expressionless exterior was broken, confusion written all over her face. He then handed her the mask.

"What is this for?" Emira asked softly, grabbing it.

"In thirty seconds, it'll be midnight," Mateo said.

"And?"

"And," he smiled, "It's Decessia. The Day of Dead." Krachelle's main holiday. They went all out, wearing masks that morphed into their beloved dead one's face. The people of Krachelle, and others around Constellatia, would put the masks on and would make the favorite foods of their deceased, and leave it out for the ghosts to feast on. It was the day when the heavens opened up, and the spirits could come and visit the physical world once again.

"But, I don't know anyone who's deceased," Emira said. Every time it was Decessia, she would be handed one of these gray, smooth, blank masks. And every time it touched her hands, it never morphed into anything. Just a blank face that she'd have to wear for the rest of the day with the other priestesses.

"I just want to see something," Mateo whispered. "Let's see if the Idols do lie, huh?" And as he did, the mask morphed for the very first time in Emira's hands.

She watched, her heart beating, as it slowly turned into the face of Priestess Irene's. *No*, Emira thought. *It can't be*. For a second, she held onto it, her mind trying to make sense of what she was seeing. Then, she dropped the mask, like it had burned her hand, and it fell to the stone ground with a metallic clink.

A million things were racing through her mind, her eyes

staring at the simulated face of Priestess Irene, the woman who raised her.

"*Who do you think you are?*" High Priestess Ethel's voice snaked its way into her mind.

The Idols don't lie.

"What kind of game is this, Mateo?" she asked, slowly looking up, her voice the personification of cold anger. She could feel her eyes burning as she studied his expression. He wasn't looking at her, simply at the mask that mirrored Priestess Irene's face exactly.

"I wasn't sure," he said, under his breath. "But, now you know."

"What the fuck did you do?" Emira hissed as she pushed Mateo, hard. He stumbled back a couple of steps, his eyes widening.

Priestess Irene's dull brown eyes were staring at her.

Her face melting off of the *bellua* flashed through her mind. Desperation settled into her chest. Her heart hammered wildly.

"What the fuck did you do to her?" she cried, pushing him once more. He, again, took a couple of steps back.

"I didn't do anything, Emira," he said, emotionless, his eyes cold. Her thoughts were racing, her heart pounding in her head. All her letters that she had written to Priestess Irene, she had never responded to any of them. Emira had thought she was busy, that there wasn't time to write her back. But... Her eyes darted towards the mask that was on the stone ground, Priestess Irene's dead face staring up at her.

"I need to go," she said, backing away from them. The six of them stared at her, like vultures in the dark.

"I need to go," she repeated, turning around.

"Emira," Mateo called after her.

"I'll go after her," Atlas said.

"No, I will," she heard Mateo say, definitively. She ran up the steps, and she could hear Mateo after her. She had the sound of his steps memorized at this point. And she couldn't breathe. She couldn't breathe at all.

Someone grabbed her arm, and she tried to rip it out of their grips. She turned around, staring straight into Mateo's mismatched eyes.

"Let go of me," she ordered. And she ordered it in more ways than one. She could feel his chaotic mind, and she shouted it into the deepest parts of him. He let go immediately, his expression pained.

"What do you plan on doing?" he asked as she turned around.

"I'm going to Aeluris," she snapped.

"How, exactly, do you plan on doing that?" Mateo said.

"I'll do what you did," she spat. "I'll use your invisible blanket, and I'll leave."

"By yourself?"

"*Yes*, by myself," she nearly yelled. She was surprised no one could hear her in the school.

"Let me go with you," he nearly begged. She bit her tongue. She bit hard until she could taste coppery blood. A part of her wanted to push him down the stairs for revealing what he did. For confusing her, for making her start to question...

The Idols don't lie, her mind insisted. Because if they did, how would she reckon the fact that she was supposed to give her life to them? How would she be able to make sense of her life up to this point? She had dedicated every year, every waking second to the Idols, to Constellatia. And if it's all... If it's all...

She couldn't think it.

"This was a cruel joke," she whispered.

"It's not a joke, Emira," he nearly pleaded. "I promise you, I'm not joking."

"I'll go with her," Silas said from behind him. Mateo looked over his shoulder at him. Silas sighed as he walked up the steps to where Emira was standing. She recoiled from him like he was a *bellua* himself. Her eyes looked him up and down.

"I don't need you to go with me," she said. He wiggled his fingers.

"I have the power of illusion," he said. Hemlock's power, the Idol of Festivity and Knowledge. He shrugged. "You might need me."

She stared at him for a long while, and then looked at Mateo who was standing behind him. He looked like he regretted ever placing the mask in Emira's hands.

"Give me the mask," she said before turning her fiery gaze towards Silas. "And fine, you can come with."

CHAPTER TWENTY-SIX

Mateo had given them the invisible blanket, reluctantly. It took him forever to find it, and Silas had wrestled with the idea of making the two of them look like they were simply squirrels running across the field. But considering the size of them both, he wasn't sure if he was going to be able to succeed in that.

Luckily, Mateo had a good memory and found the blanket. Emira immediately pulled the blanket over her and Silas. She was glad they weren't going to look like giant squirrels running out of the school. The guards would've immediately caught them.

"Don't lose it," Mateo warned. He stared at the two of them, but Emira could tell he couldn't see them.

"You can make another one if we do," Silas responded. He locked arms with Emira so that they'll be able to walk easier, and started towards the front door of Leliara.

Before they could go out the door, Mateo somehow grabbed Silas' arm wrapped in the blanket. He leaned in and whispered,

"Don't let her do anything stupid." Then, he let go of him. Emira scoffed.

"Unlike you, Cordero, I think before I act," she retorted. Mateo smirked in her direction.

"You don't think when you're angry." He gestured to her and Silas. "As we can see, from point A."

"I don't need your permission to go check up on this trickery," she spat. "Considering Silas has illusion powers, this could all be just that. An illusion."

"It's not," Silas said, quietly beside her, dashing her hopes in the process.

"I don't care if it is or isn't. I need to see with my own two eyes if Priestess Irene is... is..." Emira swallowed the words down her throat.

"Maybe I should go with you guys," Mateo muttered. Silas pulled off the blanket and looked him dead in the eye.

"If you and Emira are both missing, what do you think they'll think? Especially before the Winter Solstice," Silas said in his even tone.

"What is happening on the Winter Solstice?" Emira whispered, mostly to herself.

"The ball that the Idols like to put on in order to meet the sacrifices," Silas said.

"It's torture," Mateo said. "A photo op, really."

"I get to meet all the Idols?" Emira asked, uncontrollable excitement building up in her chest. And then it was immediately met with confusion. Excitement, bitterness, pain, and confusion. Emira didn't know how she felt about her beloved Idols, the Idols she'd been worshipping since she was young. And, for some reason, even if it were true about Priestess Irene, she wanted to meet them. How many people got to meet the Idols?

Mateo narrowed his mismatched eyes at her and then put the invisible blanket over the two of them.

"When you find out it's real, Priestess," he said, as they started out the door. His eyes met hers, though Emira didn't know how he knew exactly where she was. "Give them hell."

And with that, with the cover of night, Silas and Emira slipped out of the front door of Leliara. They shuffled down the long driveway together in silence. Snow covered the ground, and it crunched underneath Emira's boots.

Normally, she loved the snow. It was beautiful, and it hid all the imperfections of the world. And it marked her favorite holiday of the year that was coming up, the Winter Solstice. The province of Aeluris always lit up with magical little fairy lights everywhere. Colorful ornaments were hung on trees and gifts were given the day of. If any holiday felt magical, it was the Winter Solstice. But now, with Decessia being only a couple of weeks before the Winter Solstice, her favorite holiday was marred with the...

Emira couldn't think of it. Priestess Irene wasn't dead. She couldn't be dead. High Priestess Ethel promised. She promised she'd take care of Priestess Irene. Emira's hands balled up into fists.

Silas glanced over at her fists while he was picking the lock to the front gate of Leliara. He managed to get it unlocked, and the golden gates swung open.

"You're thinking about the priestess?" he asked.

"She was like my mother," Emira muttered. Night was slowly turning into dawn, everything awash in light blue. It reminded her of when Priestess Irene would wake her up.

You need to stop sleeping in, my sunshine, she would say while throwing open the curtains, *"A priestess wakes when the sun rises."*

Emira shook her head. She needed to change the subject.

"When did you learn to do that?"

"What? Pick a lock?" Silas asked. He shrugged. "I was locked up a lot as a child." She furrowed her eyebrows.

"Locked up?" That was different from what she thought about Silas' upbringing. He was Silas Silver, the son of a prominent politician family—not to mention, a legacy. He grew up here, in Astutera, but his father, the governor of Astutera, worked where other politicians worked, in Serpel. It was where the parliament and the Idols met every month to talk about legislation. So, Emira thought Silas was just another boy with a silver spoon in his mouth. A lavish lifestyle with a big, popular family. Him being locked up as a child wasn't part of the fantasy she thought of.

Silas shrugged. "Silver family secrets."

"So, you don't want to talk about it?" Emira asked. He raised an eyebrow.

"Do you want to talk about the Priestess?"

"Fair," she murmured. When the two of them reached the city, after walking down the long driveway, Silas threw off the invisible blanket. He balled it up and placed it underneath a bush. It was almost funny, watching someone ball up something that was invisible. And Emira would've laughed at the sight, if her mind wasn't filled with worries.

"Make sure I remember where I put this," he said.

"I have horrible short term memory," Emira said. "I'm like a goldfish." Silas narrowed his eyes at her, like he was trying to figure out if she was joking or not. Emira kept a straight face. In fact, she had a horribly good memory. She remembered everything, like an elephant did.

One night, she was crying after the high priestess had punished her for asking who made the Idols. Because, if they existed, they had to have come from somewhere, right? But, it was a question a priestess should never ask, and Emira was punished accordingly. Priestess Irene let her cry, Emira's head in her lap. And she brushed her hair out of her face, running her fingers through the tangled mess.

"I hate her," Emira had cried. *"I hate her because she hates me. She wishes I was never put on the temple's doorstep."*

"She doesn't hate you, my dear. She's trying to teach you, in her own way," Priestess Irene had murmured. *"Be like a goldfish, my sunshine. Don't be an elephant and hold a grudge. Forget and forgive."*

But, if the high priestess let Priestess Irene die, Emira didn't know if she could forget and forgive.

"Great," Silas muttered. He took out a gray, blank mask and put it on his face. It slowly morphed into an older lady with black hair streaked with silver. Her eyes were stone gray, and she had a kind face.

"Who was it?" she asked, gently.

"My mother," Silas answered, his tone flat. Emira had the feeling he didn't want to talk about it further. She brought out the mask that Mateo had given her and stared at the eerie face of Priestess Irene.

"It's weird, isn't it?" he said, his voice low. People were starting to come out of their houses and walk down the streets of Astutera. They all were wearing masks of their passed loved ones.

"It creeped me out, the first year," Silas said. "Wearing my mother's face. And I didn't even have a choice. My grandfather died when I was a year old, and I would much prefer to see his dead face instead of my mother's." Emira laughed along with him. But, then she immediately felt guilty for it. Her grip tightened on the mask.

"But, the mask does what it does," Silas said, quietly, as he looked at the one in Emira's hands.

"At least no one will be trying to avoid my eyes," Emira muttered, putting on Priestess Irene's face.

"She was beautiful, Emira," he whispered.

"Let's not talk about her like she's dead," she said, trying to swallow the lump growing in the back of her throat. "We don't know for sure."

"Of course," he said. "This way." They walked down the streets of Astutera without a word. Emira never got to participate in the holiday of Decessia, not knowing anyone who had passed enough for the mask to morph. Now, she felt like it was a cruel holiday. A morbid one.

The colorful buildings of Astutera were covered in snow, but even with the layer of white, it was still too colorful for Emira. She didn't understand how there was any color left in the world, when the person who painted the world for her was gone.

They walked past the town square where a bronze statue was erected in the middle. The image of Hemlock with a fox at her feet. She was dressed in her armor, a sword raised. She wondered if that was how Hemlock looked.

"Have you met the Idols?" Emira asked as they walked by the statue. Silas looked up at Hemlock.

"No," he said. "Not really. Mateo has met all of them because he was announced as a sacrifice pretty early on. But, the rest of us, we don't really meet them. Not unless we join their camp as warriors."

"Do you want to meet them?"

Silas glanced over at her. It was unnerving how he looked like a completely different person with the mask on. "If Mateo doesn't survive this, they wouldn't want me to meet them. I promise you that." His jaw clenched as he thought about it and then shook his head.

"The train station is this way," he muttered.

"Why are so loyal to Mateo?" Emira asked, catching up to him.

"Mateo saved me," he said. "He saved me and he's family."

"That's pretty vague," she said under her breath. He ignored her and walked down the steps into the underground train station. It wasn't quite as crowded as the last time Emira was there.

"Two tickets to Aeluris," Silas said to the ticket clerk. The lady, wearing a mask of the face of a dog, handed them two tickets without a word. Silas handed her some stellae in return. It burned her pride that she didn't have stellae to spend.

"I'm sorry," Emira said.

"For?"

"For making you pay," she said, her voice low.

"You don't have any stellae. You're an orphan," he pointed out.

"Okay, you don't have to rub it in my face," she retorted. He shrugged. They walked up to the ebony statue of a cat and pressed down on the paw. The cat moved to reveal the inside of the train and the two of them boarded it.

"As a sacrifice, though, you could ask for more stellae," Silas said when they sat down in their seats.

"What? I can?"

"You can ask for anything," he nodded. "Only perk of being a sacrifice."

"Pretty good perk if you ask me," Emira said. She looked out the window as the train started to take off. Darkness was the only thing she could see.

"What did you mean when you said Mateo saved you?" Emira asked after some time had passed. Silas' eyes darted towards her.

"You're not going to let this go, are you?" he asked. She shook her head.

"It'll help me get my mind off of..." she gestured to the mask on her face. Silas let out a long sigh. His mother's face looked conflicted as his new eyes darted around.

"Okay, well, he gave me a safe place," he muttered. "My family... after my mother died... Well, even before that, it was... not a safe place. And he opened up his home to me, his family."

"And his family is better?"

"Despite being the daughter of Balan, Mateo's mom is an angel," Silas said. The gray eyes on his mask lit up at the thought of his best friend's mom.

"I heard your families were good friends," Emira said. Silas snorted.

"No, our *moms* were good friends. They met at some kind of social event after my mom graduated from Leliara. Mrs. Cordero doesn't have any ichor in her, so she never attended Leliara. She was, instead, known as a socialite. So, that's how they met." He shrugged.

"So, your mom was a good person," Emira said. She studied Silas' mom's face. He didn't look much like her, just the black hair and maybe her eye shape.

"Yeah," he said, looking out the window. "Well, I try to believe she was."

"You don't think she was a good person?"

"I think a good person would stop their abusive husband from attacking their kids," he muttered. "But, she was also a good mom when he wasn't around."

"I'm sorry," Emira whispered. Silas shrugged again. They stayed silent for a moment. Then, he turned and studied the mask on Emira's face.

"Tell me about her," he said, nodding his head towards her.

"Priestess Irene?" Emira asked. She could feel her throat tighten. She wanted to tell him about her, about how she was the kindest person one would ever meet. But, she couldn't. The words wouldn't come out. Instead, she said, "You'll see her soon."

"That's right," Silas said, a small smile appearing on his mother's lips. "I will, won't I?" Emira nodded her head.

"Yes, you will." And with that, the conversation ceased. Emira hoped this was all just an evil trick of Mateo's. Something to bring her to his cause. She hoped that was all it was, so she had an excuse to pummel him once she got back.

They didn't speak to one another again until the train got to Aeluris. Usually, Emira found silence uncomfortable, but this time, she was grateful for it. She didn't feel like trying to make conversation.

"I've never been to Aeluris," Silas said when they got off the train. Her eyes lit up at that.

"Oh my Idols, I have to show you around then, if there's time," Emira said. Silas laughed a little.

"If you feel up to it," he said, a twinkle in his eye. It was the nicest he had been to her recently, and it made her feel pitied a little. Still, she was thankful for his unexpected kindness.

They exited the underground train station, which was as crowded as she remembered it being. Aeluris was covered in snow as well, and the dark, almost toppling over buildings was what Emira really felt like seeing. Silas' eyes grew wide at seeing the town.

The cobblestone streets were swept so no snow clung to it. Little lights were hung around the city, and in the distance, Emira could see the obsidian castle that housed Ophelia, the Idol of Night. Near the castle was the Temple of Night.

"Let's go," she said.

"I didn't know this town was so…"

"Great? Beautiful? Magical?"

"Dreary," Silas finished his thought. He looked around the city in horror.

"I'm sorry, you think it's *dreary*?"

"I mean, I come from a very colorful city," he said. "This… This is…"

"Easier on the eyes," Emira finished for him. He shrugged. Emira looked through a shop window in order to see the clock.

"They'll be eating lunch right now," she said. "It's the perfect time to talk to everyone." Silas followed her as they walked through the city of Aeluris. And as they did, some people bowed a little when she walked by, wearing their own masks of loved ones passed.

"I'm sorry for your loss, Priestess," they would say as she would walk by, touching her shoulder. It all made her want to explode.

The people of Aeluris knew Priestess Irene. She was always around, helping with the homeless, or shopping, or speaking the word of the Temple. And the fact that they were all telling her, even though they didn't know who she was underneath the mask, that they were sorry for her loss? Emira was simmering with anger. Anger was easier to feel. It was fiery, quick, and it burned her skin. It moved her forward.

If she let herself feel the despair, the anguish, that was starting to bloom in her chest, it would crush her bones.

Luckily, Silas seemed to know to stop talking. Emira walked even faster towards the Temple of Night, his tour being postponed.

She needed to see with her own two eyes that Priestess Irene wasn't there. She needed to hear it from the damned High Priestess Ethel's mouth.

CHAPTER TWENTY-SEVEN

Emira looked up at the dark temple. It was covered in a light layer of snow, and the two giant black cats stared at her with their sapphire jewels, like they knew what she was going to do.

"Just a reminder," Silas spoke up from behind her. "Don't do anything stupid."

"No one tells me what to do, Silver," Emira snapped. And with that newfound anger, she took the steps forward that she couldn't seem to do earlier. She entered the temple, and it was quiet, not a soul around. She walked slowly through it, like a ghost wandering through their old life.

It looked exactly like how it always had. The sconces on the walls flickered as she walked by, as they always did. The floor was newly swept, like it always had been. And she didn't understand how everything could be the same when Priestess Irene wasn't there.

She swallowed and continued to walk towards the kitchen where the priestesses would gather to eat. Her and Silas' footsteps echoed throughout the temple. Despair started to creep into every crevice inside of Emira, and she tried, desperately, to hold onto the anger, the red hot ire moving her forward.

She opened the door to the small, homely kitchen and saw all the priestesses, the priestesses who helped raise her and took her in, who were all such good friends with Priestess Irene, sitting there wearing their masks. And as they turned towards her, she could see they all were wearing Priestess Irene's face.

"Emira," she heard High Priestess Ethel say. The sound of her voice made Emira flinch. She didn't know how High Priestess Ethel knew it was her, and she didn't care. The anguish that was creeping in, escaped, and in its place was the burning flame.

Who do I think I am? Emira thought to herself, High Priestess Ethel's voice echoing from the past. *How dare I question the Idols?*

She couldn't think, her thoughts filled with only one feeling. A feeling that burned her from the inside out.

With a flick of her wrist, Emira removed all of the masks the priestesses were wearing, revealing their true faces. The masks clattered to the ground as some of the priestesses screamed. Emira pulled her own mask off of her face and stalked towards High Priestess Ethel.

"Emira," Ethel nearly begged, backing away from her. It was weird, seeing terror shining in her black eyes. *Black, like her heart,* she vaguely thought.

"Where is Priestess Irene?" Emira asked, her voice quiet and low. Ethel swallowed, her dusky eyes looking behind Emira at Silas, pleading for help. He took off his own mask and leaned against the door frame, eyeing all of them calmly. Her eyes flickered back towards Emira, averting her eyes and simply settling her gaze on her cheeks, darting back and forth.

"Emira, you have to understand—"

"Where is she, High Priestess Ethel? It's an easy question to answer. Is she in her room?" Emira started backing towards the door, like she was going to check Priestess Irene's room.

"You… You know she's not there," Ethel said, her voice barely above a whisper.

"Sorry, what? She's not here? Where is she then?" Emira asked, taking a step forward. Her eyes finally met Emira's. She didn't know what Ethel was seeing in her face, but whatever it was frightened her. Ethel took another step back until she was against the wall.

"Tell me," Emira nearly growled. "Where is she? Or, am I still not allowed to ask questions, High Priestess?" Ethel's expression crumpled at the mention, like all the regrets of how she had treated Emira flowed back into her memory. Her mouth gaped open and closed, like a fish gasping for air.

Looking at the high priestess, Emira wondered why she was ever afraid of her.

"Just tell her," another priestess said. "Tell her the truth. She deserves the truth." Ethel shook underneath Emira's gaze and closed her eyes, her wrinkles more prominent than Emira had ever seen.

"She passed," Ethel whispered. Emira's face tightened.

"How?" she asked.

"I…" Ethel sighed deeply.

"Tell me," Emira ordered. "Tell me! How did she die? Did she die naturally? Was she sick and she didn't want to tell me?" Ethel closed her eyes again. Emira grabbed her shoulders and shook her.

"Was she sick, High Priestess Ethel?!"

"She was killed." Her voice pierced through the air. She opened her black eyes, meeting Emira's. "She was executed, Emira. A couple of days after you left."

It was as if all the light and air was sucked out of the room, leaving Emira in darkness and suffocation.

She let go of the high priestess' shoulders and backed away. Her face contorted as she looked at the other priestesses in the room. At the others who raised her. At the others who were Priestess Irene's *friends*.

"Why?" her voice broke.

"She hid you. It's against the rules," Ethel said, unable to look Emira in the eye.

"So... So, you had her *killed*?" Emira couldn't understand the words that were coming out of Ethel's mouth. It was like suddenly she spoke a foreign language. A ringing appeared in Emira's ears. A ringing that she couldn't get out.

The Idol of Night said it must be done.

We couldn't fight against it.

The Idol declared it.

"Stop talking," Emira pleaded, putting up a hand while another hand went to her ear. "Please, stop."

Her hair was splayed out on the ground.

They did it in the main square.

Blood... just blood was everywhere.

The images filled Emira's head, and she couldn't get rid of them. Her vision blurred as she backed away.

The Idol of Night, the Idol of Night ordered it. The thought echoed in her brain, filling it until it was all she herself could think about.

"Curiosity will kill her." And the high priestess didn't know how true her words would become. It would kill Emira, in more ways than one. That much, she knew.

Her whole life was falling apart, being pulled through her fingers like thin pieces of yarn.

And even though it was too much, even though it was killing her, the thoughts kept coming.

The priestesses' lips weren't moving, their eyes staring at her in a mixture of horror and fear. They were huddled against the back wall, as far away as they could get from her.

And yet, their thoughts were shouting at Emira. Screaming about every little detail of Priestess Irene's execution into her mind.

An axe. A giant axe covered in blood.

Hot blood hit my face.

Priestess Irene's eyes were so lifeless. I've never seen such eyes before.

"Shut. Up." Emira warned. She felt the burning behind her eyes and glowered at the priestesses whose thoughts wouldn't quiet.

"Emira, no one's talking," she heard Ethel say out loud but the other priestesses' voices were too loud in her head.

I need to stop this, Emira thought. *I need to think. I can't think.*

Mateo's voice entered her head, cutting through all of the shouting, all the horrific memories. *"When you find out it's real, Priestess, give them hell."*

Priestess Irene's warm brown eyes filled Emira's vision, her eyes filling up with tears as Emira left the temple. *I never should've left,* she thought. *I should've never left her alone.*

I should've never trusted the Idols.

Without much energy, she raised everything in the room and threw it all at the priestesses. She heard screaming, someone fell to the ground with a thud. And with another hand, Emira lifted High Priestess Ethel high off the ground.

Ethel screamed her head off. She shouted Emira's name and something else. Maybe a prayer, Emira didn't know. And she threw her against the wall. A crack was heard, and Ethel groaned. Blood reached Emira's shoes, and she stared at it for a long while.

It was like she was back in that field with the *bellua*. Like she was trapped in the back of her mind, her feelings hidden in a box in the corner. She felt nothing. And something inside whispered that she probably should. That this wasn't normal.

"Emira, we should go," Silas whispered next to her. She stared at it and the memory of one of the priestesses entered her mind.

Priestess Irene, headless, laying on the ground of the main square. People surrounded her in horror, and blood... red crimson blood reached Emira's shoes, like Ethel's. She clenched her jaw and looked at the disarray the room was in, that she caused.

"This isn't enough," she murmured, her voice faraway, detached. Silas' blue eyes darted over towards her, curiosity mixed with his own poorly concealed fear.

"I think it is, Emira," Silas whispered.

"No," she growled. "No. You don't know what they saw. What they let happen. But I do. I saw it, all through their eyes." Emira tapped her head.

"You've punished them enough," he said, gesturing towards the room. The priestesses were obviously harmed. High Priestess Ethel was dead. But, none of them felt cold and powerless like Priestess Irene did. None of them knew what it was like to have an Idol sentence them to death, and there was nothing anyone could do about it.

"*Give them hell*," Mateo's voice echoed. Emira steeled her gaze.

"I'm giving them hell," she said, turning around. Silas grabbed a hold of her arm.

"This isn't right," he argued. His electric blue eyes pierced her soul. "They didn't kill her."

"They stood by and *watched*," Emira spat. Silas' expression turned desperate.

"What were they supposed to do? Go against the order of an Idol?" His words hit their mark. Emira stared at him for a long while. The priestesses felt sorrow for Priestess Irene, she knew that. She was their friend. And Emira could almost taste their mourning on her tongue, that's how potent it was. They didn't want her to die. They were just following orders. Like she had.

She turned around and faced the priestesses who were groaning on the floor, whispering prayers and remembering loved ones in their heads. Waving a hand, she crumbled the back wall into dust and then mentally pushed the priestesses out of the room into the white, untouched snow.

"Don't come back," she hissed at them. She started to walk out of the room, Silas leading the way. And behind her, she lifted her hand and then balled it up into a fist. The ceiling of the room came crumbling down.

"Emira!" Silas said, turning around. His eyes were wide. Emira glared at him. *Give them hell.*

No, she wasn't going to kill the lot of them. But, she was going to get her revenge.

"I'm destroying this whole temple, so you better get out," she said through her teeth. Silas took one look at her and then nodded, running out of the temple.

Emira walked through every room of the temple and destroyed it with her mind. Took it apart like how they took apart Priestess Irene. And the memories that the other priestesses had screamed into her mind played on repeat as she took the temple apart, brick by brick.

Priestess Irene, crying as she was led to the middle of the main square, her hands bound in front of her.

Priestess Irene, bowing her head for the executioner. Not fighting at all. Tears hitting the cobblestone beneath her.

Emira wanted to scream. She wanted to scream until her voice was hoarse. But, her power did the screaming for her.

A cat ran out of the way as she took down the main hall of the temple. Statues of cats turning into dust as she destroyed them. And as she got to the entrance of the Temple of Night, she stared at the giant black cats that were in the front. And with a flick of her wrist, she made the heads of them come toppling down.

She breathed heavily as she looked at the desecrated temple. Everything was quiet and the snow continued to fall, covering the horrors that had occurred.

The anger was starting to escape, the crushing feeling of despair beginning to creep into her bones. And Emira didn't know if she would survive it, if the fury went away.

"Ophelia," she heard Silas' voice say. Emira turned around to face the Idol and realized that the people of Aeluris were standing there, staring at her in horror. She swallowed as she looked at the crowd that had formed.

No one looked her in the eye. But, Emira was sure it was now for a different reason.

Ophelia smiled, showing off her canines. It still hit her in the gut how otherworldly she looked. But, mixed with the feeling of reverence, was seething anger.

The Idol of Night said it must be done. That was one of the priestesses' thoughts. It was her. She ordered Priestess Irene's death.

"Too bad you're not becoming a warrior," Ophelia finally filled the silence. "You could've easily destroyed a lot of *bellua.*"

"You ordered her death," Emira said through gritted teeth. Ophelia shrugged.

"I did," she nodded. She looked at her sharpened fingernails. "But, what did you expect me to do, little elephant? Let her pass on by with a slap on the hand?" Emira vaguely remembered Pandora also called her that, *little elephant*. But out of Ophelia's mouth, it sounded patronizing. Belittling. Like she was the dirt on the bottom of Ophelia's expensive heels.

Ophelia tsked as she shook her finger. "No, I couldn't do that. She interfered with the sacrifice."

All they care about is the sacrifice, Emira bitterly thought. *Who cares about the woman who dedicated her life to the Idols? She fucked up once, so let's kill her.*

"It was because she loved me. She wanted to protect me and maybe it was wrong but..." Emira said, instead. "She didn't deserve to die. Punished, maybe. But not *death*."

"The punishment fits the crime," Ophelia said, her ice blue eyes hardening.

"No, it doesn't," Emira argued, taking a step forward. Fury still clung to her bones, like a familiar pet, chasing away the despair that was starting to settle there.

"You forget your place, little elephant," Ophelia's voice twisted. "You don't decide that. *I* do."

Emira couldn't say anything to that. Her head was pounding. The thoughts of everyone staring at her all thinking the same thing.

Power of an Idol.

Destroyed a temple with her mind.

She killed the high priestess.

And the thoughts of the priestesses, huddled around the outside of the destroyed temple. Staring at her like they didn't recognize her. Like they didn't help raise her. Their thoughts mirroring what they saw in her.

A broken child.

A monstrous broken child.

No, Emira couldn't respond to Ophelia. She couldn't say what she wanted to say, that an Idol shouldn't get to decide whether someone lives or dies. That there should be a trial. That the crime wasn't that bad. But, she couldn't say those things. She couldn't say it without her own head being sliced off. That much Emira could retain.

So, instead, she just screamed. A wordless scream into the face of the Idol of Night. The Idol that she used to worship. Blindly worship.

Ophelia's ice crystal eyes narrowed and then she took her hand and waved it across Emira's face. Her mouth immediately closed, and Emira couldn't move. Like her whole body had turned to ice.

"Let's take them back to Leliara," Ophelia said to the Pyrinian guards behind her. Emira tried to scream, tried to move against the spell that Ophelia had put on her. But, she couldn't. It was like she had turned to stone.

Ophelia looked around Emira's body at Silas. "Your father *will* hear about this."

"Great," Emira heard Silas begrudgingly say. She couldn't see Silas' face, but she knew the hellion would never forgive her. He already disliked her, this was just icing on the cake.

The Idol of Night's ice blue eyes returned to Emira. She looked her up and down and then leaned forward so that no one in the crowd could hear her.

"You're lucky you're a sacrifice," she hissed into Emira's ear. "Or I would've executed you in the same way as your predecessor." She pulled away from her and gave her a brilliant smile.

"Do you understand?" she said in an upbeat voice. Emira wanted to throttle her. Ophelia turned to the Pyrinian guards and without another word, Emira was lifted into the air and put into the carriage. She still couldn't move at all, so she was laid down in a weird angle in the carriage. Silas sat down on the blue velvet seat, and Ophelia sat beside him.

"Ooh, that's going to hurt in the morning," Ophelia said, pointing at how Emira was lying. Emira simply glared at her. At least she still had the ability to move her eyes around.

And as the carriage started to move, the gravity of what had happened started to hit Emira. Tears burned her eyes and flowed freely down her face. Yes, Priestess Irene was killed. Yes, the priestesses just let it happen.

But, they were still her family, too. She grew up with all of them. She thought she would have a place to go back to, despite being an orphan. But she had nowhere. She had just destroyed the only home she ever knew. And High Priestess Ethel... Her blood slowly creeping towards Emira's shoes flashed through her mind. She stifled a cry.

"Are you starting to realize what your little tantrum has done?" Ophelia spat. Any niceties that the Idol had were gone. Her neat hair was slightly undone as she looked away from Emira.

"A riot just finished in Ceteria and now I must explain why my temple is destroyed and my high priestess murdered, by a sacrifice, no less," she muttered. "The press will go crazy this week." She held still for a moment and then hit the side of the carriage with an abnormal amount of force. She leaned down towards Emira.

"I will find whoever it is that you cherish the most, and I *will* murder them, sacrifice," she hissed. Emira wished she could've retorted, *"You've already done that"* but she couldn't move a muscle.

Ophelia leaned back in her seat and looked out at Aeluris rushing past.

"I loved Ethel. She was a great high priestess," she murmured. But, she didn't shed a single tear for the high priestess she supposedly loved.

She turned her attention towards Silas. "Are you the one who she cherishes the most?" He shrugged, glancing at Emira. Ophelia tapped her nose as she shook her head.

"No, no, I know who was the mastermind behind all of this," she said, smiling but without emotion. "Your best friend and your cherished one." She pointed at Silas and then at Emira.

Ophelia's cat-like eyes glittered. "Oh, but, I guess I don't need to murder Mateo. His grandfather will do that for me."

Emira tried to control her breathing. She closed her eyes.

She had killed the high priestess. The High Priestess of Night and Magic. She was still hidden in the back of her mind, feeling the tears flow down her frozen face. But the tears weren't for the high priestess, it was for herself. Because, everything she knew, everything Priestess Irene had taught her was a lie.

It was all a lie. Including herself. She didn't know who she was anymore. A murderer, a sacrifice, and what else? A psychopathic insane little girl? What did people do when their whole lives were ripped apart? Who even was she anymore? Someone who can destroy a whole building just because she wanted to? Someone who killed a person and not have a single morsel of regret about it?

Shouldn't she feel *something*?

Instead, she stayed hidden. Hidden in the back of her mind,

holding the box of feelings in her lap, hand firmly holding the lid in place.

Only one feeling was allowed to escape, the one feeling she never could quite hide away. And her fury slowly started to be directed towards Mateo. It was his fault she had to question who she was. It was his fault her life was falling apart.

Because, everything Mateo had said about the Idols... Well, was it true? Was all the knowledge Emira had acquired wrong? They lied about the fairies, she saw them with her own two eyes.

They killed Priestess Irene, and hid it from her.

The Idols don't lie.

Bullshit, she thought.

What else were they hiding?

CHAPTER TWENTY-EIGHT

"**S**o you have no idea where your childhood best friend and the classmate you've been spending an awful lot of time with could've gone?" Headmistress Alessia said, her green eyes boring holes into Mateo.

"Nope," he said, leaning back in his chair and putting his feet up on her desk. Headmistress Alessia used her pen to push his feet off of it.

"Let's not do this," she sighed.

"Do what?" he asked, innocently.

"Let's not go around and pretend like you don't know where they are and that I don't know that you know where they went," she said.

"Sorry, can't help you there, Alessia," Mateo said.

"It's *Headmistress* Alessia," she simply sighed. She put on her reading glasses and started to scribble something down. One of her assistants came in and handed her a letter. Her green eyes rapidly read over it.

"Is that it? You're not going to sentence me to three months of library jail?" he asked.

"Please leave my office," she said, waving him away.

Mateo's eyes narrowed, but he left her office and walked down the hallway towards the food hall. It was abnormal for him to be let go without a single reprimand, so whatever letter the headmistress had gotten, it must've been important. He heard whispers around him as he walked, but they would shut up as he would pass by. *That's weird*, he thought.

As he went to the table Atlas and Kanoa were sitting at, he noticed Celeste was sitting there as well. Celeste's stony face had an expression on it, which was also surprising for Mateo. Her eyebrows were pulled downward, her lips taut. If he were honest with himself, it was kind of fascinating to see the great future warrior Celeste emote at all. It was a truly rare occurrence. She was talking to Kanoa, in a hushed voice. And once he reached the table, she glowered at him.

"What?" Mateo asked.

"What did you have my cousin do?" she snapped.

"What?" he repeated, confusion wrinkling his brow.

"Ophelia is coming here," Celeste hissed. "I just heard from my mother. And guess who's with her? That girl, the new sacrifice, and Silas."

"Ophelia is coming?" He furrowed his eyebrows together and stared at the food that appeared in front of him. He stared at it for so long as he thought about what could have caused Ophelia to get involved, and then he started to laugh. He laughed at his food, and then he threw his head back and laughed even more. His peals of laughter echoed around the quiet food hall.

Celeste stared at him for a long while. "You're insane, Mateo Cordero. You've gone entirely insane." And with that, she got up and left the table.

"Gotta be insane when you're gonna die in six months!" he called after her.

"Dude," Kanoa said, shaking his head.

"She must've given them hell," Mateo laughed as he ate his food. He chuckled to himself as he thought about it some more. No wonder all those surprising things happened. Emira must've done something that was out of character, completely stopping the world on its axle. And, the funniest part of it all, they thought he had something to do with her change. As if she weren't already heading in the direction he lightly pushed her on. As if whatever she had done wasn't already a part of who she was, hidden due to her priestess training. As if this world didn't push her towards it.

Idols, he wondered what it was that she did. Just so he could congratulate her on finally becoming a person.

"You're putting Silas in danger, though," Atlas said, quietly. His words sobered Mateo up. His laughter and celebration faded, and he chewed on his food.

"Do you think he tried to stop her?" Mateo asked.

"If she has the power of an Idol, I don't think he could've done anything to stop her," Kanoa muttered. "But, what do you think she did?"

"Who knows?" Mateo shrugged. "But, whatever she did had to have been wonderfully bad if Ophelia's bringing her back."

"You know Ophelia holds grudges," Atlas pointed out. Mateo nodded his head as he swallowed his food.

"Sure," he said. "I am my grandfather's grandson. I know she holds grudges like no other. It's why she hasn't had another kid since Leliara nor spoken a word to Balan ever since."

"If she even suspects you're behind this, Mateo, you're in serious trouble. They say Balan is the most powerful Idol, but no one even knows what the limits of Ophelia's power is," Atlas said in a hushed whisper.

"What is she going to do? Make me a sacrifice? I'm already dying, Atlas," Mateo said. "Might as well give them hell on the way out."

"Ophelia is here," Mateo heard someone say as they walked past their table. Others rushed out of the food hall.

"Let's go see the damage," he said gleefully at his two friends. Kanoa and Atlas simply exchanged looks with one another.

He ran out towards the front of the school and watched as Ophelia stepped out of the carriage. She was the shortest of all the Idols, but her power always made her seem larger than life. She glanced over at Mateo, as if expecting his presence. Her ice crystal eyes didn't portray a single emotion, but they stared at him like a rat caught in a mouse trap. Like she was wondering whether to play with him for a while longer or kill him right then and there.

A guard pulled Emira out of the carriage and placed her on her feet. She looked eerily like a statue of herself. And with the snap of Ophelia's fingers, Emira came back to life.

Her violet eyes were like burning flames as she gained control over her own body again. Her blonde curls looked like golden tendrils as she walked towards Silas who had only just gotten out of the carriage. She grabbed the mask out of Silas' hands and immediately made eye contact with Mateo. She drilled forward to him, held up the mask that had morphed into Priestess Irene's face as she held it, and then dropped it at his feet.

Mateo glanced down at it before looking back up into her mesmerizing amethyst eyes. They burned through him, like that day back in that field with the *bellua*. Regal and wild.

"I hope you're happy," she hissed before bumping his

shoulder as she stalked into the school. The corners of Ophelia's lips curled upwards as she looked at the two of them before diving into a discussion with Headmistress Alessia.

What in the twelve circles of hell happened?

He stood there, watching Emira leave, until Silas came up to him. Mateo gave him a questioning look, and Silas shook his head, wincing as he looked at where Emira used to be standing.

"What happened?" he asked out loud as they started to go into the school with the rest of the crowd.

"Bro, she's… She's exactly like you," Silas muttered. "She's… angry. And she likes to hold onto it, too."

"But, do you think she believes me? Do you think she'll fight against her fate?" Mateo asked, quietly so no one around them could hear. Silas gave him a sidelong glance.

"I think she believes you. But, I don't think you understand what you've started," Silas said. He looked in the direction that Emira disappeared to. "She'll never forgive you."

"For what?" Mateo asked. For breaking the chains that encased her mind? For showing her the truth? He didn't say these words, though they burned his tongue.

He knew Emira, more than she would like to admit. No matter what it was that she had done, that wasn't what she would be upset about. She wouldn't refuse to forgive him over that. No, Mateo knew. He destroyed the world she had built up in her head. And now, life could never go on the way it had before.

He knew, because he had felt the same, all those years ago.

Silas simply shook his head, his ice blue eyes haunted for a second. Then, he pushed Mateo lightly.

"You're so lucky I'm technically a descendant of Ophelia's," Silas muttered. "She nearly murdered me. She *wants* to murder you."

"Guess she'll have to settle for Balan doing it," Mateo said. They walked side by side for a little while longer.

"You're not going to tell me what happened, are you?" he said to Silas, softly. Silas met his gaze.

"No," he said. "She needs to do that herself."

MATEO LEANED AGAINST THE BRICK WALL AT THE BACK OF THE school. He turned his fingers into flames and lit his cigarette. Breathing in deeply, he felt his body relax. And he let the smoke out, the smoke dancing in the wind. The snow was falling hard and fast as the sun started to set.

The back door opened, and Darlene slipped out, wrapping her bright red cloak around herself tighter.

"Did she say anything?" Mateo asked, without looking at her. Darlene's gaze darted towards him before leaning against the wall. She held out her empty umber brown hand. Slipping another cigarette from out of his pocket, he gave her one. She put it in her mouth and leaned forward, looking at him expectantly. He rolled his eyes and lit her cigarette with his flame fingers.

"So?" he asked after she took a long drag.

"No, she didn't say anything," she said. "Emira likes to keep things to herself." She looked Mateo up and down. "Namely, yourself."

"What's that supposed to mean?"

"The way she looked at you, fire in her eyes like that? She really is the embodiment of an Idol," Darlene wistfully said, leaning her head against the wall. She looked up at the sky. "And how she looked at you in that secret room of yours, the

Serpentes Room or whatever... No girl gets that angry at someone they don't care about."

"She doesn't care about me," Mateo muttered. "She was, rightfully, mad about what I did." He would feel the same if someone upended his whole worldview without permission. Darlene's ebony eyes glanced over at him.

"Unfortunately, for me, she does care. And I suspect she does a lot," she said, gently. "I don't think she'll ever talk about what happened. But, I have a feeling it'll show up in the news." She took another drag of her cigarette, and blew the smoke out slowly.

In the quiet, the giant snowflakes continued to fall and nestle themselves together on the ground, turning into a giant white blanket of snow.

"She can never know about us," Darlene said, suddenly, her voice hard. Mateo ran a tongue against the back of his teeth. This wasn't a conversation he wanted to have.

He liked to pretend whatever it was he was doing with Darlene and these other girls weren't really happening. Like it was someone else, not him. Someone that looked like him but on a different plane. Speaking it aloud was making it too real for him, too tangible. Because if it were real, his actions could hurt people. People close to him. He closed his eyes.

"I'm not planning on telling anyone," he responded. She smiled at him, but it didn't reach her eyes.

"We would've been really good together," she whispered.

"Yeah, if you weren't in love with one of my best friends," Mateo said.

"And if you weren't dying," she said, sadness lacing her words.

"If Emira never finds out, how are you going to get back at Kanoa?" he asked. Darlene smiled sadly, up at the sky.

"I'll find out another way to get my revenge," she said, barely above a whisper. "But, Mateo, handle Emira with care the next time you interact with her. Something bad went down in Aeluris. She's barely talking."

"Shit," he said, under his breath. He threw his half-smoked cigarette into the snow. "Silas said she'll never forgive me."

"Silas is probably right," Darlene nodded. "He is surprisingly observant at times, for an idiot." She started to go back into the school but paused before opening the door.

"Why did you decide to… pursue this?" she asked, gesturing to herself.

"You said if I ever needed the voices to stop, I should come by," he answered. Her eyes narrowed.

"So, you stabbed Kanoa in the back for no reason?" Her words hit him like a swift punch to the gut.

"It wasn't for no reason," Mateo said, quietly. "I just needed it to stop. I needed… I needed to make sure that I could never go to her."

"And I was the easiest choice?"

"You were… You were there, Darlene. And you're close to her. She won't want anything to do with me if she found out about you," he said. "And… I needed that. I can't…"

"If I knew how she felt about you, I would've never…" Darlene shook her head. "This *can't* happen again."

"I get it," Mateo answered. He shifted his weight from one foot to the other. "But, just so you know, she doesn't feel anything for me. Her and Atlas—"

"She feels something for you, for sure," she interrupted. "Whether there's something going on with Atlas and Emira, I can't tell. But there is something going on inside of her in regards to you. And it just feels… It feels wrong, knowing that. To continue…"

"Helping each other," Mateo finished for her. She nodded her head.

"Emira can never know," she pressed. Mateo nodded his head and with that, he was left alone once again. He leaned his head against the wall and watched the dusk turn into night. And he stayed until he was sure his bones were made of pure ice.

Mateo didn't know a lot of things. But there was one thing he was sure of: his whole life was just one big fuck up.

CHAPTER TWENTY-NINE

The news was out. It felt like everyone knew what happened to the Temple of Night in Aeluris. Emira could feel the terrified glances the other students threw her way. And she hated every moment of it.

"This diary is actually incredibly interesting," Shiloh said, looking over the notes she had written as she had read the diary from the hidden Room of Serpentes. "Everything we learned… I mean, some of it was true. But some of it is… completely wrong."

"Like what?" Emira asked. She didn't have any life in her voice. She felt like the undead, walking around in a haze. The only thing she could think about lately was Priestess Irene, and every time she did, guilt would bubble up into her throat and stay there.

"Well, they've always said they came from the sky as animals. When the Idols touched the ground, they morphed into the powerful beings they are now. Sent from the heavens in order to save us. But, that isn't the case," Shiloh said, in a hushed excited voice. Another student walked by. The student averted her eyes and then rushed past them, not wanting to be near Emira for any amount of time.

"What were they, then?" Emira asked. Her eyebrows furrowed together, a part of her not ready to accept anything Shiloh would have to say.

"They were humans," Shiloh said. "Like us." Emira's brow wrinkled deeper.

"What do you mean they were humans like us? They can't be," Emira said. "They're… They're godlike beings with power that is… *unimaginable*."

"Is it unimaginable?" Shiloh asked, her voice low. Her brown eyes met Emira's. Emira recoiled away from her.

"That's different. *I'm* different. I'm the sacrifice. Of course I have the power of an Idol, it's Mali's ichor. And I'm sure Mali has more power than me," Emira said, crossing her arms over her chest. She slouched a little, hoping to disappear from the whispers that surrounded them.

"They're calling it an Idol-like destruction," Shiloh said, softly. "And… E, you didn't see what you looked like when you came back."

"What's that supposed to mean?" Emira snapped. She saw a flicker of fear appear in Shiloh's eyes, and something broke within her. Emira took a deep breath.

She didn't know when her priestess training just upped and disappeared. She used to have control of her emotions, like a stone statue. She needed to reel it back in. Although anger had always been a tricky one for Emira. She wished she could go back to hiding in her mind, to stop feeling emotions. But, it would happen without her permission, and she couldn't seem to force it either.

"I'm sorry, Shi," she whispered. "I'm just… I'm very angry these days."

"It's okay," Shiloh said, gathering herself.

"What did I look like?" Emira asked. Shiloh glanced at her. "I won't get mad about it, I promise."

"You looked like an Idol on a rampage. Like one of those paintings of the Idols destroying a *bellua*. Except more… magnificent. I never really understood what they meant when they said that the sacrifice was like the embodiment of the Idol. I never understood it until I saw you the other day," Shiloh said. "And I've known Mateo my whole life. The fact that he could look like that, too, is… well… Kind of shatters my view of you guys, I guess."

"You see us differently?" Emira quietly asked.

"How can I not? I was taught to revere the Idols and here you two are, Idols incarnate," Shiloh whispered. "And then I find out they're simply humans with immense power. And it makes sense. It makes sense because you and Mateo are humans with godlike power."

"I don't think I have godlike power," Emira flinched.

"You destroyed a thousand-year-old temple with a flick of your wrist, E," Shiloh said, her voice low. "You could destroy a whole world with a simple thought. How is that not godlike power?"

Emira didn't say anything. Shiloh studied her expression and paused, causing Emira to stop in her tracks, too.

"Did it even take any energy from you?" Shiloh asked.

"What?"

"Destroying it. Did it leave you breathless? Panting? Anything?" Shiloh asked. Emira thought back on it, but even probing the memory made her want to shrivel up and cry for days. And knowing that, made her want to cry more. Because it wasn't due to her killing someone, like it should be. She murdered the high priestess who she had known all her life. She should *feel* something about it. But, no, she felt like crying for selfish reasons. Because her life would never be the same as it was before.

What kind of a priestess was she? What kind of a *human being* was she?

"No," she answered, definitively. "No, I felt the same, energy-wise." Shiloh closed her notebook of notes as they entered their next class.

"Then you have power that's boundless, Emira," she said, her voice low. "Most of us, we get tired after a while. And if you don't... Then, there's no stopping someone like you." Shiloh walked into Mr. Killian's class without another word. Emira paused there, at the door. She stared at a spot that had forgotten to be cleaned up on the marble floors. A black spot. And as her vision blurred, the spot got bigger. Corrupting the white floors of the classroom.

"Is everything okay?" she heard the low voice of Atlas say. She looked up, startled.

"Sorry," she muttered before quickly walking into the class-room. She didn't want to talk to Atlas. She didn't want comfort. She didn't want to talk to anyone, really.

The first thing Darlene had said to her when she had found out about her murdering a priestess was that she was sorry for Emira's loss. Sorry for her loss. Like she didn't murder a person.

And others, her friends, looked at her like they knew she felt bad for murdering someone. She could see in their eyes that they wanted to comfort her for it. That they believed it was an accident. An uncontrollable burst of power. *It happens to the best of us,* Emira could imagine them saying. *We all go through it some-times. Just, not when anyone else is near.*

But she didn't care that she murdered someone. She scarily didn't care because she felt that High Priestess Ethel deserved it, but she couldn't tell people that. The only thing making her feel so listless was losing Priestess Irene.

Idols, what is wrong with me?

"Today, we'll be doing duels. No power allowed to be used this time," Mr. Killian said, his hands behind his back. Complaints rose in the crowd of students, and Mr. Killian held up his hand.

"It's the new rules," he said. "To keep everyone safe." Emira felt like everyone in the room was glaring at her.

"We'll start with a cluster of duels around the room, the winners will fight the next person. Ms. Solus, if I could speak to you for a moment," Mr. Killian said. He beckoned Emira towards him while the rest of the students paired off and started to duel one another.

Emira left her books where she was sitting and walked over to Mr. Killian. He was eyeing one of the students' techniques, his eyes hawk-like.

"Yes, Mr. Killian?" Emira asked. He glanced over at her. After everyone in the school avoided her eyes the past few days, it was almost nice that someone was looking her in the eye.

"You'll be exempt from this and future lessons," Mr. Killian said.

Emira blinked. "Why?"

"You killed someone and destroyed a whole temple," he said matter-of-factly. He walked to the next dueling team, and she followed after him. He looked over his shoulder at her. "We can't have a student dying, can we?"

"So, I'm not allowed to learn to sword fight at all?" she asked, her voice small. Mr. Killian shrugged.

"You are a sacrifice, Ms. Solus," he said. He tapped a wooden stick on one of the students' shoulders. "Relax these, Mr. Wilson."

"So, because I'm a sacrifice I can't participate? Mateo gets to," Emira felt like a petulant child throwing a temper tantrum. She tried hard to swallow the feeling down. Mr Killian's hawk-like eyes darted towards Mateo who was clearly overpowering his opponent.

"Mr. Cordero has been participating since he was a child," Mr. Killian responded, giving her his full attention. She took a small step backwards. "And, if I must remind you, he has never killed a person before."

Emira swallowed, hard. "I understand." She turned on her foot and grabbed her things quickly. She didn't want the whole year to see her cry. As she walked out of the room, Mateo grabbed her arm. He was getting a cup of water, and his mismatched eyes were concerned.

"Can we talk?" he asked, his voice barely a whisper.

"Don't," she responded, twisting her arm out of his grip. She raised a finger, like she was going to lecture him. And part of her wanted to. Wanted to blame him for what she did. But, she couldn't, not when he was standing in front of her. She stood there, mouth agape, wanting to push the responsibility on the person who made her do this. But, if she were honest, Mateo didn't do anything. All he did was tell her the truth.

He stood there, his eyes expectant. He wanted her to talk to him. He wanted her to say something, anything. Emira could see it written all over his face. Could probably glean it from his thoughts. But she didn't want to hear it. And luckily for her, his thoughts weren't shouting it either.

She turned away without another word and walked out of the classroom. She could hear Mateo whisper her name like it was a prayer behind her. But, she didn't look back. She couldn't.

She kept walking until she reached her dorm room. She closed the door and rested her forehead against the cool wood.

She killed someone. Not a stranger, but someone who helped raise her. And everyone knew about it. Expected her to be distraught about it, otherwise she was cold-blooded killer.

Something in the corner of her eye caught her attention. Underneath Darlene's pillow was the corner of a piece of paper. Emira pulled at it to reveal a newspaper.

The front page was a picture of the destroyed temple. The headless cats, the only things still standing. The headline read: *Sacrifice Destroys Temple and Murders High Priestess*. Emira read through it quickly. It had witnesses of the event, interviews from the other priestesses, and the word that popped out to her was "terrifying."

She was terrifying. That's what one of the priestesses described her as. A *bellua* incarnate. And then the rest of the article was detailing what the other Idols were planning on doing with the sacrifice. Her name wasn't mentioned at all in the article, but it was obvious that it was Mali's sacrifice.

Emira crumpled the newspaper and let it drop to the ground. She laid down on the hard wooden floor, staring up at the ceiling. She stared, her eyes straining as the memories played in her mind. Silas tried to stop her. She didn't listen.

She had always been so good at listening.

What is happening to me? She pressed her palms to her eyes. She pressed hard and half-heartedly wished her brain would squeeze out of her ears. She should have never done what she did. She let her anger drive her.

Emira imagined Priestess Irene stroking her hair, like when she was younger. She could even hear Priestess Irene's melodic singing, reciting a lullaby. And with that playing in her mind, she let sleep take her.

"Emira," someone shook her awake. Emira slowly opened her eyes to see Darlene and Shiloh standing over her.

"You fell asleep," Shiloh explained.

"On the floor," Darlene said, with a hint of disgust. Emira sat up, quickly. She looked out the window, and it was clearly night. The moon was obscured by dark clouds.

"Sorry," Emira said, holding her head. "I was kicked out of Mr. Killian's class and came back here."

"And found my newspaper," Darlene said, holding it up. Emira nodded, sheepishly. Shiloh sighed and got down on her knees so she was eye level with Emira.

"We're not going to handle you with baby gloves," she said, uncharacteristically harsh. "You killed someone. You have ridiculous power. And that's sad and everyone is terrified of you, and the other sacrifices for that matter. And that's awful and I'm sorry, but you did that to yourself. We have other pressing matters to discuss."

Emira flinched. Shiloh's words were like spears dipped in poison.

"You're right," Emira whispered. "No, you're right. I did it to myself." Shiloh leaned back before standing up.

"We're meeting in the Room of Serpentes," she said. "I need to discuss what I've found."

EMIRA DIDN'T WANT TO GO BACK THERE, AND SHE DIDN'T WANT TO see Mateo. But, she didn't really have a choice. She sat down in one of the armchairs that was scattered around the room. She didn't look at Mateo when he walked in. She could feel him pause near her, and she could hear one thing in his scattered thoughts.

I'm sorry.

She ignored it. Shiloh stood in front of the others, holding her notes. She pushed her glasses up her nose, and the tips of her ears turned red once everyone directed their attention towards her.

"Okay, so this is what I found out. I'm assuming you four already know this part," Shiloh said, glancing over at Mateo and his friends. "But, the Idols are humans. Balan started this diary when he was around our age—seventeen—and he already felt like it would be used for a history book someday. There was a war, a regime that happened before the Dark Ages. Or around the Dark Ages?"

"Our guess is it happened before the Dark Ages," Atlas said.

"Okay, before the Dark Ages. But, something that I found interesting is that he doesn't mention *bellua*. He doesn't mention them at all. I skimmed further in his diary where he's detailing the war he's fighting in. But, not once is a *bellua* mentioned," Shiloh said.

"I'm confused," Darlene interjected. "What war?"

"Well, from what I've gathered is that there was a regime. Someone ruled over Constellatia. A king? A tyrant? He's not very detailed about it. But, whoever it was had gone mad, in Balan's eyes. They didn't deserve to rule. And he was a part of the rebellion fighting against the regime," Shiloh explained.

"Okay…" Darlene said, sitting back in her seat. She looked as confused as Emira felt.

"So the Idols are human," Emira said. Shiloh nodded her head. It wasn't too surprising to Emira, at this point. Her whole life had been rewritten. Everything she believed was wrong and everything that was supposed to be wrong was probably right, in this alternate universe she kept waking up in.

"Yes, but it got me thinking. The *bellua* must've showed up after the war Balan and the other Idols were a part of. The diary is very specific in regards to the war. It doesn't detail Balan's power, or how he even got it. How did twelve humans get the power of gods?" Shiloh thought out loud. "But, beyond that, if the Idols aren't from the heavens, then what lies have they told about the *bellua*?"

Mateo leaned forward. "You think the *bellua* came because of the power the Idols received?" Shiloh's eyes glittered.

"No, my theory is that the *bellua* are humans or some kind of human-like beings," Shiloh said. Mateo exchanged glances with Silas, Kanoa, and Atlas.

Silas shook his head. "No, it's impossible. Yes, the Idols are human and they didn't come from the heavens. But, our theory is that the *bellua* came about because twelve humans became so powerful. There has to be a balance in the world." Shiloh shook her own head and took a step forward, clutching her notes in her hands.

"No, you don't understand. The world doesn't need balance. The world isn't a sentient being. You're still clinging onto your religious beliefs," Shiloh said. "The Idols got power from some-where, someone. The *bellua* appeared shortly after the Idols got power—"

"History says that the Idols appeared because the *bellua* were terrorizing us," Darlene said.

"Yes, that's what the Idols tell us. But, Balan never mentions *bellua*. Never. If they were terrorizing Constellatia, and if the

Idols gained power in order to protect Constellatia from *bellua*, wouldn't he mention it? He never mentions them," Shiloh said. "I strongly believe the *bellua* are human or they are the beings the Idols got their powers from."

Emira froze in her seat. The *bellua* could talk, they talked like humans.

"You smell like... one of them," the *bellua* had told her. One of them. One of the Idols? Or...

"Or the *bellua* know where the Idols got their power from," Emira said, quietly. Mateo looked over at her.

"Either way, it looks like a conversation with a *bellua* is in order," he said, his mismatched eyes twinkling. Emira looked away from him.

"How are we going to talk to a *bellua*?" Silas asked. Emira could feel Mateo's eyes on her.

"I have a plan," he said.

"It's probably insane," Silas pointed out. Mateo flashed him a toothy grin.

"Oh, it is."

CHAPTER THIRTY

Mateo and Emira stood side by side, staring up at the massive castle his grandfather lived in. Emira's curly blonde hair was piled onto the top of her head, a few strategic curls framing her face. She was wearing a body-hugging glittery violet dress that matched her eyes. Upon seeing the Idol of Law and Fate's castle, she glanced at Mateo, anxious.

He was wearing an all black suit, even the buttoned up shirt underneath was black. He looked like an assassin, of sorts. His dark brown hair was slicked back, and it made his features look sharper somehow. Colder. He held out his arm.

Emira scoffed. "I'm not holding your arm."

He sighed. "I'm escorting you."

"I don't need an escort," she muttered. "I'm still mad at you, you know."

"Just take my arm, Priestess," he said, looking pointedly at the arm he held extended. It had been two weeks since the events of Decessia. Priestess Irene appeared in her dreams every night, replaying memories the two of them had with one another. But, even though Emira had directed her anger towards Mateo, she knew the blame fell solely on her. And, with Mateo staring at her the way that he was, it was hard to remain mad at him.

Emira stared at his arm and then resignedly took it.

They were both attending the Winter Solstice ball the Idols held. All the sacrifices were invited along with the elites of Constellatia. It was also easier to escape Leliara this way.

Balan's palace was massive. It had multiple towers piercing the sky and a sprawling staircase leading up to the entrance. Stone snakes lined the staircase, and for the Winter Solstice celebration, there was a singular green wreath hung on the unnecessarily tall double doors.

"Have you been here before?" Emira asked as they walked up the staircase.

"Balan's castle of doom or Serpel?" Mateo asked.

"Both," she said.

"I've been to Serpel multiple times," he answered as the sound of their footsteps against the stone echoed around them. "My father, despite not being a politician himself, is friends with a lot of them. He used to take me when I was younger."

"And Balan's castle of doom?" Emira asked, using his wording. He grinned at her, lopsided and boyish.

"Ah, well, here—I come here every year," Mateo said. "For the ball."

"Right," she answered. They continued to walk up the sprawling steps.

"So, the plan," she said, interrupting the all too comfortable silence between them. "Do you think it can be done?"

"Yes," he answered. He steeled his eyes. "Sacrifices like to get a little rowdy, especially the older ones. Last few months to live and all that. So, I expect this party to be a little bit more chaotic than the other ones. And we'll be able to slip by unnoticed at that point."

"Do you really think Pandora is going to be helpful?" she asked, her voice low. Mateo nodded his head, slow and deliberate, like he was asking himself the same question.

"Pandora, despite being a bit odd, is a good ally to have," he said. "No one ever knows where a magician's power lies." And yet, the lot of them had been demoted to simple party tricks.

Emira untangled her arm with Mateo's and wiped her clammy hands on her dress as they got closer to the doors. He raised an eyebrow.

"I've never met the other Idols," she muttered. "I've only ever seen Ophelia. And after the stunt I pulled with the Temple of Night... I don't want..." She couldn't finish her words. She didn't want the Idols to think of her badly. But, Mateo wouldn't understand that. She didn't really understand it herself.

"I get it," he said, surprising her. "They're still extremely powerful beings. And it's hard not to put them on a pedestal when they've been there your whole life." Her eyes darted towards him.

"I'm surprised you could understand."

"I *do* have an empathetic bone in my body, Priestess," he joked, lightly pushing her. She allowed herself to smile a little. The first smile she let herself don since finding out about Priestess Irene. They approached the double doors, and it opened as they got close. Mateo offered his arm again, an eyebrow delicately quirked. She swallowed the twisting fear that ate at her insides and linked hers with his. The moment his arm wrapped around hers, the fear evaporated. They walked in slowly. The inside was not quite as dreary as the outside.

The ceilings were high, and gold square moldings covered it.

Ethereal paintings filled the spaces between them and were on the upper half of the walls. Crystalline chandeliers hung from the ceilings, lighting the way. The floor was granite and an ornate red rug covered it, a rug she was sure was placed simply for the holiday season.

Emira's heels were silenced once she stepped onto the rug. She stared up at the palace, her mouth agape.

Mateo rolled his eyes. "Balan is excessive."

"I never thought interior decorating was an art," she breathed. "But this—this is true art." He rolled his eyes again. The guards that had let them in gestured for them to keep walking towards the ballroom. The two of them did, with others following after them.

The ballroom was just as ornate as the foyer, gold moldings and beautiful murals everywhere. The ballroom's floor, however, was black marble, but more regal than the one in Leliara's foyer. It almost looked like the vast space was on the floor below their feet, constellations and galactic auras mixing with the ebony abyss.

Emira's eyes wandered and caught Silas standing near an older man who looked a lot like him. Black hair and ice blue eyes. Standing next to Silas and talking to another politician was a man who looked a few years older, and was the spitting image of Silas' mother. Black hair and stone gray eyes.

"Who's next to Silas?" she asked. Mateo looked around the room before finding his best friend. His expression stiffened.

"That's his older brother, Cassius Silver," he said the name with reserved irritation. He glanced over at Silas who was avoiding Mateo's eyes.

"It looks like Silas is out in helping us," he muttered. "Just us and Pandora. If I can find her..." He craned his neck as he looked around the ballroom to look for the white blonde. Emira put a hand on his forearm, while untangling her arm from his. He glanced over at her.

"Why is Silas out?" she whispered. He casually walked in front of Emira so she was facing him and Silas' family.

"Do you see Cassius standing next to him?" he asked in a low voice. She glanced over at the older boy. His features were cold, like the stone in his eyes.

"Yeah, I see him," she said.

"Does he look like a nice guy? Like a guy you wanna go and get coffee with sometime?" Mateo asked. Emira stared at him. Did she really have to answer this question?

"No, not rea—"

"Exactly. Cassius isn't a nice guy. He's actually probably the Prince of Darkness himself. If you got coffee with him, he'd somehow betray you and get you murdered at the same time," he said.

"So… What does that have to do with Silas?"

"Cassius isn't going to let his kid brother out of his sight," he sighed, running a hand through his hair. "Probably because I'm here."

"And because you've escaped twenty times," she pointed out. He nodded.

"That, too," he mumbled. "I'm guessing Cassius suspects our plans, so don't make any kind of contact with him. Silas is out. I'm going to look for Pandora." He craned his neck again.

"Idols, I hope she didn't forget," Mateo muttered under his breath as he left Emira's side. Emira reached out for him, the fear finding its way back, but he was already gone, disappearing amongst the crowd of elites. She pulled her arm back into herself and held onto it with her other hand.

Emira looked around the room. She didn't know anyone around her. Beautiful people wearing the most expensive, ornate outfits, eyes glancing over at her like lions looking for their next prey. A waiter stopped next to her, holding out a plate of delicacies. She gingerly took one and planted her feet firmly. She wasn't going to go anywhere. At least, that was what she told herself.

Lystos, this is a stupid plan, she couldn't help but think. Using Pandora was unreliable at best. She remembered when Mateo told them their plan a week prior.

"It's perfect," he had said. *"We'll be able to slip out unnoticed, and Pandora will be able to get us outside the walls."*

"Pandora is a Lux. She's not going to do anything without a price," Silas said.

"You're going to come with us," Mateo had said. Silas sighed deeply at that news.

"No."

"She'll go along with it if you're there," Mateo had nearly begged. Silas and him stared at each other for a long time.

"Fine," Silas had said.

And now Silas is out, Emira thought. She didn't know why bringing Silas along would make Pandora more compliant, but she wasn't going to kick a gift horse in its mouth. But now that Silas couldn't go along with the plan, would Pandora?

Emira grabbed a drink from one of the trays and threw it back. It burned as it went down her throat, her eyes narrowing at the glass with the alcoholic substance. This plan was hanging on by a thread.

As she put the flute glass back on the tray, a man started to walk up to her. He had pure gold eyes, his dark, wavy hair was brushed back from his harsh face. And as he walked up, Emira could feel a sense of dread in the pit of her stomach. Power, unbelievable power was emanating out of him. So much so that Emira felt like she was going to be sick.

"Balan," she whispered. He quirked an eyebrow. He looked so much like Mateo, or rather Mateo looked a lot like his grandfather. And he couldn't be older than his mid-thirties. He moved like a panther, stalking towards her. *He's just a human, he's just a human,* Emira repeated in her head.

"You must be our new sacrifice," Balan said as he came up. His voice was buttery, charming. Much like how Mateo could sound.

Emira bowed low. "Your holiness."

Balan held up a hand. His lips twitched. "Please, call me Balan."

"Of course," she said, clasping her hands in front of her as she stood up straight. She regarded him as he seemed to study her. She wondered if Mateo would've looked like him if he had the opportunity to get older.

"I saw you enter with another sacrifice. My grandson," Balan said. His voice even held power. But with a lazy cadence, like other aristocrats. They all talked as slowly as possible, Emira felt. Like they had all the time in the world. In the case of Balan, that bit was true.

"Yes, Mateo and I know each other from Leliara," she answered, honestly. "He was there when I was found."

"Ah, yes. My mischievous grandson. He escapes often," Balan said. His gold eyes glittered and moved, like melted gold was being stirred within his irises. He grabbed a flute filled with bubbly gold liquid from a tray as the waiter walked by.

"Tell me, dear sacrifice," Balan said, sipping on his drink. His Pyrinian guards stood not too far away from the two of them. "Do you share my grandson's wayward thoughts?"

"Of course not," Emira answered. Perhaps a little too quickly.

She held her hands behind her back, to keep them from trembling underneath the Idol's gaze. She swallowed. "It's an immense honor to be a sacrifice."

At those words, Balan's eyes seemed to twinkle more. "Is it?" He sipped on his drink thoughtfully.

"If you think that way, what possessed you to destroy the Temple of Night in Aeluris as well as murder in cold blood the high priestess who raised you?" He quirked another eyebrow as he waited for her answer. Anger bubbled up in her blood.

"She didn't raise me," Emira bit, trying to swallow the bile burning her throat. "Priestess Irene did."

"The one who was executed," Balan said, matter-of-factly. She raised her own eyebrow. She wasn't going to shrink in the face of an Idol, her fury wouldn't let her. Not when talking about Priestess Irene.

"You're awfully well informed on what goes on in Aeluris," Emira said. "Considering Serpel is so far away."

"It's my job to keep informed," Balan said. He held out a bony, calloused hand. "Would you care to dance, sacrifice?"

"My name is Emira," she responded while taking his hand. She didn't have a choice in the matter. When an Idol tells her to do something, she would have to have a death wish to say no.

He clasped her hand in his and took her to the center of the ballroom. The music started and the two of them started to dance. Emira hadn't danced much in her life. Priestess Irene taught her the basics for a party the priestesses were invited to one time. She didn't end up dancing there, none of them did to their dismay, but the prior teachings of Priestess Irene were helping her now.

No one danced with them. It was just the two of them in the center and everyone watching.

"Emira," Balan said, her name rolling off of his tongue as

something inconsequential, unimportant. "Why did you destroy the temple?"

"Is this an inquisition?" she asked as they twirled around the ballroom.

"Let's say I'm curious," he said. "Even if you didn't believe what the rest of Constellatia does, it is of no matter. You will still be sacrificed, in the end." Emira pressed her tongue against the back of her teeth.

"The Idol of Night ordered for the one who raised me to die," she answered. There was no point in lying. She felt that Balan probably, somehow, had the power to detect it, too. She wasn't even entirely sure if he could read thoughts or not. Considering she couldn't penetrate his mind at all, she assumed he could.

"And I decided to destroy the temple and the person who let it happen as punishment," Emira whispered.

"As punishment?" Balan's gold eyes glittered. "Interesting." Emira concentrated on her feet instead of the gaze in his eyes, like he had just discovered something important about her.

The song came to an end, and Balan bowed deeply towards her. It wasn't something Idols did often, bowing to others. And he grabbed her hands in his calloused ones and kissed them, his gold eyes looking up at her.

"You really are the spitting image of Mali, my dear," he murmured against her hands. And then he flashed a familiar smile, the same one Mateo had, before walking back towards the crowd. Emira stood there as others started to dance around her. Someone grabbed her wrist, tightly, and pulled her back into the crowd who were standing on the sidelines.

"What were you thinking?" Mateo hissed as she turned to look at him.

"I was thinking, 'Hmm, I probably should dance with the

Idol of Law and Fate so that I don't *die*,'" Emira retorted. Mateo's gaze was chaotic as he was looking over towards his grandfather. The grip on her wrist somehow tightened more. She was sure it was going to leave a bruise.

"Mateo, please," she said, wriggling her wrist out of his grip. He let go.

"Don't go near him," he warned. When his face was tight like this, it reminded Emira of Balan. He looked so much like the Idol, just younger. She pressed her fingers against the edges of Mateo's lips. He looked over at her, startled.

She moved her fingers so it looked like he was smiling. His lips were smiling, but his eyebrows were furrowed together. His mismatched eyes were burning. Emira couldn't help but giggle at him as she pulled her hands away. She smiled up at him, easily, while he stared at her in horror. She felt free. Freer than she had in years.

"You drank the champagne, didn't you?" he said.

"It's actually not as bad as I thought it would be," Emira said, giggling. She kept replaying the face she made Mateo pull. He sighed and rubbed his temples. A waiter walked by with a tray of flute glasses.

"Ooh!" Emira exclaimed, grabbing one. Mateo pulled it out of her grips and placed it back on the tray.

"Are you forgetting why we're here?" he said. He had his hands on her shoulders, and she raised her eyebrows.

"You have large hands," she said. "Larger than your grandfather's."

"That's good to know," he muttered, rolling his eyes. He grabbed her arm and pulled her through the crowd.

Pandora was leaning against the wall, her dragon familiar eating one of the hors d'oeuvres that were being passed around. Her blank eyes came to life as Emira and Mateo walked up.

"You are floaty, aren't you?" she asked.

"I feel that way," Emira nodded her head. Mateo narrowed his eyes as he looked at the two of them.

"I think she's drunk."

"I only drank one glass," Emira said, holding up her finger. She pushed it into his face. He grabbed it with his hand. It was warm, too warm.

Emira's voice faltered a little as she repeated, "One."

"Lightweight," Pandora nodded her head.

"Hey," Emira scolded. "I am not."

"You are," Mateo sighed. He turned towards Pandora. "Do you know how to sober her up?"

"Water?" Pandora mused.

"Like drinking it or dunking her head in it. I'm not opposed to the latter," he said. Emira threw a glare in his direction.

"Darlene spent a lot of time on my hair," she said, her hands hovering over the pile on top of her head. "She said it made me look regal." He sighed, deeply.

"Sure," he said. "It does."

"It does?" She felt a surge of warmth in her chest as she looked up at him. He shifted uncomfortably as his eyes darted towards Pandora. Pandora put an arm between the two of them and pushed Emira backwards a little.

"Romance here is not recommended," she said. "Eyes appear everywhere."

"Romance?" Emira balked at the comment. "There's no romance." But, as she said this, the feeling of Mateo's lips on hers flashed through her mind. She lightly touched the bottom of her lip as she stared at the floor.

"What on Constellatia do we do?" Mateo hissed. Pandora shrugged.

"Water," she said. "A glass of water should stabilize it." He squinted his eyes at her as another waiter walked by. Mateo stopped him with his hand.

"Could we get a glass of water? This sacrifice had a little bit too much to drink," he explained. The waiter glanced at Emira and averted his eyes quickly.

"Of course," he said, skittering away.

"She can't be like this when they line the sacrifices up in front of the Idols," Mateo muttered.

"*She* is standing right here," Emira said, raising her hand. Mateo grabbed it and pulled it back down to her side. He glowered at her.

"You need to get it together, Priestess," he hissed.

"*You* need to get it together," she said, pressing a finger into his chest. "You're the one bringing so much attention to me."

His mismatched eyes twitched. "What do you mean?"

"Your grandfather came up to me because he saw us together. And me, the one who destroyed the Temple of Night and murdered the high priestess, hanging out with the one who's escaped a bajillion times and preaches that he doesn't want to be a sacrifice tends to raise some eyebrows."

Mateo stared at her for a long time. She couldn't tell what he was thinking. She squinted her eyes, trying to read his chaotic thoughts, but nothing came out but jumbled words. She shook her head, the confusion making her head ache.

"Pandora, watch over her and make sure she drinks water," he said. "I'm going to talk to Silas."

"I thought you said Silas was out?" Emira asked, cocking her head to the side. Mateo closed his eyes and groaned a little as a response before walking away from her.

"Silas is out?" Pandora asked, her hazel eyes wide. Emira nodded her head, sadly.

"Because of Cassius," she said.

Pandora sighed as she stared at the older Silver brother, shaking her head. "That silver cat bites, hard."

CHAPTER THIRTY-ONE

Mateo didn't want to leave Emira alone with only Pandora accompanying her, especially in the state she was in, but what she said to him was right. The two rebels hanging out with one another definitely would bring attention.

He walked straight to Silas, grabbed a flute glass as he did, and knocked it back. Silas raised his dark eyebrows at him as he walked up.

"Cassius," Mateo nodded towards the older Silver. Cassius gave a cat-like smile.

"Mateo, it's been a while," he said. "How did your last escape go? I heard it was *almost* successful."

"If I had lasted eight more months, it would've been," Mateo answered.

"If you didn't interfere in everyone's affairs, I'm sure you would've," Cassius said. His gray eyes were colder than a glacier. Silas' blue ones darted between Mateo and his older brother.

"Let's go over here," Silas muttered. He nodded his head to a corner not too far away from them. Mateo could feel Cassius' eyes scorching through his suit as they walked away.

"Cassius is as vigilant as ever," Mateo said.

"He's under the impression you're going to cause ruin to our family," Silas said.

"I'm not a part of your family. And you're hardly a part of them now," Mateo pointed out. "You come home with me every break we get."

"I'm still a Silver, especially at social gatherings like these," Silas said. "Just like how you're still a Cordero."

"Being a Silver sounds exhausting, dude," Mateo muttered. "There's no expectations being a Cordero." He grabbed a hor d'oeuvre from a tray and ate it. It melted in his mouth.

"Why aren't you with Emira?" Silas asked. They both looked over at the blonde who was across the room, giggling against the wall with Pandora.

"They look like they're having fun," Silas said, raising an eyebrow. "I don't think I've ever seen Pandora that alive in my life."

"Pandora is not helping," Mateo said, rubbing his temples once more. "Emira drank a glass."

"Oh, she's a lightweight?"

Mateo threw up an arm. "I guess."

"So, the plan?"

"It's still in motion, with or without you," he said, his voice dipping low. "It'll just be… more difficult if she keeps drinking." He watched as Emira excitedly reached out for another glass and started drinking it. Pandora was simply smiling at her.

"Is Pandora *trying* to sabotage us?" Mateo muttered.

"Why did you leave her alone?" Silas asked. Mateo stared at Emira, her violet eyes glittering in the light.

"She pointed out that she caught the attention of Balan

because of me," he murmured. He didn't remove his eyes from Emira. "I don't want him to know how close we are." Silas' eyebrows raised.

"*Are* you two close?" he asked.

"You know what I mean," Mateo said, waving his words away. "We're just friends." Silas gave him a knowing look, and Mateo shifted under his gaze. *"You love her, don't you?"* Those words of his had echoed around in Mateo's brain for longer than he wanted to admit. He swallowed. Silas glanced over at his brother Cassius who was still close by, talking to another politician.

"I don't think I'll be able to slip away," Silas eventually said, quiet anger creasing his face.

"I get it," Mateo said, glancing over at the older Silver. "Cassius is your warden." Silas snorted.

"Cassius is the right hand of a mafia boss," he corrected. He let out a long sigh before knocking back the rest of his drink. "The Idols are about to come out."

"Of course they are," Mateo said, looking up at the large grandfather clock against the back wall. The Idols came out at the same time every year. Eleven pm, on the dot.

"Why eleven?" Silas pondered. "I've always wondered that."

"Because Balan is out and about, mingling, hosting, and there's eleven of them left," Mateo said, giving him a tight smile.

"Of course that's the reason," Silas said, narrowing his eyes. The clock chimed eleven times, and the rest of the room became hauntingly quiet. Mateo put his hands behind his back as the Idols were escorted in by their Pyrinian guards. His eyes darted towards Emira who was staring, mouth open. He rolled his eyes toward the ceiling at how obviously enamored she looked.

The eleven of them met up with Balan in the front of the room, twelve ornate seats lined up for them to take.

"Happy Winter Solstice," Balan said, his face warm and inviting but his tone cold. The others said their greetings and then took their places. Mateo glanced towards Mali, the Idol of Luck and Agriculture, as she sat down. Her dark hair was pulled underneath a veil. A few dark curls framed her face which was the spitting image of Emira, but with darker features.

Mateo had seen the Idol of Luck multiple times throughout the years, but it was the first time her looks hit him like a train.

"Are you okay? You look like you've seen a ghost," Silas whispered beside him.

"I feel like it," Mateo muttered, looking at Emira. She had paled, staring straight at Mali. Who the fuck cares if people may give more attention to her if he's next to her? She was seeing what she would have looked like if she had the chance to grow older. He needed to be next to her.

"I'll see you later," he said to Silas. "When we get back." Silas nodded, his gaze following Mateo's.

Mateo walked through the crowd towards Emira. Once he was beside her, he took her hand and squeezed it before letting it go. Her hand was cold, like the blood had drained from her body. Her gaze darted up at him before settling back on the Idol of Luck.

"She looks like *me*," she whispered, her voice haunted.

"More like you look like her," he answered. She nodded her head, absentmindedly, her violet eyes still on Mali.

"Thank you for joining us for this Winter Solstice," Balan said, clapping his hands together. He stood in the center of the other Idols. "It's so good to see all of your faces." He smiled at the crowd, but it didn't meet his gold eyes.

Mateo shifted from foot to foot uncomfortably. He hated listening to his grandfather's voice. Balan always tried to mask his coldness, his indifference towards everyone, with a warm tone but it always missed its mark. It was like listening to an ancient creature try to relate to everyone else.

"As everyone knows, it's the Tenth Year this coming new year," Balan continued his speech. "And we have found our last sacrifice. Let me introduce you all to her." Mateo stilled as he gestured towards Emira's direction. Emira's amethyst eyes widened, frozen for a moment, and then she took small steps forward, her heels clicking along the marble floor. Everyone stared at her as she walked towards the center of the room, eyeing her with a mixture of awe, disgust, and envy. Mateo's fingers curled into his palms, his knuckles white.

"Meet Emira, Mali's sacrifice," Balan said, a sinister smile spreading over his lips as his gold eyes met Mateo's. "You might have heard about her in the news recently." The descendants of the first twelve families whispered amongst themselves.

Emira stood up straight, facing Balan and the other Idols. Her eyes were glazed over, like she was concentrating on something she couldn't see. Mateo's face tightened. A muscle in his jaw feathered. This was out of the ordinary.

"She was hiding, this little one, all the way in Aeluris. Isn't that right, Mouse?" Balan said, looking over at Ophelia. Ophelia nodded once, not meeting his gaze. Mateo wasn't sure they properly looked at each other in thousands of years.

"We forget the sacrifices have immense power, power like ours," Balan said, gesturing to the other Idols. "But, this is why the Tenth Year is so important. We must make sure that power is contained. And who better to contain it than the ones who saved and protected Constellatia for many millenniums." Mateo grinded his teeth together watching Balan use Emira for his self righteous speech.

"And Mali, sweet Mali who couldn't hurt a fly, will be the one to absorb this little one's power and essence. She'll live on within Mali and the threat will be contained," Balan said, his voice sickeningly sweet. Mali, who Mateo knew had hurt more than a fly, batted her eyes and lowered her head in a small bow. A conservative smile on her face.

How he wanted to kill them all.

"Let's now meet the rest of the sacrifices," Balan said, gesturing around the room. The other sacrifices came out from the crowd and stood in the middle of the room, lining up in front of the Idols that would someday take their lives.

Mateo straightened and walked towards Emira. He didn't bother standing in front of Balan, he didn't see a point in it. He stood next to Emira instead, and felt her shaking like a leaf beside him.

He met Balan's exacting gaze with a stare that he hoped would strike fear into the old man's dead heart. Balan, instead, smirked in Mateo's direction.

The crowd clapped politely as the sacrifices stood in front of them. Once Balan let the dancing recommence, Mateo grabbed Emira's wrist and led her off of the dance floor. Before he could take her to Pandora, Balan stepped in front of them, Mali diminutively beside him.

"I thought I should introduce them," he said, a small smile twitching at the corners of his lips.

"Sure," Mateo said, through gritted teeth. "Why not." Mali reached out and grabbed Emira's hands. Her violet eyes were pure jewels, pure amethyst. *Emira's only look that crystalline when she was using her power*, Mateo thought, absentmindedly.

"I've always wondered how you were doing," Mali said, her voice like a sacred whisper. "I tried not to think of you, but I thought of you every day, my dear." Emira stared into Mali's eyes, her own violet eyes guarded.

"Who are you to me?" she asked, her voice harder than

normal. Mateo wanted to take her away from there, to keep her hidden from the woman who was standing in front of her. He wanted to scream and pull her away, to keep her safe. Because he knew Mali wasn't this innocence personified she always tried to portray. She was a killer. A cold-blooded killer. Like the rest of them. Emira winced, her eyes darting towards Mateo.

"Why, dear," Mali said, her voice ever so soft. "I'm your mother."

CHAPTER THIRTY-TWO

Emira felt herself freeze in place. She slowly pulled her hands out of the Idol's. Her thoughts were swirling, and it didn't help that Mateo's were screaming at her, incoherently. She never could make much sense of Mateo's thoughts, like they were constantly racing, constantly thinking about multiple things at once. And if she could hear them without trying, she knew the woman in front of her could, too.

Mali smiled softly at her. Her violet eyes, so much like Emira's own ones, softened with a tinge of sadness.

"You left me at the Temple of Night in Aeluris," Emira said slowly. Mateo was as still as a statue next to her, but she could almost feel him humming with hatred.

"Well, *I* didn't personally put you there. I had a guard do it," Mali said, her voice like the sound of crushing clovers in one's hand. Soft and fragrant, somehow. She genuinely seemed like she couldn't hurt a fly.

"It's nice to meet you," Emira said. Her voice sounded dead, even to her. Mali's face opened up as she smiled.

"I truly have always wanted to see you," Mali said. "And I

apologize for not raising you myself." Emira couldn't help but remember what Mateo had told her before. *"In case you didn't realize from your own experience, the Idols abandon their kids. They only procreate to guarantee a sacrifice."* Emira forced a smile onto her face.

"Well, you couldn't have known I'd be a sacrifice, right?" she said. Mali's violet eyes hardened a little, portraying a thought Emira couldn't read, but her soft smile remained on her face.

"No one ever knows," she responded.

"Perhaps, since I am a sacrifice, you could put me in contact with a Priestess of Luck," Emira said, wanting to change the subject, to dispel the Idol's suspicions. Mali's eyes lit up.

"Of course I can do that for you," she gushed. "As a former priestess-to-be yourself, I'm sure you know the human instinct can really depress sacrifices." Her face was the epitome of pity. Emira forced her polite smile to stay on her face.

"It really does. But, as the priestess who raised me used to say, it's always helpful to talk to a priestess of the Idol you're being sacrificed to," she said.

"Yes," Mali said, nodding her head. "It really is. I'll make sure to put the Headmistress at Leliara into contact with a Priestess of Luck so you can talk to your heart's desire. And Emira," she grabbed Emira's hands again. Emira clenched her jaw. "I really am sorry about the woman who raised you. I would've liked to thank her for turning you into a beautiful, young woman." The wetness in Mali's eyes gave Emira pause. She pulled her hands out from Mali's once more and took a small step back.

"Thank you," she said, her voice tight. She felt disturbed by Mali's emotion. And... confused. Mateo was nearly vibrating next to her.

"You should continue mingling, Mali," Balan more ordered than suggested. Mali nodded, wiping her tears, as she disappeared into the dancing crowd. His ever-moving golden eyes fixed themselves onto Mateo.

"Where is your mother?" he asked. Mateo gave his grandfather a brilliant smile.

"She doesn't want to see you," he responded. Balan's expression tightened, much like how Mateo's would.

"Please tell her she's my favorite child," he said, his voice a decibel above a whisper. "And that I wish she would come to these functions."

"She's your favorite because you don't have to kill her," Mateo pointed out. "And, I don't think she'll ever come to anything again, since you're planning on killing her only child." Balan's gaze hardened, and Emira didn't know how Mateo didn't turn to dust right there and then. The Idol of Law and Fate didn't say another word and left the two of them.

"You're an only child?" Emira asked, lightly punching him in the arm.

"Yeah?" he said, scanning the crowd for Pandora.

"You made fun of me because I'm an only child. You said I can't share," she pointed out. The champagne still was making her feel all warm and floaty inside. Out of the presence of the Idols, she could breathe once more. She was free. She leaned forward and stared into his eyes. His mismatched eyes. One gold and one brown, but with gold specks. His brown one made him feel more human. Made him feel more safe. At least, in Emira's eyes.

"People must make a big deal out of your gold eye, but your brown one is really quite extraordinary," she whispered. Mateo leaned backwards, away from her.

"Are you still drunk?" he asked, pressing the back of his hand to her forehead. She didn't know how that would tell him if she was drunk or not. She pushed his hand away.

"I'm not, and you're avoiding my question," Emira said, pouting. He rolled his eyes.

"You didn't ask a question and I'm not avoiding it," he said. "To answer your nonexistent question, I said it because *I* can't share."

"Oh," she said, looking up at the ceiling. For some reason, it made sense to her that he was someone who couldn't share. She looked at the crowd dancing and saw the other sacrifices that were previously standing with her. Mrs. Halloway was one of them.

"Did you know about Mrs. Halloway?" Emira asked. Mateo nodded his head.

"Alexios always chooses those who are older. He'll always choose the oldest sacrifice. And he seems to be the only one to let his sacrifices live as long as they can," he explained. "The youngest of his was twenty-five."

"That's nice of him," Emira nodded along, looking over at the Idol of the Sea and Animals. He didn't really stand out amongst the other Idols. With brown hair, a lean, lanky build, he was pretty average looking, except for his eyes. Like all the Idols, his were jewel-like, brown jasper. Alexios wasn't mingling either, standing off to the side and drinking whatever it was that was in his glass. People came up to him to talk, but they didn't talk for long.

Mateo scoffed. "Nice? He still murders people, Emira." She rolled her own eyes.

"You know what I mean," she said. Mateo seemed to catch sight of Pandora by the way his face lit up. But before he could move or say anything, a large hand clapped over Mateo's shoulders. He sighed, loudly.

"Cordero! So good to see you," the large man said. He looked like he was in his late twenties. Half of his face was covered by a red beard, and his baby blue eyes twinkled at Emira. "Aren't you a beauty?"

"This is Erik Gamble," Mateo murmured.

"Pleasure to make your acquaintance, little lady," he said, holding out a large hand. He was definitely Pyrinian. Pyrinians were always easy to pick out in a crowd for their stature.

"Emira Solus," Emira said, shaking his hand. She smiled widely at him. "You look like a strong warrior." Mateo looked at her incredulously. Erik laughed, a big belly laugh. Emira didn't know if it was the alcohol or not, but she liked him. He felt dangerous, and he wasn't hiding it. There wasn't some facade or mask he put on to hide just how powerful he might be. And she liked that, the honesty.

"I like to think I am," he said.

"Whose sacrifice are you?" she asked.

His expression darkened. "Phaethon's."

"You probably can do anything, then!" Emira exclaimed. Erik stared at her and then laughed again.

"Anything physical, sure," he said. He leaned in close to her. "Do you want to see a trick?" Emira nodded her head ferociously.

"I would *love* to see a trick," she said.

"Maybe some other time, Priestess?" Mateo said, looking at her poignantly. She waved him away.

"I want to see the trick," she insisted. Erik winked at her and then stretched his arm like it was taffy across the room, grabbed a flute glass of champagne, and brought it back to him. He handed it to Emira with a smile.

"That's so cool," she breathed. She took it from him and started to sip on the drink. The burning felt comfortable to Emira. And she wanted to feel this feeling forever. Like she could forget that there was anything wrong with the world.

"Thanks, Erik, but we should go," Mateo said, pulling on her arm. "We're looking for someone."

"You trying to escape again, my friend?" Erik asked.

"You know me, always scheming," Mateo answered, dragging Emira away. Erik responded with a smile and raise of his glass. Once they were away from Erik, Mateo took the flute glass out of Emira's hands.

"Hey!" she exclaimed. He downed the rest of her drink and then placed it on a platter nearby.

"Don't trust Erik Gamble, ever," he warned. "He's not the best guy to be friends with."

"But, *you're* friends with him," she pointed out.

He gave a hard smile, cold. "I know how to handle him." She opened her mouth to say that she's just as powerful as the next sacrifice but Mateo grabbed her wrist, his eyes looking into the distance.

"I found Pandora, we need to move now," he said. His eyes were darting around, and Emira could hardly stand up straight. She felt like she was walking around like a dinosaur.

"The floating feeling is going to turn into a sick one," Pandora said once they reached her. She had been dancing with her golden dragon that had grown into a small child. It shrunk once they came up to her, resting onto her shoulders once again.

Emira shrugged. "As long as I get the floating feeling." Pandora smiled at her, like she understood.

"Silas will maintain the illusion we're still here for as long as he can, since he's not coming with us," Mateo whispered. "You two need to get it together."

"Cordero, I am *always* put together," Emira said, brushing the stray curls out of her face. "I am a priestess. Or was. And I can keep myself in check without your help, thank you very much."

He let out another sigh. Idols, he liked to sigh a lot.

"Let's just go," he said, grabbing both Emira's and Pandora's arm. They walked quickly out of the ballroom without many eyes watching them. Mateo was right. The Winter Solstice ball did get a little rowdy. Everyone was drinking and having a good time. No one was watching the three teenagers disappear behind a door. Lots of teens were disappearing behind nonde-script doors.

"How are we supposed to get outside the walls?" Emira asked. Mateo flashed her a mischievous smile.

"Priestess, how you doubt me," he said, walking quickly through the maze of hallways.

"Where are we?" Emira asked.

"Servant quarters," he answered. "I used to explore these when I was younger."

"With Cassandra," Pandora added. Mateo's expression darkened.

"Yes, with Cassandra," he muttered. He continued walking, turning a corner here and there, and Emira struggled to keep up with him. Especially in her blurry state. She peeled her heels off of her feet and held them as she padded along the cold stone ground.

He finally stopped at a wooden door. Grabbing a dark bag next to it, he pulled some items out. He handed Emira and Pandora boots and a change of clothes.

"Here?" Emira asked, her cheeks reddening once he handed her some clothes.

"Yeah," he looked embarrassed himself. "I'll turn around." He did and immediately started to pull off his suit. The heat burned Emira's cheeks as she turned around but not before staring at his back muscles. A higher being definitely created those muscles.

This alcohol was affecting her more than she thought. She shook her head. She peeled her dress off, Pandora changing beside her. And Emira pulled on what looked like hunting clothes Mateo had packed. Over top of it, she pulled on a long black leather cloak. As she felt it, she could tell it was dipped in phoenix ash.

"This must've cost a fortune," she muttered.

"The Cordero family has a lot of stellae lying about," Mateo answered. He was wearing a similar outfit that she had on. But while she felt like she looked odd and out of place, Mateo looked like the clothes were made for him. Pandora was still lacing up her boots.

"If Silas is not coming, what is my reward?" Pandora asked, looking up at Mateo as she finished with her boots, her voice slow like other elites.

"I need to think about it," he said.

"I cannot come unless I have my reward," she said, planting her feet firmly on the ground. Mateo squeezed his eyes shut. He pulled something out from the bag. It was a blue ring with gold lining it. It looked like a wave or the ocean was coming out of it. And it was beautiful. Pandora's hazel eyes widened as she took it from him.

"Magnificent," she breathed.

"It's an heirloom," Mateo shrugged, although secretly pleased that Pandora accepted it. "You really are like a dragon."

"The Lux family is," she responded, putting the ring on her finger and admiring it.

"So, you'll come with?" Mateo asked. Pandora nodded her head. At that, he opened the wooden door.

On the other side of the door was a stable of gorgeous ebony pegasuses. They huffed and stamped the ground as the three of them entered. Mateo threw Pandora a bridle, and she caught it effortlessly.

"You still remember your riding lessons?" he asked her. Pandora nodded and tapped her head.

"Nothing ever leaves," she said. She quieted one pegasus and nuzzled its snout before putting the bridle onto it. Emira stared, shell shocked, at the animals. If she wasn't sober before, she could feel herself sobering up now.

"Don't tell me we're riding those," she whispered.

"We are," Mateo said. He brought one of the giant pegasuses out. It stamped its foot and seemed to glare at Emira with its large brown eyes.

"There, there, Casper, you're okay," Mateo whispered to the winged horse. Emira clasped her hands in front of her, like she was trying to respect the beast.

"I don't know how to ride one," she said, softly. He looked over at her.

"You don't need to," he said. "You'll ride with me." He effortlessly jumped up onto the horse and held out his hand. Emira gingerly placed her hand in his, and he pulled her up onto the giant beast.

"Hold on tight," his voice vibrated through him. Emira wrapped her arms around his waist and held as tightly as she could. A vision of her falling off and becoming skewered by one of Balan's towers flashed through her mind. She held more tightly until Mateo let out an uncomfortable sound. She loosened her grip, but only marginally.

Mateo clicked his tongue at the pegasus, and it started running out of the stables. Emira could hear Pandora's pegasus behind them, and she braced herself for when the beast started to flap its wings.

"I thought you said you hardly ever visited your grandfather's castle of doom," she said into his ear.

"I didn't," he said as the pegasus started to lift off the ground. "Now the stables, the stables I visited quite often." Emira stifled a scream as Casper the pegasus climbed towards the night sky.

CHAPTER THIRTY-THREE

The night sky was dark, the moon not anywhere in sight. The winter wind was like little pins sticking to Emira's face. Half of her wondered if her skin would be dotted with little holes by the end. She squinted her eyes as the wall loomed closer and closer. They flew over the giant obsidian snake statue in the middle of Serpel. Even from a great height, it was impressive.

"Pandora! Now!" Mateo called out over his shoulder as they got closer to the wall. Emira looked over her own shoulder at the white blonde sacrifice in hiding. Her little familiar dragon was holding onto her cloak for dear life, and Pandora drew a circle with her finger. She squinted one eye, and her tongue stuck out a little as she tried to make it the most perfect shape she could.

Emira looked back in front of them, and could see a shimmer in the air. *A forcefield*, she thought to herself. But, where Pandora had pointed, there was a hole in it. Mateo aimed Casper towards the hole, and it felt like they were flying faster. Emira felt herself fall backwards and tightened her hold around

Mateo's waist. She didn't know how she wasn't cutting off his circulation.

As they went through the hole, for a moment, it was as if all the sound in the world disappeared. The wind rushing past her ears and the sounds of people celebrating the Winter Solstice below her were suddenly gone. It was for a split second and then once they were through it, she could hear the wind once more. She looked over her shoulder at Pandora who was now sitting backwards on her pegasus. Closing back up the hole in the forcefield, she figured.

Mateo angled the pegasus towards the ground, and they landed with a jolt. Emira felt herself jump into the air a foot and then came back down harshly onto the pegasus' back. That caused him to buck his back legs, and Emira flew into the air. She braced for her body to hit the ground, but she stopped an inch away. After a second, she dropped.

"Ow," she said. She looked up at Mateo who effortlessly jumped down from the pegasus. He whispered something into Casper's ear and then hit the back of the winged horse. It took off, taking Pandora's pegasus with him, back towards the wall.

"Did you catch me?" she asked him, getting up from the ground. She brushed the dead grass and semi-wet mud off of her. The snow had melted a few days ago.

"I didn't think you'd catch that," Mateo said, scanning the woods in front of them. Darkness covered them, not a flicker of light in sight. It only meant there were more *bellua* out. Emira only hoped they wouldn't be this close to the walls of Serpel.

"I didn't use my ichor so it must've been yours," she pointed out. "How did you do that?"

"Do what? Mimic your power? I saw you kill the *bellua* back at Camp Elemence," he said.

"No," Emira shook her head. "How did you have enough

power to hold a human up without... any kind of... emotion?" She didn't say the word anger. She didn't want him to know that it was what she used the most, what made her ichor flow out more easily. He frowned for a moment and then slowly smirked at her.

"What can I say? I'm just more powerful than you," he shrugged. Emira rolled her eyes. She shouldn't have said anything.

"You made the sweet winged beast leave," Pandora pouted, walking up to the two of them. Her golden dragon made its way on top of her head and it looked like it was panting, its lizard eyes wide. It said something in their soul language.

Pandora nodded. "Closer to the walls the *bellua* are not. The pegasuses would've been helpful."

"Your dragon can enlarge big enough to carry the three of us if needed, I'm sure," Mateo said. "But, we need to find a *bellua*. The faster we can find one, the faster we can leave. Riding around on pegasuses wouldn't help us do that."

"What? The wild scares the great Mateo Cordero?" Emira teased, her eyes wide and a smile playing on her lips. It was his turn to roll his eyes.

"The wild is crawling with *bellua*. Especially away from the camps," he said. "After your stint with them, you're not?" He raised an eyebrow. Emira licked her dry lips. The shadowy *bellua* with eight legs flickered through her mind.

"Okay, maybe I am," she muttered. He looked over at Pandora who was already wandering away.

"Stick close to me," he said. "Who knows when we'll find one."

"When found," Pandora said, wandering back over to them, "how will we keep it?"

"The *bellua*? That's a good question," Mateo mused. Emira sharply turned towards him.

"You didn't think about how you were going to capture the *bellua* before we came out here?" she asked.

"I figured we could wing it," he said, walking into the woods. The trees loomed over them like shadowy demons.

"You thought we could just *wing* it?" Emira asked in disbelief. He nodded his head and shrugged.

"If it escapes, we can merely kill it. Three warriors against one? I mean, I like our odds."

Emira shivered. "I don't." As soon as she said this, a bird squawked near them, and she jumped. She huddled closer to Mateo, and he glanced down at her but didn't say anything.

"We're not warriors. We're three sacrifices," Emira pointed out, taking a step away from him. She brushed her hair out of her face and pretended that a bird didn't make her jump fifty feet into the air.

"Three?" Mateo's brow wrinkled, and he looked over his shoulder at Pandora who was staring at something in the distance.

"Shit, I wasn't supposed to say anything," Emira chastised herself. She wasn't any better than Shiloh when it came to secrets. In fact, she might be worse. His gaze darted over towards her once more.

"Pandora is a sacrifice?"

"She's in hiding," Emira shrugged. "She says no one can prove what her ichor manifests as, which is true, and as far as anyone else knows, she only has transfiguration."

"Damn," he muttered. "Why didn't I think of that?"

"We might not need to travel far," Pandora called from where she was. She was parallel to them but a good twenty feet away.

Mateo rubbed his temple. "Lystos, I hope she doesn't mean—"

"I think there's one here," she said, her hauntingly high toned voice reaching them softly.

Emira peeked over at where Pandora was looking, and she saw a large creature in the distance. She didn't think it noticed them, but then its head turned, and its white, glowing eyes were transfixed on the three of them.

"Mateo?" she asked, backing slowly away. "What's the plan?"

"For now?" he said, pulling on her arm. "We should run."

"Why?" she asked, her eyes still fixed on the *bellua* in the distance.

"Because that's an *immanis*," he murmured. An *immanis*? Her eyes widened.

There were different kinds of *bellua*. There were *parum bellua*, the ones that any warrior could take out easily enough. They didn't have much power and didn't put up much of a fight. *Magna bellua* were the most common types that warriors came across. There were many of them, and they all had power of their own, with varying levels of strength. But then, there were *immanis bellua*. Those were the most dangerous. The ones with immense power that almost rivaled the Idols themselves. There hadn't been a lot of *immanis bellua* recorded in Constellatia history. And now there was one right in front of them. Hunting them.

"Run, Emira!" Mateo hissed, pulling on her arm once more. It felt like her lungs had shriveled up and she had forgotten how to breathe. She didn't realize she had frozen up and slowly started to move her limbs. They felt like ice.

"If it's this close to Serpel walls, it's sick," she vaguely heard him saying. "So it'll be more dangerous. We can't possibly—" The creature started forward.

"Elephants can't run," she heard Pandora say as she ran past her. *Yeah, that's for sure,* Emira thought to herself. But she willed her legs to move anyway as Mateo dragged her forward. She moved as fast as she could, but it was still too slow that eventually, Mateo was behind her, his hand on the middle of her back.

"Can we outrun an *immanis?*" she heard herself yell to him after a while over her shoulder. He was pushing her forward as he kept looking over his own shoulder.

"If you run like that, we can't," he said back.

"Is this really the time?" she said.

"Just—Go, Priestess! Use those Idols-given legs of yours and run *faster.*"

"If its sick, will it be more willing to talk?" Pandora asked. She was jogging like it was second nature to her, as if she weren't breaking a sweat. Emira felt like her lungs were getting clawed out of her.

She looked over her shoulder, and that was the biggest mistake she ever made. Mateo kept pushing her forward, his large hand splayed out on the small of her back. But, her eyes locked with the *immanis bellua's.* Its white eyes glowed out of its skull-like head. Its black shadowy body was sinewy and tall, almost like its limbs were tree branches themselves. Giant ebony horns growing out of its skull-like head curled downwards back towards its chin. And it was close. Much closer than before.

"I don't think we'll make it," Emira breathed. Trees were being crushed behind them, falling or splitting into two. Mateo suddenly turned around, facing the *bellua.* He held Emira's arm, and she stopped running. Both of them breathed hard, the cold air making their breath visible.

"If we can't outrun it, we'll have to fight it," he whispered, low enough that only Emira could hear. She heard Pandora stop running as well, quietly making her way back to them.

The *immanis bellua* paused once it saw the three of them standing there. Its head cocked sideways, so much so that it was unnatural. Emira swallowed the lump growing in her throat.

She was going to die much earlier than she thought she was.

It stalked forward, and Mateo kept Emira behind his back. Its white eyes glanced at her and then at him, before looking over at Pandora. Her golden dragon grew to ten times its size, to where it was as big as the *immanis bellua* standing in front of them. The bellua slowly took another step, its skull-like head cocking to the other side.

"You three smell just like them," its hellish voice whispered.

CHAPTER THIRTY-FOUR

As the *bellua* said this, an image flashed through Emira's brain. An image of three of the Idols. Kali, the Idol of Life and Fertility, Alexios, the Idol of the Sea and Animals, and Lystos, the Idol of Death and Mystery. But the three of them were caked in dirt, holding weapons in front of them, and they looked younger than they did now. Much younger. And Emira could smell the Idols. Like dirt, mixed with smoke? *Is that what the Idols smelled like to them?*

"Who are you referring to?" Mateo asked, holding a sword in his own hand. Emira furrowed her eyebrows as she regarded the *immanis bellua* in front of them. *Did I just read the creature's mind?*

The creature cocked its head unnaturally once again, its white eyes glowing brighter in the moonless night.

"Are you not them?" the *bellua* asked, its whispery words snaking around the three teenagers. Emira shivered a little, gripping the small sword Mateo had packed for her.

"We aren't," Pandora piped up. She talked like she was

having an average normal conversation with a human being instead of with the monstrous creature in front of them.

"No matter," the *bellua* breathed. "I will get my revenge this way, too." The skull-like face of it widened as the hole where its mouth should be got bigger. A smile of sorts. Emira felt her stomach churn.

With a wave of his hand, Mateo drew a circle of fire around the *bellua*. Its smile got bigger. With its large limbs, it walked over the fire like it was nothing. Mateo's eyes burned.

"What questions should we ask?" Pandora called from the other side of the *bellua*. She had the limbs of the trees wrapping around the *bellua*, but it easily broke through it, like they were thin twigs. Her dragon blew fire at the creature, and they all paused until the *bellua* stepped out of it, perfectly unharmed. Its glowing eyes were fixed onto Emira, and under its gaze, she herself felt like she couldn't move.

"I'm thinking," Mateo called back, trying another one of the powers in his wheelhouse. He cloned himself a few times, looking in pain as he did. And then there were five of him, running around the *bellua*. It turned to look at all of him, trying to hit them with its tree-like shadowy limbs. One of the Mateos got thrown into the base of the tree, his head cracking open.

The real Mateo stood a little bit away from the creature, his eyes burning bright. His one gold eye was swirling in the way that Balan's did. And his brown one seemed to be lighter and swirling around, too. Something deep within Emira wanted to hide away as she felt the amount of power emanating from him. She gripped the hilt of her sword tighter.

"It won't be able to talk once I do this," Mateo whispered to her. "Once I do it, I can hold it for a little but not for long. You'll have to read its mind. Can you do that?"

Emira nodded her head once, her eyes not leaving the creature who was still trying to bat away the other Mateos.

"All right," he muttered. With both hands, he pulled them apart from one another, and as he did, the *bellua* was dissected. Shiloh's power. Deconstruction.

The *immanis bellua's* head was pulled high above its body, shadowy tendrils still connecting it. And its black beating heart was pulled forward, the dark smoke falling away from it. It cried out in a way that was heart-wrenching. Emira winced.

"Where did you come from?" Mateo asked, not breaking a sweat as his power flowed out of him. The other Mateos phased back into him, besides the one who died at the base of the tree. That one simply turned to dust.

The creature's thoughts flowed into Emira's mind easily.

What does the human mean?

"It doesn't understand what you mean," she said to Mateo. His expression darkened.

"Where did you come from? Your kind? Did you come from the twelve circles of hell?" Mateo asked. The *bellua* laughed inside of her mind, but all of its thoughts were tinged in pain.

Twelve circles of hell? What do the humans teach you?

"It's not from there," Emira translated. The *bellua's* eyes were fixed onto her and a chill went down her spine.

"If not the twelve circles of hell, then where?" Mateo demanded. Beads of sweat started to appear on his forehead. Emira glanced at the *bellua* who was still staring at her.

The twelve humans came, the ones who smell like you three, and took from us, the creature whispered into her mind. *Left us like this.*

Emira repeated what the *bellua* thought, her eyes not leaving its horrifying face. Mateo frowned as he studied the dark creature.

"Left you like what?" he asked. The creature bore holes into Emira.

Please, kill me, it whispered. Emira could feel the essence of the *bellua* disappearing. Devolving into pain.

"I'm losing it," she said, through gritted teeth. Tears burned the back of her eyes as she felt the pain the creature was feeling. She heard Mateo let out a frustrated sigh and then rip the creature apart more.

"Left you like what?" he asked again, ruthless, as the *bellua* screamed in pain. Its glowing white eyes fixed themselves onto Mateo, and all its thoughts turned murderous.

Like monsters, it whispered.

Emira stared at the creature, at the monstrous body the bellua was in, and then closed her eyes. "They turned them into monsters."

"Great," Mateo said, his eyes narrowing. "Now, Pandora." Emira glanced over at the future magician as she threw her sword with frightening accuracy into the black heart of the *bellua*.

Emira felt the cold grips of death grab the *bellua* as it darted its gaze over at her before turning into ash. It felt like her head was on fire as she crumpled to the ground. She held her head as the last remnants of the *bellua* ripped through it.

Mateo rushed towards her, getting down on his knees, before cupping her head in between his hands. He stared into her eyes, worry creasing his own.

"What's wrong? What's going on?" he asked.

"The death took its mark," Pandora said from behind her. Emira stared desperately into Mateo's mismatched eyes. They looked normal again, not like his grandfather's with its endless swirling. She placed a hand softly onto his cheek, the side with his brown eye, before she passed out.

"How was I supposed to know she'd still be in its mind once it died?" she heard Mateo vaguely say from above her. Was she in his arms?

"She feels all that the mind feels," she heard Pandora say from beside her. Emira opened her eyes and saw Pandora's hazel ones looking back at her. She had the giant *immanis bellua's* skull head resting on her own, like a weird makeshift hat. Emira looked down at her own body. She was in Mateo's arms, and he was holding her close to his chest. His heart was beating erratically.

"She's awake," Pandora whispered. Mateo looked down at her, his mismatched eyes wide with concern.

"I'm fine," Emira managed to get out. Her voice was hoarse, like she had been screaming. "Please put me down." He immediately put her down, making sure she was stable on her feet before completely letting her go. The sun was rising, washing everything in gold and blue.

"Are you okay?" Mateo murmured close to her. So close she could feel the vibration of his voice through his body. She took a step back, away from him, and wrapped her arms around herself.

"Yeah," she whispered. "I will be." She could still feel what the *immanis bellua* had felt when it died. The cold and emptiness. And the pain. The immense pain of its soul being ripped out of its body.

She shuddered. "Eventually."

"Death isn't fun to experience," Pandora nodded her head,

the skull slipping over her face as she did. She pushed it back up her head.

"Why are you wearing that?" Emira asked.

"For proof," she answered. Emira looked at Mateo for some kind of explanation. They were walking back towards the walls of Serpel.

"We escaped the Winter Solstice Ball, they're probably looking everywhere for us. And if we explain we went outside of the walls, on a drunken whim, encountered an *immanis bellua* so close to the walls, and killed it, it'll exonerate us," he explained. Her eyes narrowed at him. It was a flimsy plan at best.

"So, for proof," Pandora said, smiling brilliantly at Emira. Emira's eyes lingered on the skull before turning away.

"What do you think they'll say about us defeating an *immanis bellua*? Just the three of us?" Emira said, her voice low. "In history, an Idol would defeat one. No one else really could."

"But it was easy peasy," Pandora interjected. "We're sure they'll understand." Her golden dragon nodded its head along with her words.

"Don't say it was easy peasy," Mateo said, turning towards her. "Make it sound like we were on the verge of death."

Pandora shrugged. "If that's what you want." Mateo and Emira exchanged a knowing glance. Without peering into his mind, she knew he was thinking the same thing. The Idols can't know the sacrifices have the same amount of power as them. Or at least, they couldn't find out that the three of them knew it.

"Brace yourself for the scolding," Mateo murmured. The walls of Serpel loomed over them as they walked closer and closer. Pandora's golden dragon walked behind them, shrinking as they neared the walls.

The black wall opened up to reveal a gate. Two Pyrinian guards stood there, glaring at the three of them.

"Greetings Constellatians," Pandora said, holding up two fingers as a greeting. Mateo rubbed his temples. Emira grabbed Pandora's wrist and pulled it down to her side. She looked over at Emira, quizzically. Emira simply shook her head.

"Where are you two coming from?" one of the Pyrinian guards asked. She looked the three of them up and down.

"The wild, obviously," Mateo said, gesturing to the area behind them. "We're trying to get back in."

"Name?" she asked. Mateo ran a hand through his brown hair. It was what he did when he was frustrated, but Emira could see that he was doing it here as a way to change his expression, which turned cold, his eyes hard.

"Mateo Cordero," he said, his usual expressive voice turning lazy and arrogant. It was odd, seeing him change right in front of her eyes. Was this the Mateo Cordero everyone else saw?

The Pyrinian guard glanced up at him and averted her eyes quickly. The other one stared at Emira, straight into her eyes. And he didn't avert them at all.

"The others?" The guard's voice was small now. She stared down at the ground.

"Does it matter?" Mateo asked. The other guard jabbed a thumb at Emira while looking head on at Mateo.

"She's got the eyes of an Idol," he said. "Seems like the both of you are pretty important."

"We're both sacrifices," Mateo answered, albeit begrudgingly. "The other is our friend."

"How did you three end up outside of the walls?" the guard asked.

Mateo narrowed his eyes. "Is that something you should be asking us? I'm sure Balan wouldn't like that his grandson and future sacrifice is standing outside of the walls." The guard's eyes widened a little and then glanced over at Pandora. His eyes lingered on the skull that she was wearing as a hat.

"Open the gates," he said to the other. The female guard raised the gate, and the three of them slipped in.

"Do we need to escort you to the Idol of Law and Fate's quarters?" the guard asked. Mateo shook his head.

"No need," he said. "We'll end up there." The male guard's eyes were still on them as they walked into Serpel.

The city of Serpel was dark, with dark green and ebony structures erected everywhere. The buildings reached the skies and were sleek and reflective in the sunlight. The people of Serpel were extremely dressed up, men wearing impeccable suits as they hurried off somewhere while the women were wearing intricate dresses, makeup done, and hair perfect as they also rushed to their workplaces. The people of Serpel barely glanced at the three of them.

"A busy city," Pandora muttered under her breath as her dragon crawled up her arm and rested onto her shoulders, like a golden lizard scarf.

"Politicians are always moving. So are lawyers," Mateo said. "C'mon. We have to get there as soon as possible." And he made a sharp turn down a nondescript alley.

"Where are we going? Isn't the castle that way?" Emira whispered, pointing in the opposite direction of where they were going.

"Oh, they're not going to be waiting in the castle," he muttered. He grabbed Emira's wrist and stared into her eyes.

"I'll do the talking when we get there, okay? Don't say a word." Normally, she would disagree with him, argue with his orders. But something in his eyes made her pause. Emira nodded, her violet eyes wide.

CHAPTER THIRTY-FIVE

The Pyrinian guards in front of the Idols' Court of Justice building led them inside. The building had columns lining the outside and the inside of it had no doors in sight. The floor was a dark forest green, and the walls were charcoal black with intricate moldings of various snakes.

Mateo kept his head high as the guards led them towards the back room, only sectioned off by columns. He knew what the Idols would be gunning towards. Having the three of them killed right there and then, so they would stop being a nuisance, a liability. He had to figure out a way to convince them not to.

"Here," the Pyrinian guard grunted. The room opened up to reveal twelve intricate chairs that corresponded to the Idols who sat in it. All twelve of them were already there, Balan in the middle. His metallic, golden eyes glared at Mateo as the three of them walked in.

"Let the session begin," Balan said once they were lined up in front of the Idols. He banged a dark wooden gavel down twice before looking back up at them.

"You're accused of illegally leaving the walls of Serpel

without permission. How do you plead?" he said, his voice cold. No one was around that he needed to woo anymore. It was now Balan's true self.

"Guilty," Mateo shrugged. He saw in his peripheral vision Emira turn her head sharply to look at him.

"Hm, you do realize the punishment for this crime is death?" Balan asked.

"Yes," Mateo responded. "But, perhaps we can work out some kind of agreement."

"Agreement?" he said, leaning forward. Balan's golden eyes swirled as he observed his grandson. Mateo nodded. He took the giant skull off of Pandora's head and presented it to the twelve Idols. They all stared at it. Only a minuscule change in their expression showed Mateo they were shocked by what they were seeing.

"What is this?" Balan asked, leaning back in his ridiculously ornate seat. Somehow, he managed to look unimpressed. Mateo's lips thinned.

"The head of an *immanis bellua*," he said. He expected whispers, someone talking, a crack in their armor, but the other Idols stared straight at him, not uttering a word.

"How is it that you came into possession of one?" Balan asked, his tone bored. It pissed Mateo off. And he knew Balan was doing it on purpose.

"We fought one," Mateo answered. "It was near the walls of Serpel. We think it was sick—"

"Lies," Phaethon loudly said. His curly, golden blonde hair fell perfectly into his piercing emerald green eyes. "It's impossible for the three of you to defeat an *immanis bellua*." Balan stared at Mateo, and it was the same feeling he got in the pit of his stomach that he felt when Cassandra was ripped away from him. That stare made his limbs go numb, glued to the spot he was at.

Balan turned towards Mali. "Is he telling the truth?" Mali winced as she looked at Mateo for a moment before closing her crystalline violet eyes.

"His thoughts are too chaotic to glean from," she murmured. "But, it seems that he's telling the truth." Balan's golden eyes darted towards Emira. Mateo felt his fingers curl into his palm at the look.

"Check the girl," he ordered. The Idol of Luck fixed her violet eyes, the same ones as Emira, onto her. She stared for a long while, her expression conflicted as her eyes darted back at Mateo. They were mildly wider, like she had figured something out.

He wondered if she got everything from Emira, all that they were learning about the Idols, or just the fact that they killed an *immanis bellua*.

Did she hear what the bellua had said?

"They're telling the truth," was all she said. She leaned back in her seat.

"The three of them defeated an *immanis bellua*?" a woman with straight, shiny black hair and pink quartz eyes said. Her unnerving pink eyes were upturned and stuck out of her skull a little, the rest of her features flat. She fixed her gaze onto Mateo. Kali, the Idol of Life and Fertility.

"An *immanis bellua* wouldn't make its way so close to the walls," a man with blue hair and sapphire blue eyes said. He looked similar to Kali, but his face was more weathered than the Idol of Life's. Lystos, the Idol of Death and Mystery.

"Not after what we did," a man with pure silver eyes and black dreads muttered. He was big, bigger than the other Idols. Taller, too. And made of pure muscle. Nyro, the Idol of War and Power.

"Killing an *immanis bellua* isn't an excuse for leaving the walls of Serpel," a woman with short orange-red hair cut at her chin and bright orange eyes said. She looked younger than the rest, but her expression was hardened by time. Hemlock, the Idol of Knowledge and Festivity.

"Quite right, Hemlock. Why should we absolve your crime just because you destroyed an *immanis bellua*?" Balan asked, turning his attention back towards his grandson. Mateo held his hands behind his back as he stared down the Idol of Law and Fate.

"Wouldn't it be better for the twelve of you to keep us alive until the sacrificial ceremony? It would be a bad look if you killed Emira and I a little too early," Mateo said, meeting each of the other Idols' eyes. He glanced back at Balan. "Could make the other citizens of Constellatia think we weren't willing. And if we weren't willing, well, it could beg the question as to why."

Balan's eyebrow twitched. And Mateo noticed him gripping the gavel a little harder than normal.

"I've been saying this process has an expiration date written all over it," a woman with soft features, ebony black eyes, and dark braids decorated with gold said. Raila, the Idol of Music, Poetry, and Light.

"As if we couldn't keep a few citizens in their place," Phaethon replied, rolling his jewel-like eyes. Balan held up a hand, and Phaethon shrank from the gesture. Balan's eyes were still on Mateo.

"You're right as well, Mateo," he murmured. "It would make things... difficult for us." He cocked his head to the side as he leaned forward.

"What possessed you to leave the walls of Serpel and steal my pegasuses to do so?" Balan asked. Mateo shrugged.

"We were drunk," he said. "Just wanted to experience it."

"Wearing protective gear?"

"We might've been drunk, but we're not stupid," Mateo answered. Balan regarded him for a moment.

"You killed an *immanis bellua*?" he asked. His breath was bated, like he was almost excited. Mateo furrowed his eyebrows together. *What was he thinking?*

"Yes," he answered.

"All on his own," Pandora piped up. Mateo glowered at the white blonde. She shrugged. Balan's gaze turned towards the future magician.

"And you are?"

"Pandora Lux, sir," she said. Then she shook her head. "I mean, your holiness."

"Of course, the Lux girl with a familiar," he said, his golden eyes swirling as he regarded her. "Funny how you aren't a sacrifice."

"Transfiguration only," she lied, wiggling her fingers.

"So, are we exonerated?" Mateo asked, trying to bring the attention back to him. Balan lazily dragged his eyes back to him and gave a small smile.

"You are the most extraordinary descendant I've ever had," Balan said. His words struck Mateo, and he shifted uncomfortably once more. He needed to figure out what the old man was thinking.

"You three are exonerated. But, you must tell no one about the *immanis bellua*," Balan said. "And you must accept your fate as a sacrifice." Mateo ground his teeth together but returned his smile.

"We promise," he vowed. Balan's golden eyes glittered as he brought the gavel down once more.

"See you in a few months," he said.

PANDORA STRETCHED UP TOWARDS THE SKY ONCE THEY WERE outside the Court of Justice. A carriage was waiting for Emira and Mateo to bring them back to Leliara. Pandora was free to do what she wished, since she wasn't a sacrifice.

"Where are you going?" Emira asked when Pandora started walking away from them.

"We're going home," she said, making her dragon wave goodbye at them to the dismay of the dragon. "It's still the Winter Solstice break." She turned back around and continued on her way.

Mateo held open the door for Emira who was still staring at Pandora. Some of her hair was falling out of her up do, she looked like she hadn't slept in days, and yet she still took his breath away. He swallowed and looked away as she entered the carriage. He sat down next to her, and the carriage started to move once more. She stared out the window, her violet eyes looking more empty than he remembered.

"Why do we keep finding ourselves in carriages with one another?" she asked, softly. Her gaze turned towards him. He tried to flash her a casual smile.

"How different things are from then," he whispered. Her eyebrows turned upwards and then she looked away, her gaze fixed on the outside.

"How our fates have changed," she muttered. He wanted to tell her their fates were fixed from the beginning. But, he didn't say it, merely keeping his gaze on her. He wanted to fill every last moment he had with her. Even though he knew he couldn't.

"We can't rewrite the stars," he murmured. She glanced over at him, knowing he echoed what she had said to him before.

"No one can," she agreed, before turning away once more.

CHAPTER THIRTY-SIX

When they arrived at Leliara, Emira immediately went to her dorm room. She wanted to write a letter to Shiloh, about what they had found out. If anyone could make sense of it, it was her. Emira couldn't get the voice of the *immanis bellua* out of her mind. *The twelve humans came, the ones who smell like you three, and took from us.*

What did it mean?

What did the Idols take from the *bellua*? How did they leave them like monsters? They were questions Emira wondered if Shiloh could answer.

Dear Shiloh, she wrote. *We found a...* She stopped and looked at the words she had already written. Her fingers felt like jelly as she remembered Balan's eyes, how they stared at Mateo. There was only one thought that she could glean from the Idol: *Power.* He looked at Mateo and thought it, and he—an Idol—was simultaneously terrified and fascinated of what his grandson could do. If he ever knew the truth... She crumpled it up and threw it away.

No, she couldn't write it down. It could get intercepted. For all she knew, the Idols were going to read every letter she would ever write until the sacrificial ceremony of the Tenth Year. In a week, it will be the New Year. And she would only have five months left.

Five months.

It was a weird feeling, knowing when one was going to die. Normally, death was out of one's control. But here she was, with the knowledge and the how of her death. There weren't any questions about what would happen. She would be engulfed by a white light and absorbed by her own mother.

Her own mother.

That was another thing she couldn't reckon with. Her mother, the person she thought of nearly every day when she was younger, the person she wondered about secretly in the quiet of the night, was an Idol. And her mother was the one who was going to kill her.

Emira pressed her tongue against the roof of her mouth as she got up and changed. There was nothing she could do. No matter who the Idols were, no matter what they had done to her, there was no where to go and no way to escape her fate, if she had even wanted to.

She didn't know if she wanted to.

She took off the hunting clothes Mateo had given her. Placing the clothes and expensive cloak dipped in phoenix ashes into her dresser, she changed into something more comfortable. She left her dorm room and walked down the spiral staircase to the main foyer.

Leliara was eerily empty. Not another soul was around for the holidays. She knew Mateo was somewhere, packing to go back to his parents' home, but other than that, she was alone. She pulled out the pins in her hair, letting it fall over her shoulders and brush against her back.

Standing outside the library doors, she used the hair pins she pulled out and tried to mimic what Silas had done with the gate door. She struggled for a moment before remembering she could just use her power.

Embarrassed, and hoping no one saw her, she used her mind to unlock the door and lightly pushed it open. It was empty.

She browsed the shelves until she found a book about the Idol of Luck and Agriculture. Her finger ran down the spine of the book before pulling out the hard covered book and sat down at one of the round tables. Staring at the cover, it was a painting of Mali. Her dark hair was pulled back in a veil, like she was a priestess herself. And, Emira had to admit, she was the perfect image of innocence.

When Mali sifted around in her mind, back at the Court of Justice, Emira could feel the essence of her. And it was soft, like little padded paws flipping through memories of hers like they were files in her brain. And she went through a lot of them, quickly, and without much emotion.

She had lingered on a memory with Priestess Irene. It was when Emira was younger, and it was fall. The leaves were raked up, and Priestess Irene would lift Emira and then drop her into the leaves, Emira shrilly laugh-screaming from the action. It was when she was young. Very young. Emira had forgotten that particular memory until Mali drudged it up. She wondered why the Idol of Luck was interested in the memory. The only other memory she lingered on was the one of Mateo kissing Emira. That one made the Idol of Luck feel dangerous. It was a memory Emira wanted to keep hidden from her. But, it was the only one she looked at with Mateo in it, like she had accidentally came across it and didn't want to know more.

But the essence of Mali made Emira curious about her biological mother and future assailant. She opened the book, the smell of old paper filling her nose. And she started to read about who Mali was.

The book didn't talk about any battles, only that Mali helped when it came to the judicial system in Constellatia. She helped Balan develop it, and she used her ichor to see if anyone was telling lies. *She really should be called the Idol of Truth,* Emira thought.

Mali oversaw the province Sapiem, a province filled with rolling hills and farmland. Emira looked at the picture provided and traced the hills with her fingers. It looked peaceful, like a wonderfully quiet place to grow up. *Why did she put me in Aeluris?* Emira wondered. *And why didn't she look at the rest of the memories with Mateo?*

"What are you doing?" she heard Mateo say. She nearly jumped out of her seat as she closed the book she was reading. Emira glowered up at him.

"Couldn't you have given me a warning? A little hint that you were here?" she said, annoyed. She brushed her hair out of her face. Mateo smirked.

"I didn't realize I'm that quiet," he said. He took the seat next to her and pulled the book towards himself. "Must've been really into this book." He held it up and raised an eyebrow. Emira snatched it away from him.

"It's not a crime to want to know what my mother is like," she muttered. He worked his jaw and then glanced at the book.

"The books don't describe her nearly as well as Balan does in his diary," he said, his voice soft. It didn't match his gaze though. It was a hard glare, staring straight at the painting of Mali on the cover.

"Hopefully I'll get a chance to look at that," Emira said, looking pointedly at him. He shrugged and gave her an easy smile.

"It could probably be arranged," he said. Emira looked at him, her eyes darting to his gold eye to his brown one. And she remembered what he looked like when he was using all of his ichor, how much power emanated from him. How it made her want to expel anything still sitting in her stomach. How his irises swirled and how his eyes became more vibrant. How they burned. Like Balan's.

She shuddered. "What are you doing here, anyways? Aren't you leaving?" His smile faltered.

"Yeah, I am," he said, nervously scratching the back of his head. Emira raised an eyebrow.

"What are you doing talking to me then?" she asked. His expression was boyish, almost sheepish. It was a stark contrast from what he looked like when he was in the Idols' Court of Justice. Emira remembered the fear that flashed through Shiloh's eyes and what she had said: *"You didn't see what you looked like when you came back."*

Now she had an idea.

"I was wondering, since you have nowhere else to go," Mateo started. He looked up to the ceiling, like what he was about to say pained him.

"Go on," she said, resting her head on her elbow as she smiled at him. She could guess what it was he wanted to say, but she wanted him to do it. Especially since it seemed like it was a difficult thing for him to say.

"You're really going to make me say it?" he asked. She nodded her head.

"Mhmm," she said, her smile getting bigger.

"Do you want to come back to my place?" he asked. And then he added quickly, "Silas is there, too."

"Silas being there interests me less," Emira pointed out. She remembered the icy glare the youngest Silver brother kept giving her.

"He'll be on his best behavior," Mateo vowed, his mismatched eyes softening. Emira hugged the book about the Idol of Luck and Agriculture to her chest. She gave him a side-long glance. Part of her wondered what it was like for Mateo growing up. She wanted to see who his parents were, the probably grand house he was born in. The other part of her just didn't want to be alone.

"Sure," she said. "I don't have anywhere else to go, like you said." Mateo gave her a wary smile. A smile that didn't quite reach his eyes.

"You didn't think I'd agree," she guessed. He shrugged.

"I never know where your head is at," he said. "You hate me one day, you tolerate me the next." Emira felt her own smile fade. She looked away from him as she got up from the chair.

"I don't hate you, Mateo," she said, her voice barely above a whisper. "I've never hated you." She glanced over at him, his mismatched eyes were wide, but his hand was curled up into a fist. His jaw worked once more, and he turned away from her.

"Great," he said, his voice colder than normal. "I'll be waiting in the carriage."

She looked over her shoulder at him before leaving the library. He was still sitting there, staring out into space, his hands in fists. His broad shoulders were tense. And she wondered what he was thinking about. Why did her staying at his place for the New Year make him viscerally upset?

She placed a finger onto her lips as she headed back to her dorm room. *Maybe he regretted it,* she thought. Maybe he wished he never kissed her. And she wished she could regret it, too. That she could get it out of her mind.

CHAPTER THIRTY-SEVEN

Emira looked up at the pristine white house with golden details. Her eyes wandered around the estate they were standing on, becoming more self conscious by the second. It was on the outskirts of the city in Vismary, Phaethon's province, where all the rich businessmen lived.

She glanced down at what she was wearing. Nothing really to write home about. She brushed the wrinkled sweater she was wearing down and gave Mateo a pained expression.

"I didn't know you were, like, uncomfortably rich," she muttered. He quirked an eyebrow, a whisper of a smirk playing on his full lips.

"I'm a Cordero," he responded. "A descendant of one of the first families. It would be odd if I wasn't uncomfortably rich." He shrugged as he entered inside.

"Master Cordero," a servant said, bowing low as Mateo entered.

"Lila, as we've talked about before, please stop calling me that," he said. The older woman still stayed bowed.

"Of course, Young Master Cordero," she said. Mateo sighed. Without energy, he gestured towards Emira. Emira gave him a glance and mouthed *Young Master Cordero?* He let out another long sigh.

"This is Emira. She's going to be staying with us until the break is over," he said. Emira raised a hand and gave Lila a small wave. Lila didn't meet Emira's eyes, but nodded once at her.

"Another sacrifice," she said, her voice small. Mateo nodded his head, almost absentmindedly.

"Lila, where's Si—" Before he could finish his sentence, a woman who had wavy brown hair, streaked with gray, ran into the foyer.

"Mateo!" she cried. Her gold eyes were filled with tears as she engulfed him. "How I missed you!"

"Mom, please," he said. She pulled away and stared at him for a long time, like she was committing his face to memory.

"It's cruel they don't let you come home more often," she said. Emira couldn't see Mateo's expression, but she saw his body tense at his mother's words.

"Mom, this is Emira," he said, changing the subject. He moved slightly and gestured towards her, and she immediately wished she was wearing something else. Wiping her hands on her pants, she held one out.

"Hi, it's nice to meet you. I'm Emira Solus," she said, inwardly wincing when saying her last name. Mateo's mother's eyes widened at hearing her last name and glanced over at Mateo before turning her attention back to Emira.

She took Emira's hand and shook it before pulling her into a hug. "It's always nice to meet anyone who's friends with Mateo." She pulled away and looked at Emira, staring straight into her eyes.

"Mateo gets in so much trouble. It warms my heart that he has such loyal friends," she said.

"Thanks, Mom," Mateo grumbled. "Is Silas here?"

"He got here after the Winter Solstice ball," Mrs. Cordero answered. She pointed upwards. Then her attention was back on Emira.

"I'll get a room set up for you," she smiled warmly. She simultaneously looked like Balan and didn't. Her features were softer and warmer. Emira wondered if Balan ever looked that human before.

"Lila, please take her belongings and put new sheets in the guest room near Silas' and Mateo's," Mrs. Cordero said. "And then, I'll see you tomorrow." Lila nodded, took Emira's small suitcase right from her hands, and then disappeared into the massive house.

"Be ready for dinner," Mrs. Cordero said, her friendly face turning stern. "Your father is going to be here." Mateo looked like he was halfway through rolling his eyes before stopping himself at his mother's gaze.

"All right," he said. He turned towards Emira. "C'mon." He started up the stairs and Emira followed after him. She looked at the pictures on the walls in the hallway as they walked towards wherever Silas was staying. In an instant, she watched Mateo grow up through them.

"You lost both your front teeth at once?" Emira asked, pointing at a picture of a young Mateo grinning. He couldn't be more than six or seven. He moved and stood behind her. Emira was very aware of Mateo's presence, and she tried to even her breath.

"Yeah," he said, chuckling a little. "Silas and I got into a fight. He won. Last time that happened."

"It's because I let him win now," Silas said, standing in a

doorway not too far away from them. "Can't injure the precious sacrifice."

"How was the rest of the Winter Solstice?" Mateo asked, doing a complicated handshake with Silas before entering the room. Emira quietly followed after him. Silas' guest room was pristine. White with some pops of blue in places.

Silas closed the bedroom door. "Awful."

Mateo raised his eyebrows. "That bad?"

"After they figured out the three of you stole some pegasuses, the ball was over," Silas said. "I was questioned."

"By who?"

"Who do you think? The seeker of truth herself," he muttered.

"Mali?" Emira asked. Silas looked taken aback.

"You know about her?" he asked.

"She probably got it from that book she was reading," Mateo said. He was settled onto the floor, his back leaning against Silas' bed. Emira sat down on the ground across from him.

"I did," she answered. "It said she helped build the judicial system and she's used in big cases."

"Big cases? She's only used when the case gets put in front of the Idols," Silas said.

"Wouldn't that be a big case?" Emira retorted. Silas narrowed his eyes at her, his mouth opening to dispute what she had said, but Mateo interrupted him.

"Does she know? About what we're up to." Mateo's voice was hard as he looked up at Silas. Silas sat down on his bed and shook his head.

"I know how to keep my thoughts scattered," he said. Emira furrowed her eyebrows and hugged her knees to her chest. Mali had flipped through her own memories so quickly, she wasn't sure if she knew what they were up to or not. But, if she had to guess, she would assume the Idol of Luck knew.

"Mali doesn't work like that," she said. Silas looked at her, his blue eyes piercing.

"How does she work?"

Emira shrugged as she picked at the stray string hanging from her sweater sleeve. She pulled it and watched as it bunched up before ripping the strand off. "She goes through your memories like they're in a filing cabinet. She doesn't only see your thoughts that are at the forefront."

"Can you do that?" Mateo asked. His mismatched eyes seemed to be searching for something in her violet ones. Emira shook her head.

Idols, did she wish she could. Because maybe she'd be able to understand what was going on in his head all the time.

"I'm sure I could if I tried, maybe someday," Emira said. "But, I don't know how to do it at this point."

"So, scattering my thoughts…" Silas' voice trailed off.

"She'll find whatever it is she's searching for," Emira finished for him. "Unless all of your memories are jumbled like that." *Like Mateo's,* she almost said. She glanced at him as he and Silas exchanged looks. Did he already know Mali's ichor worked like that? Was his essence purposefully chaotic or did he do it by accident?

"She might know," Silas muttered.

"It won't matter to her too much," Mateo said, shrugging the failure off. "As long as she gets her sacrifice, what does it matter if we know the truth?"

The three of them were silent for a moment, the sacrificial ritual blanketing over them. A death knell waiting to be rung.

"How was the wild?" Silas asked, changing the subject. Emira could tell he looked uncomfortable. Disappointed, worried. His blue eyes kept darting towards Mateo, like he was concerned he failed him.

"We caught a *bellua*," Mateo said. "It gave us answers but also many questions." Emira wondered why he didn't tell Silas it was an *immanis bellua*. Did he believe Balan's threat?

"What did it say?"

"'The twelve humans came, the ones who smell like you three, and took from us,'" she repeated, having committed the thought to memory. "The twelve humans have to be the Idols. But, what they took and who the *bellua* are, we still don't know."

Silas looked lost in thought. "It died before it could tell you more?"

"It was in a lot of pain," Emira whispered. She still could feel it, the *bellua's* mind as it died. Was that how Ethel had felt when she took her life? She squeezed her eyes shut and shook her head. "It didn't tell us more than that."

"I'll have to talk to Shiloh or Atlas about it," Silas murmured. And then the conversation turned into talk about the most recent Volani game. Volani was a sport where people with wings, mostly from Fonsia, fly around chasing after a ball. Emira was never really interested in it, and she tuned out of the conversation.

She watched the two of them talk to one another. Noticing the way Silas tended to search for Mateo's validation. She wondered what exactly happened to Silas in his upbringing.

"*I was locked up a lot as a child,*" he had told her. Is this the reason why he turned to Mateo for confirmation? It was as if he couldn't trust his own judgment.

"I saw Isla leaving our room the other day," Silas said, his eyebrows raising quizzically. She watched as his blue eyes darted towards Emira, like he wanted her to hear this particular segment of the conversation. She focused back on the conversation. Her inner self whispered to peek into Silas' memory, to listen to his quiet whisperings. But, she refrained herself. She wasn't Mali. She wasn't going to invade someone's thoughts on purpose. Not unless she had to.

Mateo stiffened and quickly glared at Silas. The youngest Silver simply flashed him a smile in return. Mateo glanced at Emira before answering.

"She's..." his voice drifted off.

"Who's Isla?" Emira asked the question she knew Silas was wanting her to ask.

"Oh, she's Celeste's friend. In the year below us," Silas answered. "You've probably seen her around."

Ah, the redhead, Emira vaguely thought. She looked over at Mateo and met his eyes. The redhead that was in his bed that one time.

"You get around, huh Mateo?" she said, smiling. But it didn't reach her eyes. She didn't know why it pained her, to think of him with another woman. She didn't understand it. But the pain was there, always constantly there when she looked at him.

"I don't date," he said, his eyes almost pleading with her. Emira blinked. "She's just a good friend."

"It doesn't matter to me," she said, quickly. Mateo looked away.

"I didn't think it would," he said, but his voice seemed solemn. Silence stretched between them.

Silas cleared his throat. "Should we go down and grab dinner?"

Mateo's dad didn't look like him at all. He had curly brown hair that was graying greatly. And his eyes were brown. He wasn't as tan as Mateo, a paler complexion. And he looked tired, much more tired than Emira expected him to look.

He was reading a newspaper at the table, the front page discussing the Winter Solstice ball at Balan's palace. The picture was the one of the twelve sacrifices standing in front of the twelve Idols. The Idols all looked serene and friendly, but still unapproachable. Emira stared at the back of her head in the picture in the newspaper.

"Why didn't you stand in front of your grandfather as is custom?" Mateo's dad asked as he closed the newspaper to pointedly look at the picture. Mateo shrugged as he ate his dinner.

"It's the last year," he said. "Wanted to switch things up."

"You know your actions reflect on the whole family," Mr. Cordero said, his brown eyes cold as he looked at his son. Emira immediately felt like she shouldn't be privy to this conversation.

"You and Mom didn't come to the party," Mateo pointed out. He met his father's gaze. "I wonder how that was taken." He was acting like he did in front of the Pyrinian guards and in front of the Idols. Cold. Distant. Not like Mateo at all.

"Your mother couldn't bring herself to, and I wasn't going to leave her at home all alone," Mr. Cordero said. The two of them stared each other down until Mrs. Cordero cleared her throat.

"Let's have a good meal, please?" she said. "This is one of the last times Mateo will be home before..." She turned away from the table. Her eyes were wet and filling up more as the seconds ticked by.

"If you'll excuse me," she whispered, leaving the table. Mr. Cordero threw a glare in Mateo's direction, like it was his fault his impending death was mentioned, before getting up and following after her.

"I'm guessing your dad and you don't get along," Emira said as servants took her plate away and replaced it with another course. Dessert. Emira's favorite meal.

"We never have," Mateo said. "He's all for tradition but my mom and I, we're rebels at heart." He gave her a smile that should've stopped her heart.

Stop it, she thought to herself. *So he's unbelievably beautiful. Heart-wrenchingly so. So what?*

"Do you guys need me to leave you two alone or...?" Silas said, his voice lazy. He glanced up from his plate and pointedly stared at the two of them. Emira felt the heat rush to her face and stared intensely at her own plate.

"You're really trying to start a fight, aren't you?" Mateo murmured. Silas shrugged and leaned back in his seat.

"Just trying to help," he said. He gave Mateo a toothy grin and looked over at Emira. "Do you want to watch the Volani game with us?"

"I'll pass," she mumbled. "I'm not a fan." The two boys stared at her like she stabbed one of them in the back.

"What?" she asked.

"How can you not be a fan of Volani?" Mateo asked.

"I don't like watching blood gush out of someone's nose or someone's limbs breaking," Emira said. And also, she had only ever seen TVs from the windows in storefronts, never in someone's own house. But, she didn't want to admit that little tidbit of her past. And she didn't want the two of them to see how enamored she'd look in front of one.

"That's the best part," Mateo said, aghast. She rolled her eyes.

"I'll be in my room," she said. "I'll see you two tomorrow." She finished her dessert and then climbed the steps to the room

Lila had shown her to before leaving for the day. She counted the doors until she reached the tenth one.

Emira grabbed the book she stole from the Leliara library and laid down on the bed. Stole was a harsh word. She was going to give it back once school was in session once more.

Flipping through the book, she consumed everything there was to know about Mali, her biological mother.

CHAPTER THIRTY-EIGHT

Emira tossed and turned on the bed. The *immanis bellua's* pain screaming into her mind remained in the recesses, reminding her of it every time her eyelids shut. And no matter what she did—counting backwards from one hundred, clearing her mind—the screaming wouldn't leave. She tossed to the other side. The mattress was too soft, the pillow underneath her head had too much volume. And the room was too...

Emira sat up, rubbing her face as she looked at the early hours of the morning through the window. The Cordero estate was large and sprawling. A garden that was probably the crown jewel of the estate during the spring spread out in the backyard. In the winter, however, it looked like a graveyard of plants past their prime.

Emira got up and opened the wardrobe in her room. The whole house and estate was too much for her. Obnoxiously expensive objects in every room, and she could always find them, like they were calling out to her to say: *look at me! I'm expensive and you would never, ever be able to afford me!* The difference between the upbringing of her and Mateo was stark. It almost made her look at him different, like they were two different species. *Almost*. She grabbed a cloak and pulled it over her body. The fabric felt like it was worth more than her whole life.

She made her way outside, the cold waking up her tired limbs. Emira touched the dead plants as she walked through the large, dead garden. The dew was frozen on the plants, a glaze of frost, and eventually her hands became painfully red. She didn't know how long she walked outside, but the dark sky was becoming a twilight blue.

The *immanis bellua* was still in her head, even whilst awake. The cold feeling of winter was comfortable for her because it was the same pain as the death the *immanis bellua* had felt. What stuck with Emira was that the feeling the *bellua* had in its final moments felt so human to her. Pain mixed with longing. Longing for someone.

She wondered if that was how she would feel when death came for her. If in her final moments, she'll yearn for someone. Mateo's mismatched eyes and boyish grin flashed through her mind.

She wondered if High Priestess Ethel longed for someone in those last seconds, or if all she felt was pain and fear. Emira shuddered from the cold as it started to snow once more. She stared up at the sky, the white frozen liquid falling onto her face and hair. Freezing her even more.

Eventually, she made her way back inside, shaking the cold off of her. A servant was already at the house and averted their eyes immediately after seeing her. Inwardly, Emira sighed, but outwardly she said a polite, "Good morning," and made her way upstairs.

How many doors was it to the room again? Emira counted to the eighth door and then opened it, wringing the snow out of her hair. She didn't realize she was in the wrong room until she opened the wardrobe to take off her cloak and saw clothes unfamiliar to her. Emira glanced over at the bed, and Mateo was lying in the bed, sleeping.

His dark, curly lashes were long against his tanned skin, his mouth slightly open as he breathed deeply. His whole face was relaxed, serene, like he hadn't a care in the world.

He looks like a child when he's sleeping, she thought. Quietly, she made her way to him, like he was gravity and she couldn't help but be drawn to him.

She kneeled down by his bed and brushed a small piece of hair resting on his forehead. And as she did, his eyes flickered open. She started to move backwards, and took her hand from his face, but he grabbed her hand before she could and pulled her closer.

She was filled with his scent. Mint and cedar mixed with laundry detergent. His eyes anchored her to the spot, unable to move away from him.

He gingerly touched her frozen cheek, tracing down her face and her jaw. Staring at her lips, he softly traced over them as well before looking into her eyes.

"Even in my dreams, I can't have you," he murmured. And his mismatched eyes looked somber as he laid back down in his bed, falling fast asleep. Emira kneeled there for a moment more.

What he did warmed her more than a fire ever could. She wrung her hands together, night finally placing its heavy blanket over her. Barely able to keep her eyes open, she curled up on the ground, using her arm as a pillow, and fell asleep.

In her dreams, she was the *bellua*, ripped apart as Mateo's swirling gold and brown eyes glowered at her.

"PRIESTESS?" EMIRA WOKE UP TO MATEO'S SHOCKED AND confused voice. Her eyes flickered open, the morning sunlight blinding her for a brief second before fading to see Mateo's mismatched eyes staring down at her from his bed. He looked… horrified.

She sat up quickly, causing her head to hit his. They both groaned and rubbed their heads as they pulled apart from one another.

"*Ow,*" Mateo said, pointedly.

"Oh, like you haven't hit me on the head before," Emira rolled her eyes. His jaw dropped.

"I've never hit you on the head."

"Do you remember that one sword fighting lesson where the sword fell on my head and I was sporting a nasty bruise for a week?" she retorted.

Mateo stared at her. "That was from *you* dropping your *own* sword."

"Yeah, but you're the one who taught me that move," she said, shrugging. His eyes squinted.

"What are you doing in my room?"

"I don't know what you mean," she said, focusing on the pattern on the rug in his room. *Why didn't I move a few feet over and sleep on the rug?* She couldn't help but think.

"I mean, what are you doing sleeping in my room on the ground?" he repeated. She winced as she continued not to meet his eyes. She wanted to hang and quarter her past self.

"I couldn't sleep," Emira answered. "And so I went outside and walked around your yard, which is massive by the way I don't understand how one person can own this much land and not farm on it, like you should sell some of it to people at a fair price so others can live on this land—"

"Just get to the part where you somehow ended up in my room," Mateo interrupted.

"Well, I was walking around and then I went to go back to my room but I forgot how many doors it was until it was *my* room and I opened this one and didn't realize you were there actually," Emira laughed awkwardly. "And then I was so tired that I fell asleep on the floor."

Mateo stared at her. Emira looked away, deciding to focus on how his room looked. It was plain, a gray paint color on the walls, white moldings making little squares around his room. There wasn't much… of Mateo in it.

"You didn't notice I was here and then fell asleep on the ground," Mateo said, summarizing what Emira said.

"Yup," she said. "So, nothing weird is happening right now."

"Did something weird happen earlier?" he looked genuinely concerned.

"Nope," she lied. "Nothing weird."

"Okay," he said, his expression showing he wasn't convinced.

"Okay," Emira said, nodding her head. They stared at each other for a moment more.

"Could you leave my room?" he asked. She nodded her head again, getting up from the ground.

"Yup, I'll leave now," she said, quickly going to the door.

"And Priestess?" he called out once she opened the door. She turned and tried not to look him in the eyes.

"Yeah?"

"If you need something to be able to sleep better, you can always ask me," he said. "I can get whatever it is that you need."

"Yeah, I can see that," Emira said, gesturing to his room. He looked around his room, confused.

Instead of figuring out what it was she was talking about, he said, "Your room is two doors down from this one. I'll see you later."

"Yeah, I'll see you," Emira said quickly and then left his room. Once she closed his door, she lowered herself to the floor and put her head into her hands.

What in the twelfth circle of hell was that? Why were you acting like that?

She groaned inwardly before getting up and going a couple of doors down and opening it. Luckily, Mateo was right, and it was her room.

She laid back down on the too soft bed with the too much volume pillow and stared up at the ceiling. Her heart was pounding as she replayed what happened in Mateo's room.

"Even in my dreams, I can't have you," he had said. She touched her lips in the way Mateo did, tracing over them.

"You would've been important to me," he had told her before kissing her that one time. *"You're important to me."*

Emira placed an arm over her eyes, obstructing her view of the ceiling. And in the dark, she could see Mateo's eyes, his lips.

She could feel everything he felt when she touched his mind. And she knew, she knew what it was that he felt for her. What he felt for no other before.

And she wished things were different. She prayed, silently, for him to find solace in someone else. Because she could never return his feelings for her.

Because if she did, she knew he would never stop until he could save her. But, he couldn't. Nothing he could do could save her. And it would get him killed.

And she wouldn't be able to save him. It would be a vicious cycle.

And she knew what their future would hold. Loving him would be like loving a house of cards. Constantly waiting with bated breath for it all to fall apart.

CHAPTER THIRTY-NINE

Emira was careful to make sure Mateo and her were never alone for the rest of the week. She and Silas would play chess with one another while Mateo read as much as he could about *bellua*. They all would watch TV with one another, even if it was a Volani game, which was just as brutal and violent as Emira thought it would be. Half the time, she was watching with her hands over her eyes. And neither Emira nor Mateo brought up her sleeping on the floor of his room or what he had said to her, if he even remembered it.

But, sometimes, she could feel his eyes on her when she pretended not to notice.

New Year's Eve came quickly, and Mrs. Cordero apparently had always thrown a huge party. This year was no exception. The servants were hanging decorations, and Emira was helping in the kitchen with Mrs. Cordero and the chef.

"Thanks for helping out, Emira," Mrs. Cordero said, smiling warmly. Emira piped the filling on top of the bottom part of the macaroon. She continued down the line.

"I like doing stuff like this," Emira answered. "It reminds me of when we would get the temple ready for some kind of event." Mrs. Cordero's golden eyes glazed over when Emira mentioned the temple. Her golden eyes never swirled. They were instead flat and metallic, not a hint of ichor within them. Sometimes, they unnerved Emira.

"You had good memories in that temple?" she asked, her voice too nonchalant. Emira bit her cheek as she continued piping.

"Yes," she said. "I know I destroyed it, but I did have great memories there."

"Then why destroy it?" Emira glanced over at her, at Mrs. Cordero's frank question. Would she understand? Would anyone? Emira swallowed the knot building in the back of her throat.

"It felt fitting," she answered, honestly. "It didn't feel right that it was still standing when Priestess Irene was..." Her voice drifted away. She didn't know why she was telling Mrs. Cordero this. But, it was cathartic. Like she was confessing to someone for one last time.

"I understand," Mrs. Cordero said, quietly. "When my mother died, I went to my father's house and wanted to destroy the room that he kept her locked in." Her eyes looked pained as she smiled up at Emira. "But, I couldn't do anything. Sometimes I wish I did do something."

"You're not afraid of me?" Emira asked, ever so quietly. Mrs. Cordero's eyebrow twitched.

"You killed someone, Emira," she said, her voice a little cold. "If I wasn't scared of your anger and power, I wouldn't be human." The words were like little knives piercing her lungs.

"Of course," Emira whispered. She didn't want Mateo's

mother to be scared of her, but she did what she did. And she couldn't even say she regretted it. Emira wanted to utter those words, to say: *I regret killing the high priestess, of course. It was just a momentary lapse of anger.*

But, it wasn't the truth. She never regretted killing Ethel. She didn't think she ever would.

Perhaps, she wasn't human, anymore. Perhaps, she never was one.

Mateo's mom put the tops of the macaroons on the places where Emira piped. "Not to change the subject, but what's your relationship with my son?"

Emira accidentally piped too much onto one macaroon. She panicked and then piped the space beside it as well. She grabbed a towel to wipe it up, and Mrs. Cordero took it from her and fixed it.

"Was that too personal of a question?" Mrs. Cordero asked as she wiped up Emira's mess. Emira could feel the blood rush to her head.

"No, no, not at all," she said, quickly. "I understand wanting to know, since he's your son and all and I'm... Well, me. But, um, we're just friends." Mrs. Cordero glanced over at her, her golden eyes searching.

"Friends?" she asked, her eyebrows furrowed.

Emira nodded. "Just friends. Maybe, someday, *good* friends. Before our untimely death, I mean." She gave a nervous laugh. Mrs. Cordero studied Emira. She didn't like the way Mateo's mom was looking at her, searching for something in her expression.

After a while, she didn't seem to find what it was she was looking for. Her shoulders dropped a little.

"I see the way he looks at you," she finally said, returning to her work. "Friends don't look at each other like that." She smiled at Emira, a smile that didn't quite reach her eyes, as she wiped her hands on her apron and then proceeded to take it off.

"I left a dress in your wardrobe," she said, her smile turning warm and genuine towards Emira like they didn't just talk about how Emira killed someone and how Mateo apparently looks at her as more than a friend.

"Be sure to wear it," she said, pointing at Emira and then leaving the kitchen. Emira stared down at the piping bag in her hands. The chef offered to take it from her, but she continued to pipe the rest of the macaroons and then put the tops on them.

She didn't want to think about what Mrs. Cordero said to her. Emira tried to box up her words and hide them into the back of her mind. A box marked with the words "Do Not Open," filled with memories of Mateo.

But, no matter what she did, the box was overflowing, spilling into the forefront of her mind. And the closer the sacrificial ritual came, the more she thought about him.

Emira decided she definitely was going to steal some glasses of alcohol at the New Year's party. Because she wasn't going to last the whole night being near Mateo sober.

She made her way upstairs to get dressed before the party started. Opening the wardrobe, a dress made of crushed ebony velvet was hanging there. It was floor length, and the neckline dipped lower than Emira was comfortable with. It was a simple dress, and yet it was the most beautiful dress she'd ever seen.

She felt the fabric in her hand and watched as it glittered a little in the light. A diamond necklace was hanging from the hanger as Emira took out the dress. It was ornate and lined with gold.

Emira put the outfit on and looked at herself in the floor

length mirror. The diamonds were clustered like frozen tears around her neck, and the dress only kissed the ground. She didn't know what to do with her hair besides a singular braid down her back. It was the only hairstyle she had mastered that Darlene had taught her.

She quickly did her hair and then looked at herself again, her violet eyes standing out on her light face. Did she always look like this? An otherworldly alien hidden in a slouched teenage girl's body. And part of her wondered what Mateo would think and then shook her head. It didn't matter what Mateo would think because her goal was not to be alone with him the whole night.

She couldn't be. It would ruin everything.

A quick and short knock appeared at her door. Emira looked over her shoulder and called for them to come in. Silas opened the door and stopped, quiet surprise written all over his face.

"What? Is it too much?" Emira asked, looking down at her dress. "Mrs. Cordero insisted that I wear it. I can change into something else. I don't know how fancy this party is going to be." Silas raised his eyebrows and gave a small smile before fully coming into the room. He hardly ever smiled around Emira so the expression took her off guard.

"No, it looks," he cleared his throat, "it looks good... on you."

"Was that as painful for you to say as it was for me to hear?" Emira asked. He nodded his head and let out a laugh.

"Yeah, it was," he said. "People are starting to arrive. Mrs. Cordero asked me to come get you."

"Oh, thanks, Silas," she said walking towards the door. The two of them walked down the stairs to the beginning of the party. As Emira walked into the room, she grabbed a glass from one of the many trays being passed around, and downed the contents quickly, wincing as the liquid burned down her throat. Silas threw her a sidelong glance.

"What?" she asked at his judgmental gaze.

"You need some liquid courage or something?" he said, pointing to her empty glass.

"Something like that," she muttered.

"I've been looking for you two," Mateo said from behind him. "These parties are just a lot of talking to—Oh, yes, hi. It's been a while." His words got interrupted as an older woman with red hair and her husband came up to him.

They made pleasant small talk for a little while until the older woman pointed out a girl across the room, her clone but younger, "Oh, Isla is here, too. I remember you two being good friends." Silas snorted.

Mateo threw a glare in his direction before resuming his polite, cold exterior. "Yes, we hang out at school."

"Of course you two do," the woman said before seeing someone else she knew and excitedly going over there. Her husband followed after her. Emira didn't think he said more than two words in the whole conversation.

She glanced over at Isla who was talking to Celeste. Her gaze washed over the redhead. Her hair was neat, straight, and shiny like a red gloss. She was wearing a crimson red dress that accentuated her figure nicely. Emira's hand unconsciously went to her unruly curly hair, only tamed by a single braid.

"I need another drink," she muttered. Mateo's mismatched eyes glanced over at her. His gaze dipped down towards the necklace that hung around her long neck before meeting her eyes once more.

"I don't know if that's a good idea," he murmured. With the liquid courage already coursing through her veins, she glared up at him.

"I don't care what you think," she said before turning on her heel and walking away. She found another tray with a glass of alcohol and downed it. Mateo, from across the room, grabbed a glass next to him, downed it, grabbed another one, and knocked that one back as well, his eyes on her the entire time. Emira made a face at him.

"The Astorias," someone said. And Shiloh walked in with her family close behind her. Emira let out a breath of relief and ran up to her. Her chestnut brown hair was pulled into a beautiful updo, and she was wearing a sage green gown.

"I'm so glad you're here," Emira gushed, hugging her friend. Shiloh hugged her back and looked at her.

"This dress looks like it was made for you," she said.

"Mrs. Cordero got it for me," Emira said, almost guilty. "She's been very kind to me."

"Dahlia is one of the kindest socialites around," Shiloh agreed, her eyes searching for the hostess.

"Is Darlene, Kanoa, and Atlas coming?" Emira asked, her voice hopeful. She needed some allies, someone to distract her. Shiloh shook her head.

"These parties are for the first families only," she said. "Celeste probably could've brought Kanoa with her, but her family wouldn't approve."

"Wouldn't approve of Kanoa?" Shiloh nodded her head. "But why?"

"He's not from a great family," she explained. "Plus, dating isn't exactly allowed for us."

"You're not allowed to date?" Emira asked.

"It's complicated," Shiloh muttered. Her eyes narrowed as she finally looked at Emira properly.

"Are you drinking?" she asked. Emira shrugged.

"I may or may not be," she answered, her lips curling upwards. Shiloh rolled her eyes and then smiled at her.

"You're going to be a handful tonight," she said.

"You could say that again," Emira muttered, looking through her lashes at Mateo who was flitting around the room. Playing the part of the perfect hostess' son, for one last time.

"What happened during the Winter Solstice ball?" Shiloh asked, her voice dipping low. Emira's eyebrows furrowed as she remembered the events from a week ago. The *immanis bellua's* pleading echoed in her mind: *Please, kill me.* She flinched.

"Why weren't you there?" she answered with a question of her own.

Shiloh shrugged. "I told my parents I didn't feel like going. Plus, with all of us there, it would've been more chaotic."

"We escaped and found a *bellua*," Emira said, her voice lowering. "It spoke to us but died shortly after." She didn't know why she didn't tell Shiloh it was an *immanis*. For some reason, she wanted to shield the information from her. Not because she was worried about Balan, but because she was worried about how Shiloh would start to look at her.

"You didn't see what you looked like when you came back," Shiloh had said to her. And Emira still remembered the fear that lingered in her brown eyes.

"You didn't get it to talk more?"

"Well, it was going to kill us," Emira shrugged.

"What did it say?" Shiloh's eyes were lit up, excited about solving the puzzle that was laid out before her.

"'The twelve humans came, the ones who smell like you three, and took from us,'" Emira whispered the memorized words to Shiloh. The brunette bowed her head at hearing the words and nodded to herself.

"When school starts again, and if we have the chance, we should go to the National Library in Astutera," Shiloh said. "The *bellua's* words… I'm sure I've read a book that might be an answer."

"I'll come with you," Emira said and then clicked her tongue in frustration. "If I'm allowed to leave Leliara once we get back." Shiloh narrowed her eyes.

"What happened?" she asked.

"It's a long story," Emira muttered, watching Mateo talk to Isla and Celeste. Isla batted her big brown eyes and played with her hair and… *Idols, I need a drink.*

Shiloh followed Emira's gaze and then looked back at her as Emira grabbed another glass and knocked it back. The burning felt like some sort of cathartic punishment.

"I didn't know Mateo and Isla were close friends," Shiloh said, like she was testing the waters. Emira laughed and nodded her head.

"Oh, they're closer than close," Emira said. "I saw her in his room. Without any clothes on." Her voice was becoming shrill as she laughed some more. Shiloh gave her a look marred with pity, her own eyes darkening as she glanced over at the leader of the hellions.

"I'll get you another glass," she said after a while.

"Sounds good," Emira nodded.

After seven glasses of various types of cocktails, Emira could hardly stand up straight as she walked down the long, dark hallway. The people downstairs were starting to count down to midnight, the New Year.

Her head was pounding and she was tired, exhausted. Shiloh and her had danced the whole night, drinking and laughing about various things. And Emira's legs felt like jelly, she needed to lay down. Shiloh had offered to come with her, but Emira had waved the offer away. She pulled the heels she was wearing off of her feet and continued down the hallway.

Squinting, she saw two figures in the distance. She wondered if it were Silas and Mateo but as she squinted more, the figures were much too close to one another.

"Three, two, one! Happy New Year!" the party goers shouted downstairs. And Emira watched as Isla planted a kiss onto Mateo's lips.

CHAPTER FORTY

Emira stared, frozen in place. Cheers erupted downstairs, and she felt her heels slip out of her hands and clatter to the ground, her stomach twisting. Mateo and Isla pulled away from each other, and the look Mateo gave her… She wanted to rip it out of her memory.

She should've taken Shiloh's offer, it was all she could think about.

"Emira?" he asked. His voice seemed to echo all around her, suffocating her. Emira shook her head, backing away from the two of them.

His eyebrows knitted together as he took a hesitant step towards her, and it was enough to make her run away. She didn't want to look at him, she couldn't see that look in his face.

The image of Isla pressing her lips against his was burned into her memory, blurring her sight. She ran, barefoot, into the gardens outside, Mateo calling after her.

The snow was so cold that it burned her feet as she ran. The winter air suffocated her lungs and sobered her up more. Tears burned her cheeks and she wiped them quickly away. She tried to run faster when she heard Mateo's footsteps behind her, but instead of moving her legs, she ended up tripping over her own feet.

She fell to the ground in the most ungraceful way and just held her head in her hands.

Why Lystos, why? It was all she could manage to think through the noise of her mind.

"Emira," Mateo said, panting as he looked down at her. He kneeled down and peeled her hands away from her face. His mismatched eyes were wide and were stirring slightly, like they always did. And Emira imagined she probably could get drunk staring into them for too long. More drunk than she was right now. His eyes flickered towards her bare feet.

"Where are your shoes?"

"In the hallway, I reckon," Emira said, bitterly.

"Why—" He stopped himself and shook his head, like he was dealing with a child who was trying to make life difficult for him. Mateo tried to take his shoes off, and she recoiled away from him and managed to stand back up on her own two feet. The world felt like it was spinning.

"Emira, please put on my shoes," he nearly begged.

"I don't need your stupid shoes," she cried out.

"What's wrong?"

"What's *wrong*?" She repeated his question like the answer was obvious. He was standing there, his hair slicked back, his suit impeccably black as always. And he was beautiful. The most beautiful being in all of Constellatia. Her eyebrows pulled upwards as her eyes widened, almost pleading with him. She opened her mouth, and then closed it, tightening her lips into a line. It was as if she were trapped inside her own rib cage, banging against her chest with her fists.

"Nothing's wrong," Emira mouthed, trying to walk away

from him. His hands wrapped themselves around her wrist and turned her around.

"Can you—please, just talk to me," Mateo murmured. His voice, not much louder than the wind.

"What do you want me to say?" she asked, her expression crumpling. *Don't cry, don't cry. Don't, especially in front of him.*

"Is this because of Isla kissing me? Because I—"

"I couldn't care less who you kiss or sleep with. Sleep with and kiss whoever you want. Kiss to your heart's content. Why would *I* care?" Emira nearly shouted. She took a deep breath and wrapped her arms around herself.

Mateo stared at her for a long time. Emira didn't know how much time passed as her words seemed to take root in his brain.

"Why *do* you care?" he asked, his voice low.

Emira felt the tears burn her eyes. *Idol of Life,* please *don't cry.* "Don't you have to go back to your—whatever she is to you?" He frowned, his mismatched eyes starting a fire in the pit of her stomach.

"Why do you care?" he repeated, softer this time.

She looked away. "I don't."

"Don't you and Atlas have something going on?" he asked, taking a step forward. Emira furrowed her eyebrows together.

"Me and Atlas? There's nothing going on with me and Atlas," she said. "Atlas is—" She stopped herself. It wasn't her place to tell him.

"Atlas is what?" Mateo asked.

"Atlas is no one," she finished, her voice barely above a whisper. "We're just friends."

"So, you're not with Atlas," he said. It looked like he was processing something, like this was new information.

"Did you think that I was?" Emira asked. "*Me?*"

"Why do you say it like that? It's an obvious conclusion," he said.

Emira laughed without emotion. "An obvious conclusion? Maybe to someone with half a brain. You think it's obvious that I like Atlas?"

"Well," Mateo scratched the back of his head. "I don't know."

"I don't have any feelings for Atlas," Emira said. "We're hardly around each other." She pleaded internally that she didn't have to say it. That he would just figure it out himself.

But, it didn't look like that was going to happen. She wiped away the tears that slipped through her grasp.

"Never mind," she muttered. "Just leave me alone." She started to walk away, and Mateo quickly stepped into her path. His mismatched eyes were pleading.

"Priestess," he whispered that stupid nickname to her. The stupid nickname that she found herself looking forward to hearing. His thumb wiped away a stray tear as he stared deep into her violet eyes.

"Do you *really* think I want to kiss anyone else?" he murmured.

"Then why?" Emira asked. He looked pained.

"Because," he fingered a stray curl of hers, "Because it was the only way to get you out of my mind. I thought…" His hand lightly made its way around the back of her head and held her there, staring into her eyes. And his own were swirling around, like how they were in front of the *immanis bellua*. Dangerously powerful.

"Idol of Life," he whispered. "You're going to ruin me."

And then his lips crashed onto hers. And it was as if universes exploded and were remade between them. And she let herself go, her hands entwining in his hair. Pulling him as close to her as she could.

She could feel his mind, his thoughts exploding around her. Like his essence was trying to consume her. And for the first time in a long time, Emira felt safe. Truly, utterly free.

And then, there was a churning in her stomach that progressively got worse as time went on, and she abruptly pulled away. Mateo's expression was contorted into concern, and Emira doubled over and threw up on the shiny black shoes he tried to make her wear.

She wiped her mouth, looked up at him apologetically, and then felt the spinning bring her closer to the ground. She saw him roll his eyes before he caught her. Just in time, as she was about to collapse into her own puddle of vomit.

She shivered from the winter air, and Mateo lifted her off of her feet and cradled her into his chest. He carried her through the party, and surely they got a few weird looks but Emira couldn't care less, and put her into her own bed.

Emira reached up and touched Mateo's brow as he tucked her in. He gave her a pained smile, his eyes going from warm to cold, like he wasn't sure how he was supposed to be feeling.

"We can't be together, can we?" she whispered. His expression contorted. He held her hand and pulled it away from his face. But, he kept holding it as he studied her.

They were both sacrifices, they couldn't be together. And loving each other... It would be dangerous. Even in Emira's intoxicated state, she could recognize it.

"Do you remember when I met you?" he asked, his low voice barely above a whisper. Emira nodded her head, cuddling into her blanket.

"I knew then that you would be my undoing," he murmured. Emira gazed up at him, the alcohol making the lines around his head fuzzy. Like there was a glow around him.

"I hope they kill me before you," she whispered. A thought

that she had kept boxed up, a thought that she never, ever wanted to admit to herself, let alone him. But the thought slipped out, hung there like a dagger between them, waiting for someone to grab it. She felt him stiffen, and he let go of her hand.

"I don't think I could watch you die before me," she explained, her eyes closing. "But, I want you to still be with me, in the end."

"Why would you say that to me," he barely breathed. "Why would you curse me with that?"

Emira's eyes opened and looked at him. He hung his head, his brown hair shrouding the side of his brown eye. His gold one was looking down at her blanket, searching for something in the pattern.

She reached out her hand and gently touched the top of his.

"We can't rewrite the stars," she whispered. "But, I wouldn't mind."

"You wouldn't mind what?" Mateo asked, not looking at her.

"I wouldn't mind loving you until the end," she breathed. Her fingers wrapped around the metaphorical dagger in her mind's eye and plunged it into the middle of his chest with her next words, the words she had kept hidden from herself.

"Because, I think I might be a little bit in love with you, Mateo Cordero." And with those words, she felt sleep whisk her away.

In her dreams, she felt Mateo kiss the top of her forehead.

"I think I'm a lot a bit in love with you, Emira," he had whispered. And it turned her dreams into a whisper of baby pink.

CHAPTER FORTY-ONE

When they got back to Leliara, Emira avoided Mateo like the plague. Anytime she saw him in the hallways, he'd raise a hand to greet her, and she'd run the other way like a madwoman. Because, once the floaty feeling disappeared and the harsh light of day creeped in, she realized she had made a terrible mistake admitting what she did.

She was a sacrifice. No matter who the Idols were, no matter what Constellatia was found on, no matter who she was becoming, she couldn't be in love with Mateo Cordero because she was going to die. And, if she admitted it to herself, she didn't know what she was capable of doing.

"Why are you desperately avoiding Mateo Cordero like he has three heads that are going to eat you alive?" Darlene asked one day at dinner.

"No reason," Emira said, shoveling in food. Shiloh took the spot next to her.

"Probably because she puked on him at the New Year's party his mother threw," Shiloh teased, bumping her shoulder. Emira closed her eyes as she felt her stomach drop. *Does everyone from the party know what happened?*

"I can't believe I didn't get an invite," Darlene moaned. She didn't even comment on the puking, which only meant she had already heard about it. *Great.*

"The Cordero New Year's Eve party is always the first twelve families and anyone who's anyone only, and any plus ones the others bring," Shiloh said. "It's stupid and elitist, but our families, unfortunately, stick together."

"Was Kanoa there?" Darlene asked, as nonchalantly as possible.

"He wasn't," Shiloh confirmed. Darlene's eyes brightened and glanced up to see Kanoa eating with Celeste, and her obsidian eyes darkened once more.

"Why don't you just tell him?" Shiloh asked, softly. Darlene threw a glare in her direction. She started talking about something or other, but Emira didn't hear it as the noise around her disappeared when she saw Mateo walking straight towards her.

His mismatched eyes were large and open, vulnerable, as he walked up to her. *"I think I'm a lot a bit in love with you, Emira,"* his words echoed around in her head. She immediately grabbed her things, stuffed more food into her mouth, and got up from the table just as Mateo reached it.

"Hi," he managed to say. His voice could nearly bring Emira to her knees. With her mouth full, she gave a quick wave and then booked it out of the food hall.

She heard Darlene say, "Idols, Mateo, what did you do to her?" as Emira fled the scene. All she could think about was that moment with Mateo. Their second kiss together and a proclamation of love, but what was that going to do?

Emira didn't want to hold his hand (she did, desperately) and she didn't want to kiss him (again, she did very much) but even if she did, what was she supposed to do about it? They would get attached and then he would watch her die, or she would watch him die, and it would become a bloodbath.

Even if the Idols were liars, they still protected Constellatia. Wherever the *belluas* came from, they were still a terror to all citizens. The Idols protected the walls. She couldn't let anything happen during the sacrificial ritual. It would change the world as they knew it. It had to go as planned. She *needed* it to go as planned. Because if it didn't, she would've lost every part of herself she thought she knew.

And Emira could tell, if she let Mateo get attached, he would do anything to save her.

"You remind him of his cousin," Silas had said to her. And he didn't save his cousin, Cassandra. He couldn't. He was only eight years old. And an eight-year-old couldn't be a hero. A seventeen-year-old very much could become one. Or become a radical. A revolutionary.

She shook the thoughts out of her head as she entered her dorm room. Because the Breaker of Bones competition in Pyrinia was starting to take place, since it was the month of Nyria, their history teacher, Mrs. Hawthorne, assigned a research paper to be written about the competition. Emira needed to concentrate on that. On graduating.

On at least accomplishing something in her short life.

She held her pencil above the sheets of paper and thought about everything she had learned and read about the Breaker of Bones. It was created after the second Tenth Year had occurred. And it was a way to get the people of Pyrinia to show off their physical prowess. But, it was a hard competition. A competition where they would fight to the death. The strongest, the fittest, would be the lone survivor of the whole competition. It was brutal.

"Are you writing the history paper?" Shiloh asked, slipping into the room. Darlene wasn't with her.

"Well, trying to," Emira said, turning to look at her. Shiloh took a seat at her own desk and pulled out a bunch of books.

"I was thinking," she said, "We could use the research paper as an excuse to go to the National Library in Astutera."

"That's a good idea, actually," Emira said, nodding her head. "And we could also do actual research for the paper. I need a source on why the Breaker of Bones even started."

"I'm sure it's just because there wasn't a war anymore and Nyro was bored," Shiloh said, surprisingly rough.

"You don't believe we should follow the Idols anymore," Emira guessed, her voice low. Shiloh shrugged.

"Balan's diary... I mean, it shows all his inner thoughts, his desires. And power, power was above everything else. Even the woman he loved was below it," Shiloh said. "I don't trust that he or any of the others have our best interests at heart. I think they're just playing god."

"Don't say that," Emira said, her voice stern. "You can't think like that. When I'm gone—"

"Yeah, I've been thinking about that a lot, actually," Shiloh said. "I don't think you should go quietly into the light, E." Emira stared at the blank pages in front of her, the white filling her vision. She looked over at Shiloh. Her friend's gaze was exacting, determined. It frightened her.

"What?"

"I think you should fight back against it," she clarified. "You have all the ichor of Mali. And yeah, she's had years to hone her power, but you could do the same thing. You could fight back. At least make it hard for her. Show the viewers and the rest of the country the inhumanity of the Idols, and a revolution will start."

Emira went quiet. She turned away from Shiloh and stared out the window. The outside was awash in a white powder.

"I don't want to be the start of a revolution," Emira said, quietly. She could feel Shiloh's disappointed gaze on her.

"They ordered for the woman who raised you to die," Shiloh pointed out. "Just for hiding the fact that you had ichor from them."

"It's against the law for a reason," Emira muttered. "No, I don't think she should've died. And I want to pull the intestines out of Ophelia."

"But?"

"But, if there's a revolution, if I start one, think about everyone who would die. You, Silas, Kanoa, and Darlene—I'm sure—would join the revolutionary efforts, and your lives will be cut short. I want to die knowing that the rest of you—that you guys can live long lives and have your own families," Emira said. "That's why I'm doing this. Because it's for the good of Constellatia. If there's a revolution, Shiloh, war is brutal. There is no good or evil, there is no more innocence. And we'd be taking it from the world. The chance at life."

"That's nice," Shiloh said. "That's a lovely dream, E. But, what about *our* lives? What about all the future lives to come? Because having a family? That wouldn't happen for us either. I have ichor. The person I marry—if I marry—will probably also have ichor because the only people I will be able to meet would be the other warriors that I work with. That I am protecting on a daily basis. Our kids would have a huge chance of having ichor. And what if my kid has all the ichor of one of the Idols? Am I supposed to give them up after knowing they're hoaxes?"

"Shi…"

"You might not want to start a revolution. But, it's going to start with or without you," Shiloh said. "I would hope you'd want to save yourself instead of letting yourself die for no real reason."

"We don't know who the *bellua* are or where they came from, Shi," Emira said, turning fully towards her. "We don't know what the Idols took from them. We, honestly, don't even know the full extent of their power. You'd be starting a war that you would know you'd lose."

"Well, I have a plan for that," Shiloh said, her eyes steeling.

"Really? And what would that be?"

"When we find out what it is the Idols took from the *bellua*, and where the *bellua* came from, you can take what it is they took. You and Mateo. And then the two of you would be just as strong as the Idols. Perhaps stronger, because of all the years of genetic mixing, who knows what the extent of your power is currently. With whatever they took, you two would be unstoppable," Shiloh said.

"You'd want us to take what they took? Damn the *belluas* more?" Emira asked. Shiloh knitted her eyebrows together.

"Damn them?"

"There's something else the *immanis bellua* said," Emira confessed. Shiloh's eyes grew wide.

"Holy shit, Emira. An *immanis bellua*? You never mentioned that," she said.

"I wasn't supposed to," Emira muttered. "But, after it told us about the Idols, it said they left them like this. Like monsters."

"So, what the Idols took from the *bellua* left them like how they are now?" Shiloh asked, leaning forward. Emira nodded her head. Shiloh pulled out her notebook that she was using to take notes on Balan's diary and started to scribble something in there.

"Interesting," Shiloh said, scratching her neck. "I think I have a theory on who the *bellua* are. But, the hellions are going to call me crazy."

"Who do you think they are?"

Shiloh leaned over her notebook and started to write something more. "I don't want to reveal it now. Not until I can confirm it." She pushed her glasses up her nose as she glanced up at Emira.

"It's only a hypothesis," she insisted. Emira looked at Shiloh, at her flushed cheeks and her wide brown eyes, and goosebumps started to appear on her arms. Whatever it was Shiloh was thinking, it excited her. And with the way her friend's thoughts were heading towards...

"For the record, no matter who the *bellua* are, I'm still not going to steal whatever it was that the Idols stole, and I'm not starting a revolution," Emira clarified. The feeling of the *bellua's* mind when it died snaked its way back into her bones. She shuddered. Shiloh gave her a long stare.

"I think you'll eventually change your mind," she said.

EMIRA, DARLENE, AND SHILOH STOOD IN FRONT OF THE GRAND orange and white building called the National Library of Astutera. It was the biggest library in all of Constellatia, and Emira was surprised she was even allowed to go. Headmistress Alessia had been wishy-washy on whether the three of them could go for their research paper.

"*Aren't there adequate books in the Leliara library?*" she had asked.

"*The books in the school library only touch the surface on the national phenomenon of the yearly Breaker of Bones competition,*"

Shiloh had argued. *"How are we supposed to write a compelling research paper with the poor things that you call informative books?"*

Headmistress Alessia couldn't argue with that so the three of them were taken to the National Library.

"I've never seen you so passionate over something," Darlene said to Shiloh as they walked into the National Library. There were ceiling to floor bookshelves filled with books. And as Emira looked up towards the high domed ceiling, there were floors and floors of them.

"I think arguing might be my calling," Shiloh said. "If this revolution thing doesn't work out for me, I might end up in Serpel after my warrior days, being a lawyer." Darlene didn't even flinch at Shiloh mentioning a revolution, which told Emira the two of them had already been talking about it. Perhaps, extensively. She pressed her tongue against the back of her teeth.

"You'd make a good one," Darlene said, smiling. "And after my warrior days, I'll be a famous actress, and I'll hire you as my personal lawyer, in case anyone tries to sue me."

"Why would anyone sue you?"

Darlene shrugged. "Your guess is as good as mine. But mark my words, it'll happen."

The three of them walked up to the library desk, and Shiloh showed her library card. Emira and Darlene exchanged looks.

"You just happen to have a National Library card?" Darlene said.

"I don't *happen* to have it," Shiloh said. "I got it a while ago."

"How? Only researchers get those privileges," Darlene said, putting a hand on her hip. "I thought we'd have to use our seductress powers to get in."

"Seductress powers?"

"You know what I mean. How did you get it?" Darlene insisted.

Shiloh rolled her eyes. "You know how."

"Ah right, why need researcher privileges when you got daddy privileges?" Darlene muttered. Shiloh threw her a dirty look.

"I know I get things handed to me, but at least it's helping us," Shiloh said, under her breath. Darlene gave Emira a look which Emira understood.

The first twelve families got whatever they wanted. They had a shit ton of stellae, and they could buy their way into office, into being the head of a company, really into anything. It wasn't fair at all. But, it wasn't as if the citizens of Constellatia had much choice in their future anyway. It really depended on where you were born.

A Pyrinian, even if they're gifted in the arts, would most likely become a guard to scout the walls and protect the Idols and anyone else that needed protection or a police officer, or even a blacksmith. But never a painter.

An Astuterian, even if they've dreamed of becoming a doctor, would most likely become a teacher, or librarian, or a researcher because that's what most Astuterians did.

There were only a few that would step out of the mold. It was something that happened fairly rarely. It was why Emira was convinced she would become a priestess, even if that's not what she had wanted. She didn't really have a choice. No one did. Except, of course, the twelve families.

Shiloh stopped a librarian's assistant. "We're looking for books on the ancient species, the ones that inhabited Constellatia before humans." The librarian's assistant looked at the three of them, her eyes lingering on Emira. Emira was wearing sunglasses in order for people not to recognize her as Idol adjacent or as the sacrifice that murdered the High Priestess of the Temple of Night and destroyed the temple with her mind.

"Sunglasses aren't allowed in the library," the librarian's assistant drawled, her tone bored.

"I have pink eye," Emira lied. It came so naturally to her now, breaking the rules, lying.

Who even am I?

The librarian's assistant narrowed her eyes. "It's still not allowed."

"The books on the ancient species?" Shiloh asked, interrupting the stare down the librarian's assistant was doing.

"The elven race? It's on the fourth floor," she said, throwing Emira a glare. She motioned for Emira to take the sunglasses off and Emira, reluctantly, did. The librarian's assistant's eyes got big once she saw Emira's violet ones.

"I'm pretty sure they don't call themselves elves," Shiloh muttered to herself, not noticing what was going on around her. "Let's head to the fourth floor." Darlene linked arms with Emira, smiled brilliantly at the librarian's assistant that was frozen to the floor by fear—or reverence—and followed after Shiloh.

"Idol of Life, if I had people looking at me like that every time I left the house, I would become a recluse," Darlene said, looking over her shoulder at the panicked librarian's assistant. "I mean, you're still a person. Just because your eyes are all unnatural and—"

"Thanks, Darlene."

"You know what I mean! Your eyes might be abnormal, but you're still a human being with *feelings*," she said. Shiloh turned around once she reached the staircase, her hands on her hips. Emira had never seen Shiloh so authoritative before.

"Could you guys please hurry up? We only have an hour here, and I want to read as many books as I can," Shiloh said.

"Why don't you use your fancy schmancy National Library card and take some books out?" Darlene retorted.

"We told Headmistress Alessia that we were researching the Breaker of Bones competition. If I bring back books on the ancient species, she'll know we lied to get here," Shiloh said. Darlene twisted her lips.

"I guess you're right about that."

"So, let's pick up the pace, please and thank you!" Shiloh exclaimed as she ran up the steps.

CHAPTER FORTY-TWO

Before coming to Leliara, climbing four flights of stairs would've been hard for Emira. After training her body for the past few months, the four flights of stairs were still incredibly difficult to climb, but not as bad as it would've been. Shiloh and Darlene barely broke a sweat.

"Oh, here is the elf section," Shiloh muttered to herself, turning sharply. She ran her finger down the spines on the shelves and then grabbed what seemed like random books. She handed Darlene some and some to Emira and grabbed a pile for herself.

"All right, we divide and conquer, okay?" Shiloh said once they sat down at one of the tables. The library was comfortably quiet, and the three of them tried to keep their voices to a whisper as there were others around reading and researching at the wooden round tables.

Emira opened up the first book she had in her pile and started reading. Shiloh was right. The elven race didn't call themselves "elves" but rather *dryadales*. They inhabited Constellatia before humans were even a thought in the universe, supposedly. There were a few facts about their civilization, and how they were community driven. They weren't traveling creatures, opting to stay near giant mountains or dormant volcanos.

In all of Emira's teachings, she had never heard about them. Humans were the beginning of history for her, the Idols saving them from extinction once the *bellua* came about. Her head ached as she tried to reckon with the new information when it went against everything she had ever learned. Was any of it true? Or was everyone in Constellatia learning only carefully constructed lies? She put a hand to her temple, leaning it against her hand as she flipped through the pages and found a drawing of one of the *dryadales*.

Pure white hair, like the snow that covered the ground outside, with little braids throughout the curtain of white and skin that was charcoal black with an undertone of blue. Their arms had bands of blue tattoos on their skin and the tips of their pointed ears were dipped in blue ink as well. Some of them had blue dots around their eyes and some had them on their necks.

Emira had never heard about them. Never did Priestess Irene ever talk about a race that existed before the humans. She flipped through more pages and read the final note about the *dryadales*.

The dryadale race was destroyed when a
meteor hit the world. Unfortunately, they were
reduced to ash, as well as their inventions
and way of life.

"Here," Emira said, showing Darlene and Shiloh the words. "It says here they were destroyed before humans were in the picture." Shiloh gave Emira a look.

"What?" Emira asked, slowly putting the book down.

"The Idols write the histories," Shiloh said. "We can't believe that it's the truth. They probably still exist outside the walls."

Darlene showed the book she was reading, her eyes lighting up. "Look, it says that the *dryadales* had jewel-like eyes. Crystalline in nature. Sound familiar?" She looked over at Emira as if to compare her eyes to the description in her book.

"So, whatever it was the Idols stole, it changed their physiology," Shiloh murmured, poring over the pile of books she had herself.

"You know, now that we're talking about their physiology changing," Darlene whispered. "It says here that the *dryadales* were known for their height. That they were incredibly tall."

"And who else is incredibly big and tall?" Shiloh said, her own eyes lighting up. They both glanced at Emira. She bit her tongue as the realization dawned on her.

"The Pyrinians," she breathed.

"So, does this mean Kanoa is part elf?" Darlene said, one of her eyebrows raising. She seemed to like that idea.

Shiloh turned towards Emira. "You've seen Nyro, right?"

"I have," Emira said. She remembered what the Idol of War and Power looked like. Large, big, and had an overpowering presence. As well as abnormally unnerving silver eyes.

"Did he look like the *dryadales*?"

"I mean, we've seen paintings of him. He doesn't, really, does he?" Darlene half-answered and half-asked. A delicate eyebrow of hers raised.

Emira shook her head. "He had dark brown skin, but it wasn't charcoal black like this. He's just... he's big. Like all Pyrinians."

"His stature might've changed when they took whatever it is they stole," Shiloh mused.

"And it must've been passed down in the genes as all Pyrinians are pretty big and tall in stature," Darlene pointed out.

Shiloh groaned as she closed another book. "We just need to figure out what it was they would have stolen."

"And why stealing whatever it was turned the *dryadales* into *bellua*," Darlene added.

"If the books are written by the Idols, or under Idol supervision, would they ever mention it?" Emira asked. "Wouldn't they hide whatever it was they stole so that no one would be able to figure it out?"

Shiloh twisted her lips as her brown eyes glazed over in thought. She lit up as she closed the books that were in Emira's and Darlene's hands. She brought her voice down to barely a whisper.

"The special edition section," Shiloh said.

"Special edition section?" Darlene asked, bewildered.

"Yes, there's a section that only the descendants of the twelve families can go into," Shiloh said. "Although, only my father can enter."

"Why?" Emira asked.

"He's the head of the Astoria family. Only one person can go in per family."

"So, how are *we* going to get in?" Darlene asked. "I don't suppose your father is around, is he?"

"Why do you think it'll be in there?" Emira asked.

"My father knows things. Things that aren't in books. He likes to brag about his knowledge, it was how I knew about the ancient species in the first place, before coming across a book which mentioned them. I'm guessing the Idols have to clue some people into their ruse in order for this to have gone on for so long. The first twelve families had to know what was going on, in reality. They would've known the Idols didn't come from the heavens. And Balan's diary details some kind of war with the last regime," Shiloh explained. "The truth about the *dryadales* may very well be in that section of the library."

"Okay, that's great and everything, but again, how are *we* supposed to get in?" Darlene asked. Shiloh's smile faded a little.

"It's a risk, but I could say I'm going in place of my father. He is pretty busy," she said.

"Yeah, representing the Inficium province in parliament," Darlene said.

"Exactly," Shiloh smiled. "He needed to send his only, and filial, daughter to the National Library to look over something and bring him notes. It makes sense."

"And no one really knows you're friends with Mateo," Darlene pointed out, starting to get the idea. "So, they wouldn't suspect you at all."

"But, Darlene and I wouldn't be able to come in," Emira said. Shiloh nodded her head.

"It would only be me." Darlene exchanged a look with Emira.

"It could work," she finally said. A twisting feeling appeared in the pit of Emira's stomach. As if something felt wrong about this plan, like something bad was going to happen. She bit her tongue and tried to will the feeling away. They were in the National Library of Astutera. What could happen to a prominent politician's daughter in the special edition section of the library? It was, most likely, heavily guarded if it carried the secrets of the Idols.

And yet, the feeling wouldn't go away.

The three of them got up, returned the pile of books on *dryadales*, and started towards the special edition section of the National Library.

As they walked closer to their destination, the twisting feeling in her abdomen turned into a weird one, one that filled all of her limbs and made her feel alert, like she was being watched. She looked over her shoulder, but no one was looking her way. Darlene's expression contorted as she looked over her own shoulder as well. Their gazes met, eyes both wide.

"Does it feel like someone's watching us?" she whispered to Emira. Emira nodded. The hair on her body was standing up, her skin pickled in goosebumps. Someone was watching them. And she felt like she was being hunted.

"Okay, you guys wait here, I'll be back in a second," Shiloh whispered, not noticing their hushed conversation. She walked up to the person guarding the special edition section of the library, flashed her ID and her National Library card, and the guard led her inside. The orange ornate doors, murals of foxes on it, closed with a resounding thud that echoed throughout the library.

Darlene's head was on a swivel as she looked around them. Her eyebrows were furrowed, and she looked like she was going to be sick.

"What's wrong?" Emira asked.

"We're being watched," she whispered, her voice losing any of its upbeat-ness. "I can *feel* it."

"It might just be because of my eyes," Emira mused. "I'm sure it's fine." Darlene's gaze was hard as she looked at the people around them. No one was watching them, their heads stuck in books, but Emira also couldn't shake the feeling.

"I hope you're right," Darlene said. "I just… I have a bad feeling." She shook her head and rolled her shoulders back before opening her eyes once more.

"You're probably right," she repeated. "It's probably nothing." At least, Emira hoped it was nothing.

She changed the subject, just to get the feeling out of her

mind. "How were the holidays?" Darlene rolled her eyes at the question.

"Oh, it was the worst. Family drama, you know? First of all, getting to Fonsia is *such* a pain," Darlene said. She was right. Fonsia was the only province which floated in the air. There weren't walls around Fonsia because the only way to reach the province was by hot air balloon or if you had wings.

"I heard those lines are massive," Emira said.

"*Massive!*" Darlene exclaimed. "And so I wait for hours to hitch a ride home, then my mother starts going in about my grades, and then she had a panic attack when she realized how close to graduation I was."

"Your mom isn't excited about you graduating?" Emira asked. Darlene's gaze turned to stone.

"My mom was a warrior," she said, her voice flat. "She never wanted me to have the same fate."

"But, being a warrior is such an honor! You're protecting Constellatia and the citizens in it," Emira said. Darlene gave her a sidelong glance.

"You've fought two *bellua*, right? Easy enough for you and Mateo, sure. But for the rest of us… Imagine fighting *bellua* day in and day out, your closest friends die and you couldn't do anything to save them but somehow *you* survived," Darlene said. She looked away from her. "There is no honor in war, Emira."

"I'm sorry," Emira said, under her breath. "I didn't realize."

"Some warriors are better at compartmentalizing. After they're released, a lot of them go on to live good, normal lives. My mom… My mom fell apart," Darlene said, staring into space. "She couldn't handle it."

"Are you worried about becoming a warrior?" Emira asked. Darlene looked suddenly interested in a book on the shelf next to them. She fingered it, running her pointer finger along the spine, over the raised puckered letters.

"I try to practice compartmentalizing, to not give into my emotions. But, I'm an emotional person like my mother. And sometimes… Sometimes I have nightmares that I'm stuck in my own head like she is," Darlene whispered. "I'm worried that I get too attached."

Emira nodded her own head. "That's why you do the no feelings thing." Darlene looked up at her, chewed on her cheek, and then nodded.

"If I'm attached, and I lose them in the future, I don't think I'll ever recover," she breathed. "I think I'll hear their dying voice for the rest of my life, just like my mother."

"Is that why you push Kanoa away?" Emira asked, softly. Darlene narrowed her eyes and then sighed.

"What exactly did Shiloh tell you?" she said. "I swear to Lystos, that girl can't keep a secret to save her life."

"She said you two slept together," Emira answered, honestly. "And that you were crying a lot about it last year."

Darlene looked up towards the ceiling, her fingers curling into her palms, and then let out a long sigh.

"Yes, Kanoa and I slept together. I thought it would be like everyone else, you know? Just… a warm body," Darlene muttered, fingering the bracelet on her wrist. "But, it wasn't like that. It was… deep. Like he reached the core of me and made a home there."

"And you didn't want to get attached," Emira guessed. Darlene shrugged.

"He said that it was meant to be. That he never felt like that before. That there was an invisible string tying us closer and closer together. And the worst part? I could feel it. I knew what he was talking about," she whispered. Her ebony eyes shimmered with tears. She quickly blinked them away.

"But, I don't want to become my mother. I don't want to lose him and then fall apart. So, I told him I wanted nothing to do with him. And… yeah, last year was hard." *So, she rejected Kanoa, not the other way around,* Emira thought.

"But, you don't like seeing him with Celeste," Emira pointed out. Darlene breathed in deep.

"No," she said. "I don't. But it's better that he's with her and continues twisting the dagger into my heart than me getting attached to him. Than me losing myself someday." She let out her breath, and gave her a small smile. "You probably don't understand." Emira understood more than she wanted to admit.

Emira was about to reveal her own complicated feelings when Darlene's head whipped up. She was staring hard at something.

"Emira, I think we're—" And then a white mist appeared around them. Emira breathed it in and watched as Darlene crumpled to the ground. She tried to hold herself steady, grabbing the bookshelf next to her, as whatever it was she breathed in was starting to grab hold of her. But the world was spinning, and not in a good way. Before she knew it, her face was hitting the ground and darkness fell over her.

CHAPTER FORTY-THREE

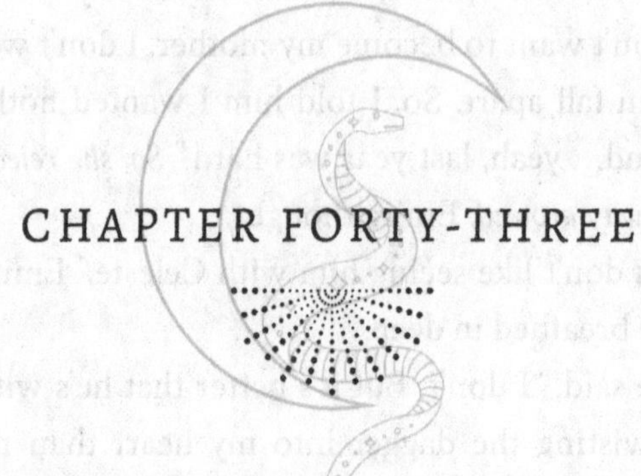

When Emira awoke, she found she couldn't move her arms. They were shackled to the ground. She rattled against it, her heart hammering in her chest at the claustrophobic feeling filling her. Biting her tongue, she tried to breathe in slowly through her mouth, trying to calm the heart that beat against her rib cage. She squinted in the darkness but couldn't see much besides a figure next to her.

"Darlene?" Emira whispered, her voice full of worry and desperation. Half of her didn't want to be alone, didn't want to be lost in the darkness without her friends. But, the other half hoped her slight, fairy-like friend wasn't here, wasn't going through the same emotions she was. In the end, she hoped it was someone else.

To her mixed disappointment, Darlene groaned a little.

She looked around for Shiloh, but didn't see the brunette anywhere in her field of vision. Emira silently hoped Shiloh got away.

Using her legs, she nudged Darlene with her foot. Her eyes were adjusting a little to the absolute darkness, but she still could only barely make out Darlene's small figure. Darlene's head lifted a little, another groan escaping her lips.

"Darlene," Emira whispered, more desperate this time. She seemed to lift her head up more sharply, and started to look around.

"Shit," she whispered. She moved her arms and found they were also shackled to the ground, the chains clanking together as she pulled with all her might.

"Emira?" she asked, her voice betraying her anxiety.

"I'm right here," Emira said, quietly.

"Shit," Darlene said more intensely. "I can't believe I'm going to die before I graduate."

"It's a little earlier than I was planning but..." Emira tried to joke. Darlene shook her head. She was quiet for a long time, but Emira could hear her straining a little.

"What are you doing?" Emira asked.

"I'm trying to use my light, but these chains, I think, are causing us not to be able to use our ichor," Darlene said. "I've never seen anything besides potions be able to do that."

Emira saw something move ahead of them. "I don't think it's the chains," she whispered.

"If it's not the chains then what..." But Darlene's voice faded away as they heard someone unlocking a door.

Two figures walked in, sconces on the walls lighting up as they did. They both wore black robes that covered their bodies and silver masks over their faces. The only human feature Emira could see on them were their eyes.

"You better let us go," Darlene said, her head held high. "I don't know if you've noticed, but you've captured a sacrifice. I don't think the Idols will take kindly to that."

The two figures didn't say anything, and Emira took the opportunity to look around their cell. It was made of some kind of sandstone. There weren't any windows, and the only objects in the room were what was keeping their arms chained to the ground.

The two figures parted to reveal a third figure, wearing the same set up. The third figure's eyes were orange. Much like the Idol of Knowledge and Festivity's but less jewel-like.

Still, they had to be a relative. Emira wracked her mind to try and remember what it was Hemlock's ichor was. Silas had her ichor, but only the illusion part. The other was creation. But, this person could be related without having a lick of her ichor as well.

But this figure's eyes, their eyes were emptier than Mateo's. Emira swallowed the fear that began to claw its way up her throat from the depths of her stomach.

The third figure walked over to Emira and placed a cane underneath her chin, lifting her head to look directly into their eyes.

"What are you planning?" the figure said. It was a male voice. Emira swallowed, her mouth going dry.

"We're not planning any—" Before she could finish, the man used the cane to hit the side of her head. Emira's head whipped to the side, stars filling her vision. She vaguely heard Darlene yelp from the action.

"Let me ask a different question," the man said. "What were doing reading about the elves?" Emira blinked the stars away, trying to face the man. She felt something warm dripping down the side of her head where she was struck.

"Researching," she managed to get out.

"Researching what?" the man hissed, getting close to her. She focused on the light headed feeling that was filling her and reached out for the man's essence.

It was chaotic. Like Mateo's.

She tried to push through. But the only glimpse she could glean from his thoughts were golden eyes. *Balan*, she thought. She tried to hold onto the essence, mold it. But her mind was moving so slowly, like her thoughts were moving through earth. And before she could hold onto it and whisper a command into his mind, the man jolted backwards, like he had been electrocuted. The man's chaotic essence slipped through her fingers like little pebbles of sand. He narrowed his orange eyes at her and stared for a long while, like he knew what Emira had been doing inside of his mind. He struck her again, and this time Emira would've nearly fell to the side, if it weren't for the chains keeping her arms in place.

"You can't do that to her!" Darlene cried out. "She's a sacrifice! Do you know what the Idols would do to you if you hurt her?"

"I think they're working for the Idols," Emira said, spitting out blood. "Or at least, one of them."

The cane was underneath her chin again, moving her head to look at him. His orange eyes were crinkled, like he was smiling underneath his silver mask. "Look at you, able to use your ichor somehow." Emira merely grimaced at him.

Without tearing his gaze away from her, he called out, "Aetos, keep closer to them." One of the figures behind him moved so that they were a few feet away from Darlene and Emira.

Aetos? Emira thought. *A legacy?*

Once the figure with the last name Aetos moved closer, the light headed feeling Emira had managed to hold onto disappeared. She felt something twist inside of her as she glared up at the figures. The man laughed when he caught her gaze.

"We have a fighter on our hands, boys," the man called out. He leaned in closer, his orange eyes hardening.

"What were you researching?" Emira stayed silent. With a quick movement, the man reached out and grabbed Darlene around the neck. Any rebellion within Emira evaporated. Darlene struggled against the man's grip, but he tightened it, without even looking at her. Emira's eyes darted towards Darlene as she made these guttural sounds. Her face started to have a blue tint to it, and her eyes were wide, desperate.

"We were researching *dryadales*," she finally said, the words escaping her lips felt as painful as if the man pulled out her fingernails, one by one. The man squeezed harder and Darlene involuntarily let out a whimper.

"Why?"

"I don't know," Emira said, quickly. "I don't know. We have this theory."

"Who does?"

"Darlene and I. Just Darlene and I," Emira cried. Her eyes burned, desperate to do something but unable to even reach out for Darlene. How weak she was without her ichor. She never wanted to feel this helpless ever again.

The man cocked his head to the side and then released Darlene. She gasped for breath, her head hanging as she tried to fill her lungs.

"You came to the library with another," he said. Emira wracked her brain. *Orange eyes, orange eyes.* If Aetos is a legacy, this man probably was, too. Orange eyes meant he was related to Hemlock, the Idol of Knowledge and Festivity. If he was also a legacy, he most likely was related to…

"I don't think you want me to reveal it," Emira said, her voice so low she wondered if he could even hear her. The man's eyes narrowed once more.

"Hm, perhaps letting you stay longer in here will convince your tongue to loosen," he glanced over at Darlene and then withdrew. He gestured for the other cloaked figure to follow after him. Aetos, as the man called them, stayed behind, sitting only a few feet away from them.

Emira's brain quickly replayed the moments that had just occurred, trying to find some kind of weakness within the man's gaze. But, she couldn't find a single moment. Even mentioning the library, he didn't flinch when Emira implied it would be a family member.

Or, perhaps it didn't occur to him that the other person was.

Darlene coughed, her charcoal eyes glittering as she looked at the cloaked figure left behind.

"Aetos, is it?" she said, cocking her head to the side, her voice sweet as honey. Her long neck was filled with red marks that looked more dark crimson on her complexion. The cloaked figure didn't move to look at her at all.

"I know a few Aetoses," Darlene cooed. "I've never heard of an Aetos who can erase power. Though, that family *is* pretty large."

Aetos continued not to say anything, leaning their head against the wall. Darlene's face twisted as her lips curled into a smile that chilled Emira to the bone.

"Although, there is one Aetos that was said to have died at a very young age," Darlene said. "Zahir, right?" The figure stiffened. Darlene's smile widened.

"You're Zahir, aren't you?" The figure, who Emira was sure was who Darlene said he was, got up and walked over to where they were. Darlene stared straight into his masked face as he dipped down and grabbed hers. He squeezed her cheeks together with his gloved hand and brought his masked face close to her.

"If you keep talking, I'll give you something that'll shut you up," he whispered. His voice crawled underneath Emira's skin and clawed at it. She wished she could wrap her arms around herself, to give her some kind of protection from the man in front of them.

So disgustingly helpless, something in her bitterly whispered. *A slave to fate.* She wanted to disappear into nothing.

Darlene merely glowered at the man and kept her mouth shut. But she was working her jaw and Emira didn't have to be able to read her mind to know her thoughts were murderous.

Zahir Aetos, the name didn't ring any bells in Emira's head. But, she didn't know much about the twelve families. They were so far above her growing up there was no point in knowing all of them or how they worked. But, Darlene knew all the gossip. And if he was said to be dead, how was he here in front of them, alive?

Emira moved her foot so it was lightly touching Darlene's, as some form of comfort. Darlene tapped her foot against Emira's, her dark eyes still fixated on the man most likely named Zahir.

Emira closed her eyes and tried to calm her beating heart. If her theory was right, which it very much might not be, the man in charge here was an Astoria, which meant he was related to Shiloh. If he was close to Shiloh, he might not want her to be involved in this. But, that's only if Emira's theory was correct.

"Darlene," she barely voiced, distinctly aware of the man sitting not too far away from them. Darlene's eyes darted towards her but then fixed themselves back onto their captor.

"Is there anyone in the Astoria family directly related to Hemlock?" Emira whispered. "They're the family that got Hemlock's ichor, during the Dark Ages, right?"

Darlene furrowed her eyebrows and glanced over at Emira. Her black eyes were glazed over, lost in thought. The Idols usually only procreated with the descendants of the first families they gave their ichor to. Not always, like with Mateo's grandmother, but usually. Emira now knew it was in order to further guarantee a sacrifice.

"No talking," Zahir ordered. Darlene glared at him.

Barely moving her lips, she said, "Half-brother." Emira's eyebrows knitted together, and Darlene glanced at her and tried to emphasize what she had said with her eyes.

"Shiloh's?" Emira mouthed. Darlene barely nodded her head.

"Is he dead?" Emira whispered. Darlene darted a glance over at their captor, but his head was leaning against the wall, and it didn't seem like he could hear them too well.

"Deader than dead," Darlene barely spoke. "Body burned in the seas of Krachelle and everything."

Emira glanced at the man who was suppressing their powers. The sconces slowly turned off, leaving them in pitch darkness.

Zahir Aetos was rumored to have died at a young age. Emira had never even heard of anyone being able to erase powers, just from their presence. It wasn't in the wheelhouse of any of the Idols. Which meant, he was something that was coveted. And Shiloh had a half brother, which Emira was pretty sure was the man with orange eyes. And he was rumored to be dead, too.

What was Balan doing with a bunch of supposedly dead people?

One thing Emira was sure of. The fact that she and Darlene were kidnapped because they were reading about the *dryadales* meant that was exactly where the Idols got their power.

The question was, how?

CHAPTER FORTY-FOUR

Emira didn't know how much time had passed. Only that her throat was dry and her stomach was caving in on itself. She didn't know if she slept but her neck was sore, making her think she might've.

The lightheaded feeling was starting to come back to her, in bursts, which meant their captor was losing energy as well. All she could glean from his mind, during those bursts, was the same thing as the man with orange eyes.

Gold, swirling, dangerous eyes. Balan. But not a single hint as to where they were.

She couldn't see Darlene's features, only that she was there. She tapped her foot and Darlene tapped her back, indicating that they were both still there and alive.

Any little noise made outside the cell sent cold fear through Emira's veins. She didn't want to see the man with orange eyes again. And, selfishly, she didn't want to get hit with his cane once more.

The liquid that was dripping down the side of her face had dried up a long while ago. Though, she didn't know how long it had been. It felt crusted when she moved her jaw.

She shuddered, involuntarily, when the lock started to open again. The two cloaked figures with their silver masks entered the room. The sconces lit up.

"Aetos," the man said. "Here's some food." Zahir started to inhale the food the man brought him. It had been a while for him to eat as well.

Emira couldn't see the masked man eat, his back was turned to them. But she could hear it and smell it. Like fresh bread with butter and cinnamon. And, involuntarily, her mouth started to salivate.

"I hope you're ready to talk," the man with orange eyes said. He held the cane underneath Emira's chin once more, forcing her to look into his eyes.

"Who was with you in the library?" the man hissed, leaning forward. Emira felt her head jerk backwards at his movement, and he hit her ribs with the cane. She tried to stifle the cry, but it still escaped her lips.

I will never let someone terrify me like this again, she vowed. *Next time, if there is one, I'll be strong. I won't be a slave to fate.*

You already are one, her inner voice retorted.

"I'm not going to ask again," he whispered. Emira's lower lip started to tremble as she tried to open her mouth. She hated how the fear overtook all her limbs, her nerves. She reached for the fury always hidden within her, but it was gone. Fear suffocating it to oblivion.

"Malachi, isn't it?" Darlene interrupted. The man with orange eyes froze, his eyes turning murderous.

"What did you call me?" he nearly growled. Darlene's eyes were clear, almost as dangerous as his were.

"Malachi," she said, rolling the name off of her tongue.

"Malachi Astoria." The cane disappeared from underneath Emira's chin. She hadn't realized she was holding her breath until the cold air replaced where the cane was.

Emira glanced over at Darlene. She was smaller than Emira, less powerful than her, too, when her ichor was able to manifest. And yet, here, in the face of sure death, she was strong. Resilient. And she wasn't going to back down to anyone.

Emira wished she could go kicking and screaming, too.

You were going to go quietly anyways, something whispered from the depths of her mind. Emira squeezed her eyes shut.

The man, probably named Malachi, got up and leaned down to look at Darlene. He put the cane underneath her chin, lifting her head painfully until she was staring up at him.

"You're a little gossip, aren't you?"

Darlene shrugged. "You call it gossip. I call it valuable information." His eyes hardened, and he hit the side of her head with the black cane. It had a gold fox on the top of it. Emira didn't notice it before. But it was all she could stare at so she didn't have to see Darlene's bloody face. Emira felt herself start to tremble, like a leaf hanging on for dear life in the wind, and she took in a shaky breath. A part of her wondered if she was going to die here.

Darlene turned and smiled at him, her ebony eyes wide and crazed. Blood was dripping down her forehead into her mouth, and she spit it out before smiling at Malachi once more.

"I'm best friends... with Shiloh Astoria," she said, enunciating every word. The man with orange eyes froze, his cane still slightly in the air.

Something within Emira stirred. *Weakness*, her mind cried out. *There is weakness in him.* She leaned forward, memorizing the look in his eyes.

Darlene's smile widened, like she caught a fly in her web.

"You want to know who the other person was in the library? You want to know who has a theory about the *dryadales*?" She leaned as forward as she could muster with the chains still holding her back and lowered her voice dramatically, "It's your sister."

Just as she said this, the cloaked man behind Malachi started to scream. Emira looked over at him and his body was being pulled apart, like how Mateo did with the *bellua*. Except with a human, Emira could see all his muscles and bones being stretched and torn apart. And in an instant, the cloaked man exploded. His hot blood and guts hit Emira's face, and she couldn't help but echo the man's scream.

"Looks like she found us," Darlene said, throwing her head back and laughing. Her laughter sent chills down Emira's spine. Down the steps was Shiloh, her hands splayed out, and they were trembling slightly. Behind her were Mateo, Kanoa, Silas, and Atlas.

Malachi looked over his shoulder, stared at his half sister for a long while, before turning into himself and disappearing. Emira stared at the empty space the man with orange eyes had been.

There were two Kanoas running down the steps, running towards Darlene, but they were forcefully pulled into one Kanoa, which made him stop in his tracks.

"What the hell?" he muttered, looking around the room. His eyes fixed onto Zahir who was pressed against the wall.

"He erases power," Darlene accused. Mateo's mismatched eyes were locked onto Emira as he walked forward.

"Great," Mateo said, not looking at the man. "That means I have that power, too." With a flick of his wrist, Emira could feel her ichor start to course through her veins again.

And with another flick of his wrist, Zahir was set on fire.

Zahir screamed at the top of his lungs, trying to put the magical fire out. He pulled off his silver mask, and Kanoa took that opportunity to cut his head off with one fell swoop of his sword.

Zahir's head rolled across the room until it was right in front of her, his eyes wide and his mouth hanging open. Emira stared at it, intensely. He wasn't much older than they were.

"Are you okay?" she heard Mateo murmur. He pressed a warm hand against her cheek as he studied her face, but Emira didn't answer. Her eyes were fixed onto the decapitated head. She wondered if High Priestess Ethel looked like that, when she killed her. Odd and unnatural, without life animating it.

Mateo's other hand hovered over the wound on her head. Kanoa, beside them, was using his sword to break the chains that were keeping Darlene's arms down. His black eyes looked murderous as he took in the blood running down Darlene's face.

"I'll kill whoever the fucker was," he snapped. "Slowly."

Darlene rubbed her wrists above where the manacles still were. She looked over at Shiloh. "It was Malachi." Shiloh's face blanched.

"Atlas," Mateo ordered, his eyes still on Emira. She could feel his mismatched eyes burning, his gaze violent as he took in her wounds.

"Just a second," Atlas said to Mateo. He turned to Darlene, "Stay still." From Emira's peripheral vision, she could see Darlene's wound start to heal.

"But, Mal is dead," Shiloh whispered.

"Not anymore," Darlene said, her voice hard.

"Kanoa," Mateo ordered. He gestured towards Emira's chains. Kanoa quickly brought his sword down on them. Emira didn't realize she was still trembling until Mateo held her hands in his. His eyebrows were upturned as he searched her eyes.

"Are you okay?" he asked, again. Emira opened her mouth and realized tears were starting to fall down her cheeks. She closed them. It wasn't a question she could answer honestly. Not to him.

"I'm fine," she said, her voice hoarse. Mateo's gaze hardened. He helped her up to her feet, and Atlas appeared by her side.

"This won't hurt," he said, in his quiet way, as he healed up the wounds in her head and jaw.

"My side," Emira managed to get out. Atlas furrowed his eyebrows as he took a look at her ribs. He inhaled sharply and then got to work on that as well.

"There's more coming," Silas said from the door. She finally looked up at Mateo who was staring at the door, his eyes swirling around like they were in front of the *immanis bellua*. Power emanated from him, and from as close as she was, it made her head spin and her stomach flip over. Mateo wasn't the Mateo that Emira had gotten used to. No, he was Mateo Cordero, now. A legacy with all the ichor of Balan.

He grabbed Emira, and held her up as they started up the stairs. His arm around the small of her waist. They met Silas at the top and just as he said, there were more cloaked figures wearing silver masks.

"These things are creepy," Kanoa said, holding Darlene up with one hand. She glowered at him and tried to push him off of her but he held on.

Mateo didn't say anything, but there was something dark emanating from him. Darker and more dangerous than she had ever felt. Without any kind of motion, the ground opened up where the silver masked people were running on. They fell in and then the ground swallowed them, while they were still alive.

He walked over their twitching limbs that were above the ground and continued to pull Emira along. Emira stared in horror at the limbs and then looked back up at him. His mismatched eyes were swirling, faster than she had seen it before.

"Did you see the one with orange eyes anywhere?" Mateo asked Silas, his voice cold, detached. Silas shook his head. His blue eyes worryingly roved over his best friend.

"He disappeared into thin air. I've never seen ichor manifest a power like that," Silas muttered.

"Just like how I've never seen someone able to erase powers," Mateo muttered. "I saw the dude do it. I should be able to teleport then."

"Do you really want to risk it?" Silas asked. Mateo glanced down at Emira who was staring up at him.

"I think she's in shock. We should get out of here as soon as possible," he said. "Hold onto me."

Shock? Was I in shock?

The others grabbed hold of Mateo and in the blink of an eye, they were in the Room of Serpentes at Leliara.

Emira started to collapse to the ground, but Mateo reached out and grabbed her before she could reach it. He gently guided her to a chair, and she let the armchair engulf her as she looked around the well lit room.

Was it just a dream? Emira thought. *Was the whole time simply a terrible nightmare?*

Mateo moved to place his hand underneath Emira's chin in order to look at her better, but she flinched, and he pulled away.

"What happened?" he asked, turning towards Darlene. She was fussing with Kanoa who was insisting to help her take all the guts and gore of the man who exploded out of her hair.

"Kanoa, I can do it myself," she hissed.

"I don't know how you're going to get all the pieces out," Kanoa mumbled, still picking stuff out of her hair. She batted his massive hands away as she turned her attention to Mateo.

"What happened? I don't know, really," Darlene said, bitter, finally answering his question. "We were in the National Library, Shi went into the special edition section, and I swore we were being watched. I could feel the hair stand up all over my body, but I couldn't see who it was."

"And then?" Mateo asked, his voice still disturbingly detached. Power was still oozing out of him, but it was slowly fading away. The choking feeling around Emira's throat fading with it. She let out a slow, shaky breath.

"Then, I saw a man with a freaking silver mask on blow something out of his hands and when I woke up I was in a cell," Darlene said. She pointed at Shiloh. "And it *was* your dead brother."

"In his mind, I saw Balan," Emira whispered. Mateo's jaw clenched.

"Of course," he snapped. "Of course you saw Balan."

"Why did they kidnap you two?" Silas asked.

"I don't know," Darlene said. "Something about the *dryadales.*"

"The what?" Kanoa asked.

"It's what the elven race called themselves," Atlas spoke up. He was leaning against the wall, his arms crossed over his chest.

"The elven race? There was an elven race?" Kanoa asked, bewildered.

"They were called the *dryadales,*" Shiloh said. "They supposedly existed before humans were even a thought in the universe. Apparently, they all died out when a meteor hit the world."

"I'm guessing you don't think that's the truth," Atlas mused. Mateo's eyes were still locked onto Emira, and she was staring at him as well, while the others were talking. Like she couldn't look away. Like all she wanted to do was memorize all the features in his face. She didn't want to admit she missed him, but Idol of Life, did she miss him. Even if she was avoiding him before.

"It's not," Shiloh said. "I think that the Idols stole something from the *dryadales* and whatever it is they stole, it turned the *dryadales* into *bellua*." Darlene leaned forward.

"Don't tell me you didn't find anything in the special edition section," she said through gritted teeth. Shiloh's cheeks flushed a little.

"There weren't any books in there about the *dryadales*. I think it was taken out before we got there," Shiloh said, quietly. Darlene clenched her jaw and looked away.

"We were reading those other books for a while," Emira finally said, clearing her throat. She tore her gaze away from Mateo and looked at the rest of them. "If someone was watching us, they would've figured out what we were looking for from the beginning."

"So, we don't know what they stole, we don't know what caused the *bellua* to become *bellua*, and apparently there's a secret group of dead people running around kidnapping others and wearing creepy masks," Darlene said, throwing her hands up. "Did I miss anything?"

"The trip wasn't a complete loss," Shiloh said, nearly pleading with Darlene. "I mean, we at least know they definitely stole something from the *dryadales*. Look at how they reacted."

"It wasn't a loss?" Darlene stood up. She took a few steps toward Shiloh. "Your *dead* fucking brother *kidnapped* us, *starved* us, hit both of us in the head, *broke* Emira's ribs, and you think it wasn't a *loss*? You think knowing that they're keeping the precious information about *dryadales* secret proof that we have something? We have *nothing*, Shiloh."

"Hey," Kanoa said, grabbing Darlene's arm and pulling her back a little. She focused her glare on him. "It's not Shiloh's fault that happened, Darling. I know that what happened was traumatic, but don't—"

"Darling?" she laughed, an emotionless empty laugh. "Darling? Don't fucking call me that, Kanoa. And don't tell me how I should feel about what happened to me." His dark eyebrows furrowed together.

"Darle—"

"You and I are *nothing* to each other," Darlene continued in a fevered frenzy. "I don't even know why you came." Kanoa stared at her for a moment, something appearing deep in his dark eyes.

"You know why I came," he whispered. Darlene's eyes widened and she looked panicked, like something was going to come and squeeze her neck once more. Her free hand fluttered around her throat, and she opened her mouth, closed it, and opened it once more.

"I fucked Mateo," she snapped, glaring into Kanoa's eyes. Something cold and slimy settled into the pit of Emira's stomach. She glanced over at Mateo who had froze, his eyes as wide as a deer caught by a hunter.

Darlene stood on her tiptoes so she could be as close to Kanoa's face as she possibly could. His expression tensed, and Emira watched his eyes dart towards Mateo for a moment.

"You... What?"

"I. Fucked. Mateo," Darlene said, enunciating every word. "I fucked him a good handful of times." Kanoa's hand let go of Darlene's arm. Darlene took a step back, stared at his crumpled expression, a flicker of something unreadable crossing over her face, and looked back at Emira over her shoulder.

"Sorry, E," she whispered before running up the stairs out of the Room of Serpentes. The room was silent as the tension grew. Kanoa stared up the stairs for a long time.

"Kanoa," Mateo finally said, breaking the silence. Kanoa's head turned, his eyes cold.

"You slept with Darlene?" he whispered. "*My* Darlene?" Mateo held his hands up as Kanoa took a step forward.

"Kanoa, man, I didn't know you even liked her," Mateo muttered, but something in the tone of his voice felt like a lie. "And, I was just… I was…"

"You were what?"

"I was sabotaging myself. That's what I was doing," he said, his mismatched eyes glancing over at Emira. Emira looked away quickly. She held her hands together tightly, like holding her hands together was going to keep her from falling apart.

Her mind was struggling to follow, still on what Darlene had said. "*I fucked Mateo.*" Emira closed her eyes, trying not to imagine the two of them together.

"You didn't know Kanoa liked her?" Atlas spoke up, his expression in disbelief. He narrowed his eyes. "He's called her Darling since he's met her and always talked about marrying her someday."

Mateo swallowed. "I didn't… I didn't know. Or… I just… I didn't care. And I'm sorry."

Kanoa stared at him for a moment longer, his cold eyes getting more and more icy by the second, before splitting into five of him. Each of them walked over and punched Mateo in the face.

The sound of flesh on flesh made Emira flinch, five times. She felt herself start to tremble, the sound eerily like the cane hitting the side of her face, the side of Darlene's face.

Then Kanoa walked away, all five of him phasing back into

himself as he walked up the stairs. Mateo rubbed his jaw. His lip was split open and the left side of his face was starting to swell.

"If you think I'm going to heal that, you're sorely mistaken," Atlas said, his expression contorted into disgust. "You can go to the nurse and explain how you got that."

"She only did it because she doesn't want to get attached to Kanoa. If she slept with Mateo, he would never go back to her," Shiloh explained. Atlas shook his head, the full force of his glare on Shiloh.

"I don't care what Darlene's reasoning was," he bit. "What I care about is that Mateo has known all of us since we were five." Atlas turned towards Mateo, his dark eyes taking him apart, bit by bit.

"He was supposed to be like a brother to you, remember?" Atlas said, his voice low. "Or do your selfish needs always have to come before everyone else?"

Mateo didn't say anything, merely stared at the ground as Atlas left the room. Silas walked up to Mateo, patted his shoulder, and then followed after Kanoa and Atlas.

"She didn't mean anything by it, Emira," Shiloh said, her eyes big. "She told me that she stopped once she realized you had feelings for him."

Emira froze, her gaze slowly rising to meet Shiloh's. Her brown eyes looked desperate, pleading for the friend she had known for over a decade. A friend that would always come before Emira.

"You've known all this time?" she asked, her voice trembling. She looked at Shiloh, a person that she considered her friend. "You didn't tell me?"

"It wasn't my place," Shiloh responded, unable to handle the betrayal written in Emira's eyes. "And she swore me to secrecy.

Plus, I didn't know if you even liked Mateo. She was convinced of it, but me... I couldn't tell. It didn't seem like it."

Emira felt herself scoff. "I thought you were terrible at keeping secrets." Shiloh looked up, hurt flickering through her brown eyes. Then she closed them and started up the steps.

"I'm sorry, Emira. But, I don't think your anger should be directed towards me or Darlene," she muttered before leaving.

Emira sat there for a moment longer, her fingers gripping the armchair. Mateo kneeled down and looked into her eyes. And she hated that her heart hurt at seeing his face all messed up.

"Emira," he whispered, with that voice that spoke to the deepest parts of herself. "Emira, I never meant—"

"It's fine," she interrupted. "It's not like we were anything to each other."

CHAPTER FORTY-FIVE

"You know that's not true," Mateo said, his eyes imploring. Emira scrunched up her face as she looked away from him.

"You know how I feel about you," he continued. She looked up towards the ceiling and closed her eyes.

Of course she knew, it was why it hurt all that much more. She could feel it, in his thoughts. And if he felt that way about her, how could he… How could he possibly…

She shook her head.

"How do you feel about me?" she finally said, turning to look at him. Mateo placed his hand on top of hers.

"You're the air that I need to breathe, Emira," he said, his voice quiet. "I don't know how else to describe it."

"Then why?" Emira asked. "Why would you…" She couldn't say the words. She wanted to shout at him, but she didn't have the right. She wasn't with Mateo. She was actively trying *not* to be with him, so what did it matter if he had relations with Darlene? Did it hurt? Yeah, but seeing him with Isla hurt, too.

"I hear voices," Mateo finally answered. "I hear voices, and we were just… we were helping each other. We vowed never to talk about it."

"I don't care that you slept with Darlene," Emira whispered. "I just wish you didn't treat me like a toy that you bring out sometimes and then put me away when it's too much for you."

Mateo's mismatched eyes darkened. "*I* do that." Emira licked her dry lips, her eyes widening at the force of his words.

"I think so."

His eyebrows furrowed downwards as he stood up. His veins in his arms and hands popped out. "Priestess, you did that."

"I don't know what you—"

"I told you I was in love with you and you avoided me for the past week or so," he said. "I told you I was in love with you in more ways than one, and you didn't want to hear it. You still offered yourself up as a sacrifice and you didn't want anything to do with me." Slowly, his injured face was healing itself, his ichor doing it for him. She didn't think he even noticed it was happening.

"That's not true," Emira said, standing up so that he couldn't look down at her like that anymore. He was still much taller than her, but at least she wasn't taking it sitting down.

He took a step forward, but Emira held her ground. His expression had changed. The hardened face and cold eyes of what everyone else thought the grandson of Balan should look like. And something in her heart broke.

"What is the truth then, Priestess?" he asked, his voice so low that Emira wasn't sure what she heard.

"I couldn't not offer myself up as sacrifice. I knew I was one and I wasn't going to run away from my fate. Unlike you," Emira spat.

"I apologize if being slaughtered isn't my cup of tea,"

Mateo growled. Emira took a step forward and pressed her finger against his chest. They were inches away from one another.

"You slept with Darlene and Isla and who knows who else because you were afraid. You were running away," she said.

"From what? From you?" he gave an emotionless grin. "Were you not running away from me?"

"I was running away from you not because I didn't want to accept my fate, Cordero. But because I knew that if I let this—whatever this was—happen, then you would've done anything that you could to save me. But, I didn't want to be saved. I *still* don't want to be saved," Emira said. She stared up at him, her eyebrows knitting together as she studied his expression.

He leaned his head down minutely. "Tell the truth, Priestess."

Her jaw tensed. "That is the truth."

"No, it's not," he said, a cold smirk on his lips. "You just didn't want to get hurt. Just like me."

Emira rolled her eyes and took a step backwards, crossing her arms over her chest. "You're delusional. The reason I told you is the truth."

You're lying, she whispered to herself. She bit her tongue until she tasted copper.

"No," he let out an emotionless laugh, his mismatched eyes swirling. "You just didn't want to get too attached. We're a lot more alike than you think, Priestess." She glared up at him.

"Too attached? What? You think I didn't want to get too attached to the Winter Solstice pig that was going to eventually get slaughtered and eaten?" Emira hissed.

Mateo's eyes widened. "Wow, you hit it on the nose." She rolled her eyes and glowered at him.

"Just admit that you were afraid," Emira said.

"I was," he retorted. "But, you are too."

"I wasn't afraid of falling in love with you," she muttered. "I was afraid of what you would do."

"See, Priestess, the difference between you and I is that I know what I am. I know how I feel. You don't have the slightest clue who you even are anymore. Priestess. Sacrifice. But, you don't want to be either, do you? Your world has shattered around you, and you don't know who you are and what you're capable of," he hissed. "You think you were afraid of what *I* would do?"

He took a step forward and leaned down until all she could see were his gold and brown eyes. "You're afraid of what *you* would do."

"I'm not afraid of myself," Emira murmured, the lie easily escaping from her lips.

"Aren't you?" he whispered. She felt her legs tremble a little. Closing her eyes, she turned away from him. She heard him take another step forward, but she still didn't open her eyes.

"You told me you wanted to die first, that you didn't want to see me during the sacrificial ritual," Mateo murmured. "And that's why you offered yourself up as sacrifice, even when I begged you not to."

"I don't ever want to see you again," Emira whispered, opening her eyes to look at him.

It didn't deter him, didn't stop him from ripping her apart, showing her that he saw right through her like a pane of glass. "You offered yourself up as sacrifice not because you wanted to save Constellatia, not because you wanted to protect a baby, and not because you wanted to feel important. But because you knew that I would die. No matter what, I was going to die. And you would have to watch it happen. Because you knew. You knew how you felt about me."

Emira turned away and walked quickly towards the exit. Mateo grabbed her arm and forced her to look at him.

"You think *I* treated you like a toy? You think what *I* did was cruel? Making sure the last thing I see is the life leaving your eyes is more than cruel, Emira. It's heartless."

Emira ripped her arm away from his grip and ran up the stairs. She felt like she couldn't breathe in the same space as him. She ran as fast as she could up the spiral staircase and towards the girls' dorm room. But, his words followed her.

Making sure the last thing I see is the life leaving your eyes is more than cruel, Emira. It's heartless.

She went straight to the communal bathroom and took off the clothes that were covered in dried blood and guts. Turning the knob so that the water was scalding hot, she washed the blood out of her hair and off of her body.

The blood pooled around her feet, diluted with water. And she felt herself hyperventilating, but it was like she was outside of her body. Hiding away in the recesses of her brain, simply watching what was happening. Watching herself break down.

Mateo was a selfish asshole. Even his friends said so. He only cared about himself. And yet...

We're a lot more alike than you think.

Emira grabbed the sides of her head and squeezed, like she was trying to keep her brain from falling out.

The worst thing was he was right about her. He was right. She watched in horror when she saw him open the ground up and swallow all those people, killing them in an instant. But, it wasn't because she was disgusted at what he did. It was because she knew she'd do the same exact thing. Actually, she probably would've done worse, made their deaths slow and painful for what they did to him.

She wasn't afraid of what he would do if he got attached, she was afraid of what *she* would do. If she had to watch Mateo die, she knew something dark would possess her. And she wouldn't be able to find her way back to herself, whoever it was she was now. She knew.

Emira closed her eyes as the hot water burned her skin. He could see right through her, as if she were transparent. And she hated it.

CHAPTER FORTY-SIX

"It's good you were able to escape, alive," Headmistress Alessia said. She handed Emira a cup of tea and smiled warmly at her. "We were all so worried."

"How long were we gone?" Emira asked.

"A few days," Headmistress Alessia said. "But, that's not why I called you to my office." Emira already suspected why she had been ordered to the headmistress' office. The newspapers were already talking about the rumors that the Tenth Year sacrificial ritual had been moved up due to the fact a sacrifice had been kidnapped.

"I guess the rumors are true then," Emira muttered, looking down at her cup of tea. It was brown and swirling, like Mateo's eye.

The headmistress gave a tight smile which made the wrinkles on her face more prominent. "Yes, unfortunately, Balan has decreed that the Tenth Year be moved up to next week."

"Okay, thanks for telling me," Emira said, her voice monotonous.

She had vowed to herself she wouldn't be a slave to fate, and yet, here she was. Again, unable to do anything about it. Dragged through her own life without a say. She vowed to be strong. But, what strength does one girl have against a whole society? Against the Idols?

"It's too dangerous, now that you've been kidnapped. You could've died, and then the Tenth Year wouldn't be complete. It's important for the good of Constellatia," Headmistress Alessia explained. Emira nodded her head. She once thought like that. That it was important for them to be sacrificed so the Idols could continue protecting the citizens, so that the Idols' already long lives could be more prolonged. She once thought like that. She wasn't sure if she did anymore.

"If there's anything you want to do, or need, let me know," Headmistress Alessia said, her eyes the epitome of pity. It made Emira dig her nails into the palms of her hands.

"I will," she said, without emotion. And then she left the room. Shiloh was waiting outside of the office for her.

"What did she say?" she asked.

"The Tenth Year has been moved up," Emira said, not letting the news sink in because if she did, she thought she might explode.

"To when?" Shiloh asked.

"Next week." She stared at Emira as they walked down the hallway to the food hall. And she placed a comforting hand on Emira's shoulder.

"I'm so sorry," she whispered.

"It's not your fault," Emira said, her voice detached. "There's nothing that can be done."

"You said Balan might be behind you being kidnapped," Shiloh said, her voice low. "Do you think he did it on purpose?"

If she knew anything about the Idol of Law and Fate, it was

that everything he did was deliberate. As to why he kidnapped her and Darlene, she wasn't sure.

"What do you mean?" Emira asked, turning towards her.

Shiloh shrugged, and adjusted her glasses. "It's just too much of a coincidence. Balan knows we're researching about the *dryadales* and then you get kidnapped for a few days? You don't die, when they could've killed you. And then he announces that, because the safety of the sacrifices is in question, that he's moving up the ritual?"

"Well, even if he did it on purpose, there's nothing we can do about it," Emira murmured. Shiloh looked lost in thought as they entered the food hall.

"Maybe there's something. I have to think about it more," she muttered to herself.

As Emira stared at Shiloh, she found herself wondering if under the silver mask, the man with orange eyes had the same features as her. Did they have the same nose? The same lip shape?

If Shiloh lived for long in this world, found out more about the truths that the Idols were hiding, would her brown eyes eventually look as empty? Was that why Mateo's looked like that? Silas'?

"Can I ask you a question?" Emira asked as they sat down at their table. Shiloh nodded her head.

"When did Malachi die?" Shiloh's face lost color, and she focused on the food that appeared on her plate. She cleared her throat.

"He died when I was five. I had just entered Leliara, and he was ten. I didn't know how it happened, I still don't. But one day he was alive, and the next..."

"He's related to Hemlock, right?"

Shiloh nodded again. "She's his mother. My father had a love affair with her before he married my mom."

"But, his ichor…"

"He was categorized as being under Phaethon's umbrella. But, I didn't know his ichor manifested into that," she lowered her voice, "Into teleportation."

"Do you think anyone knew about it?" Emira asked.

"The adults, probably," Shiloh muttered. "It's an unusual power. I haven't heard of anyone with it."

"Just like with the guy who erases power," Emira said, under her breath. Shiloh looked over at her.

"Do you really think it was Malachi?" she asked, quietly.

"Darlene seemed pretty sure. And when she said his name, he had a visceral reaction to it," Emira said.

"I can't believe he's alive," Shiloh breathed. "I watched his body burn in Krachelle." Emira's eyes wandered to Darlene who was sitting by herself. She was looking out the window, not touching her food.

Emira had hardly seen Darlene that morning. She was gone before Emira woke up, and she ate breakfast by herself. And now, she was also eating dinner alone. On the other side of the room Kanoa was sitting with Atlas and Silas, but Mateo was nowhere to be seen. A part of Emira, a very small part, wondered if he had eaten.

"She doesn't want to talk to you," Shiloh said, following Emira's gaze.

"I'm not mad at her," Emira said. It was the truth, she wasn't. If anything, Emira was more mad at herself. Mad at Mateo. Mad at the situation of it all.

"I know, but she doesn't believe that," Shiloh said. She sighed and watched Darlene. "She's so punishing towards herself."

"I understand why she did it," Emira said. "I'm not mad at her at all. And I hope I get to talk to her before…"

"I wouldn't pray on that," Shiloh muttered. "I think it would hurt her more if you forgave her right before your death. The guilt would eat her away until there was nothing left."

Emira looked over at Kanoa once more. Celeste was sitting with her friends, throwing daggers through her eyes at the Pyrinian. The rumors had spread fast throughout the school.

Kanoa didn't even need to break up with Celeste. In the hallway before first period, she was screaming at him, telling him that he never loved her and she'd always been second to his precious Darlene. And he stood there, his expression blank, as she cried her heart out.

Both Kanoa and Darlene were two people who didn't care who was swept into their hurricane. They didn't care who they used for collateral damage, as long as they were hurting one another.

"Do you think after this there's any hope for them?" Emira asked. Shiloh shrugged.

"Kanoa and Darlene always find their way back to one another," she said. She glanced at Emira. "But, I feel like you should make up with Mateo before… everything." Even the matter-of-fact brunette couldn't say it.

"I'll do that when the twelfth circle of hell freezes over," Emira muttered. Shiloh sighed, again. Emira felt bad Shiloh was stuck in the middle of everything. But, then again, she was the one who put herself there.

They ate in silence for a moment before Shiloh interrupted it, "Do you think you would be willing to practice something with me?" Emira glanced over at her and shrugged.

"Sure," she said.

"THIS IS NOT WHAT I MEANT WHEN I AGREED TO PRACTICE something with you," Emira said, crossing her arms over her chest. Shiloh pleaded with her big, brown eyes. They were outside underneath the willow tree next to the lake that was frozen over.

"I'm not asking you to do anything outrageous. Just to peek into her brain and stop her from keeping the other sacrifices from not being able to do anything," Shiloh said.

"You're starting to sound more and more like Mateo," Emira said, shaking her head.

"Do you want to be frozen, unable to even fight back?" Shiloh asked.

"I don't know why you think Mali stops the sacrifices from fighting. They're all willing," Emira pointed out. "Plus, if they wanted to stop the sacrifices from resisting, they could give them potions for their ichor and tie them down."

Shiloh narrowed her eyes a little and then let out a sigh. "You don't know what really happens, do you?"

"Is there something different that happens? You get absorbed by the Idol and disappear after a flash of light. It's painless and—"

"That's not what happens," Shiloh said, her voice quiet.

Emira stared at her for a moment. "What do you mean?"

"There's no flash of light, and it isn't painless. That's only what they broadcast to the rest of Constellatia," Shiloh said, almost matter-of-fact. Like it was something that everyone knew.

"How do you know what happens, then?" Emira asked.

"I was there when Cassandra died," Shiloh muttered, pulling her cloak around herself tighter. "It was by accident. I was in a phase where I liked to sleep in carriages. They're small and… safe. I accidentally fell asleep in the carriage Cassandra left in. Mateo had snuck in and found me."

Shiloh let out a breath and looked up towards the gray cloudy sky. "Mateo told me to stay in the carriage, but I got out and followed them in. I was small and was able to fit in places that I shouldn't have been. I saw it happen. And… Emira, it was a bloodbath." Emira stared at her friend, the memory of Cassandra glazing over her brown eyes. She adjusted her glasses under Emira's gaze.

No wonder why Cassandra had haunted Mateo after all this time. He was eight years old. Eight years old and witnessed a bloodbath. Emira pressed her tongue against the roof of her mouth, closing her eyes.

"So you've known all this time?" Shiloh looked up at her.

"Yes," she said. "But, I've always believed that it must be necessary for the Idols to continue protecting Constellatia. Until, I found out the Idols weren't gods."

Emira tried to process the information Shiloh was giving her. She shook her head and turned away from her. It was the last thing she had been holding onto. The last thing she knew to be true. And even that was a lie.

She wouldn't live on within the Idols, would she? None of them would.

"Tell me exactly what happens," she whispered.

"They slit their throats, one by one, and then they drink their blood," Shiloh said, her voice matter-of-fact despite the horrific things she was saying.

"Their blood?" Emira asked in a hushed breath. She turned to look at Shiloh, her eyebrows pulling upwards, her eyes straining, and Shiloh shrugged, her emotional armor washing over her.

"I have a theory that's how they get the power," she said. "Because power is the most important thing to them. Or, at least to Balan."

"More power is important to the Idols," Pandora had said to Emira. Her voice echoed inside of her head. It must've been why they chose those who had all their ichor instead of those who simply had one of their powers. Because one with all of their ichor, one with as much power as theirs, would give them more of it.

The sacrifices were Idols incarnates, as earth-shatteringly powerful as the Idols themselves. To consistently consume that much power every ten years...

"You think more power is what prolongs their life," Emira said, quietly. Shiloh nodded her head, her eyes widening.

"Yes," she said. "That's exactly what I think. Why else do they drink the blood of people who have the same amount of power as them?"

"And what makes you think Mali is controlling the sacrifices? How do you know they didn't give them potions beforehand?" Emira asked, her voice flat.

Shiloh shrugged. "If you were considered a god for centuries, you'd be arrogant. Arrogance allows for mistakes."

A flash of Mateo's throat being slit by Balan, and Balan's mouth covered in Mateo's blood went through Emira's mind. She curled her fingers into her palm and steeled her gaze as she looked at Shiloh.

"So, you're sure I'll be able to control what Mali does?" Emira asked. Shiloh looked her up and down, as if noticing the change in her disposition.

"You can do anything Mali can do," she said. "What's to stop you from controlling her as well?" Emira bit the inside of her cheek, remembering the soft padding Mali did around her mind back at the Idols' Court of Justice. How she could see everything that made Emira who she was.

Something dark settled into the depths of Emira as she realized what that power meant. If Mali could see what it was that made a person who they were, it meant she could easily take it all away.

"She goes through minds like they're a filing cabinet. She doesn't just see your thoughts in the front of your mind, she can see your memories. She's probably able to whisper compliance into the core of who you are, so that's probably why the other sacrifices don't move at all," Emira explained.

"So, you need to be able to combat that," Shiloh responded. Emira nodded her head.

"And be able to do it back to her," she whispered. She gave Shiloh a sidelong glance. The idea made her sick, made her stomach churn, but it was the only thing she could think of. She opened her mouth and then closed it again.

Shiloh's gaze hardened. "Emira, I'm here so I can practice with you."

"I don't want to do this to you, Shi," Emira said, barely above a whisper. "I could accidentally mess you up."

Shiloh gave her a small smile. "E, I'm already messed up."

CHAPTER FORTY-SEVEN

"I'm sorry to be the bearer of bad news, Mateo, but the Tenth Year has been moved to next week," Headmistress Alessia said. The wrinkles around her eyes crinkled ever so slightly, but her sad smile looked more like a grimace. She had watched Mateo grow up, he would be surprised if she didn't feel any sort of way about it. But then again, how many kids did she lead to the slaughterhouse in her time as headmistress?

"When next week?" Mateo asked.

"The eighteenth of Nyria," the headmistress said, very softly. Mateo stared at her for a long while and then let out an emotionless laugh. *Of course.*

"My grandfather is a sick man, isn't he?" he said through gritted teeth.

"I'm sorry, Mateo," she said. And for once, he believed her words. He looked away from her, his jaw clenching. He noticed the lines in her wooden desk and followed them with his eyes.

"Can I go see my mom one last time?" he asked.

"You're a flight risk. I can't have you—"

"You can send me with guards who won't let me leave their sight. Like Milo. Milo and I are very well acquainted, and you know he won't take any nonsense from me," Mateo nearly pleaded. He closed his eyes, stilling his expression.

"My mom was expecting to see me for my birthday. I think it's wrong to not let her be able to say one last goodbye," he muttered. Headmistress Alessia stared past him, over his head as she contemplated his request.

"Fine," she finally said. "But, you must be in Serpel the day before the ritual."

"I will," he promised. Headmistress Alessia grabbed the black telephone on her desk and started to dial a number. Not many people in Constellatia had telephones, only those with enough stellae to burn.

"Could you send Milo here and have him pack Mr. Cordero's things? Thank you," she said into the phone.

"Wait outside my office, and Milo will come shortly," she said, putting the receiver back into its cradle. Mateo got up and walked towards the door. As he touched the doorknob, Headmistress Alessia cleared her throat. He looked over his shoulder.

"I will miss the shenanigans you were always up to," she said, quietly, like she was admitting a buried thought. She looked uncomfortable with what she was saying to him, like it was being tortured out of her. Mateo flashed her a smile.

"Thanks, Alessia," he said. She sighed and rolled her eyes, but smiled in the end.

"It's *Headmistress* Alessia, to you," she corrected, for one last time. Mateo opened the door, but looked over his shoulder once again.

"I never did get to know your first name, headmistress," he muttered. She looked at him, almost offended.

"You didn't hear about my quests?" she asked. He shrugged. She let out a small sigh and gathered some papers on her desk.

"It's Charlotte," she said. "But, my friends call me Charlie."

Mateo grinned, "It was nice knowing you, Charlie."

She stared at him for a long time. "Get the hell out of my office, Mr. Cordero."

MATEO WAITED FOR MILO TO COME GET HIM. HE WASN'T allowed to pack his own stuff, in case he grabbed something that would be considered a weapon. Momentarily, he thought about whether he should say goodbye to Silas, Atlas, and Kanoa.

Kanoa's cold black eyes flickered through his mind. The betrayal riddled within his irises. He didn't look very shocked by it, only hurt, as if he had always known Mateo would stab him in the back one day. That look Kanoa had given him would be burned into his memory until the day he died. It was a look Mateo never wanted repeated. He closed his eyes and leaned his head back against the wall behind him. He knew what he did was worse than a betrayal to Kanoa.

Emira's violet amethyst eyes flashed through his mind. The glare she gave him, the way she had looked at him. She was shocked. She couldn't believe the betrayal. She never expected it, never saw it coming.

Because she didn't really know him. He curled his fingers into his palms.

"How did things get so fucked up?" he muttered to himself. Maybe it was a good thing he was going to die. Get out of everyone's hair.

"He was supposed to be like a brother to you, remember?" Atlas

had said. *"Or do your selfish needs always have to come before everyone else?"*

Atlas was right. He always was. Mateo made his problems the biggest thing. He only ever thought about himself, and his friends were always cleaning up his mess. He never really asked about their families, never asked how they were doing, how they were coping. He made them learn the truth about the world and didn't care how it affected them. Was he ever a good friend to the three of them? The three boys he had always considered the brothers he never had? He thought about Silas, about how he let him stay with his family after finding out what had happened to him.

"I can't live there anymore," Silas had said to him, twelve years old and his mother was barely cold in her grave.

"You can stay here," Mateo had said, letting him come in. *"You always have a place here."*

He never knew what happened to Silas growing up. He would sometimes come back from breaks skinnier and bruises in random places on his body. But, Silas didn't want to talk about it. He never wanted to talk about it. And Mateo never asked about it either. Should he have?

Mateo opened his eyes when he heard heavy footsteps coming towards him. Milo was holding a bag filled with his stuff over his shoulder. Part of Mateo sank.

"Let's go, sacrifice," Milo said.

"Man, I know you know my name," Mateo muttered, following after him. Milo didn't say another word.

"I'M GOING TO SEND HIM A LETTER," MATEO'S MOTHER SAID, HER voice almost frantic after he had told her the news. Her hands shook as she reached for some paper. Mateo put a hand over hers.

"Mom, it's fine," he murmured.

Her golden eyes flashed. "It is most certainly *not* fine. He's going to kill you on your birthday? Your *eighteenth* birthday? I can't even have that?" She angrily grabbed the piece of paper and a pen, tears wetting her eyes.

The Corderos had a landline they could use, and usually his mother would talk on the telephone, but she never did with her father. She always preferred to write letters to him. Mateo suspected it was because she didn't want to have to deal with his response over the phone. Or maybe, she didn't like hearing his voice. He sure didn't.

"I'm going to give him a piece of my mind. He loves to talk about how I'm the only child of his that he likes. Well, he better do this for me," his mother said, stomping off to the living room. She sat down and started to scribble angrily on the paper. Mateo was surprised it wasn't tearing apart with the amount of force she was writing this letter.

"I don't think writing to him is going to change anything," he said. "He's using the kidnapping of a sacrifice to move the Tenth Year up."

"Oh," she said, absentmindedly, "I heard about that." She finished scribbling, put it in an envelope, and handed it over to Lila.

"Make sure it gets to him as soon as possible," she implored. Lila nodded and then left the room in a haste.

"Was it anyone you knew?" she asked, finally looking at Mateo.

"It was Emira," he muttered. Her eyebrows furrowed together.

"That girl…" her words drifted off. She sighed and ran a hand through her graying brown hair. "I know how you feel about her. But, she goes and destroys a temple, *murders* a high priestess, and then is surprised she gets kidnapped? And because of her, my darling boy…"

"Mom," Mateo moved away from his mother's hands. "It isn't Emira's fault the Tenth Year was moved up. It's mine."

Mrs. Cordero gave him a quizzical look. "Your fault? I don't think I understand."

He shook his head. He didn't feel like explaining everything. How could he explain to his mom that he basically challenged his grandfather? Forced his hand by making people learn the truth about the Idols. It was always going to end this way. And his mother wouldn't understand the reason as to why he did it. Why he was trying so hard for people to understand. This was how society had been for thousands of years. She wouldn't be able to comprehend why he felt *he* had to be the one to change it.

No, he didn't need to discuss that. Because there was a reason he was back at the Cordero Estate, more than just seeing his mother for the last time.

"Do you know anything about people wearing silver masks?" he asked. "Specifically some kind of secret network amongst the twelve families? Did you ever see them around Balan or when you were growing up in Serpel?"

His mother's eyebrows knitted together. She shook her head, slowly. "What is this about?"

He thought about telling his mom, telling her about the cloaked figures wearing silver masks who kidnapped Emira, but he shook his head. There was a possibility that, even though she was the beloved daughter of Balan, that Balan wouldn't hesitate to kill her if she knew too much. He never hesitated to murder his other offspring.

"Nothing," he said. "Never mind." The inner corners of Mrs. Cordero's eyebrows raised as she looked at him.

"I'm glad that I at least get a week with you," she whispered, placing a hand over his. Mateo wasn't one for crying, but seeing his mother so broken made the back of his eyes burn.

"Yeah," he said. "I am, too."

MATEO'S FATHER WAS NEVER SOMEONE HE FELT PARTICULARLY close to. Lorenzo Cordero was hardly home, always working at the Cordero corporation, or other business stuff he attended. And he seemed to hate Mateo in a way. Especially after it was announced he was a sacrifice.

Mateo always figured it was because his mother had a hard time with the news. When they were told he had ichor in his blood and was going to have to attend Leliara, Mrs. Cordero broke down. His father had to hold her as she sobbed on the floor. At five years old, Mateo didn't understand what was going on. He couldn't comprehend why his mother was so distraught over him getting to go to a special school. Over finding out he had powers. Mateo, at the time, was excited about it. He was special. How many people got the chance to fight monsters? Now, he understood.

His mother knew that if he had ichor, he might become a sacrifice. The boy that she had prayed to have for years and finally did. Her miracle child. And he was going to be ripped away from her by her own father.

When it was announced that Mateo was the next sacrifice after Cassandra was "absorbed", his mother barely ate and slept all day or stared out the window. She hardly talked to anyone. Balan came a few times during that period.

"He'll live on within me, my nugget," Mateo had heard Balan say to her one time. He always called Mateo's mother that nickname. The only child of his that he was able to remotely connect with since he didn't have to kill her.

After that, Mateo's relationship with his father went downhill drastically. And Mateo understood why. His father was always going to put his mother above everyone, including their own child. He understood it, but it didn't stop the bitter taste in his mouth whenever he saw his father.

So, it was odd that he was leaning against the door frame of Mr. Cordero's office, waiting for him to notice his son was standing there. Mateo watched as his father pored over papers on his desk, intensely writing things down, and then putting them in a pile when he was finished. He didn't know how long he was standing there, watching his father. He wondered if this was what he would do if he were able to live longer. Would he also work for the corporation? Would he be working late hours and hardly be home? Would he even choose to work at the corporation, or would he continue to climb the ranks as a warrior once his contract was done?

They were decisions Mateo would never be able to make.

He cleared his throat. "Dad?" His father looked up and his eyes widened momentarily at seeing his son standing in the doorway.

"What's going on?" he asked, leaning in his chair and facing him. He took off his reading glasses and placed them on his messy desk.

"I just had a question," Mateo said. He took a step into his father's office. A place he never really dared to step into when he was younger.

His father studied him with aged brown eyes before nodding his head once. "Go ahead."

"Did anyone in the Cordero family who had ichor die at a young age?" he asked. His father's eyes narrowed ever-so-slightly.

"A lot of us have died at a young age," he answered. "Due to the Tenth Year." Mateo shook his head, taking another step closer.

"I mean, really young. Like…" he thought about Shiloh's half brother who was said to have died at the age of ten, "Like around ten years old. When their ichor started to manifest itself."

Mateo's father stared off into the distance as he thought. The corners of his lips tugged downwards as he shook his head. "Not recently."

"But, there's been a time before," Mateo more said than asked. Mr. Cordero nodded his head.

"Yes, my sister," he said. "She died when she was nine years old, right when her ichor was manifesting." Mateo didn't even know his father and his uncles had a sister.

"Do you know what her ichor was?" he asked. His father shook his head.

"No," he said. "But…" His eyes glazed over in thought. "But, I swore I saw her on the streets of Vismary wearing a black cloak. Right after you had escaped for the fifth time. And when I tried to go to her, she was gone."

Mateo's father was always someone who had a stone, cold face. Nothing penetrated his armor, his mask. But, his father's expression crumpled. Filled with sorrow at remembering his deceased sister.

Mr. Cordero shook his head. "Your uncles thought I was crazy. And, perhaps I was, at the time. Your mother was..." He finally met his son's gaze, his expression returning to how Mateo had always seen it.

"Why do you ask?" he said. Mateo shrugged, backing out of the office.

"No reason," he murmured.

CHAPTER FORTY-EIGHT

Mateo spent the rest of the week with his mother. He would play chess and walk around with her in the garden. She told him about what had been happening in her life, the gossip with the other twelve families. Occasionally, his mother would tear up and look away, stopping their conversation. They would sit in silence with one another while she would try to swallow her sorrow.

Mateo never knew what to say when his mother would get overcome with sadness. So, he would just hold her hand as she would tremble and choke back sobs. Sometimes, at night, he could hear his mother crying, as if he were already dead. And when he would hear them, he would retreat back into his room and stand near the slightly ajar door until her sobs were quieted by sleep. Only then was he able to fall asleep himself.

His mother would ask about his friends, and Mateo would lie and say that he said his goodbyes already. He didn't want to let her know what he did. How he fucked everything up. And perhaps, he did it on purpose so that they wouldn't miss him. At least, that's what Mateo told himself. That he subconsciously was trying to save them from the pain.

On the last day before he had to arrive in Serpel, someone knocked on the door. He opened it, casually, eating an apple, and nearly dropped it upon seeing the person standing there.

"Can I come in?" Silas asked. Mateo slid to the side wordlessly, letting him come through. His mother came into the foyer, having heard the knock, and wrapped Silas into a tight hug. Tears filled her golden eyes as she pulled away from him.

"It's so good to see you, Silas," she nearly whispered. She covered her mouth with a slightly aged hand and turned away.

"Excuse me," she said and left the room. Balan had never answered his mother's letter. And as the seconds ticked by, she was devolving more and more into an emotional puddle.

Mateo stared at him, and Silas studied him as well. He wondered why he was here. For a second, he thought perhaps something had happened. He stilled his expression, steeling his eyes.

"Do you want to come up to my room?" Mateo finally asked. Silas nodded, and they wordlessly went up the stairs.

He closed the door and hoped his mother wouldn't come into his room while they talked. Silas looked around before sitting down on the armchair in the corner.

"What are you doing here?" Mateo asked. Silas looked up at him, his blue eyes somber.

"You're still my best friend," he muttered. "No matter what you did. None of us want you to go without being able to make up."

"I don't see Atlas and Kanoa here," Mateo said, almost under his breath. Silas gave him a pained expression.

"You know how Kanoa is," he said, looking down at the dark brown hardwood floor. "And Atlas is weirdly loyal to Kanoa.

You know the two of them have always been closer. Plus, the headmistress would only allow one of us to go. She thought if all of us came that you would escape again." Mateo felt himself relax and roll his eyes as he sat down on his bed. Nothing had happened. *Thank Kali.*

"No letters?" Mateo asked, half joking. Silas smirked at him.

"Can Kanoa even read?" he joked. They both laughed.

"I guess Atlas didn't want to..." His voice drifted away as he remembered Atlas' expression marred with disappointment and disgust. Silas' smile faded and then took out a note.

"He told Kanoa and I something. He wanted to tell you, too," he said, handing Mateo the note. Mateo unfolded it and started to read.

Dear Mateo,

You have always been a person that I looked up to and I couldn't believe that someone like you would want to be friends with me, a nameless nobody.

I've been replaying the last words I've said to you for the past few days. I never thought this day would come, honestly. I've always believed that you would escape your fate.

I meant the words I said to you. You are selfish. You do put yourself above everyone else. But, I know it's, partly, out of survival.

I've thought a lot about what you did to Kanoa. And I've come to the conclusion that you did know. And that you did it on purpose, so that you wouldn't have to say goodbye to us. Well, sorry, buddy. We're still not going to say goodbye to you. Because I still have hope.

Shiloh told me she's been helping Emira practice something. She said it might change things. Might be able to save the two of you. But, she isn't sure if Emira would go through with it. She told her what she saw that day with Cassandra. You never told us she was there, too.

So, have hope, Cordero. Go out fighting until your last breath.

Also, Kanoa wants me to tell you that he'll never forgive you so you have to survive and make it up to him.

Sincerely your good friend,

Atlas

P.S.

I don't want this to change our friendship, but I'm gay. I've been gay since I was born. Stop asking me about women. And yes, I'm telling you this in case you do, in fact, die.

MATEO STARED AT THE CHICKEN SCRAWL THAT WAS ATLAS' handwriting for what felt like an eternity. He looked up at Silas' expectant gaze.

"No wonder why he was always so annoyed when I asked him about his secret relations," he muttered. He put the letter in his pocket and looked off into the distance for a moment, thinking about one thing from Atlas' letter. Emira was practicing something that would save them.

He turned his attention back towards Silas. "What is Emira practicing?" Silas shrugged.

"She's trying to look into the mind, the way that Mali supposedly does. Shiloh is under the impression that Mali uses her power to make the sacrifices compliant. Whispers into their mind or something," Silas said. "She has a theory that Emira could do the same thing to her."

"They tied down Cassandra," Mateo said. "I don't know where Shiloh got the idea that—"

"Did you notice the other sacrifices at the time? Were they tied down?" Silas interrupted. "Shi said they weren't."

431

Mateo tried to think back to when Cassandra was sacrificed. But, in his memory, he could only see her. And then all the blood that trickled to his shoes. He felt his limbs start to go numb. He couldn't let himself think about the rest, or the voices… Mateo shook his head.

"You're right, I don't remember the rest," he said, quietly, his voice hoarse. His head was starting to hurt. "I was only focused on Cassandra."

"So, Shiloh might be right," Silas said slowly.

"Would Emira really…" Mateo let the question drift off as he thought. If Emira can control Mali, it would be difficult. And she would only be able to control one Idol with the amount of time she had to practice.

"What exactly is the plan?" he asked Silas. Silas shrugged again.

"There isn't really a solid one. Shiloh just wanted to give the sacrifices a fighting chance. If Mali is disposed of, the rest of the sacrifices won't be frozen in place. They'll be able to fight back," he said.

"What changed Emira's mind?" Mateo asked, softly. Silas met his gaze.

"She didn't know how it actually happened," he said. "She thought that you all would be absorbed by a white light. Shiloh told her the truth."

"And she believed her?"

"She can read minds now," Silas pointed out.

"How is she practicing this? She would have to practice on a real brain," Mateo said. Silas opened his mouth and then closed it. He looked away.

"Yeah, she's been practicing on Shi," he muttered. "It's been… messing her up a little. Atlas does his best to heal parts of her brain, but even for him, it's difficult." Mateo swallowed as he thought about the brunette. She was always quiet, keeping to herself. Her and Atlas were close, that he knew. But, she never talked to Mateo much. The fact that she was giving her all to stop the sacrificial ritual said a lot about her.

"I hope she's okay, in the end," he whispered. Silas nodded, steeling his gaze.

"She'll be okay," he said. "She's a fighter." Mateo nodded at those words. He didn't know Shiloh all that well. Not as well as he knew the others. But, to offer herself up to be experimented on by a girl with all the power of an Idol, he had to admit she was brave. Though, all the Astorias were known for their bravery and quick thinking. It shouldn't surprise him that Shiloh was the same, no matter how quiet she was.

"So, there's a chance. A chance we could survive this," Mateo said, carefully. A part of him wondered if it would be ripped away from him. This hope.

Silas nodded his head and held Mateo's gaze.

"The revolution is starting," he said, leaning forward. "And we'll be the ones to ignite it."

CHAPTER FORTY-NINE

Emira hugged Shiloh goodbye, Darlene behind her. She grabbed her things and started towards the door. Turning around, she looked at Darlene who still wouldn't meet her gaze.

"Will you just hug me?" Emira asked. Darlene looked up at her, and her dark brown, almost black, eyes quickly filled with tears. She jumped towards Emira and they wrapped their arms around each other.

"I'm so sorry, E," she whispered into Emira's hair. "I'm so sorry."

"I never really cared, Darlene," Emira said, pulling away from her so she could look at her face. "Mateo and I weren't…"

"Don't bullshit me," Darlene said, pointing a finger in her face. "You love that boy. And I'm sorry I didn't realize it sooner. I'm usually so good at realizing who's in love with who, and I missed it. Under my very nose."

"Darlene, really, I don't care," Emira emphasized. And it was the truth. She was facing her probable death. Who cared who slept with who? It all seemed trivial at this point.

"I'm all right." Darlene looked at her with her big doe eyes and then nodded her head, finally letting it sink in.

"Go kick some Idol butt," she said, smiling at her. Emira let her lips curl into a smile, but it didn't quite meet her eyes, and nodded. She still didn't know if she'd be able to overpower Mali. And it frightened her that all the work she did, all the damage she did, would be for nothing. She turned towards Shiloh, whose brown eyes were glazed over slightly. Looking at her brought pain to her chest.

"Do you remember the plan?" Emira asked, softly and slowly. As if she were talking to a child. Shiloh's eyebrows crinkled together.

"What plan?" she asked. Emira swallowed the apologies down her throat. There was no point in trying to. In a few minutes, Shiloh would forget why she apologized and then soon would forget the apology itself.

There were times when Emira was practicing whispering commands into every part of who Shiloh was, tearing everything that made her Shiloh, for the command to be the only thing left, where Emira would pull away, and Shiloh would look at her with confusion written all over her face.

"*Who are you?*" she would say, terror built up in her voice. High and child-like. "*Why am I here?*"

Other times, there were moments where Shiloh would start screaming, screaming like someone was slicing her brain, holding her head together as if it were going to fall into pieces. She'd look up at Emira with tears running down her face, her nose bleeding, and beg her to stop.

"*Please,*" she would plead. "*Please.*" Like she didn't understand why Emira was torturing her. That was when they had to involve Atlas. And he would be there, trying to heal the damage Emira did to her brain. But, there were some things her friend would never recover from. For one, Shiloh was completely compliant to Emira. And anything about the revolution, she would forget within minutes. Emira wasn't sure why that was.

Her heart hurt as she looked upon Shiloh before leaving. Her friend was a shell of herself. All because she wanted to help Emira. Because she wanted to save Constellatia from the Idols' tyranny. And if Emira failed…

Darlene put a hand on Shiloh's arm. "I'll watch over her. Don't worry."

"I'm so sorry, Shi," Emira whispered, taking her hands into hers. She was unable to hold back the useless apologies. "I'm so sorry." Shiloh stared at her with an empty gaze.

"It's okay," she said, though Emira knew she didn't know what she was apologizing for. Just that she saw Emira look conflicted, hurt, and wanted to comfort her.

"It's okay," she repeated. She took her hands out from Emira's and patted the tops of them. Darlene's expression tightened.

"Atlas said he'll keep working on her," she muttered. "He said he might be able to get her back to normal. But, it'll take a while." It was a hope that she could hold onto. But, Emira knew it was a very small chance. The damage she had done would always leave its mark. Even if Shiloh ended up going back to normal, she'd never fully be back to who she was.

"Hopefully, I'll see you guys later," Emira whispered. Darlene nodded, and Emira left their dorm room. The dorm room she'd never go back to.

It was the early hours of the morning. Headmistress Alessia was standing next to a black carriage flanked with four Pyrinian guards. She smiled sadly at Emira as she entered the carriage. It was the day of the sacrificial ritual.

The day that would either change Constellatia forever or that would mark the end of Emira's short life.

She closed her eyes as Astutera rushed by. She hoped what Shiloh and her did was enough. That it was enough to stop an Idol.

Because Emira didn't think she'd be able to live knowing that it wasn't, and that she ruined Shiloh's life forever.

EMIRA LOOKED UP AT THE IDOLS' COURT OF JUSTICE. IT LOOKED more menacing than when she had stood in front of it prior. She never knew that the Tenth Year took place here. She knew it was in Serpel, but she didn't realize the last time she had seen the Idols was going to be the same place where she was supposed to die. She had thought the building looked morbid before, like a giant mausoleum, but now the feeling was really settling in. The Pyrinian guards surrounding her pushed her forward a little.

There were other sacrifices arriving to the Court of Justice, also flanked by four Pyrinian guards. The Idols weren't taking any chances. She tried to look past the guards and find Mateo.

The last words she said to him were, *"I don't ever want to see you again."* She squeezed her eyes shut. He was gone the week before, she was told he went home. She didn't have a chance to right things with him. And, even if she couldn't, even if she wasn't going to be able to tell him the truth of how she felt—sober, this time—she at least wanted to be able to see him. The way that he looked at her in the Room of Serpentes... She wanted the boyish Mateo, the carefree one stuck in her memory. Instead, his cold, mismatched eyes were seared into her eyelids. The last thing she saw from him.

Praying that it wasn't the last time she'll see him, she continued to desperately look through the Pyrinian guards to find him.

"He knows what's going to happen," Silas had said the night before after he got back from Vismary. *"He'll be ready."*

Cameras were arriving for the broadcast. Journalists weren't allowed in the Court of Justice during the sacrifice. But, they were all lined up outside of it, ready to interview the Idols for their newspapers.

The Pyrinian guards led her into a nondescript room. They handed her a plain, white gown to change into. It was satin, expensive to the touch. She fingered it for a moment, waiting. Emira stared at the guards.

"Could you please turn around so I can change?" she asked, her voice as quiet as a mouse. The four Pyrinian guards stared at her, almost bored.

"No," one of them said. "We're under orders not to take our eyes off of you." *Wonderful.* Emira bit her tongue until she was sure it was going to bleed.

Heat filled her face at the thought of them looking at her. She had always been overly covered, modest. Her life as a priestess made it such. And now, strangers were going to see her. She felt less than human. Less than an animal. She turned around and tried to quickly change, trying to do it so as little skin showed as possible.

She pulled her curly, blonde hair into a singular braid, as she normally did. And looked down at herself. The white gown was so pristine that not a mark was on it. And Emira knew that soon it would be covered in blood. Her own blood. She closed her eyes once more.

"Are you ready?" one of the Pyrinian guards said. Emira nodded her head, once, and they opened the door. She followed them to the center of the Court of Justice, where there weren't any doors in sight, simply columns separating the spaces from one another.

As they led her towards the center of the courtroom, she saw Mateo with his own guards. His mismatched eyes fixed onto her. And in those eyes, Emira found some sort of comfort. They weren't cold and hard. They were warm, searching. The Mateo she knew. She took in a shaky breath.

She had to pass by him in order to stand where she was supposed to be in the line up. His hand reached out a little and brushed the back of hers. She glanced over at him, but he wasn't looking at her. Instead, his gaze was straight ahead, hardening as time went on.

Emira stood in front of where the Idol of Luck was going to be, a guard holding her arms behind her back. Terror hid in her joints, and she felt herself start to tremble a little.

You can do this, she thought to herself. *You are an Idol incarnate. You can do this.*

"Hey, little lady," a familiar voice said beside her. She looked to her left and saw a large man with a red beard and baby blue eyes.

"Erik," she said, remembering him from the Winter Solstice ball. He smiled, though it didn't quite reach his eyes.

"Glad we're next to each other," he said. "At least we can keep one another company until the end." Emira nodded her head, the fluttering in her chest not letting her speak much. The Idols started to come in, wearing traditional robes that were golden and beautifully embroidered.

And again, Emira could feel herself getting sick from the amount of power coming into the room. Her stomach churned, and it was hard to concentrate on anything. Pure, boundless power flowed out of the twelve beings. And her vision blurred. She swallowed the bile that threatened to escape her body.

She looked around, wondering if anyone else was having such a physical visceral reaction to the Idols, but no one else looked fazed.

Balan stood in front of Mateo, the last of the Idols, and gestured to one of the guards. The Pyrinian guard obediently came to him.

"Tie him up, please," Balan said, adjusting his ostentatious robe. "I don't want him doing anything." Emira tried not to look over at him. Not while Mali was staring into her eyes whilst talking to the Idol of Life next to her.

"Why must we wear these things?" she heard Ophelia say from somewhere in the lineup. "It is heavier than it should be and quite uncomfortable."

"It's tradition," Phaethon said, standing up tall in front of Erik, though he didn't reach the sacrifice's height. "It's only heavy for you because you're so small, Mouse."

Ophelia made a face. "Or maybe it's so light for you because you have impossible strength." Phaethon smiled at her, a smile that didn't reach his emerald eyes.

"Thanks, Mouse," he said. "I'm glad you're finally admitting I'm stronger than you." Ophelia grumbled to herself, adjusting her robes again.

It was weird, for Emira, to watch these Idols act like humans. To act like they were just on an outing, or were getting ready to do some kind of photo op. If she wasn't aware, she wouldn't have realized they were about to kill twelve people.

Emira looked at the other sacrifices. They were all from different walks of life. Some of the former warriors were struggling against the Pyrinian guards, but once they did, something washed over them and they were as still as a lake. Emira glanced at Mali, who was looking at them like they were mischievous children. She tsked lightly under her breath before continuing her conversation with Kali.

"I mean, I don't understand why they're always trying to fight against it," Mali muttered.

"Instincts," Kali had said, cracking her fingers. The both of them barely looked at the sacrifices in front of them. At that thought, Mali suddenly looked over at Emira, her violet eyes—so much like Emira's own—burning, like there was a crystalline fire hidden behind them.

"Emira," she said her name the same as Balan had said it before. Insignificant. "Did you ever get a chance to talk to that Priestess of Luck? I had recommended the high priestess to your headmistress."

Emira shook her head, her throat dry. "No, your holiness. Unfortunately, I never had the time." Mali's gaze hardened.

"Pity," she said, shrugging a shoulder and continuing to whisper things to Kali, completely ignoring Phaethon on the other side of her. She was different than when Emira last saw her. Emotionless. Lethal. Emira couldn't believe that this woman was her biological mother, looking at her like she was merely an insect in her path.

The last sacrifice finally walked in as the cameras were getting set up. The little girl was bigger than most five-year-olds, but her cheeks were shiny from the tears that she had shed. *Poppy*, Emira thought. The sacrifice from Pyrinia. Erik followed Emira's gaze, and she felt him stiffen beside her. The girl was the youngest of them all.

The Pyrinian guard carefully guided her to stand in front of Elemence, the Idol of Healing and Fire. The Idol's blonde, with a tinge of strawberry, hair was tied back into a low ponytail.

Emira thought Elemence probably had the kindest face out of all the Idols. She was older than the rest, and something about her made her look trustworthy. But, Emira knew the truth about Elemence. She may look kind, however in history, she was one of the fiercest warriors. Creating an army of the undead.

Elemence's ruby red eyes darted over towards her, like she could feel Emira's curious gaze on her, and Emira quickly looked away.

"Are the cameras ready, yet?" Balan said, his impatience clear. One of the Pyrinian guards nodded their heads, and then Emira felt something in her mind. A quiet probing, into every part of her being. Flipping through all of her memories, taking apart what made Emira who she was. Somehow, the Idol knew what it was that kept Emira together, even if Emira didn't know herself.

Stay, it whispered. She looked into the eyes of Mali who was standing in front of her, sure that betrayal was written into her own. Emira's eyes darted around, frantically, as she lost control over her own body. And in every memory she ever had, Emira lost control. Standing there, as if that's all she'd ever done in her life.

She closed her eyes as she tried to pull her ichor forward, to feel the lightheaded feeling that she could hold onto. Lightheaded with a mix of fire bubbling in her veins. Her eyes snapped open once she realized she couldn't hold onto it. That anytime she would feel it even a little, it would evaporate away. Her heart started to flutter again in her chest, beating against her rib cage. If she couldn't get a hold of her ichor, everything she and Shiloh did, it would be for nothing. All these people, they would end up corpses. And...

Mateo.

Mali's eyebrows twitched and the corners of her lips pulled downwards as she studied Emira. The Idols were being handed golden daggers, and Mali didn't look away from Emira until the guard bumped her with the pillow the dagger was resting on.

Emira looked around, barely able to see Erik standing beside her in her peripheral vision. She tried to imagine Mateo was by her side, and not tied up next to Erik. If she concentrated hard enough, she could kind of see his profile. But, Erik was so large, and he was in the way.

She mentally took a deep breath and tried to steady her beating heart. From what she remembered of the Tenth Year, they would go down the line. Alexios was first. But, the process was quick in the broadcast she had seen when she was eight. The light would absorb the sacrifice fast and then it was the next one, and down the line they went.

I have time, Emira thought. *I have time to fight against her order.* But, it wasn't enough time to save everyone. She tried not to think about that as her teeth ground together. Mali glanced over at her once more, her frown more apparent on her face. Emira had time to save herself since she was third to last. But, she wouldn't be able to save Mrs. Halloway, her Creatures teacher who was first in line.

"Let's begin," Balan's voice was heard throughout the court-room, despite not being very loud. Emira heard her heart pounding in her head. She saw Alexios murmur something to Mrs. Halloway, and then her neck was slit, blood pouring out of her.

She watched through her peripheral vision, frozen, as Alexios put his mouth to her neck and sucked the life out of her. And then it was Lystos and his sacrifice.

Her mind was racing, unable to think at the horror she was witnessing. Her breath came out in short bursts.

Concentrate, Emira thought to herself.

"You have power that's boundless, Emira," she remembered Shiloh telling her. She kept the image of Shiloh in her head. She had boundless power. Power that couldn't be contained. Not by any Idol. Not by anyone but herself.

I will never be weak again, she thought, the thought growing bigger in her mind.

Mali's eyebrow twitched, her grip on her dagger tightening until her knuckles were white.

She watched as the little girl, with tears streaming down her face, had her throat sliced by the seemingly kind Elemence. Crimson blood ran down the front of her dress, staining it red. A gray film started to cover her eyes as Elemence drank her life away.

It was almost Emira's turn.

She glowered at Mali and whispered to herself. *My power is boundless.* And in every memory of Emira's, she whispered it to herself, the same mantra. Because what would it have been for? The damage to Shiloh's brain. Her friend would never be the same, and she would be damned if it were all for nothing.

Emira was going to fight until she was dead. For herself. For Mateo. For Shiloh and the rest of Constellatia. And suddenly, she could feel Mali's essence. Mali lifted her knife, out of order, and Emira knew she could feel her in her mind, and Emira whispered into the Idol's soft essence. Flipped through all the millions of memories Mali had in her unnaturally long life.

And she repeated the same order to her. *Stay.*

Mali froze, arm in midair, gripping the golden dagger. Her violet eyes wild and frightened. Phaethon glanced at Mali and then his emerald eyes darted towards Emira, danger lurking beneath them. His gaze, protective.

Emira, with her mind, pulled the dagger out from Mali's

hand and pushed the dagger Phaethon was holding out of his before he could react. She saw Erik stretch upwards, cracking his back, as he winked at her, like he was expecting this moment, before turning his arm into taffy and pulling himself away.

"What is going on?" she heard Raila—the Idol of Music, Poetry, and Light—say, her voice shrill. Emira grabbed the dagger and felt her powers start to melt away. Similar to when she was locked up in the cell.

Of course Balan had that power, Emira thought. But she wasn't going to let that stop her. She took the golden dagger and sliced it across Mali's slight throat, her violet eyes desperately pleading with Emira.

And she let the blood gush out, staining the golden robe she was wearing. Silence washed over the room. Everyone froze until Mali fell to the ground. The sound of her body hitting the floor echoing throughout the mausoleum-esque facade of a Court of Justice. The Idol of Luck and Agriculture was dead.

Then everything erupted into chaos.

The other sacrifices, that hadn't been murdered yet, started lunging towards their Idols. Raila sprouted wings from her back and started to fly upwards.

"I told you this was going to happen someday," she bitterly called out to no one in particular. Emira reached towards Mateo, his mismatched eyes anchoring her. But before she could, Balan pulled Mateo towards him. The action caused Mateo's white frock to move a little, and Emira saw a silver necklace around his neck spill out, a moon crescent charm at the end. Her necklace. The necklace she thought was lost forever. Her heart nearly stopped.

Without a word, just a simple cold look, Balan pulled a silver mask out from underneath his golden robe and pressed it against Mateo's face. And then, he turned inward into himself until they were both gone, his gold eyes glittering.

"Mateo," she whispered, though she wanted to scream it. Her arm was still reaching out for him, wishing she could tell him everything, all that she felt for him.

"Get out of here," someone told her, pushing her away from where Mateo was once standing. She looked around the room, the corpses of the sacrifices she couldn't save lying on the ground in the pool of their own blood. Lifeless, grayed eyes staring right at her.

Emira blinked, walking backwards. Ornate golden dagger still in her hand, dripping Mali's blood onto the floor.

Run, something in her shouted into her mind.

And Emira ran for her life.

Gold. Freedom. Those were the words Sybil Yuka had said to her months ago. Emira didn't know it when Sybil Yuka had said it, but Mateo turned out to be her freedom. Her freedom from herself.

-To Be Continued-

ACKNOWLEDGMENTS

First, I'd like to thank my wonderful husband, Quan, for listening to me talk about this book for so long. Thank you for helping me build my confidence and for encouraging me to put out another book. You are the light of my life, and I appreciate everything you do for me.

I'd like to thank my parents for believing in me. You guys believe I can do anything, to a fault. And because of you two, I am delusional enough to put out my own books. You two gave me an imagination that makes life worth living for.

Thank you to my two childhood best friends, Olivia and Anna, for letting me read this book to you in the car on the way to the beach. Your input was seriously invaluable, and it definitely made the book better. It also gave me confidence to keep working on it!

I'd also like to thank my beta readers for reading this book and for giving me feedback on it. Micha, you added such great plot lines and added to the story immensely. I loved all of your suggestions on how to make Emira's character arc more defined. Madelyn, all the feedback you gave me was amazing. You definitely made this book better and helped make the characters jump off the page more. You both are some of my favorite people, and I appreciate all you've done for me in helping this book be the best it could be!!

Thank you to my street team for helping me promote this book and for loving it as much as I do! You guys are amazing and I adore all of you so much!!

And last, but not least, thank you to the readers who bought this book and gave it a chance! You all are the best!

ABOUT THE AUTHOR

Bianca K. Gray is a mostly fantasy author, but likes to dip her toes in different genres. She graduated from the University of Virginia with a Bachelor Degree in English. Bianca also received a Master Degree from the same institution in English Education. A former 8th grade English teacher, Bianca has always had a love of literature that she wants others to discover and cultivate within themselves. She currently resides in New York City with her husband, rambunctious shih-tzu, and the most adorable kitty cat. If you want to keep up to date with her future endeavors, follow her on Instagram (@biancakgray.author).

instagram.com/biancakgray.author

* 9 7 9 8 9 8 5 9 0 4 6 7 3 *